London is the place to be ... the
spring air is vibrant and alive with excitement in
anticipation of the unveiling of the magnificent
Crystal Palace. But can a star-crossed love
finally bloom in the midst of the tumult?

Mimi Marsh has adored the brilliant and dashing
Nathan Price in secret for years. One brief, raptur-
ous moment is all they have shared, and she
yearns passionately for more. But since that
night, Nathan has known the exhilaration of triumph ... and the pain of personal ruin. How can
Mimi hope to win back his trust and affection in
light of all Nathan has been through? With her
soft gaze and gentle words she invites him back
into her soul—and Mimi sees the desire that
burns in his eyes whenever she enters the room.
The only woman ever to have captured this
wounded man's love, Mimi is now the only one
who can save him. But will proud, wronged
Nathan ever embrace the power of her passion—
and open his guarded heart to a miraculous,
once-in-a-lifetime romance?

———————

"Adele Ashworth is a thrilling new discovery.
Someone Irresistible is the most enthralling
reading experience I've had in years.
Her novels are moving and beautifully
written. ... She is certain to become one of
romance's most beloved writers."

Lisa Kleypas

If You've Enjoyed This Book,
Be Sure to Read These Other
AVON ROMANTIC TREASURES

ADELE ASHWORTH

Someone Irresistible

An Avon Romantic Treasure

AVON BOOKS
An Imprint of HarperCollinsPublishers

This is a work of fiction. Names, characters, places, and incidents are products of the author's imagination or are used fictitiously and are not to be construed as real. Any resemblance to actual events, locales, organizations, or persons, living or dead, is entirely coincidental.

AVON BOOKS
An Imprint of HarperCollins*Publishers*
10 East 53rd Street
New York, New York 10022-5299

Copyright © 2001 by Adele Budnick
ISBN: 0-380-81806-X
www.avonromance.com

First Avon Books paperback printing: December 2001

Avon Trademark Reg. U.S. Pat. Off. and in Other Countries, Marca Registrada, Hecho en U.S.A.
HarperCollins ® is a trademark of HarperCollins Publishers Inc.

Printed in the U.S.A.

10 9 8 7 6 5 4 3 2 1

Iguanodon

lived 120 million years ago
England
lives in marshes and swamps
found in sandstone and clay
eats shrubs and horse tails
Early Cretaceous
lives in the horse tail swamp

—*Helpful notes as written by*
my eight-year-old son, Andrew, 1999

This one is dedicated to you,
my sweet, inquisitive angel.

Hers was certainly distinctive, he decided, now that he studied it closely. Her jaw was a bit too square to be considered perfect, he supposed, and her forehead was on the high side. But her skin was fair, creamy, and flawless, and her mouth was full, pink, and . . . arresting. She was listening intently to an older gentleman Nathan didn't know, nodding vaguely at something the man said, and Nathan couldn't help but stare at those two rose colored lips as they parted in a conscientious smile. Strange that he hadn't noticed the uniqueness of her face—and especially those eyes—before tonight.

Mentally shaking himself, he dropped his gaze to the crystal champagne flute in his hand. His preoccupation with Miss Marsh was likely caused by the drink. He'd already downed one glass, probably more than he should have, and that would never do. He needed to remain focused on the night ahead, certainly not on her, or on any woman, for that matter.

Nathan lifted the flute to his lips, swallowing the remaining contents in two easy gulps. It was quite good, but that was about all he detected of the champagne's quality with his nerves as jumpy as they were. The greatest moment of his twenty-seven years, the moment when he would become a shining star in the scientific world, was nearly upon him. In less than an hour, he would be unveiling a precious jawbone, the greatest treasure he had ever uncovered from the depths of the earth—or had ever seen, for that matter—and every eye in the scientific community would be focused on him and his extraordinary prize.

She'd also grown breasts, he observed with a sort of confused fascination, as his eyes drifted upward again unintentionally. How had he missed that, last he saw her? Or maybe it was just her particular low-cut evening gown enhancing something he'd never had the opportunity to assess until now. She had to be at least twenty years old, and still slender, though tonight she seemed . . . proportioned. Like a woman. Odd that he'd never really considered Mimi Marsh a woman before.

But those were very definitely breasts jutting from her gown in two pale, softly smooth handfuls. It was an uncomfortable notion, thinking of Mimi as a woman with breasts, with a body he might be eager to explore. Especially since she stood next to her very ordinary sister, Mary, and several gentlemen, including her father, Sir Harold Marsh, the famous, talented dinosaur sculptor. It was Nathan's opinion that no lady should be scrutinized so thoroughly when standing next to her father.

Her gaze flickered in his direction, and one side of that pink mouth turned up coyly when she captured his eyes with hers, just briefly. He nodded once to her, minutely, before she turned back to acknowledge something her father said.

Suddenly he sensed the bothersome prickling in his groin that he had no business feeling for any female right now. Chastising himself for allowing his mind to wander, Nathan swung around purposefully and placed his drained flute on an empty exhibition table next to the glass wall.

This was the opening night of what was termed the Great Exhibition of 1851. The night the grand exposition began inside the Crystal Palace in Hyde Park, and probably the greatest night for scientists in recent memory. Designed by Joseph Paxton, a gardener for the Duke of Devonshire, the enormous glass structure had the look of a greenhouse, but it encased, among other things, the most amazing assortment of recently discovered dinosaur bones ever recovered in this country. And tonight he, Nathan Price, one of England's finest and thoroughly well-respected paleontologists, would be making his mark in scientific history.

The hall had been filling steadily for more than six hours. The Marshes had arrived late that afternoon for the celebration, along with Justin Marley, Nathan's friend and fellow paleontologist. He was speaking to Sir Harold and several others, while Nathan stood in the distance, next to his draped display, watching for any sign of the great Richard Owen, the anatomist who, along with Prince Albert, had made this night happen for the good of England. Owen knew more about dinosaurs, the new breed of beasts, than anyone in the country. Probably more than anyone alive. He would be arriving shortly for the unveiling, there to donate an unspecified amount of money to Nathan for the English Natural History Museum and Professor Price's intended exhibit, of which his newly found jawbone would be the crowning part.

Mimi laughed softly at something Justin said, gently tossing a delicate, pale hand in the air. Of course Nathan was a good ten feet from her, and the milling scientists, socialites, statesmen, and wives blocked his view of her. Yet Nathan noted the protruding bones of her wrist and her tapered fingers, straightened his backbone for better observation when she tilted her head to one side, revealing an elegant throat free of jewelry, a shapely ear from which hung a dainty earring to match her dark blue gown.

He'd heard rumors that Mimi was as talented a sculptor as her father, but of course he had no idea if this was true, since he'd seen none of her work. She didn't appear to have the hands of a sculptor, though he had no idea if a sculptor's hands would look different from anyone else's. Maybe he found himself suddenly intrigued by her because he'd always considered Mimi a child. Maybe she fascinated him now because he was a hunter of sorts by profession: it was in his blood. Yes, he concluded, this surprising interest in Sir Harold's daughter had to be simple, natural male instinct. A man attracted to a woman biologically.

She stood on the other side of his covered glass case, within an ever growing cluster of people ambling through the displays at this end of the Crystal Palace. Nathan had placed himself near the far glass wall, in part because he usually grew quiet in crowds, but also because standing among them was Carter Sinclair, an anatomist who frequently made Nathan's anger rise with his unsound scientific pronouncements and arrogant nature. Carter didn't like Nathan any more than was necessary, either, but they remained on cordial terms when the need arose. He smiled at Mimi, Nathan noticed, but it was a pleasant smile, not one of a man with any great interest in what she was actually saying. But then Nathan understood that. Most women of his acquaintance weren't all that interesting, either.

He placed his hand possessively on the velvet-covered glass beside him, fingering it thoughtfully. Inside lay notes, drawings, and his prize. All his. A jawbone discovered and dug up by his own sweat-drenched body in an ancient rock bed in Oxfordshire last year. He'd worked for it, labored for it, cared for it. Nobody had seen it, either, aside from the few workers at the excavation site, but they weren't noblemen or scientists of his caliber, so they were not, naturally, a part of this great exhibition at the Crystal Palace. He was the only one here tonight, the only one in London, who had seen this treasure of his, and everyone would be envious of his showing. In less than an hour the unveiling would reveal it to the world.

"It's lovely to see you again, Professor."

The softly spoken words came from behind him. Nathan pivoted around to see Mimi standing at his side, one corner of that pink mouth curved up, those enormous brown eyes sparkling at him.

He blinked, momentarily disconcerted by her surprising nearness, by the scent of spice in something she wore on her pale skin, then annoyed that he would let such frivolous things affect him. Straightening, he attempted to be charming.

"You're looking . . . well, Miss Marsh."

Her smile deepened but she didn't comment on his rather standard attempt at polite conversation. Instead she turned to the case at his side.

"May I have a peek?"

"No, you may not."

She nodded as if she expected this reply from him, lifting the fingers of her left hand to glide them sensually across the top of the red velvet casing. But the smile never left her lips.

"I've heard you found a monster."

He cocked his head to one side, studying her earrings as they glimmered from the bright gas lights. "You've heard correctly. Though it would be more accurate to call it an ancient lizard."

"Mmmm." Her forehead creased gently. "What part?"

"I beg your pardon?"

"What part of the lizard did you discover?" she repeated graciously.

Of course. "The jawbone, top and bottom," he replied, knowing her interest was strictly due to her father's association with the upper scientific circle. He'd never met a proper lady yet who found his work truly engaging. But she was trying to be courteous.

She waited. "It's inside the case?"

Her tone was mischievous, but startlingly smooth. It had an addictive quality that would no doubt be very arousing under the right circumstances. He wondered for a moment if she knew that, if she ever used her voice on purpose to tempt a man.

"Yes, it's inside," he answered levelly. "I'm awaiting the arrival of Professor Owen before I reveal it, however."

She took a sip of champagne, and he studied the way her throat moved when she swallowed.

"Is that why you're standing here all alone, Professor Price? You're waiting for Professor Owen?"

Her voice fairly purred and it made him suddenly uncomfortable, especially the way her vivid eyes returned to capture his frankly. He refused to let her know how she flustered him, though.

"In part, Miss Marsh," he replied with deliberate intent and a gentle nod. "I've also made my introductions to those in the room and am now only concerned with the evening ahead. I'm not here to mingle."

"Indeed," she acquiesced. Then, "I suppose you'll have it sculpted, so I'll see it eventually, won't I?"

"The jawbone? I imagine so, yes. I'm hoping it will be part of the English Natural History Museum when it's completed, but a sculpture by your father will remain here in the Crystal Palace until this marvelous building is dismantled."

"I see. And the museum is the one to which Professor Owen is donating funds."

She said it as a statement, but he nodded in answer. "Right again."

Suddenly feeling awkward standing alone with her in the crowded hall, Nathan really wished he had something to do with his hands, especially now that he didn't have a drink. He clasped them behind his back.

"It's getting so noisy," she remarked, glancing around the room, "and warm." She fanned herself with her fingers in front of her chest, drawing his attention again to those full, prominent breasts.

Nathan tried not to ogle them as he forced himself to look at something else. Her dark blond hair was piled high on her head in two long, coiled plaits that were fastened expertly with a jeweled comb at her crown. Her cheeks were dewy, soft, but then it was June, and the Palace suddenly felt very stuffy.

"Would you care to walk with me out of doors, Miss Marsh?" he asked tentatively, and quite by surprise, trying to hide the shock from his own question, as he added, "I'm sure the air temperature is much more pleasant out in the open."

She grinned broadly and took his extended arm with her right palm. "I'd be delighted, Professor Price."

Nathan hesitated for the slightest second, but decided reputations wouldn't matter since the grounds were teeming with people. Of course it would be getting dark soon, but they wouldn't be gone long. Just a little more than thirty minutes until the unveiling. Another thirty minutes to find something to take his mind off the wait for the splendid reaction to come. Mimi took an unconscious deep breath, and he quickly concluded he could easily look at her and her amazing figure tightly corseted beneath royal blue silk for the next thirty minutes.

"Come, Professor," she said with a subtle tug on his coat sleeve, her eyes once again shining impishly. "I'm certain Mr. Marley or my father will look after the exhibit, if someone were to be rude enough to attempt to steal a look."

Nobody would, he knew. Most didn't even know what he had inside, and of course the gentry always restrained themselves, at least in public.

"Your argument is persuasive, Miss Marsh."

She placed her champagne flute next to his empty one on the table beside her. Then he gestured with his arm and she began gliding toward the exit beside him.

With little notice from others, she led the way through the huge, crowded corridor filled with formally dressed patrons, large and small science exhibits, even live growing trees that extended to the high clear ceiling above. The walk was a good ten minutes to the arched glass exit, and they traveled it in superficial conversation. Soon they were standing in the fresh breezy June air, and she stopped beside him, closing her eyes and taking a deep breath.

"Yes, this is much better," she said.

"Much."

What a stupid reply. Why in God's name was he acting so oafish with her? He was older than she by at least seven years, more experienced, a man. She was lovely, though, and Nathan didn't often come across lovely women who clung to his arm, regardless of how well he knew them.

She started to lead him down the path toward the southeast side of the building and he strode beside her at a steady pace.

"Mr. Marley speaks well of your accomplishments in the field," she said.

Nathan inhaled deeply, forcing himself to relax. "Does he? We're good friends."

"Ah, but you're being modest, Professor Price," she countered, squeezing his arm playfully. "Professor Owen wouldn't be donating money to someone he could not trust to succeed."

Nathan knew this was true, and was actually a

little surprised that she'd considered it. "He trusts my work."

"Mmmm."

Mimi had to step closer to him to allow a round woman in heavy hoops to pass on the path, but she didn't move back after the woman strolled by. She held to his arm discreetly, knowing without doubt that her closeness might send signals to others that they were more than acquaintances. Nathan wondered about that but didn't question it. The hair on top of her head was very nearly touching his chin and he liked the way she smelled—clean, spicy, and feminine.

"It's been months since you've been to visit my father," she carried on as if they were discussing something quite ordinary.

"Until just recently, I've been digging at the Oxfordshire quarry, Miss Marsh."

She stopped abruptly and turned toward him, never letting go of his arm.

Her smile grew cunning. "You've known me for several years, Nathan. I don't think it would be at all indecent for you to call me by my given name, especially when we are alone."

Why are we alone? he suddenly wanted to ask, but didn't. Of course their actions weren't improper, and certainly wouldn't cause speculation among family and friends. But it did seem like an unexpected turn of events to find himself isolated, arm in arm, in the cooling dusk, with Mimi Marsh.

She turned again at his continued silence and began a steady stroll, seemingly unruffled by his lack of comment to her statement.

"You don't care for Carter Sinclair, do you?"

Her probing question made him pause. "Why do you ask?"

She lifted a smooth, bare shoulder in a light shrug. "He's not altogether fond of you, and I wondered if the feeling was mutual. I'm also curious as to why there is such animosity between you."

Nathan drew another long breath. "We've been rivals for a long time, Mimi."

She didn't look at him when he said her name, as if she expected that he would.

"But he's an anatomist, not a paleontologist. Your work can't be that similar."

"It crosses over frequently, but in general, no, it's not," he confirmed with a little irritation in his voice. "But our ideas on science differ greatly. He's a backward thinker, completely disregarding new theories because he's arrogant."

"He's asked my father for my hand," she stated quietly, somewhat wistfully, staring away from him and across the green landscape of Hyde Park.

With those words something he couldn't define stirred deep within him. Gradually she stopped walking and turned to him, starkly gazing into his eyes, hers darkened to black in the growing nightfall.

"Have you accepted?" he heard himself ask huskily, curious as to why this topic was even spoken between them. He'd known both her and her father as acquaintances for years, but this was really a private matter and none of his concern.

"Not yet," she admitted, watching him closely.

Nathan was confused, more by her candor than by her desire to discuss a marriage with Carter Sinclair. The match would be a perfect one socially and financially, as Sinclair was from a wealthy, well-respected family. But the news bothered him irrationally. He didn't like confusion. He was a scientist and he preferred answers.

He dropped his voice to a deep whisper. "Why are you telling me this, Mimi?"

Her eyes narrowed and her chin jerked to the side just negligibly. "Don't you know?"

No, he didn't. At least, he didn't think so. But he was beginning to suspect there was more to this conversation than she'd revealed.

She released his arm and stood back a foot, into the shadows beside a high secluded hedge.

Nathan stilled as clarity washed over him. Then his pulse began to speed with uncertainty. He dropped his gaze to her breasts again, eyeing the full curves openly, then looked back into her eyes.

"What do you want, Mimi?" he whispered.

Without hesitation, she silkily replied, "I want you to kiss me."

Could it be as easy as this? Stealing a kiss behind a hedge in back of the glorious Crystal Palace? They couldn't be noticed; at least this end of the park was void of people and darkness was closing fast. But the dare pushed that biological, primeval urge to the forefront of his good intentions. He couldn't turn away from such an invitation.

Nathan lifted a palm to her throat. Her skin felt hot to the touch, but she never moved or averted her eyes. Only her breath came quickly.

For moments his hand remained steady against her. Then, when he could no longer deny himself, he leaned forward and brought his lips to her softly parted ones. Immediately, she placed her palms on his shoulders and pulled him closer.

Her pulse beat fast beneath his fingertips; wayward curls tickled his cheek; but it was her moist, coaxing mouth that nearly brought him to his knees.

He didn't invade it with his tongue, and she didn't press him for more. He led, she followed, while he tasted and touched and stroked her lips with his.

Seconds later, he pulled back, dazed, delighted, and irrationally languid from the contact, considering that his body had become rigid from head to toe.

He stared at her closed eyes, her dreamily relaxed face.

Nathan flattened his thumb against her mouth one last time and she rubbed her lips sensually against it, sighing but never lifting her lashes.

It was as if unreality had set in. He suddenly felt as if he knew her intimately, as if kissing her were as natural as breathing. And as needed for survival as fresh air.

"Nathan," she whispered.

He dropped his hand and placed his palms on his hips, inside his gray pinstripe frock coat, steadying himself, attempting to control his own heart that beat like a hard, heavy rock against his chest.

He felt pulled from both ends. He needed to get back inside, to his waiting exhibit, to science and facts and the prestige that was about to be his. But he wanted to touch her more, and that thought was so carnal in its simplicity it alarmed him.

"Mimi, you're—" He didn't know where to begin. He cleared his dry throat to voice something else, something practical, and in that time she opened her bold, luscious eyes to his.

"Think about me," she murmured softly, intently, before she let out a deep exhalation and moved past him onto the path in the direction of the Palace entrance.

Nathan watched her retreating back for a moment, then followed silently, more stupefied by this turn of events than he could put into coherent words.

All eyes remained centered on his display. Nathan stood erect, chest out, hands behind his back to hide his nervousness. Next to him were dinosaur experts from across the country, Professor Richard Owen, and several other distinguished dignitaries. After a brief announcement of where his fossil was discovered, under what circumstances, and what effort it took for Nathan and his co-workers to get it to the Crystal Palace tonight, he lifted his right hand and placed it on the velvet cover.

"Here, ladies and gentlemen," Nathan informed them proudly, "is a superb example of a fully intact jawbone of the Megalosaurus reptile."

With controlled fingers, he lifted the cover and pulled it from the glass case.

Lights shone brightly; a single gasp could be heard, followed by a low rumble of whispers.

Nathan could only stare, his smile of jubilation dissolving, feeling an instantaneous sinking in his belly, a crowning humiliation to replace his moment of triumph.

Aside from two small bone fragments, the glass

case stood empty. His notes, his drawings, and his most valued prize had vanished.

Anger, red and hot and seeping from his pores, replaced his shock, suddenly threatening to undo him. He would not, however, show his outrage. This was theft, pure and simple. How and when the jawbone had been stolen he could not now be sure, but it was certainly gone. He would explain, question the guests.

Then the snickers began. Confusion for some, enjoyment for others, and Nathan was numbed by a dark understanding.

They didn't believe it existed. Nobody had ever before found an intact Megalosaurus jawbone, and not one of these men here tonight believed that he had. And with his notes and drawings gone as well, he had nothing to show for his months of work. Whoever had stolen them knew that. He had been ruined intentionally.

His fellow paleontologists enjoyed the joke they witnessed, not knowing that for Nathan this was the end. From Owen he saw only pity, embarrassment in the man's eyes, perhaps a sense of disbelief.

There was no possible explanation. No money would be forthcoming; no exhibit for the Crystal Palace, for the museum. Only rumor and gossip from his peers, followed by disgrace.

As Nathan strode from the exhibit, shoulders back, ignoring the murmurs and stares of sympathy mixed with satisfied amusement from his contemporaries, he couldn't even look at Mimi Marsh.

Chapter 1

October, 1853

Mimi Sinclair sat at her workbench, in her private studio in back of her Chelsea townhouse, studying the paperwork that accompanied the Pteranodon skull she was ready to draw and sculpt. It was an amazing discovery, this one, a rare fossil found by a French archaeologist, turned over to her for processing by her father. He still kept his studio behind his home in Holland Park, but he was out of the country with Richard Owen at the moment. It was all for the better that she do this sculpting anyway, as her father's eyesight had deteriorated considerably in the last few years and his arthritis had recently begun to worsen. This replica had to be ex-

17

act and without flaw for a year long display at Owen's Zoological Garden, so Mimi had accepted the work for her father. Of course nobody but those in her family knew that she did the craftsmanship herself, but that was beside the point. As a woman, she wouldn't be able to receive great acclaim for her efforts, though in this small regard she accomplished something both worthy and praised. Artistic talent ran deep in the family, in the blood, and she took pride in hers, even if it came in little, sometimes insignificant, amounts.

She'd been working a great deal more of late, and she liked that. It kept her mind active and was time well spent. Since Carter's death she had found less and less to do while in mourning, aside from household management. Calling on friends was inappropriate, and Mimi despised not being social and attending a party or two each month. God should never have made her a widow at so early an age, but obviously God hadn't asked for her opinion on the matter when he'd taken her husband so suddenly. Art and sculpture were all she had now, as she was still in half mourning. Soon, though, she would be able to regain her social gregariousness. It wasn't in her nature to be quiet and solemn anyway. In truth, she despised the somber nature she'd been required to accept these last two years.

Laying her sketch pad on her lap, she began to draw with her pencil. The afternoon sunlight shone a brilliant, pale yellow through the long clear west windows behind her, illuminating her drawing as she worked. She had placed an old cushioned settee in her studio for such a purpose so that she didn't have to carry whatever fossil she might be sketching at the moment to her living quarters just to be able to sit comfortably. It was peaceful, too, in the solitude. Rarely did anyone bother her here.

The sketch soon took on a shape of its own. The Pteranodon was a relatively small creature and would be easy enough to construct. She would start it tomorrow, probably. With notes from Monsieur Lamont, the French archaeologist who found and delivered the fossil, she should be able to build a very good likeness. It was all they had anyway. There really was no definite way to mold a reptile millions of years old with any precision, or at least that was her opinion. Much of it was guesswork, although the scientists were getting better every day as more and more fossils were recovered from deep beneath the earth.

The Pteranodon fossil sat across from her, on a wooden four-legged table that had lost its polish years ago. She studied the angle of the jaw, the long, sharp beak. The jawbone wasn't very large, and she'd heard that this particular beast was something of a birdlike dinosaur, which was how she intended to portray it when she finally got to the sculpting— as a bird, with wings spanned wide. Mimi was looking forward to it.

"Mrs. Sinclair, there is a gentleman to see you. Are you at home?"

Mimi glanced up to find her parlor maid, Stella, standing at the doorway, her starched gray uniform signaling to all the half mourning status of the household. Her reddish-brown hair looked slightly unkempt, her cap tilted to one side, but then for Stella this was custom. She was an attractive girl, as was required of a parlor maid, but regardless of the negative impression she might give because of her constant flustered look, Mimi kept her because she liked her.

Without stopping the motion of her fingers on the pad, she replied, "A gentleman?"

"Yes, ma'am. He's waiting in the morning room. Said he wants to discuss a bit of work." She raised her brows and lowered her voice. "Very nicely dressed, he is, too, though he didn't have a card."

Mimi wiped the back of her hand over her left cheek, brushing stray hair off her face, curious because Stella rarely offered opinion on callers since it was not of her station to do so. He must have made an impression. Handsome, probably. The work part, however, intrigued Mimi more. He likely wanted a sculpture for home or yard decoration. But she remained extremely selective about her sculpting, creating only from fossils and other scientific drawings, and only a few people in all of England knew she did this kind of artwork. She didn't care at all about pottery birdbaths, clay bowls, or metal statues, but she would decline his offer personally.

"I'll see him, Stella."

Her maid curtsied and walked away, her light footsteps tapping on the wooden floorboards as she returned to the front of the house.

Mimi stood and tossed her pad and sketching pencil on the chair. Then she smoothed her boring gray work skirt, rolled down the sleeves to cuff them, and brushed her blond hair with her fingertips until all loose ends fit neatly inside the bun at her nape. Following that, she hurried as fast as was proper to the front of her modestly fashionable home to meet the waiting gentleman.

The day was warm for October and the windows of the house had been cracked open to allow fresh breezes to enter. She walked into her morning room, decorated in light peach and lavender silks and brocades, colors Carter had disliked but that she favored, to find the stranger standing rather than sitting. He faced a large oil painting of Hyde Park in late autumn, studying the colorful leaves blowing across the lake from a mild wind. The man was tall, with broad shoulders and narrow hips, his clothing expensive, but his dark hair too long to be fashionable.

Mimi smiled, standing straight, hands to her sides. "Do you like it? My mother painted it. She used to adore sitting in the park, and had a good eye for symmetry and color . . ."

Her voice trailed off as he slowly turned around, his dark brown eyes locking with hers, expressing a mix of emotion too vivid to be real.

"I've seen this spot in person," he remarked intently, his voice cool and deep, "only the last time was June, I think." Carefully, he glanced down her figure, then up again. "It's as lovely as I remember."

She didn't know whether he meant the painting anymore, but that hardly mattered in the least. Only a few small feet away from her stood a very aloof, challenging, totally changed Nathan Price.

Mimi swallowed then clamped down with her teeth to keep from gaping. He was still as handsome as she remembered, even more so, if that were possible. He wore an immaculately tailored suit in deep olive, and a starched white linen shirt, topped off with a Byron necktie in pale green, knotted precisely. The colors enhanced his hair and eyes, and especially his smooth bronzed skin. Standing comfortably in her morning room, he looked elegant and sophisticated. For a moment Mimi was speechless.

He didn't smile at her shock, didn't move as he waited for her response.

In an attempt to remain composed, Mimi reached out to her side, grabbing the padded back of a peach brocade chair to steady herself. Hopefully he wouldn't notice how she swayed, how her instantly speeding pulse made her body grow hot all over. She just hoped to God her cheeks weren't red.

"Professor Price," she returned in greeting. "How . . . kind of you to call." A ridiculously formal thing to say in their situation, but she felt of a sudden like she'd temporarily lost her mind. Better to stick with formality.

He didn't alter his rigid stance, but he nodded once. "How kind of you to receive me, Mrs. Sinclair."

The measured way her name rolled off his tongue meant something, but she didn't want to speculate on that. His voice, though, she would never forget. It had been two and a half years since that fateful night at the Crystal Palace and yet as the memory came flooding back it seemed incredibly like yesterday. Except for him. Professor Nathan Price, standing here before her. Every sharp edge of her remembrance of him was exact, and not a day went by that she didn't think of him in some regard. But that was a secret she would never reveal.

She motioned with her palm to the settee next to the fireplace. "Won't you please be seated?"

It was seconds before he turned and stepped toward it, but when he did, she followed his fluid, graceful movements with candid eyes. His clothing accentuated his strong physique and dark coloring most becomingly, and she mentally scolded herself for yielding to his sheer attractiveness. He was not cattle on display, and she was still in mourning. She had no business staring at a man as if she hadn't been with one intimately in years. Which she hadn't—but then, that was beside the point.

She sat across from him on a matching settee, awkwardly, or so it felt, adjusting her plain gray skirts around her feet before folding her hands in her lap.

"What can I do for you, Professor?" Immediately, at the slight raising of his brow, she wished she hadn't said that. It made her vividly recall that marvelous and confusing night when he'd seemed to notice her as a woman for the first time, that utterly romantic and splendid kiss behind the hedge. Now she simply tried not to show how uncomfortable she was, how angry she still felt over his complete dismissal of her following his horrid showing at the Crystal Palace. How the memory of him stirred her inside even as she sat across from him, waiting for his reply without dropping her frank gaze.

"I have a request of you," he began without

pause or affectation. "A mutually beneficial request that involves sculpture."

He wanted her to ask him to explain, she knew that intuitively. But she refused. "I see."

"Do you?"

The words were spoken simply, to entice her. He goaded her on purpose, though why, she couldn't be sure. From the wry twist of his lips he seemed to be enjoying how unsettled he'd made her by his unexpected presence in her home.

Sighing and lifting the side of her mouth whimsically, she replied, "I suppose you'd like me to ask you about it."

"That's irrelevant," he returned bluntly. "I think you'll do it anyway."

That irritated her a little, and she ground her fingers into her palms. "Perhaps you should get to the point, Professor."

His dark eyes narrowed minutely, and he leaned back to relax on the settee, but he never dropped his gaze.

"I'm very sorry you lost your husband," he said coolly.

She blinked from the abrupt change in subject, but otherwise she never wavered. "Are you?"

That unexpected rudeness didn't faze him. "Of course. I knew Carter for years, as a colleague. His death was unfortunate."

"Yes," was her simple reply, an attempt, especially with this man, to keep her pent up emotions out of her voice. He didn't deserve an explanation, but she felt like giving him one anyway. "It was sudden and entirely unforeseen. Blood poisoning, or so the physician said. He'd cut himself badly while working in the field and it didn't heal properly." Through a deep exhalation, she added, "We were only married for a few months."

He nodded and looked away for the first time, toward the cold fireplace. After a moment, he murmured, "And you never had a child?"

That made her fidget, feel hot again, and she adjusted her body on the settee. She refused to be baited, though, and so gave the standard answer. "No, we were not blessed in the short time we were together."

He tossed her a quick glance but added nothing.

"Did you ever marry?" she asked, unable to help herself.

He smirked but didn't look at her. "No."

Mimi liked that simple answer to an uncomfortable degree. She was also growing tired of the absurd formality. Aside from their last intimate encounter more than two years ago, they knew each other better than this.

Boldly, she lifted her chin, angling her head in question. "Exactly why are you here, Nathan?"

Without pause, he looked back at her and stated, "I'm here for your services, Mimi."

Her eyebrows rose faintly. "I beg your pardon."

Grinning slyly, he added, "I need your help."

"With a sculpting project?"

His smile broadened, though it wasn't a particularly happy smile. Then he folded his hands in his lap. "Precisely."

For a reason unknown to her she had trouble believing him. "I'm not sure what you want, Nathan, but if it's to sculpt a dinosaur, I think you'd better speak with my father—"

"Actually," he broke in, "I'd prefer your work."

Her palms began to sweat and she rubbed them lightly on her gown over her thighs. "I don't readily sculpt dinosaurs, Nathan."

"Well, now, that's interesting." He cocked his head to the side. "I've heard that you do."

"From whom?" she blurted.

He leaned forward to whisper, "It doesn't matter. It really doesn't. What's important is that I *know* you do, Mimi, and I need you to help me with the skills you possess. Should you choose to keep it all a secret for the rest of your life, nobody will ever hear from me that you were the sculptor."

Her heart began to beat fast again. Nobody knew she sculpted reptiles save her father and Mary, and her father's continued reputation was paramount. Nobody had broken the silence. Nathan had to be guessing.

Still, the whole possibility that others knew of her work agitated her, and she found herself at a loss for words. Nathan must have assumed as much, for at that moment he stood again swiftly, his legs brushing her skirt, his large bearing filling the space between them so that she had to lean her head back and look up to see him. He immediately turned and began to walk slowly around the settee, away from her, the fingers of one hand rubbing his clean-shaven jaw.

"I'm sure you'll recall the night of the Exhibition opening," he started, voice bland.

Mimi was certainly glad he wasn't looking at her because she simply *had* to be blushing now. "Of course—vaguely."

He gave something of a sarcastic snort, then glanced at her askance. "Vaguely? Don't you remember kissing me, Mimi? I most certainly remember kissing you."

How could she ever forget? "As I said, vaguely. It was a very exciting time and much was going on around us."

Snickering, he added, "I'm sure you remember luring me outside."

Her forehead creased as her mouth dropped open. "Luring you? I didn't *lure* you anywhere. It was *you* who asked *me* if I'd like to walk outdoors."

"Ahh. So you do remember spending time with me that evening," he drawled.

"Spending time with you?" She swept her arm across the room in amazement. "I remember your arrogance, your elusiveness, and, in a moment of distraction, my begging you to think about me—"

"Begging?"

"—Which you obviously didn't do. I wrote you three times, Nathan, and never got a response. I was truly sorry about what happened to you, but if you're looking for sympathy now, you've come calling two years too late."

She'd lost her composure at last and he knew it. He faced her fully again, stretching over the settee opposite her, his palms resting casually on its back. "I like you better this way, full of passion and fire. The calm widow pose doesn't suit you."

That completely undid her. She stood to meet him squarely. "I'm rather busy today. It was nice of you to call, Professor Price."

"Let's get back to the request I have of you," he directed with utter confidence, completely ignoring her dismissal. His smile deepened, his eyes took on a reckless cast as they probed hers. "I would like you to sculpt a jawbone for me, and I'll need it by December. I'll give you notes, sketch it, and pay you reasonably for your labor." He leaned over the settee back to add pointedly, "I know you've been sculpting for Sir Harold for at least two years, and that he didn't sculpt a single reptile that now sits within Owen's Zoological Garden. I'm certain you can do this for me, Mimi."

That acknowledgment thoroughly shocked and appalled her. He was blackmailing her without saying so and they both knew it. She had never known Nathan Price to be anything but a gentleman, but he had hardened since his downfall. He was cynical now, shrewd, and she didn't like the change at all. But she absolutely could not allow him to announce to the world that she'd been doing her father's work for years. Sir Harold's reputation had to be maintained at all costs. The Nathan Price she had known before his disastrous ruin at the Crystal Palace was not the man in front of her now. This man was older, more sure of himself, more calculating. Ruthless.

"The jawbone of what?" she finally asked, her tone spilling over with resentment and anger. She didn't want to appear to be giving in easily, without a fight. And she was deathly afraid she already knew the answer.

He thought about that for a moment, his expression harsh. Then he shoved his hands into his coat pockets and began to pace behind the settee, staring at the lavender carpet at his feet.

"The opening night of the Exhibition I was humiliated, Mimi," he began, subdued. "At eight o'clock in the evening I was an admired, respected paleontologist; at five minutes past eight I was the Palace jester. Early that afternoon I had personally transported a perfect, one-of-a-kind Megalosaurus jawbone to the Crystal Palace for the world to see; not six hours later it was missing, stolen by someone who wanted to see me fail, and fail well in front of the most important scientists in England." He drew a long breath as he dropped his head back, and closed his eyes to the ceiling. "Suddenly I had no reputation and my career was all but destroyed. I also received no funding for the museum I had been given to manage. Instead, that money went to Carter Sinclair for his study of monkeys in habitat."

Mimi felt the blood drain from her face. "Carter didn't steal it, Nathan," she admonished in deadly quiet, unable to voice anything more.

His eyes popped open and he abruptly turned to her. "Perhaps he didn't, Mimi," he said, only hinting at untold bitterness. "The Carter Sinclair I knew was, in general, a smart man, but he wasn't calculating in his cleverness. I don't think he could have planned such a scheme and carried it through with the precision it had to have taken—at least, not on his own. It's also true that he wouldn't have known Owen would donate the money to his research instead of the museum if I'd failed to win it. We weren't exactly competitors. Fierce rivals for personal recognition, maybe—but not competitors in the field."

Mimi crossed her arms over her breasts and glanced away uncomfortably, toward the open window with the clear view of Mrs. Ines' red rose covered trellis. Guilt bubbled deep within her as she considered that at the time of the Palace opening she was very much hoping that Carter would be in competition with Nathan for her, Miss Mimi Marsh, Sir Harold's daughter. She'd never told Carter, and now it hardly mattered. Nathan, of course, would never know it, either.

"Do you suspect anyone at all?" she asked moments later, her uneasiness building.

She heard the floorboards creak beneath his feet as he moved again around the settee toward her, but she never altered her stance.

In a clear, direct voice, he murmured, "Yes, I suspect Sir Harold."

Her head flipped around as her mouth dropped open. "That's outrageous!"

"It's also logical."

"How dare you come into my home and accuse—"

"Think about it, Mimi," he cut in, undaunted, stepping closer still. "Who else would gain? Who else knew what I had under the velvet cover, what I stood to lose? He was also the only one close enough to Owen to know that if I failed that night Owen's money would go to Carter, the man who had just asked for his daughter's hand in marriage."

"It's impossible and unthinkable," she fairly

shouted. "Any number of individuals at the opening could have done it. What you suggest is insulting, Nathan." Seething, she lowered her voice to add, "You also have no proof of anything or you would have accused him years ago."

He reached out and grasped her upper arms tightly. "Maybe," he agreed, passionate with his purpose. "But I've been waiting more than two years to clear my name, Mimi. I now know of a way to do it, to discover and expose the man who disgraced me publicly. If you're so sure it wasn't your father, then help me. Help me if only to prove it *wasn't* him." He relaxed a little and smiled cynically. "If nothing else you should enjoy the challenge."

That confused her. The entire incident confused her. His inappropriate nearness had her suddenly dazed, too, with his earthy scent assaulting her senses and his probing eyes drawing her complete attention. Immediately, she jerked herself free of his scorching grasp and took a step back in unconscious self-protection.

He didn't like that, though she wasn't sure why. His smile vanished and his demeanor darkened as his body stiffened beside her.

Mimi looked away from him, toward the fireplace mantel, staring down at all of the silly and useless little trinkets her mother-in-law occasionally sent her to beautify what the woman felt was a less-than-elegant home. Aside from Mimi's occasional sculpting that nobody knew she did, this had become the greatest entertainment for her since Carter's death and her necessary state of mourning—

wondering what little bauble her mother-in-law had wrapped this time in a gaudy box. How absurd, but terribly typical for ladies of her station.

He was right. She'd adore a new challenge right now, and especially one opposing the enigmatic Nathan Price. The idea alone renewed her with a vigor she hadn't felt in a very long time. But could she allow herself to get involved like this? She supposed she must, since it concerned the little issues of blackmail and family dishonor. To save her father a future public disgrace, she would need to prove his innocence of the scandal more than two years ago. She never would have believed for a moment that the Nathan of her past would actually humiliate them all, but she couldn't say certainly that he wouldn't. That minute thread of doubt left her no other choice. She needed to learn what he knew.

Seconds later she felt her anger seep from her skin to leave her drained, numb. "What do you want sculpted, Nathan, and why?" she asked quietly, glancing his way again.

"I need an exact replica of the Megalosaurus that was stolen from the Crystal Palace."

She had assumed as much, and almost laughed at such a preposterous idea. Perhaps he knew it, too, for his dark eyes blazed with the gravity in his request.

"It's important, Mimi."

He was completely serious, and it worried her.

"Nobody believes it existed," she returned briskly. "What are you going to prove with a replica of a fossil nobody's ever seen?"

His cheek twitched. "I'll worry about that when the time comes to produce it."

"And when is that time?"

"During a scientific function, but I don't have details as yet. I need the Megalosaurus first."

She paused, watching him closely, studying his taut expression. He needed a haircut badly, and his face was deeply tanned for this time of year, apparently from working every day under bright sunshine. He'd been gone for a long while, digging for fossils on the Continent, or so she'd heard through the little gossip she'd received. That he was back suddenly and asking—no, *forcing*—her to sculpt the Megalosaurus made her curious, even suspicious. It was a very unusual request. Yes, indeed, the man had a purpose in mind, and although she knew she would have to give in to his demands, she also realized fully that if she wasn't careful in her approach, they would all suffer at the outcome.

"And if I refuse?" she asked coyly, enticing him to argue.

Very slowly, he shook his head, glaring down at her. "You won't. That's the beauty of our little arrangement."

That made her mad again, and he knew it. She could almost see him hold back a smile of satisfaction as heat suffused her face. Fortunately for her, he didn't comment on it.

"I'm staying at the boarding house at Four-forty-seven King's Road," he said instead, "right here in Chelsea."

She knew which one. Quite fashionable and quaint.

But then, most of Chelsea was. She wondered for a moment if he could afford it, then swiftly decided the state of his finances was none of her business.

"Take time to think about how you'd like to begin," he suggested reasonably. "I'll be back in a day or two with notes and drawings of my own, and we can then discuss getting started."

His rich brown eyes probed hers for seconds longer, then dropped to linger on her body, her breasts, before he tipped his head in a gentlemanly gesture. "Good day, Mrs. Sinclair."

Without reply, Mimi stared at his wide back as he strode confidently from her morning room.

Chapter 2

The table had been set as usual for the Sunday meal. Their father would be absent again this week because he was still gone from the country with several of Professor Owen's advisors, inquiring about endorsements from the European elite for research grants. Although due back sometime the following week, he was in Belgium at the moment, or so Mimi had heard. With her father's arthritis, he had trouble writing and refused to dictate for fear someone might discover how physically disabled he'd become from his affliction. News from him, then, tended to be sporadic.

Today, however, even without Sir Harold's presence in his home, the best china had been laid, along with the finest linens and silver for the late breakfast she and Mary would share together, as they did each Sunday after church and had done for as long as Mimi could remember.

She sat at the northern end of the oblong table, in her conservative Sunday gown of deep purple—the only colorful apparel she wore while in half mourning. Mary sat directly across from her, backlit from cloud-filtered daylight seeping through the dining room windows, wearing a plain but striking dress in the becoming shade of green pears. For an unmarried lady of twenty-eight years, her sister carried herself with a surprising amount of grace and sophistication. In small measure, Mimi had always been somewhat jealous of Mary and her elegant, serene beauty and clever wit. Even after she'd married Carter she'd been a little bit in awe of Mary and her ability to remain dignified and worldly in the face of probable spinsterhood. A shame, that, but then Mary enjoyed the life she'd made for herself and indulged her desire to care for their father after their mother's unfortunate death from a weak heart twelve years ago. Mimi also felt, perhaps too romantically, that Mary deserved love and intimate companionship as well, though trying to convince her sister of that went beyond the impossible. Mary seemed happy and content as she was, and Mimi respected her sister's decision in that. At least for now.

She knew she had been rather quiet all morning, waiting for the right time to broach the subject of her unexpected visitor of two days ago. Mary hadn't commented on her unusual silence, thankfully, and even now seemed preoccupied with her own thoughts as she chattered on about the Sunday service and the week ahead. Mimi listened with only half interest as she watched her sister stir sugar into her tea with graceful fingers while a servant leaned over her plate and began cracking the shells of her boiled eggs.

"I've never heard such absolute drivel as that piece played this morning, have you?" Mary carried on without expecting a reply. "I mean, really. Mr. Goodall has certainly been tutoring Priscilla Nagolt long enough to teach her a bit of Handel done properly, don't you think? The worst part, naturally, is that I'll have to attend the poor girl's piano recital next week if I'm going to secure the position I need with Lady Tesh. I'm *sure* she'll be there." Mary slid her spoon gently across the edge of the teacup and shook her head, glancing up mischievously as she lowered her voice to whisper across the table. "I've heard the lady wants silken bed sheets made in the most scandalous shade of red." She giggled. "Two sets to match her most unusual set of—"

"Nathan Price is back in town, Mary," Mimi broke in, deciding in a rush that it would be best for all concerned if she just came right out and plainly divulged the news.

Mary's mouth went slack; then she blinked hard and sat straight up in her chair as her spoon fell from her fingers and onto the saucer with a loud *clink*.

"What?" she blurted, dumbfounded.

For Mary to lose her poise in any situation meant she had been taken fully by surprise, and Mimi couldn't begin to describe the shock she witnessed on her sister's pale face. She supposed that's how she must have looked to Nathan two days ago when he came to her house. How utterly embarrassing.

"It's true," she maintained as nonchalantly as possible. "He's returned to London."

Mary sat back hard, staring at her, ignorant of the servant placing sliced ham and buttered toast on her plate.

"How do you know?" she mumbled. "Did you see him?"

For the last day and a half, Mimi had considered how much to reveal to her sister, finally deciding she would simply have to tell all. There would be no way to hide the fact that she'd be working with Nathan during the coming weeks, and Mary would certainly wonder why she bothered.

"Actually, he came to my home Friday," she admitted through a long sigh, sitting back in her chair as well. It was now her turn to be served, and she waited until ham, plain toast, and scrambled eggs, her preferred choice, were placed on her plate.

Mary continued to stare at her, stunned. "And you received him?"

She lifted a shoulder in a shrug. "He arrived very properly, impeccably dressed, with a request. He wants me to sculpt a dinosaur for him."

For a moment Mary appeared confused, then her forehead creased gently with concern. "He wants to *hire* you? However does he know you sculpt the beasts?"

"I've no idea," she answered honestly, "and he didn't say. I believe he knew I sculpted as a hobby and is now assuming I can create a fossil replica."

Mary paused, rubbing her fingertips back and

forth slowly along the edge of the table, then said, "I'm sure you declined his offer."

Mimi shifted her attention to the jar of strawberry preserves, reaching for them. "Not exactly."

"Mimi!"

"Not yet anyway," she stressed. "But I am considering his request."

"Good heavens, why?" her sister asked, lifting her fork as she remembered her food at last.

Mimi spooned preserves onto her toast, purposefully avoiding Mary's agitated gaze. "He . . . implied that if I don't, he'll make certain all of England knows I'm the sculptor of the works that grace the halls of the Zoological Garden."

She expected to hear a burst of outrage, but it didn't come, which surprised her. Instead, her sister took particular notice of her breakfast and began to eat in earnest.

"He can't know anything," Mary insisted after swallowing a bite of egg. "And since he hasn't told a soul that we know of, he's likely got no proof whatsoever that you're the sculptor. Nobody would believe him anyway should he reveal this to others."

Mary had a point, but she didn't know the full of it. Mimi swallowed ham that tasted particularly salty and unpalatable this morning, then calmly remarked, "He also believes Papa was the one to steal his notes and jawbone from the Crystal Palace two and a half years ago."

If she expected shock again, she didn't get that reaction. Mary continued to eat without looking at her, but her head was shaking now, her full lips thinned with growing disgust.

"That's outrageous."

"Exactly what I said."

"The man should be charged with slander."

Mimi sighed. "For heaven's sake, Mary, he's smarter than that."

Her sister looked up sharply. "Smarter than what?"

"Nathan Price didn't actually *accuse* Papa of a crime. He has no proof or he would have done so years ago." She reached for her tea and leaned forward, over the edge of the table, to stress her point. "No, he just wants to clear his name, to rebuild some sort of reputation that he lost that night, and he's asked me to help."

"Threatened you, is what it sounds like," Mary corrected through a tone of disgust. "And I can't believe you're thinking of doing it."

"Papa didn't steal the jawbone, therefore it can't hurt to help him." Mimi's mouth curled up in smile. "I think I might enjoy the challenge of proving Professor Price wrong in his assumptions."

Mary tapped at the corners of her lips with her napkin, then motioned for a waiting servant to pour her more tea. "What does he want sculpted and why?"

Mimi knew this question was coming but she took it in stride, avoiding her sister's eyes as she concentrated on her plate of food. "He has some function to attend in late December where he'll present a replica of the Megalosaurus jawbone that was stolen from the Palace—"

Mary's sudden laughter cut her off, and her head jerked up.

"What do you find particularly humorous in that?"

Mary stared at her, an odd combination of incredulity and amusement expressed in her delicate features.

"He can't be serious."

She realized Mary's stupefaction was merely due to Nathan's audacity rather than a question of her talent. "Oh, I think he is most definitely serious," she countered after a deep inhalation.

Mary gazed at her for another few seconds, then scoffed with dismissal and lifted her cup to her lips, finishing the contents.

"The whole thing sounds ridiculous. I cannot imagine why on earth he should need a replica now."

Mimi considered that for a moment, biting into her toast and chewing without tasting. "He's been humiliated publicly, Mary, and wants to repair the damage done him the night of the Palace opening, I believe. What's wrong with that?"

"Repair the damage?" she repeated. "The man is a fraud."

She shook her head. "That is not proven. Just because he's not of your taste—"

"Not of my taste? What does my taste have to do with it?"

Mimi scooped eggs onto her fork with her toast, wondering at her sister's heightened aggravation. "He is not a completely refined gentleman, true, and I expect he's from a lower class—"

"He *is* from a lower class," Mary cut in again, "and has always had expectations above his station, but that is beside the point." She placed her fork and knife on her plate, then folded her hands together, wrists on the edge of the table, and leaned forward. "He was arrogant and foolish, from what I remember of him, and far too sure of himself. He probably created his own downfall."

Mimi smiled, refusing to be baited. "He's still arrogant, but I . . . admire him. Like him, oddly enough. He's a contradiction of a man. Unique."

"Is he married?"

That question came out of nowhere, and Mimi tried not to squirm in her chair. "I don't believe so, no," she said after a moment, attempting to sound blasé about the matter.

Mary grew silent after that, though Mimi could tell she was thinking shrewdly with her brows gently furrowed and her dark gray eyes narrowed in disapproval. Weak sunlight bounced off the blond braids hooped around her ears as they moved with a very small shake of her head.

"You like what you see, not what you know," Mary warned very carefully. "I've never understood your attraction to that man, Mimi. He is wrong for you in every way."

She felt a creeping warmth in her cheeks and lifted her lace napkin to her lips as a measure of coverage should her sister notice. "My *former* attraction to Professor Price, as you know, was the stuff of adolescent fantasies, and there is absolutely no reason for him to be *right* for me now. I simply admire his work. I want to help him."

"Of course you do," Mary agreed too sweetly, purposely batting her lashes.

"He is a fascinating gentleman," Mimi reasoned,

which brought no response at all. "And since he is innocent of the ruin thrust upon him, he deserves to have his name cleared."

Mary stood suddenly, tossing her napkin on her plate, her breakfast unfinished. "I think it's a foolish thing to do, but then you're headstrong and have hardly ever listened to me. You've obviously made up your mind." She dropped her voice and leaned forward, palms flat on the tabletop. "Just be careful and remember to keep your distance. He is an un-married man and you are a widow still in mourn-ing. Not only is that dangerous socially should others learn of your working . . . connection, it could be personally ruinous. As reckless as you sometimes are, I don't want to see you hurt."

With that, Mary stepped away from her chair and swept past her, highly angered, Mimi knew, because she never left the table until they were both finished.

It hardly mattered. She had given Mary only half-truths regarding her objective in helping the man anyway. Of course Nathan also remained ignorant of what she knew, and of her motives, those she'd now taken two days to evaluate. She had no prob-lem assisting him in his desire to clear his name and proving her father's innocence, if only to Nathan. No, the greatest part of this little endeavor would be finding out if he still desired her as he did two years ago, the night he kissed her so beautifully, with such utter bewilderment at his own feelings. It truly was a shame that men were so unaware of their roman-tic needs.

Mimi finished the remainder of her tea; then, smiling with satisfaction, she rose, brushed down her satin skirts with her palms, and walked from the dining room to the parlor to get her things. She had her own demands if they were going to work together, and it was time to reveal her terms to Professor Price.

turn to keep his mind off Mimi Marsh. No, Mimi *Sinclair*, he kept reminding himself, which was proof enough that his attempt at concentrating on work-related material wasn't enormously effective.

It wasn't as if he'd been unaware of the few women in whose presence he'd mingled during the last two or three years, or hadn't been involved in two or three romantic interludes. But it was a fact, indeed, that Mimi was the only woman to make him think of nothing but her for days—weeks—after seeing her, just as she had that fateful night at the Crystal Palace. She was the one woman who possessed the uncanny ability to immobilize his thoughts, both day and night. And during the last two nights his sleeping thoughts of her consisted of erotic overtones that were surely defeating his purpose of remaining objective and clear-headed about his return to London after all this time.

Not only did this inability to control his lascivious musings and dreams concern him, it made him rather angry at himself. He didn't have time for it. He had so much to consider now in clearing his name, in reinstating himself within the upper echelon of the scientific world. For the first time in nearly three years he had hopes of a professional future worth something more than what he gained by digging in the ground. It wasn't that he didn't appreciate working with the soil on his hands and knees, his sweat-drenched body taking pride in the finds, the discoveries, but what he ultimately wanted for himself was intellectual achievement, prestige. Nobody in his family had ever achieved greatness, and he wanted to be the first. This had al-

ways been his ultimate goal. Simply laying eyes on
Mimi Sinclair again two days ago made him momentarily forget the important strategy ahead, and
what he could not understand was how one average English lady managed to do that to him.

The problem, he decided, was that she was just so
very *removed* from average. Perhaps her life as she'd
lived it thus far had been appropriate for a lady of
her station, but as an individual she was unique.
He'd noticed that about her when they'd initially
met eight or ten years ago, though at that time she
was a child and he'd given her little more than brief
acknowledgment. But she'd always had a look
about her that suggested an unlimited number of
intricate thoughts roaming around mischievously in
her very female mind. Nathan didn't know much
about females, coming from a family of dominant
males and a mother who lived as a proper,
unassertive mother should, but he knew just by
looking at Mimi Marsh that she was colorful and
shrewd beyond what was customary for a lady of
quality.

Nathan groaned and leaned his head against the
wall behind him, draping his forearm across his
closed eyes.

Widow Sinclair. The title made his stomach turn,
though he wasn't exactly sure why. He'd expected
her to look different upon seeing her again, older,
rounder with her married status. Matronly. Instead,
when she'd walked into her morning room to greet
him, he'd had to force himself to keep from staring.
She was certainly a vision, even in drab work clothing, though the ridiculous shade of gray she was

forced to wear didn't do her justice. It wasn't a good color for her at all. He wasn't sure how he knew that, either, since color was something he rarely noticed when it came to women and their attire.

She was also sexually . . . there. Always. Regardless of what she wore. Her sexuality remained centered, the focal point of everything she said or did, whether she knew it or not, and after their meeting of two days ago, Nathan doubted that she did. Her sexual appeal wasn't forced or intentional, it was simply a part of her, like her hair color or the length of her legs. She possessed an aura of allure that ruffled a man's feathers when she happened to be near him, especially when she spoke in that soft, velvety voice of hers. When she grew passionate with purpose, eyes flashing, color bright, she was beautiful. Simply beautiful. Carter had probably noticed this about her, too, had probably enjoyed the spicy scent she always wore, enjoyed watching her, touching her, savored tasting her for the first time—

Nathan stood abruptly, the chair behind him shoved back loudly on the bare wooden floor, annoyed at his continuing line of thought when he had so much work to do. He pushed his hands through his hair with hard fingers, then walked to the window.

The sky had become fully overcast, the day gray and dreary, which fit his mood. From his second floor room he saw only tall white or red brick buildings on all sides of him, caught a slim view of the busy street, and the small garden with its narrow path just below him, its flowers all but lying dormant for the coming winter.

The boarding house suited his purposes nicely, and it was marvelously convenient, a four block walking distance from Mimi's stylish townhouse. His room was perfectly functional, his bed warm and soft, especially when he compared it to sleeping on cots or the ground, as he'd been doing off and on for the last two years. The wallpaper was a bit too ornate for his taste, but then that was irrelevant. The thick burgundy drapes that matched the coverlet hung loosely at the window and completely shaded the room from outside light if closed for daytime sleep. He also had a gas lamp and fireplace, which were certainly more comforts than he was used to. Soon, however, he would be ready to look for a home of his own, as long as his funds didn't run out. That concern alone made restoring his reputation paramount.

In many ways he'd been glad to return to his father's country—*his* country—and to the city life and excitement of London. But he regretted leaving the warmth of Southern France where he'd spent the last eighteen months, losing the freedom to move around as he pleased and to answer to nobody, giving up the space and sunshine and good, honest work for an honest day's wages. He would miss it, but the time had come to pick up his life as he was meant to live it and press on. It was time to reestablish his good name in the community and reclaim his honor. He only wished he didn't need Mimi's help to do it. It would be so much easier not to involve her.

But then she was the center of it all.

Nathan swore softly and crossed his arms over

his chest. Leaning the side of his head on the glass, he stared vacantly out to the bustle of traffic on King's Road.

He'd thought of her frequently during the last two years, and had all but come to the conclusion that it was that one sweet kiss between them that had not only shredded his reason, but had allowed his defenses to fall, driving him toward his ultimate ruin. Yet he accepted full responsibility for it because he'd yielded to her wonderfully perfumed smell and dark, beckoning eyes that led him not only outside that night, but to his downfall. Still, he knew that wasn't exactly correct. For weeks following the Crystal Palace opening he'd wanted to blame Mimi for setting him up to fail in front of the greatest group of scientists ever to be assembled in one building, though logically he realized that probably had not been her intent at the time. Probably. The jawbone had to have been stolen earlier, not when she'd followed him out to the open air. That would have been too risky, and the timing wrong. But he couldn't altogether dismiss the coincidence. He believed wholeheartedly that Sir Harold Marsh was the catalyst behind his demise, therefore he also had to suspect the man's enticing daughter because she was the one who'd won in the end. It was possible the entire affair was her father's doing without anyone else's knowledge, but Mimi was the only one who'd triumphed totally by his failure that night. Technically, he supposed, she was now living off funds that should have been his. In the end, this bothered him more than he could put into words.

Of one thing Nathan was certain: whoever had destroyed him the night of the Palace opening would be made to pay, and his irrational, albeit undeniable, lust for a striking, sensual woman meant nothing to him when his restored reputation was at stake. Women came and went in a man's life, but honor remained with you beyond the grave, and he would have his returned to him. If Mimi knew what happened that night, or where the jawbone was now, supposing it still existed, he would discover that information, regardless of what he had to do to get it. Triumph would ultimately be his.

Suddenly his eye caught the movement of dark purple skirts on the street below, and he sharpened his attention, his gaze narrowing on the lady's swift walk and upturned head until she disappeared from view at the front of the building.

Mimi. She'd come to discuss their arrangement with him.

The shock of seeing her here, now, on a Sunday afternoon, quickly turned to amusement, which overshadowed the steady rise in his pulse. Nathan ignored that reaction as a slow smile crept up one side of his face. He knew enough about her to realize her being here was complete submission to his demand while attempting to regain control of a situation she didn't like. Very bold of her, but she didn't stand a chance and he relished the thought of explaining that to her.

Nathan stood where he was for a full minute, making her wait, until he heard the knock on the door.

"Professor Price," came the sturdy voice of Mrs. Sheffield, the owner's wife. "There is a lady below who wishes to speak with you."

"I'll be down in a moment," he gruffly replied. When he heard Mrs. Sheffield retreating with heavy footsteps, he finally straightened, rolled down his sleeves, and buttoned the cuffs before he made his way to the door and descended the stairs.

She'd be waiting in the parlor, he assumed, and just before he entered it, he took a deep breath and combed his fingers through his hair a final time. No point in looking unkempt.

She stood by the arched window gazing out to the tiny garden path between the buildings, her back rigid with purpose. She'd piled her dark blond hair loosely atop her head, but the ends of it were covered by a purple narrow-brimmed beaded hat. She turned when she heard him walk in, and once again he was struck by the vivid darkness of her large, brown eyes as they dauntlessly locked with his. Her eyes were something he had never forgotten.

"Professor Price," she said evenly, a pleasant smile firmly planted on her face. Then she glanced to his attire, looking him up and down, and delicately frowned.

Nathan couldn't decide if his general appearance bothered her, since he wore only casual pants and an inexpensive linen shirt, or the fact that he'd not buttoned his shirt to the neck. Frankly, he didn't care, but her unvoiced disapproval did annoy him.

He strolled into the parlor proper and stopped about three feet away from her, legs spread wide, arms crossed over his chest.

"Why, Mrs. Sinclair," he drawled. "How delightful of you to visit."

Her lips thinned and she pulled her body erect, clutching her beaded reticule with both hands in front of her small, corseted waist. "Oh, for heaven's sake, Nathan, stop calling me that."

The fact that she snapped at him took him a little by surprise since it was, in fact, her name, but he tried not to let it show. Actually, her appearance surprised him, too, although he supposed a widow of her class would be appropriately dressed in purple. But this gown clung to her bosom exceptionally well, the fabric a fine . . . silk, he believed, the rich color enhancing her pale skin perfectly. Yes, if Mimi Sinclair knew anything it was how to dress to be noticed, even in half mourning.

"Mimi," he started again, dropping his voice and forcing a polite grin, "it's lovely to see you. Would you care to be seated?"

He could have sworn she huffed when she drew her gaze away from his and swept past him to lower her body into a wing chair near the slow burning fireplace. But he noticed more clearly the way she smelled when she passed by him—clean and fresh and . . . arousing. No perfume today, but he could tell she'd recently had a bath. It had been a long time since Nathan had experienced the scent of pure, clean woman, and it made him irritable that he encountered it now, here. From her.

Instead of following her lead by sitting, he remained standing, though he moved a good distance away from her, positioning himself near the window and holding his hands behind his back.

"So," he carried on, watching her adjust her skirts for what appeared to be a lengthy stay, "what brings you to King's Boarding House on a peaceful Sunday afternoon?"

Sitting comfortably, with a gracious tip of her head and a wry smile, she replied, "I think you know why I'm here, Nathan, so let's just get to the business at hand."

His brows rose and he glanced briefly to his scuffed, worn shoes. "Excellent suggestion, I suppose, but I did say at our last meeting that I would call on you." Clearing his throat purposefully, he tried again, his words a bit more succinct. "What I want to know is why you came here today when you knew I would be returning to your home in another day or so."

She waited long enough for him to realize that this line of questioning plainly took her aback. Shifting her bottom in the chair, she turned her attention to the wall at her side, her gaze resting on a well-done floral painting.

"I suppose I simply wanted to get these issues out in the open as quickly as possible." She shrugged lightly. "Why wait until tomorrow when what one needs to have done can be done today?"

That silly answer pushed him to the edge of laughter, but he held back to pleasantly agree, "Why, indeed?"

She looked at him again, her eyes wide and bright, lips turned up in a half-smile of certain conquest. "I've considered your . . . request, Nathan, and although I find it in many ways troubling, I believe I have no choice but to prove you wrong."

He leaned his shoulder casually against the window frame and crossed one shoe over the other. "Oh?"

The tight line of her mouth was the only sign that his brief reply wasn't what she wanted to hear. Of course he didn't know if she expected a show of anger on his part, or frustration, maybe something else. She should know, however, that he had to have considered everything before he went to her in the first place. He knew exactly how she would respond, and as the skin on her cheeks suddenly began to flush, he enjoyed the fact that she was just this moment putting this together in her mind. Still, he remained silent, letting her brood.

She straightened her shoulders even more, if that was possible, though he couldn't tell if it was for her own sense of confidence or his visual benefit, since her breasts pushed out against her silk bodice nicely and his concentration on her face faltered for just an instant as he stole a fast glance at them. She couldn't be that astute at knowing how to distract a man, he didn't think. Then again, she'd briefly been married.

"The first requirement if I am to help you," she began in earnest, chin held high, "is that you must tell me how you learned who exactly is sculpting the dinosaur models that now sit in the halls of the Zoological Garden."

He wasn't expecting that, but he understood her need to know. It made him smile, actually, his first true smile of pleasure in days. "And your other requirements?"

"We'll get to them. I want this answer first."

Very tactful. He nodded as he drew a deep

breath, capturing the scent of something roasting in the nearby kitchen. Dinner would be served soon, but for now they were alone in this part of the house. Even Mrs. Sheffield had disappeared, though he knew she was likely nearby, eavesdropping if she could. Mimi obviously suspected this as well or she would have been more direct with her question. How did he know *she* was the dinosaur sculptor? Maybe she was a good deal more clever than he'd first supposed. Amazing, for a woman.

Nathan strode to the small sofa that faced both her and the grate, and sat comfortably, one arm relaxing lengthwise across the short back, one leg crossed over the other, his foot resting on his knee. He realized she likely had a list of specifics she needed answered, and if she were anything like his mother, this could take hours. He groaned inwardly.

"I guessed you were a reptile sculptor, Mimi," he replied at length. "I've known of your artistic talent for years, and I simply deduced that you'd follow in your father's footsteps."

She clearly didn't take that acknowledgment at face value, and her expression of flat disbelief told him so.

"Really, Nathan. I think you owe me the truth considering that my father's reputation is at stake."

Immediately his blood ran cold, and just as quickly she realized she shouldn't have said that. Her eyes never strayed from his, but her fingers tightened noticeably around her reticule.

"The truth?" he repeated, his tone dropping a degree with measured coolness. "The truth is that I've been digging with a team of French archeologists and paleontologists in southern France for the last eighteen months, Mimi, because it was the only work I could get. About a year ago I came upon some wonderful discoveries that were my very own. One was a marvelous fossilized tail of a Stegosaurus, the molding of which now sits in the Zoological Garden."

He could see the light come on in her eyes as they opened round with growing shock and understanding, and he simply had to grace her with a cunning grin to complete the blow.

Leaning forward, elbows on his crossed leg, palms together, he slowly murmured, "I also discovered a Pteranodon, nearly complete and in perfect fossilized condition. I believe it lies in your studio, the likes of which you're sculpting now."

Her lips parted with a sharp inhalation as her upper body tensed, her fingers practically white now as they clutched the twisted strings of the bag in her hand.

Cautiously, she whispered, "I don't understand."

"Yes, you do." He stared intently into her eyes, no longer caring whether Mrs. Sheffield heard anything. "In order for my plan to work, I needed to discover if you sculpted, Mimi. I suspected that you did, but the only way I could possibly prove it, since I was certain you'd deny the fact if I simply asked, was to set you up so that you had something to sculpt. A rather brilliant idea on my part, I think."

Her brown eyes flashed hotly. "I think it's rather arrogant."

He nodded gingerly in agreement. "I've been known to be arrogant from time to time."

"How humble you are as well, Nathan."

Her sarcastic connotation did not go unnoticed and he smiled again. "Regardless of my tact, my plan had merit. It worked." Sitting back against the soft cushion once more, he carried on. "Soon after I discovered them, I sold both fossils, the Stegosaurus and the Pteranodon, outright to French archeologist Pierre Lamont. I knew with his connections to your father, Sir Harold would be the Frenchman's first choice to sculpt it, which, ultimately, would lead to you. I planned the commission to take place at the precise time I knew your father would be absent from the country, and then I waited for Monsieur Lamont's treasures to be presented at the Garden after being sculpted. I now have full confidence that you can help me. There is no way for you to deny your skills, Mimi."

For a second or two she looked as if she might cry. She blinked several times, her features sagging. Then not an instant later she shook herself and lifted her chin, clenching her jaw. Her face flushed and Nathan could sense that she'd become fiercely mad at him. It didn't faze him. It's what he expected, and how he would have felt in her position.

"You used me," she whispered tightly.

He shook his head negligibly. "You were paid adequately to do what you do well. That's all. You were never used."

"You're using me now," she seethed through closed teeth.

"I need your help because I know you can do what I need done, Mimi," he countered gravely. "I trust your talent."

With obvious disgust, she glanced around the parlor, taking in its peach painted walls behind oil paintings in gilded frames, the rich, brocade drapes, plush carpeting, and new cherry wood furniture.

"And I suppose selling the fossils is how you—"

Sharply, she looked back at him, understanding dawning.

How I paid for this luxury, Mimi? For the quality suit I wore to greet you? For my temporary return to your social class? He didn't voice the thoughts, though, because they didn't need to be said. The fossils were incredible finds and she knew that perfectly well. Monsieur Lamont would be well on his way to establishing his name in the field because he had bought the right to say he'd found them. Their sculptures would sit in the Zoological Garden alongside Professor Owen's, in the name of France. Yes, Mimi now understood what he'd lost through his temporary financial gain. Silence paid very well, indeed.

She continued to stare at him for several long seconds, intensely angered. Then swiftly she rose, tossing her reticule in the chair and crossing the floor to the window, her back to him, arms clutched together in front of her.

"Those fossils could have restored your reputation, Nathan," she said, staring out to the darkening sky. "And yet you readily sold them."

"Yes, they were good finds, and with them, along with continued research and the passing of years, I could have begun to rebuild my name as a renowned paleontologist." He pushed himself up to a standing position, but didn't move away from the sofa. Passionately, arms to his sides, he added, "That isn't enough, Mimi. It could never be enough. Reputation can be easily gained or regained, but not honor. The only way I can have my honor as a man returned to me is to be good at what I do, and to prove that I was *wronged*. I must discover who set me up for professional ruin in front of the most important people in my field on the night that I was to gain final, undeniable respect. And above it all, I want to know why."

She didn't argue or say a word when he finished his fervent disclosure.

They both knew she wanted to exclaim that it wasn't her father who could have done such an ignoble deed, but she'd been defeated in a manner and it would do no good if she tried even a modest defense of him now. Nathan had to admire her poise in that.

A loud clatter of dishes in the kitchen broke the settled quiet between them, and they both turned toward the noise.

"It's getting late and I must be going," she said at last, pivoting to face him squarely. "I have two more requests of you, however, if we are going to be working together."

Her demeanor had changed subtly so that she looked slightly weary, even remotely concerned, but every bit as determined as she was when she'd walked into the boarding house just a few minutes before.

He waited, folding his arms across his chest. "Go on."

She drew a long breath. "You must give me your word that my father will not be humiliated in any way. That would be tantamount to my helping you to ruin him."

He couldn't promise her that, which she likely suspected. Nevertheless, he nodded, attempting to evade the issue. "I need the sculpture by New Year's Eve. I'm attending a formal banquet given by Professor Owen. Several statesmen and dignitaries, and nearly every paleontologist in England will be there."

Her face went slack as her eyes opened wide. "How do you expect to get an invitation?"

"Through Justin Marley," he revealed, only because he believed it wouldn't matter if anyone knew. "Justin and I have been in contact these last two years, more friends than colleagues, really. He'll be attending, certainly, and it was, in fact, originally his idea."

"And what do you propose to do with the sculpture?" she asked a bit dubiously, tilting her head, her brow creased in a frown.

He began to step toward her. "Show it to everyone."

She attempted to hide a smile, but didn't press him for detail. Instead, she asked, "Will my father be attending?"

When he stopped directly in front of her, he admitted, "Probably. But I will not reveal who the sculptor is, Mimi. That has nothing at all to do with my intentions."

She gazed into his eyes a moment longer, evaluating, calculating the difficulties ahead, perhaps the possibilities, shielding her worries the best she could.

Nathan watched her candidly, taking in the smoothness of her skin, her full mouth that he remembered so well, a few strands of her straight, clean hair that had fallen loose to peek out from beneath her hat. If there was one thing he now knew with certainty it was that she truly did not believe her father to be guilty of his downfall. If she suspected it at all, she would have immediately denied him the chance to redeem himself at the banquet. Her father would be there, Owen would be there, Justin and other top English scientists would all be attending. She fully understood what was at stake. The only other possibility was that *she* had been involved with the theft and instead confidently knew this was something he would never learn. She'd agree to help him not to protect her father but to see him fail again. Ultimately. That thought alone sickened him more than he wanted to acknowledge.

With a final look of acceptance, she lowered her gaze and swept past him, her skirts brushing his legs as she moved to retrieve her reticule.

"I also need you to be there for the sketching, Nathan," she informed nonchalantly, lifting her bag and pulling the strings over her right wrist. Turning to face him again, she added, "And for the sculpting as well."

It was his turn to be surprised, and he surely expressed it in his features, for she smiled, somewhat condescendingly.

"It's something nobody has ever seen," she explained, "and you're the only one who knows the true dimensions of the beast. If you want others to be convinced of its authenticity it will need to be exact, perfect. I'm sure you understand."

Nathan felt his body stiffen. He couldn't be sure if she mocked him now as others had in the past, or spoke in honesty, but it irked him just the same.

Audaciously, she waited for his response, watching him closely. Slowly he lowered his eyes to her breasts again, concealed behind a snug layer of silk, only hinting at their beauty. Teasing. Just like her face, her eyes, her voice. Hinting, teasing, never revealing what lay beneath, inside.

He stepped toward her, moving closer, raising his eyes again. She was blushing now; she'd realized where his thoughts lay, felt the pull of attraction as he did, but she was bold enough to stand her ground and ignore it openly. Good for her.

"I haven't had time to sketch anything yet, Mimi," he said softly, intently, working the lie splendidly. "And of course I'll need to be there for the sculpting. When would you like to begin?"

"When you are ready, Nathan," she replied at once, sweetly. "I work in my studio during the week, from ten in the morning until teatime. You may join me whenever you wish, starting tomorrow if you like." With only the slightest hesitation, she reached out with her hand. "Do you agree to my terms?"

Her terms? He swallowed a laugh. How odd that this one female had such an extraordinary ability to turn everything to her apparent advantage. He couldn't decide if that was an affliction of her character, or a gift.

"I agree." He clasped her hand firmly with his. Her skin felt hot, soft, and he rubbed his thumb once over the delicate bones of her knuckles, daring her to withdraw. The contact startled her, he could tell, and sent a jolt of unexpected arousal through his body, but he stood his ground, marvelously satisfied that a simple touch from him could unnerve her.

She blinked and drew an uneven breath. Then she pulled back and he released her.

Without further comment, looking away from him at last, she turned and walked with head held high, shoulders back, to the parlor entrance.

"Until tomorrow, Mrs. Sinclair," he bade her softly.

She paused briefly in her stride but didn't acknowledge him as she lifted the latch and stepped through the front doors into the gloomy late afternoon.

Mimi waited till nearly midnight, then quietly climbed the stairs to the third floor rooms, most of them closed off tightly for the coming winter. In slippered feet, she made her way to the far end of the corridor, then reached into her nightdress pocket for the single key she owned to the attic door. She hadn't been inside for months, as there was really no reason for her to enter the small, dusty enclosure. The contents within were of little use— some rare books in boxes, Italian glassware of her mother's that she treasured and wanted left undisturbed, paintings she had no desire to hang at the moment. And Carter's things, including a few pieces of jewelry and clothes not given to the poor, his personal notes and scientific journals that he'd kept at home.

She turned the knob and stepped nimbly inside, closing the door behind her. A musty odor struck her immediately, though that was to be expected, and without hesitation she turned up the light on the lamp in her hand to have a look at her surroundings.

Everything remained as it should; nothing had been disturbed since her last visit. Cobwebs drifted down from the wooden beams at the ceiling, but otherwise the tiny room was clean, save for a layer of dust coating everything. Mimi placed her finger beneath her nose, pausing for a moment to stifle a sneeze, then got immediately to her task.

She moved quickly around piles of useless things to the west wall, where crates of her prized items sat undisturbed. Placing the lamp on a small wooden stool to her side, she began shifting small boxes around and out of her way until she stood in the farthest corner.

It was there. Exactly as she'd left it.

Lowering herself to her knees, Mimi reached out to touch the crate's cold, dry wood. Then she placed her palms at the edges and shoved them upward—two times—before the top gave way and opened with a gentle creak.

Here it rested, undisturbed after two years. Mimi stared at black velvet for several moments, then slowly lifted the soft edge to reveal her treasure. The chill in the room pressed against her; the silence sliced through the night, and she centered her mind on the wooden floor beyond the attic door for the sound of a servant's footsteps, her heart pounding loudly in her breast with the thought of being discovered, with the fantastic notion of what she'd now decided to do.

At her fingertips lay the ancient Megalosaurus jawbone, stolen from Professor Nathan Price at the Crystal Palace. Large, sturdy, hidden, it remained the one piece of evidence that could restore the man's lost reputation—or ruin them all.

Gingerly she stroked the top of one of the greatest discoveries of paleontology, its worth immeasurable but not denied, noticing again how it felt like cool wood, the edges so delicate they could crumble if disturbed. It had taken her a weekend of careful consideration, but now Mimi had a plan. The jawbone had remained untouched all this time, but in a daring move she at last knew what to do without anyone learning the truth. Nobody could ever know what she knew.

Nobody.

Chapter 4

Mimi paced the floor of her studio, hands clasping her upper arms as she looked at the clock. Half past eleven, and Nathan had yet to arrive. She scolded herself for caring, too; she had other things she could do while she waited, perhaps even work on the Pteranodon, though she really didn't have the desire. Certainly she didn't need his approval or appraisal to begin a project, but so far this morning she'd had difficulty concentrating on the process ahead simply because he wasn't there to oversee it. It disgusted her that she'd yielded her entire schedule to Nathan and his authority, or, one could argue, his cool, singular charm.

Again, she glanced at the clock. Thirty-*one* minutes past eleven. Her preoccupation with the man and his lateness was getting ridiculous. Then again, she'd more or less told him to come at his convenience by not specifying that she wanted him there *precisely* at ten. He'd evidently read what he wanted into that.

Sighing loudly with her impatience, Mimi dropped her arms, shook them out, and wandered to the west-facing oblong windows, resting her bottom on the back of the settee to take in the view of her small but orderly backyard. The autumn season had arrived at last, and leaves now showed a definite change to fall hues, from golden yellow to russet. Her workshop had been added on to the west end of the house, which was why her garden, where she spent much of her time in summer months, was so very tiny. Already her rather insignificant cluster of prized flowers had gone dormant. But the view from her studio still provided plenty of color, and she gazed with only half regard at a lilac bush that needed trimming. It reminded her again that she should be doing something worthwhile with her time now, like cutting back overgrowth for the coming winter, instead of waiting for a man to arrive so she could start her workday.

She rubbed her temples with her fingertips. Stupid woman. Or maybe just stupidly obsessed.

A blend of rustling skirts and footsteps echoed in the hallway suddenly, and Mimi turned to the doorway, her pulse quickening as the sound grew louder. At last he was here, she knew, because Stella had been given instructions that she not be disturbed in her studio until Professor Price arrived. She glanced again at the clock. Thirty-four minutes past eleven. The man needed a lesson in timeliness.

"I beg your pardon, Mrs. Sinclair," came Stella's voice, only slightly shading her curiosity. "Professor Price is here."

Then, before she could respond to her maid, in he walked, all six marvelous feet of him, filling the room with his broad shoulders and commanding presence as if he belonged there, a black leather case tucked under one arm. Today he wore casual cloth-ing, a gray linen shirt, buttoned conservatively, navy trousers, and the same work boots he'd worn yesterday. He'd also finally received a haircut, though it was still a little too long in back to be con-sidered fashionable in the upper circles of society. But if visiting his barber had put him late for their meeting this morning, she would forgive him. He was just so terribly handsome, and the trimming did wonders for his overall appearance. Then his clear, brilliant eyes drew her attention away from everything else, and for a moment she was dumb-struck, as she typically was at the first sight of Nathan. Still, refusing to let it show, she planted a pleasant smile on her lips and nodded once to her almost-grinning maid.

"We wish to work undisturbed, Stella," she said a bit sternly. "We will take luncheon at one o'clock."

Stella's expression went properly flat, and she curtsied slightly before offering a humble, "Yes, ma'am," to her employer. Then she quit the room.

Nathan stood silently, obviously waiting for her to invite him in to sit.

"Well, Nathan," she began through a long, exaggerated exhalation, "I'm so glad you could make it today."

"Mimi," he drawled, eyes narrowing, "I'm so very glad I could, too."

His deeply smooth voice made her shiver inexplicably and, she hoped, unnoticeably. But she substituted that reaction in favor of her annoyance at his late arrival.

Smiling pertly, she clasped her hands behind her back. "You look . . . well this morning."

Now a brow rose faintly. "As do you."

"I was rather hoping you'd be here sooner," she pressed for detail.

He nodded as if he expected this. "I apologize for keeping you. I had a scheduled breakfast with Justin Marley this morning and it ran late. I should have mentioned that yesterday when you so unexpectedly graced me with your lovely presence."

She wasn't sure if that was a cutting criticism of her intrusive visit to his residence, or just a simple compliment. It was offered so blandly, however, that it made her shift uncomfortably from one foot to the other.

"Oh, I see," she acquiesced. "I hope your breakfast with Mr. Marley was engaging, then."

He tipped his head toward her. "It was, thank you."

He had yet to offer any word of conversation, or look around the room, and the way he was gazing at her so frankly made her a bit anxious. She wore her usual modest gray work dress, but he scanned her up and down, his eyes pausing a trifle too long at her bosom.

For a reason unclear to her Nathan seemed overly fascinated with her breasts. His eyes strayed there every time they met, which in turn made her insides liquify sinfully. She didn't understand his preoccupation with them, frankly. Carter had never been so tempted by her breasts, and had actually preferred her female parts a bit below them—incessantly and sometimes deliciously, she remembered now. Immediately, she felt her body heat along with her maddening sexual thoughts—thoughts no lady should consider, especially in the presence of a man who was not her husband.

"Would you care to get started, Nathan?" she asked after a firm clearing of her throat and a soft shake of her head to free her mind, ignoring the flush he surely noticed in her cheeks.

His knowing, boyish, half-grin made her knees go weak, but thankfully he stopped staring at her at last and took his first few steps into the room, finally regarding his surroundings. With unwarranted nervousness, she followed his gaze.

Her studio was typical of a sculptor's, square by design, similar to a conservatory in structure, with windows on part of the angled ceiling, connecting to those on the west wall. This brought in a good amount of natural light, which she preferred to work by, from late morning till dusk. On the north wall were cupboards and racks for storage, drawers containing tools of various kinds, and a small broom closet where she kept cleaning materials. Opposite, in front of the south wall, stood an airtight, metal box for clay, alongside a double, wide-opening door that led to the garden entrance. This she used for moving large pieces from the house to the street, where they could then be carried to museums, should the need arise. Her room also contained a trash bin and flat work station beside the sink on the east wall, next to the doorway leading to the main house. The settee sat quite cozily in front of the window, but she'd moved her old worktable, on which now sat the Pteranodon fossil, to the far corner, where both would remain until it was time to sculpt.

She'd also picked the place up a bit for Nathan's visit, though she noted suddenly that dust still sprinkled the floor in corners, several fossil samples sat conspicuously on the counter top, and her most recently used papers and tools remained scattered beside the sink. She was never born to be a housekeeper, and certainly it was her workshop to do with as she pleased. This was the first time, in fact, that she felt slightly embarrassed about its somewhat sloppy appearance. But then as a man, Nathan probably wouldn't notice these things.

"Quite a complete and functional workshop, you have," he commented after a moment, without a trace of sarcasm in his voice. "Impressive."

Mimi felt the tension lift from her shoulders a little, and she smiled in a measure of pride. "Thank you. I've grown rather fond of the room, myself. It's the only place in my home that I feel is totally mine to do with or keep as I like."

"Meaning . . . cluttered to your taste?"

He'd noticed. But at least he seemed amused by it, not repelled.

"Sometimes," she admitted, disguising her abashment with a casual air.

He nodded and looked back at her. "Did Carter not spend much time in here, then?"

He always managed to bring Carter into the conversation, and it made her hesitate before answering, wondering why he did that, or why he cared. "No, not really," she replied slowly, her smile reduced with her thoughtfulness. "Most of the time he was bored with the notion of my desire to sculpt, although he allowed me the time to do as I pleased." Providing her duties as his wife came first, but she didn't feel it appropriate to mention that to Nathan. He'd probably assume as much.

"Did he know you sculpted dinosaurs for your father?"

"No," she said at once. "He knew I helped my father from time to time, but I didn't really begin doing complete dinosaur sculptures until after my husband's untimely death."

He waited, staring at her candidly, then said, "I suppose that was all for the best."

She didn't know how to take that; his tone held no color, but his words held a world of meaning. Before she could respond, however, he began to walk toward her, turning his attention to the black leather case he carried at his side.

"I've still got a few notes that weren't stolen two and a half years ago," he remarked coolly, his manner direct. "Thank God they were in my office at the time, but they're hardly complete. We'll more or less have to start from the beginning." He glanced up again as he stood at her side at last. "Where do you want me, Mimi?"

He smelled heavenly—clean, with the lingering scent of musky soap. He'd obviously had a bath this morning, too, and her first thought was that he could sit next to her all day if he wanted. She wouldn't put it quite like that to him, however.

"You'll need to be close while I'm sketching," she answered nonchalantly, brows furrowed, fingers squeezing her knuckles as she glanced over her studio. "So you can watch to make sure I draw dimensions properly. I suppose the settee will be adequate."

"Indeed," he said, only hinting at a sudden underlying amusement. "It appears to be all we have, anyway."

Then why did you ask? she wanted to blurt, but didn't out of courtesy. Instead, she turned away from him, grinning to herself, pleased he'd decided not to argue but not wanting him to know that. From the edge of the counter top she grabbed her large sketching pad and a charcoal pencil, then settled into the cushioned seat of the settee. He followed and sat after she did, beside her, his leather case on his lap.

Mimi adjusted her body so that she wasn't touching him knee to shoulder, although her skirts blanketed his right leg, which he didn't seem to mind. She hoped he appreciated how difficult it was for her to keep her distance like that, as well, since the settee was especially small with him in it.

She peeked up at him sideways. He sat perfectly

straight, facing forward, and didn't interject the fact that they'd both likely be more comfortable if they had separate chairs. That filled her with a guilt-laden rush of satisfaction.

He unfastened the gold snaps on his case, reached inside, and removed four or five papers. Then he lowered the case to the floor while studying the pages in front of him in earnest as he organized them. She clutched the pencil in her lap and tried to remain focused on the work ahead.

"The Megalosaurus was an enormous beast," he began, "larger even than the Iguanodon. There's some debate as to whether he stood upright or bent over, especially when he walked, but how he walked has yet to be proven, and it's doubtful that it ever will be. We're fairly certain he was a meat eater, and I believe he was, given the shape and size of his teeth—" he turned his paper over, studying it— "each one sort of like a wild cat's, curved with cutting notches on the edges, and about four and a half inches long."

He handed her the page, and she took it. Definitely a rough drawing, but she supposed it looked remotely like teeth.

"This looks as if his teeth were imbedded in the jaw," she offered. "Is this how you want it portrayed in the model?"

"Yes, actually," he said, eyes opening wide, a bit taken aback by her keen observance. "The jawbone stolen from me showed this to be obviously so, and that's exactly how I want the model. Megalosaurus means 'great lizard,' but in point of fact its teeth were imbedded like a crocodile's, unlike those of the Iguanodon that were more precisely like the teeth of a common lizard. Ultimately, as more Megalosaur fossils are discovered, scientists will continue to be confounded by this, I believe. I find it merely fascinating."

"Scientists do tend, as a whole, to be stuck in their beliefs, don't they?"

He nodded, frowning. "Foolish, I think, but then my forward thinking approach hasn't always won me honors and accolades."

Mimi smiled, charmed by his bluntness, his eagerness, and especially his desire to discuss this with her as if she were not a simple female but an interested individual with an understanding of scientific notions. Then again, maybe he was just concerned that she get his drawings and model correct. She would probably never know for sure.

"I don't think anyone will ever be able to prove how fast the Megalosaurus itself could move," he continued looking back at his notes, "even under the best conditions. Most paleontologists think he was a very, very slow mover, given that he was extremely large and, as most believe, reptilian in nature."

"It would be a monumental achievement if you could prove them wrong, Nathan," she maintained, a mischievous tinge of excitement in her words. "That would certainly return you to the forefront of the scientific world, forward thinking theories and all."

He shifted his attention to her once more, his intelligent eyes examining her closely as he took in every feature of her face, lingering for a moment on her lips, her cheekbones and forehead, her carefully plaited hair now coiled atop her head. Then he met her gaze again, and such frank, probing assessment made her flush warm to her toes.

"It would most probably be impossible to prove," he countered, his voice contemplative, quietly intense. "But now that I have you and your talent at my side and disposal, Mimi, I won't need to."

That, with its multitude of hidden meanings, made her stomach flutter. For a second she thought he might lift a hand and touch her cheek, run his thumb slowly across her lips as he had that night in Hyde Park. Wishful thinking on her part, evidently, for his eyes darted quickly back to his notes.

"I've drawn a sketch of how I envision the beast, based on the various fossils I and others have discovered," he said, pulling out another sheet from the stack. "A few parts of the Megalosaurus have been found and pieced together, but as far as I'm aware, I'm the only one to discover the completely intact fossil structure of an entire head. Since I'm a deplorable artist, I'll let you have a go at copying my drawing."

She was distinctly aware of the underlying mixture of pride, accomplishment, and sadness in his words but decided against making any remark. Instead, she reached for the sketch he passed to her, lowering it to her lap to study his own depiction of the lizard. He was right; he was a horrible artist.

"It shouldn't be too difficult to work with," she lied after a moment, turning the page around in her hands. "But I do think you should be here while I do so. I won't be able to make mistakes if you're sitting beside me and observing my actions, Nathan."

"There's nowhere else I need to be, Mimi," he murmured softly in swift return. "And of course watching you work should prove both enjoyable and engrossing."

At those words, she refused to look at his face, now only an inch or two from hers, because she knew he would be able to detect subtleties and perhaps even advances not only from her previous statement, but in her eyes, regardless of whether those advances were there. She was smart enough to realize that if she looked at him often, or for long, he'd see very plainly the core of her long-felt attraction to him.

Withholding even a quick glance, she said through a sigh, "Then let's get to it, shall we?" Lifting her pencil, she began to make a rough copy of his drawing on her sketch pad, working silently for two or three minutes. After that first quick draft was complete, she tore off a brand new sheet from her pad to begin anew, this time clarifying her actions.

"What we usually do first," she explained, "is section the paper in quarters for dimensions, like this." She folded it, pinched the creases, then opened it fully again. "In this case, since I'm going to assume you know what you're talking about, Nathan, I intend to draw the beast as an upright reptile, though leaning over, in the unlikely event you're wrong." He half-snorted at that, and she smiled to herself. "You can please everyone this way."

"Nobody will see these drawings but us, Mimi," he argued.

She shrugged, brushing over that as she started the sketch. "But perhaps I'll sculpt the neck as well, which would be . . ." she paused in thought, though her fingers continued to work expertly. "Like this—a straight line from the tip of the nose to the tail. Like so. This way, as you display the sculpture to scientists at your little function in December, they can each one speculate as to whether you think him an upright dinosaur leaning forward, or one that walked on four legs."

"Clever."

She didn't know if he meant her, or her decision to draw the beast in such a way. She decided he meant her.

For nearly three quarters of an hour she worked diligently, using his numerous suggestions, drawing several copies of the Megalosaurus at different angles, with various body structures, though always with the same neck, head, and shape of jaw, at Nathan's insistence. Regardless of whether other great minds believed his now infamous jawbone had actually existed, the man beside her knew what he wanted from her drawings, as well as the coming sculpture, and likewise knew exactly what fellow scientists would think as they viewed it. Her depictions were very good and intricate, and he commented more than once on his approval of her ideas.

Finally Mimi placed her sketch pad on the floor next to the settee and held out the final copy she'd drawn of the Megalosaurus for Nathan's inspection.

"These are very good," he interjected after a moment of analyzing her drafts.

She beamed.

"Do you think you can build this and keep it a secret while you do so?"

Her prideful smile faded. He was blatantly challenging her. He'd asked, in essence, not *Will you make my jawbone and keep it a secret as you've done with all the others?*, but *Are you skilled enough to make this jawbone and then manage to keep your mouth shut about the details to family and friends?* And he also knew she understood his meaning perfectly well. He'd more or less insulted her, she supposed, but then he probably realized she'd never refuse a challenge like that when it came to her dinosaur sculptures.

Mimi set her jaw and narrowed her eyes in response to his arrogance but she refused to be baited, or to appear as annoyed and uncertain as she felt. Beneath everything Nathan asked, behind every word he spoke, lay calculation, repressed bitterness, and an anger greater than her own. She had to remember that. As desirable as she found him to be as a man, as a scientist he was using her.

She smiled in feigned sweetness. "Whatever you need, Nathan, I'm sure I can humbly accomplish for you and your big, lifetime event. And I will be discreet where family questions are concerned."

"And I suppose you'll want me here every day until the model is complete," he said matter-of-factly.

"Of course. I'm sure you wouldn't dream of allowing me to slave over the work without your scholarly presence to cheer and guide me," she replied. "How utterly boring for me, and unforgivable, should I fail at my appointed task."

That pushed him near the brink of laughter, she

could tell, as his eyes flashed with humor and he tightened his lips to keep from grinning outright.

"I imagine I'm rather boring, too, Mimi," he ventured without inflection.

"Then you can watch me suffer as I wallow in the thick of your pompous, dull character, Professor," she said through an enhanced sigh, stretching out a bit, one arm lengthwise on the settee's armrest, the other propped on its back, next to his outstretched hand. "Since you know yourself so well, it should make you feel sufficiently guilty for using me for this uncertain scheme of yours."

He knew she was teasing him and he chuckled softly at that, which in turn made her grin broadly, matching his jovial mood. Then, for the first time in her life, Mimi dared to allow herself to linger in her appraisal of a man who was not an intimate, unconcerned that he should notice. Her smile dwindled as she focused her concentration on the man who sat not a foot away, lounging, more or less, on her settee.

Her eyes grazed his face, examining every feature closely, and she found herself mesmerized once more by his dark, satiny lashes, his angled, clean-shaven jaw, the very masculine structure of his physique.

She lowered her gaze from his wide, firm shoulders to his chest, observing its slow rise and fall with every breath, its solid mass barely discernable under conservative gray linen fabric, wondering if it was covered with soft, dark hair. His thighs were thick and hard as rocks, she could tell, but lean. He had rugged arms that lengthened to large hands and long, strong fingers, tanned and callused from physical labor. She'd never before seen a man's hands that were not soft, and fingers that were not manicured, and Nathan's hands were coarse and hard and thoroughly different from her own. That in itself intrigued her.

It had been a long time since she'd visualized any man's beautiful, strong form that lay hidden beneath layers of clothing, and she yearned for just a brief touch, to feel the strength of Nathan's build under his very appropriate shirt. She caught herself, though, before giving in to such an embarrassment, bringing her own hands together in her lap once more, and squeezing them tightly.

But her greatest mistake, she realized, was taking the time to analyze the man so openly, and then looking back into his eyes.

His face had lost all humor, and his expression waxed grave in a sure signal of . . . distrust? Apprehension? Maybe both. She couldn't be sure, but he studied her own features now intently—lips, cheeks, brows. Every line and curve of her face.

And then it hit her that he clearly understood where her inane and unwanted thoughts were leading. He witnessed an interest beyond the appropriate, maybe even sensed that it had always been there.

"Be careful, Mimi," he murmured, his voice husky and low. "There's work to do here."

"Be careful?" she repeated, dazed.

He bit down hard. "Careful how you look at me." Stunned at that certain warning, of what it implied, she blinked quickly, and then slowly raised herself to stand back from him, perfectly still. She held her entire body rigid, hands to her sides, all the while never looking away from his dark, knowing eyes.

The room felt stuffy suddenly, crowded, thick with tension. Then Nathan gazed beyond her, toward the doorway, and instantaneously there was a tangible shift in mood. His expression turned from dark to bleak; his eyes filled with an animosity he couldn't conceal.

Mimi turned, trepidation seeping into her skin, as she noticed the proud, stately bearing of her father looming over them, or so it seemed, from the small entrance to the house.

She blushed crimson, she knew, from being caught . . . what? Doing nothing. Working. Working with Nathan Price.

"Papa," she mumbled breathlessly, running her palms down her gown at her hips. "I didn't know you were back." And she hoped to God he hadn't heard Nathan's last words.

Sir Harold inhaled deeply, which made his jowls widen and his white side whiskers flare. "How are you, my darling daughter?"

She adored hearing his gruff voice again and wanted to run to his arms. She loved him immeasurably and hadn't seen him in nearly three months, but Nathan's conspicuous presence held her back. He stood beside her now, stiff as stone, large and predatory, and never had she felt more uncomfortable about a situation in her life. Her father, bless his intuitive heart, sensed her predicament and saved her humiliation.

Stepping a few paces into the studio, he pulled down on his waistcoat and acknowledged Nathan with a nod.

"Professor Price, is it? I had no idea you'd returned from the Continent."

Mimi couldn't decipher her father's mood, his initial thoughts, but she imagined he was likely more concerned at finding Nathan alone with her in her workshop, than shocked at his being back in England. Nathan however, remained resolute in his stance.

"Sir Harold," he said formally. Then, without waiting for reply, he turned to her. "I shall be on my way, Mrs. Sinclair. Until tomorrow."

He reached down for his drawings, and with a curt nod to both of them, left the studio.

Seconds later, her father cleared his throat. "Well." He ran his palms down his chest. "That was certainly awkward."

Mimi lowered her body heavily onto the settee, dismayed, confused, and a little bit saddened that he'd left so soon, so quickly. They hadn't even eaten, and she had been hoping Nathan would want to stay for luncheon. But that was beside the point now.

"It's wonderful to see you, Papa," she said warily.

He grunted and strode toward her. "I told Stella I'd be staying for luncheon, but I guess Price won't be joining us." Shrewdly, he looked down at her upturned face. "Are you going to tell me why he was here?"

"Yes, of course." She rubbed her brow with her

fingertips, feeling terribly guilty that she wished her father had not come to visit because she'd rather, at this moment, be eating with Nathan alone. What kind of daughter did that make her?

Then she rose again, wearied, but planting a smile on her lips before she lifted them to her father's cheek. "Shall we eat? We'll talk then. I want to hear about your trip as well."

But as they left the workshop together, Mimi's main consideration wasn't his trip or her stomach, but her breasts. Since that was what Nathan so admired about her, she'd simply have to wear something tighter in the bosom tomorrow.

Chapter 5

The very distinguished Sir Harold Robert Marsh waited, however impatiently, for Justin Marley, in the man's small but tidy home near Regent's Park. His impending visit with Marley was unexpected and perhaps hasty, but it was also crucial. He paced upon new, dark gold carpeting, in a parlor decorated with excellent taste in rich colors of bronze and teal, sporting spectacular artifacts from Marley's frequent travels to the Continent. Yet for all the room's striking appearance and comfortable feel, Harold couldn't bring himself to sit. He strode back and forth in front of the fireplace, ignoring the heat it offered from its shooting sparks, his head down as he rubbed his palms together in front of him.

Damn Nathan Price for coming home only to stir

things up again. Damn Carter for dying unexpectedly and leaving his daughter widowed to fall prey
to a clever, wily man. And damn the scientific establishment for creating this concern in him that, in
only the last three hours since his visit with Mimi,
listening to all her startling revelations, had begun
to grow into alarm.

Price had been wronged. Harold believed that.
He had known Nathan well enough in '51 to accept
without question that the man had indeed found an
intact fossil which was consequently stolen, starting
the dark, downward spiral to his ruin. Still, regardless of Price's lowered professional status, or his
sudden eagerness to regain his honor, however
courageous that might be, Harold didn't want the
man in any of their lives, especially Mimi's. She was
impulsive and always had been, and her odd devotion to a disgraced scientist below her social station
unsettled him. He was her father, after all, and he
wanted what was best for her. That had been Carter
Sinclair until the man had passed on to an early
grave. Perhaps his visit to Justin now proved that he
was jumping to conclusions, responding to his
building distress rather than confronting it, but then
this was always the reaction he had when the course
of troubling events turned its attention to Mimi.

Sir Harold stopped pacing abruptly and pinched
the bridge of his nose with his forefinger and
thumb, shaking his head.

Mimi. His loving daughter. Such a delightful,
charming child turned woman—when she wasn't
sidestepping her place, interjecting her unasked-for
opinions, and sticking her darling presence into

business that did not involve her. Now it was happening again, as it always did where Nathan Price was concerned. If only he had not returned, Harold mused, but then such direction of thought was entirely moot. He would now be forced to focus on the professor's intent.

Harold looked up and straightened to the appropriate bearing when he heard the returning footsteps of Marley's aging, flawlessly dressed butler.

"Mr. Marley will see you now, Sir Harold," he said languidly. "In his study. This way, if you please."

Harold followed immediately, taking only half-notice of his surroundings. He'd been in Marley's home once or twice before, but it had been a long time ago, right before Carter and Mimi were married, if he remembered correctly.

Near the back of the ground level, the butler ushered him inside a room of dark paneled oak walls and forest green furniture, got assurance from his employer that there would be nothing more, then made his silent departure.

Justin sat behind his large, sturdy desk, the top of which exposed a scattering of papers. He wore a white shirt of fine quality, sleeves rolled up, forearms on the flat surface, but focused instantly on his arriving guest. Slowly, he stood as Harold moved confidently into the room.

"Good afternoon, Sir Harold," he remarked without inflection. "Care for a brandy?"

It was far too early to imbibe. "Thank you, yes," he replied, deciding time was unimportant when it came to his primary concern.

Justin motioned for him to sit in the straight-backed leather chair across from the desk while he walked to a sideboard, pulling a bottle and two snifters out of the cupboard beneath it. They both remained silent until he handed over the light brown liquid, which Harold took and lifted at once to his lips.

It was fine and smooth, and he held himself back from swallowing the contents in one gulp. God knew he probably needed it.

"Well," Justin began after once again lowering his body heavily into his cushioned rocker behind the desk. "I suppose you're here to discuss Nathan."

Direct and to the purpose. Regardless of the fact that Justin, the son of a distinguished British Lord, remained on friendly terms with a disgraced scientist, Harold liked him. He liked Nathan, too, he supposed, at least he had when he had known him better years ago, but he would never admit that to anyone. His feelings for the man were irrelevant.

After a deep inhalation, and another long swallow of his brandy, he nodded and plunged right into the reason for his unannounced visit. "Yes, in fact that is precisely why I'm here." He shifted his stout frame in the chair. "He's requested a mold of a dinosaur fossil, to be sculpted by my daughter Mimi, and I want to know why."

Justin's brows rose fractionally. "I had no idea Mimi sculpted reptiles."

Harold was afraid of that and he squirmed a little. "From time to time she's been known to take an interest in the process. She's quite talented."

"Indeed. How very fascinating," Justin replied

without further inquiry, neither surprised nor dubious. "But why not ask Nathan of his interest?"

"That would not be appropriate at this time," Harold answered, mouth thinning grimly. "Quite frankly, I want to know what you know. I'm concerned for Mimi."

Justin placed his snifter on the desk and leaned back in the rocker, lacing his fingers together over his stomach.

"I suppose I understand your need to shelter your daughter, Sir Harold, but I'm sure Nathan is not out to do the lady harm."

"Of course not," he snapped, annoyed at his own irritation. Justin, however, didn't seem to notice or mind his surliness, or was simply too gentlemanly to comment.

With hard, aching fingers he rubbed his right temple. "I don't imagine the man is here to hurt Mimi directly, only that his presence in her life during such a vulnerable time could be"—he waved a wrist— "distracting for her. She is still a widow in mourning."

"Ahh." Justin's eyes grew wide with understanding. "I see."

Harold could feel his face reddening, but he refused to look away from Justin's probing stare. Instead, he pressed for information. "Have you any idea what Nathan is planning?"

Justin blinked, then reached once more for his brandy, gazing down at the liquid for a moment as he swirled it around in the snifter. Harold wondered if he were stalling or simply attempting to organize his thoughts. He hated his suspicions.

"He's only confided a little in me, Sir Harold,"

Justin said at length, "and none of it had much to do with Mimi." He took a sip, eyeing his guest again with shrewd, narrowed brows. "But his final intention is to attend Professor Owen's dinner party on New Year's Eve."

Harold felt a chill creep under his skin. "For what purpose?"

Justin took a long sip of his drink, swallowed, then licked his lips. "I'm not at all certain of the details, but I believe he wants, in front of a score of paleontologists, anatomists, and selected dignitaries, to expose the man who ruined him."

Sir Harold went still to the bone, his brandy snifter cold in his hand.

Impossible. Nobody would be that brazen, including Nathan Price. "He told you this?" he asked, his throat unnaturally scratchy.

"In so many words, yes," Justin admitted with a slight nod, his mouth turned down. "In a method unknown to me, he's planning to expose the man who set him up to fail at the Crystal Palace opening. Most everyone who was at the opening will also be at the dinner party, as I'm sure you know."

"Including us," Harold mumbled aloud.

Justin leaned forward as he lowered his voice. "Including us. But we have nothing to worry about since neither you nor I stole the jawbone in 'fifty-one."

Justin's tone implied warning, but Harold ignored it, his mind racing with uncertainties. Sitting a little straighter in his seat, he then, in two quick swallows, finished off his brandy and placed his glass on the desk in front of him.

"Will his . . . scheme work?" Harold asked skeptically, his voice low.

"I've no idea. He didn't give me the details, as I said." Frowning, Justin added, "Have you any idea who took the jawbone, sir?"

Harold jerked back a little at that bold query, totally unprepared for it. "No ideas that matter now," he replied at once. Seconds later he let out a long, solid breath to add, "None of it matters now, actually. I don't see how the man intends to prove anything. And how will he get an invitation? Owen certainly won't invite him, and he couldn't possibly arrive unannounced for dinner. I know he's not on the guest list."

Justin placed his forearms on the desk, turning his snifter around in his hands, the creases in his frown deepening as he concentrated on the clear glass at his fingertips. "I've agreed to take him as my guest."

"That's absurd," Harold quickly bellowed.

Justin shook his head and looked back at him. "I don't know who ruined the man, Sir Harold, but somebody did. That's obvious. Nathan is a friend, and if there's some way I can help him, I will. I don't care what Owen thinks at this point. I didn't steal the jawbone, so I've nothing to lose by bringing Nathan with me. If you didn't steal it, neither should you. The only ones who could possibly be injured by this would be Nathan and the person who purposefully destroyed his reputation. If Nathan wants to take the chance, then I'm willing to assist him."

Uncomfortable in his thoughts, Sir Harold stared at Justin for seconds longer, then stole a glance around the room, pretending to take particular interest in the large charcoal watercolor hanging over the mantel, the picture of it a blur.

"Have you any idea what his intentions are regarding Mimi?" He knew that came out a bit too rushed and plagued with worry, but he couldn't help exposing his concern. She was his daughter.

Justin drew a deep inhale before replying. "I've no idea."

Harold turned back to his host, his gaze now penetrating, probing for untruths. "He's said nothing about her?"

Now he saw a flicker of amusement on the younger man's features—a twitch of his lip, a subtle thinning of his lids—passing almost too swiftly to notice. However, it took a long moment of deliberation before he answered.

"He did say that he found her lovely, Sir Harold, but then so do I, and I have no intentions toward her."

Quite a letdown when he'd hoped for more, but it's all he should have expected. A statement in answer shedding light on absolutely nothing.

Harold cleared his throat. "You're saying then that the man has intentions toward her?"

Justin looked surprised. His brows lifted as he sat back a little. "I said nothing of the kind."

"I see." He tapped his painful, arthritic fingers together in his lap. "Then I suppose I won't worry in her behalf."

"I know of no reason why you should," Justin replied very properly with a tilt of his head. "If nothing else, Nathan is a gentleman. That he finds her a beautiful woman is no wonder, but he won't take advantage of her. That I can promise."

Sir Harold believed it, but he knew Mimi. She was attracted to the man, as he and Mary had discussed briefly upon his return, and Harold was quite afraid it would be Mimi taking advantage of Professor Price, not the other way around. That would never do, and he would put a stop to it if he could. The core of his trouble, he realized, was going to be convincing Mimi what was best for her and their family. He'd never been able to do that well. It was times like this that Harold truly wished her mother was still alive.

"Well then," he said, subdued, "I suppose there is nothing more to say. Thank you for the brandy, Justin. It was very fine, indeed."

"It has been my pleasure," Justin returned, standing as Harold did, taking no offense in his guest's quick departure. "I shall look forward to seeing you at the New Year's Eve party, then. It will be a smashing success, I believe."

"Yes, and a night to remember, I'm sure."

Justin chuckled and crossed his arms over his chest. "Nathan knows what he's doing. Although I'm not privy to the details, the unfolding of his plan may be the highlight of the evening." He dropped his voice to a deep murmur of caution. "The man is smart, Sir Harold. I'd venture to say, even with his common blood, he's smarter than the rest of us."

That's what I'm afraid of.

"I shall take your good word for it." He nodded once to his host. "Until the party then, Justin."

Justin nodded back. "Until then, sir."

Harold made his way to the front of the house, retrieved his overcoat and hat, then walked onto the porch, pausing a moment as the butler closed the door behind him.

A light drizzle of rain had developed and droplets tapped his shoulders and hat, the dark, low cloud cover making the day seem later than it was. Gloomy. He shivered from the cold dampness in the air, then took the stairs slowly, one at a time, to the busy street where he would hire a hansom cab—if one was available with the steady rain. He'd rather ride, if he could. The walk would be long and tiresome with his joints aching as they were. Funny, how the pain he felt seemed trivial now with his mind centered on something that could prove perilous to his beloved daughter and his own good name.

Chapter 6

~~~

It was going to be a long, hot day, Nathan feared, and it wouldn't be because of the weather.

Sitting in Mimi's studio, on her plump settee, he watched her gather tools to begin their work—or rather, *her* work. It was an interesting process, watching her in action. And a somewhat erotic one. She glided across the floor in a plain but tightly waisted gown of thick gray muslin, her hips gently swaying, her breasts pushed up and out by an obviously well-designed corset, her silky hair caught up in a neat chignon at her crown. Still, he tried very hard to disassociate himself from his bodily urges, though that was difficult to do when they made him physically uncomfortable. It had been ages since he'd been alone with a woman, so close, on a daily basis.

He'd arrived at her townhouse just a few moments ago, at ten minutes past ten—fashionably late, which would have made his mother proud, but to him was strictly a matter of arrangement. He didn't want to appear as if he'd bow to Mimi's wishes, but he didn't want to keep her waiting, either. She was a demanding woman—an enticing, demanding woman. A combination he had trouble reconciling.

He was surprised by how anxious he'd been to get started in her home today as well, especially after his rushed departure of the afternoon before. Sir Harold's unexpected appearance had shaken him up, though. He hadn't anticipated leaving her side so early, at least not before luncheon, but he just couldn't let an awkward moment pass without action. And he couldn't, right now, look Sir Harold in the eye without betraying his bitter emotions. He wasn't ready for that. Soon, yes—but not now.

It was Mimi the woman, however, who stirred his blood this morning. Her individual scent had drifted his way the minute he'd walked into her workshop. Such a base initial reaction to being in the same room with her again had made him practically snort with shame. He was no better than an animal, which would no doubt give credence to the obscure theory that man and apes were somehow related. Apes were affected by scent, sniffed each other of habit. Right now, sitting in her warm studio, on her softly cushioned settee, staring at her gently sloping backside, Nathan felt the overpowering urge to rise, walk toward her, grab her around the waist—from the back, so he could press himself against her bottom—place his face in the crook of her neck, and sniff her. He squirmed in his seat from his libidinous thoughts. He'd never noticed the way a woman smelled before, at least not in a positive way. Mimi made him think unusually, and he didn't like it. His constant musings of her were appalling because they were just so totally, unexpectedly arousing.

"So what did your father say about your new sculpting project?" he asked to break the quiet, and further, to turn his mind to more practical matters.

She smiled vaguely, though she didn't look at him as she concentrated on the materials in front of her, placing instruments in order on the ugly brown table. "I only told him what was necessary. Not everything."

"Meaning?"

She raised her shoulders negligibly. "Meaning that he now knows you've hired me to sculpt, in his name—"

"What?" he chimed in, incredulous and sitting forward.

She ignored his outburst as if she expected it, still looking away from him as she tacked two of the Megalosaurus drawings of yesterday onto an easel.

"I told him you'd learned somewhere in the field that I sculpted and you have a function to attend for which you need a sculpture." She paused and glanced at him, her gaze roving briefly down, then up his body before she looked away again. "I didn't think it was necessary to tell him you're blackmailing me, Nathan."

That hit him right in the stomach. He really shouldn't be so swayed by her words, though, and it annoyed him that he felt such sympathy for the woman he'd put in a particularly tight spot both with family and professionals. He really couldn't understand her reaction, either. He'd expected her anger, pure outrage, maybe even hatred for attacking her father's name in an attempt to prove the man was responsible for his failing. But she wasn't angry at all, and that, Nathan had to admit, confused him. Then again, she'd said she felt sorry for him when he'd lost his social and professional status. She was thoroughly confident in her sculpting ability, and perhaps that confidence extended to her desire to prove him wrong. This in itself would account for her rather relaxed demeanor around him. Feeling suddenly agitated by his wandering thoughts that explained nothing, Nathan stood again and moved closer to her.

"Tell me what you intend to do here," he said, crossing his arms over the front of his white woolen shirt.

She smiled again. "Well, let's see. First, after arranging necessary tools, I'm going to study the drawings we made yesterday and consider how best to copy them into small clay models."

He relaxed beside her now, feeling the heat of her body and smelling that spicy woman scent of hers. "I see."

"Later I'll take the best one and make it life-size,"

she continued, pulling up two small wooden chairs for both of them to sit at the table, "though since we're not making a whole dinosaur, this shouldn't take too long."

"Good," he added, noting the contour of her ear and that she wore no jewelry. And was that a birthmark beneath the lobe? A tiny pink oblong mark the size of—

"Most sculptors use wooden spoons, knives, rolling pins, and such to work with," she informed him easily, pushing her tools to the side of the table and sitting in her chair. "I'll use those for the first miniature clay models, then move to larger items for the actual life-size model you'll need for the dinner party."

"Mmm." He sat beside her, in his chair, folding his arms over his chest again and leaning back, observing that her lashes were quite dark compared to the color of her hair. It made the brownness of her irises stand out, which of course was why they were so noticeable even at a distance. Her eyes were the loveliest part of her face, really. Or at least the most striking.

"Now," she continued in explanation, sitting squarely, "when we get to the life-size model, we'll no longer use clay for construction, but what we need of bricks, iron columns and hoops, tiles and concrete. The sculpture of the finished jawbone will be quite large, naturally, which is why I have a door to the garden entrance. That's how we'll transport everything from the house."

"Fascinating," he murmured, observing her closely as she rolled up her sleeves to start. Again he was taken with the small bones of her wrists, the smoothness of her pale skin, the length of her fingers and her short, tapered nails. The fact that such smooth, delicate hands and fingers could make prized sculptures amazed him.

"Nathan?"

He blinked and glanced up. She was looking at him strangely, and then he realized she'd asked him a question. "Pardon?"

Her pink lips turned up minutely. "I asked you if you wanted to help with the initial sculpting."

That surprised him, but what else was he to do? And it would, in fact, give him the opportunity to sit by her side and smell her all day.

He leaned forward and placed his forearms on the tabletop, never dropping his gaze from hers. Softly, he replied, "I was hoping you'd ask."

That took her aback. Or confused her. She straightened even more, pulling away from him a little, her forehead creasing into two tiny lines.

"Really? Well—good. Let's get started, then, shall we?"

She turned her attention to the clay at her fingertips, dug in, and handed him a chunk of it. He had no idea what to do with it, so he followed her actions and began massaging the cool, pliable material. It was hard but moved easily enough with gentle pressure.

"So," she said after clearing her throat, "where do you think the dinosaurs came from, Nathan?"

"Which dinosaurs?"

"*The* dinosaurs. All of them."

"Oh." He hesitated briefly, lifting his eyes to view

her curiously, deciding to use the standard answer he'd used on various ladies of his acquaintance. "I've no idea, really. I spend most of my time just analyzing their structure and habits."

Mimi, being unlike the typical ladies of his acquaintance, didn't for a moment accept that.

"Well, naturally you don't know, but I mean"—her forehead creased even more deeply as she considered her words—"what do you think about their appearance on this earth? Are they God's creatures? The Devil's, as some believe? When did they live and die? I'm sure you're aware of what the public thinks."

He sucked in a heavy breath as he shifted his attention once again to the clay in front of him. If she wanted greater depth in his explanation, he would supply it. She was, after all, the daughter of Sir Harold Marsh, a respected researcher in the study of Dinosauria. Certainly she'd heard more about the science of paleontology than the average lady of quality.

"The public are generally confused when it comes to science," he started slowly, cutting his clay into two portions as he watched her do. "They tend to be less open to new thought and scientific developments, especially those that contradict biblical accounts."

"And you think the dinosaurs do," she stated rather than asked.

"Of course," he answered without pause. "Most people believe God created the world only a few thousand years ago, and yet these giant lizards are proof that he did not. But to think or announce that belief is blasphemy. This is what the public find so fascinating about it, which keeps me—or kept me—employed."

He glanced up to find her nodding, though her concentration was clearly focused on her model. But she seemed to grasp his reasoning. Recently, especially with the success of the Crystal Palace, it seemed as if the entire world were in a great debate of history and its relation to the Church. This by itself kept the masses intrigued, which in turn led to funding by the elite for more research by the scientists. It was the enjoyment of it for those in upper social circles that kept those of Nathan's class and education employed, lecturing, and creating more theories. She had to know that.

"Professor Owen doesn't believe in the theory of transmutation, does he?"

Nathan stopped his hand movements and stared at her, amazed that she could even pronounce the word. Tiny wisps of blond hair unfurled themselves at her forehead, two strands getting very near her eyes, and he fought the urge to wipe them back for her with his clay-coated fingers.

"You're familiar with the theory of transmutation?" he asked.

She peeked up at him, her lips cocked into a half smile. "Words like 'transmutation' are tossed around from time to time in my family, Nathan. You shouldn't be so surprised."

Feeling annoyed at that slight rebuff, he looked back at the mass of nothing he was constructing on the table. "Owen disagrees with the idea that life on earth has become progressively more complex over time, yes, which is basically the theory of transmutation. He instead subscribes to the idea that dinosaurs were more complex creatures than we give them credit for, and that they were, in their anatomy, superior to those reptiles we see today."

"And you?" she probed casually.

He wiped his hands on a damp cloth on the tabletop and sat back, eyeing her erect, trim form carefully. "It is probably the one area of disagreement between Owen and me."

She nodded, but didn't look away from her creation. At least hers was beginning to look something like a sculpture. She leaned to her side and lifted a bowl of water from the floor, pushed her free hand inside, then sprinkled both of their clay with a few droplets, to keep it moist.

Features growing serious again, avoiding his gaze, she admitted, "Carter didn't believe it."

He shifted his body uncomfortably in the hard, small chair, hands now folded in his lap. "Didn't believe in the theory?"

"Yes, but for different reasons than Sir Owen, I think. That's why he studied monkeys. He wanted to prove how different we are, not how similar. That God created man as he is, above the animal world."

"That's the view of most people, Mimi," he said slowly. "There are a good number of scientists who study their work not to discover new information, but to prove their ideas are correct."

She glanced up to him momentarily. "And this is what you think?"

He sighed and shrugged lightly. "I'm always open to new ideas."

She didn't offer another comment, but went back to her project with vigor.

Topic of conversation aside, it was suddenly clear to Nathan that Mimi had difficulty talking about Carter beyond the superficial, though he couldn't begin to guess why. She appeared troubled by her thoughts whenever his name was introduced into the discussion, and suddenly Nathan found himself impatient to know the cause of her feelings— even if it meant learning that she simply missed him terribly.

Running the fingertips of one hand along his clay mound, he broached the personal subject. "Tell me about your marriage, Mimi."

That clearly startled her. Her head shot up and her eyes opened wide. "About my marriage?"

He smiled nonchalantly. "Were you happy?"

Her lids narrowed, holding his gaze breath for breath. Then, very gradually, she grinned, her mouth parting seductively, revealing clean white teeth, which he took note of immediately. The tip of her tongue darted out to graze her lips, to slide first across the top, then the bottom. That small, insignificant action made him go instantly hard. Embarrassingly, irritatingly hard, and he stretched out as best he could in the tiny chair, wishing to God he'd never brought this subject up.

"I married Carter because you didn't ask me first, Nathan," she revealed in a deadly soft purr. With that, she turned back to her work.

Nathan gaped at her for a moment, dumbstruck. Could she possibly mean that? After seconds of consideration, he doubted it. She knew nothing about him, really. She was probably just putting him and his prying questions in place. Obviously Mimi Sinclair was used to being in charge of the conversation—and the mood.

Feeling awkward and a trifle unsettled, but refusing to let her have the final word, to get the best of him, he asked as evenly as possible, "Did you enjoy kissing him?"

For a fraction of a second her fingers paused in their movement, but her casual smile never wavered. "I think he enjoyed kissing me," she murmured.

Nathan grunted. "You didn't answer my question."

Lifting her right shoulder in shrug, she added, "What specifically do you want to know?"

She was baiting him, he knew, but there was no turning back now. Lowering his voice to a soft whisper, he asked, "Did you enjoy kissing him more than kissing me?"

He watched her cheeks pinken a little, but it was the only visible betrayal of her thoughts. "I only kissed you once, if I recall."

"And it was a spectacular kiss, if memory serves, so no doubt you and Carter had a very . . . lively relationship."

He couldn't believe he said that once it was out of his mouth, and neither could she apparently. A large piece of clay fell out of her fingers, and before picking it up again, she rubbed the back of her right hand along her hot cheek, leaving a grayish-red streak above the bone.

Flustered, but refusing to look in his direction,

she admitted, "I imagine our marriage was typical, Nathan, and of course we were quite happy."

"Of course," he remarked flatly, feeling at once defeated. He rested his wrists on the edge of the table and tapped the tips of his fingers together. "What did you think of the kiss you and I shared?"

Her casual bearing changed abruptly. Her mouth hardened and she stopped her hand motions, closing her eyes briefly before opening them wide again and giving him her full attention. He waited for her response, unduly nervous and chiding himself for it.

Seconds passed before she sighed and said, "Honestly, Nathan, that was a long time ago—"

"—And you remember it as if it were yesterday, don't you?"

She couldn't respond to his whispered words right away, though she continued to stare into his eyes, hers dark pools of contemplation, cheeks flushing beautifully, lips moist. And then, very, very slowly, she smiled at him again, rich and lovely, as she always seemed to do when he least expected it.

"It's none of your business," she whispered in return, confidently. "But if you must know, I don't remember ever enjoying a kiss more."

That made his insides turn to pulp. "Than mine?"

She shook her head and leaned toward him. "A gentleman has no business asking such things of a lady."

He moved closer to her as well, only the edge of the table between them, the heat of her face touching his. "Than mine?" he whispered again huskily, succinctly.

His breath brushed her cheek and made the hair on her forehead stir. She glanced over his facial features as if contemplating the question to great lengths. Finally, she brazenly replied, "Your kiss behind the Crystal Palace opened the world for me, Nathan. My only regret was that it didn't last a lifetime. It was heavenly."

That shook him deeply, unexpectedly. He didn't, in fact, know precisely what she meant by such a statement, or even if perhaps she only teased him because he so adamantly wanted an answer. No woman had ever before complimented him on his kissing ability, either.

Quickly, he jerked his body back to an upright position, and she responded in kind by straightening and returning to her mold, which was all but completed, he supposed. Then she leaned her head back, her face to the ceiling, eyes closed, giving him a delicious view of her creamy white neck.

"It's so warm, isn't it?" she casually commented, shifting her head from one side to the other.

She fanned her face with her fingers, and then, to his utter shock, lowered her hand to her neck and unbuttoned the first three—no, *four* buttons on her gown.

Nathan didn't move, didn't utter a sound as he watched her intently, trying to reconcile his feelings of total disbelief in her brazen actions with the overwhelming desire to touch her, to place his thumb on the spot at her throat that pulsed with life, to draw it slowly down . . .

"Mimi—"

"You're not doing a very good job, Nathan," she cut in, the right side of her mouth turned up in a wry grin as she lifted her head and gazed at him through her lashes. "You're not keeping up with me at all."

Her words left him mystified, but he managed to murmur, "I'm not much of an artist."

"Indeed," she agreed in a casual sing-song tone. "Some of us are artists, some of us are scientists. It might prove more useful if you simply watched."

Suddenly she raised her body and stood over the tabletop, angling toward him so that he could see the pressing action of her hands. With nimble fingers she leaned toward him to pat down a fraction of her clay model—and the top of her gown dropped open just enough for him to view the lacy edge of her corset.

His body went rigid again. Thankfully she wasn't looking at him, but at her creation, which gave his eyes ample opportunity to linger on the two soft mounds of flesh that pushed up so perfectly against red satin.

Red satin. Jesus.

Nathan bit down hard and briefly closed his eyes, scrubbing one of his hands over his face, making every attempt to erase the thought of Mimi, standing before him, clothed in nothing but a red satin corset. Red satin against pearly white skin. Red satin as the only barrier between full pale breasts and hard red nipples—

"There," she said matter-of-factly, standing back. "This is how I envision the side of the jaw—sort of curved at the tip, though still with enough room for the teeth, which I'll get to later. What do you think?"

She sounded normal, and Nathan braved a glance at her face.

She looked at him innocently, giving him that damn smile again.

"It's fine," he managed to croak out.

Her smile faded. "You didn't even look at it."

He dropped his gaze to the mold on the table. "It's fine," he repeated, rubbing his sweating hands together in his lap.

Several long seconds passed in deathly quiet before she softly asked, "What did you think about our kiss, Nathan?"

He looked back into her dark eyes, his breath catching from the intensity he saw in them as they probed his. And that was the moment everything fell into place. The moment he knew exactly what she was doing.

Anger hit him hard, and then just as quickly it dissipated and something more potent replaced it. Something carnal. She was playing with him, though how far she'd take her game was anyone's guess. Still, he now understood deep within exactly what she wanted, and it startled him more than he could ever put into words.

With full comprehension at last, he drew a long breath and raised his body to stand before her, his face only inches away from hers, his erection probably visible, should she look in that direction. But she didn't; she kept her glorious eyes locked with his.

Smiling dryly, he leaned toward her until his knuckles rested on the tabletop. "Every second of your lips on mine was kissing at its perfection, Mimi," he whispered. "And I, for one, will never forget that perfect moment."

Her jaw dropped open a little and she took a step back, blinking in sudden confusion, a blush creeping into her cheeks once more.

"Oh," she managed on a slight breath of air.

She'd never expected such a detailed disclosure on his part, and he took a large measure of pride in his ability to disconcert her.

"But the problem as I see it," he continued, his voice low and harsh, "is that our relationship, if one could call it that, is built on mistrust, resentment, and calculated awareness that will only take us nowhere. The fire you started the night we kissed is banked. Let's keep it that way."

Standing rigidly, he gazed down into her fierce brown eyes. "I think I'm done here for today. I have an appointment elsewhere and sadly must leave your company."

Her features went immediately slack in surprise, then tight with an irritation she couldn't mask, but she said nothing. Brimming with satisfaction, he pushed his chair back and brushed by her, striding to the door.

Pausing at the threshold, he placed his palm on the knob and turned back to her. "I'll be here tomorrow precisely at ten, Mrs. Sinclair."

She stared at him without comment, which made him swallow a bitter chuckle. She might have

him, dressed in standard clothes of the middle class, talking over pints of ale and a meal of beef stew, cheddar cheese, bread, and pickles.

Their dialogue had been rather mundane thus far, as their discussion moved from the nasty turn of weather, to local interests, to politics. Justin stayed clear of mentioning paleontology-related matters, probably because he knew first-hand how Nathan didn't exactly enjoy discussions about the elite scientific establishment and their new discoveries and theories right now. But he wasn't there to discuss that anyway.

Nathan swallowed a chunk of cheddar, followed it with two large gulps of ale, then relaxed against the wall behind his head to admire the view.

A luscious barmaid, probably no more than twenty years of age, flirted with a man who sat among four companions only two tables away. Strands of her long hair fell loosely from her chignon and over her bold cheekbones, the blond, silky tips spilling into the man's drink, still in her hand, which he didn't seem to notice or mind. Her hair wasn't quite as dark as Mimi's, but it was thick and pretty. So was she, in a rather robust, loud way. Her voice was more high-pitched than Mimi's, and her teeth were already starting to yellow, as he'd noticed when she'd served the two of them. But then she had a hard look about her, as many common women did when they were forced to work. Mimi's loveliness would naturally outlast this woman's, though Mimi would always lead a sheltered life, remaining in the background of experience while assuming her position at the forefront of protected society. Just like all ladies of her station. For a second Nathan considered how very sad it would be to exist without the freedom to explore all facets of the world, an opportunity he had been given at an early age, not from income or social status, but from desire. It was his opinion that women of Mimi's natural vitality should be given that opportunity as well—within reason, of course. Not all ladies deserved the liberty, surely, and most of them probably wouldn't want it. But ladies with intelligence and stamina, and especially those with inborn curiosity like Mimi's, merited such an independence, in his opinion. The amusing thing was that he didn't know one other man who believed that.

The barmaid burst out with rowdy laughter as one of the men playfully grabbed her breast, and she swatted his hand away lightly. Her breasts were marvelously large, which she showed off to their full advantage. Mimi's weren't so full and round, and they likely hadn't been groped by strangers, either. Warm, smooth, and perfectly fitted to his palms, that's how he imagined Mimi's breasts to be. Their mystery simply fascinated him, and he wondered for a lustful second what the Widow Sinclair would do if he grasped her in a playful gesture like that. But then Nathan had never found time or interest in playing with a woman. Bedding her was one thing, but playful teasing was something he didn't understand or take much pleasure in.

Still, he could envision Mimi swatting his hand away in fun while she laughed and encouraged him in a husky, coaxing tone. She would be frisky before a good round of lovemaking, and although it shocked him to think of her like that, he couldn't seem to stop himself. She'd tease him, then moan loudly when he took her nipple in his mouth. It would taste—incredible, and again his mood darkened when he considered that Carter Sinclair had been the first, and possibly the only, man to taste and hold and caress those nipples . . . nipples Nathan had very nearly seen this morning, or might have with one simple lift of his hand, one touch of a finger to push that red satin aside. One stroke—

Stretching out long on his bench, Nathan clasped his hands together on his lap to cover his erection brought on by his drifting thoughts of red corsets and blond females, annoyed with the whole bloody bit of it. He needed a woman badly, he supposed, but he was not going to tell that to Marley in so many words.

"Where the devil is your mind today, Nathan?"

He turned to his friend, who watched him curiously from across the table.

"My mind?"

Justin smirked as he wiped a hunk of bread along the inside of his bowl, gathering up remnants of his stew. "I've been talking for minutes about the damn market and you haven't said a word. What's getting at you?"

Nathan had no idea to which "market" Justin was referring, but he didn't mention that. Instead he eyed the man carefully, considering how best to broach this delicate subject while admitting to himself that further delay was futile. He needed advice and he had no one else in London to ask. And Justin, ever the good, calm, rational friend, waited patiently, stretching out on his bench seat as well, one leg propped up on the wood, his back to a window, arms crossed over his chest while he chewed, focusing on Nathan with bland curiosity expressed on his full, pinched brow.

"I fear I'm going mad," Nathan finally said, straight-faced.

Justin chuckled, reached for his mug, and took a long swig of ale. "The lovely widow, eh?"

Nathan shook his head, averted his gaze and lifted a chunk of cheese. "It's very little to do with her."

"Really," Justin stated with clear disbelief.

Attempting to relax a little, Nathan took an unwanted bite of cheddar for something to do and chewed slowly to give him time to consider his reply. Seconds later, smiling sheepishly, he admitted, "It's obvious, I suppose."

"That you're besotted with the lady? Not at all."

Nathan's lips curled into a wry grin, and he raked the fingers of one hand through his hair, watching the buxom blonde's swaying backside when she finally moved off to the other side of the room.

"I'm not besotted with anyone," he countered. "Just—needy in a general sense."

Justin followed his lingering gaze, then nodded in understanding. "I see. So what are you doing here talking to me? Or rather, I should say, pretending to listen to me? You should instead be looking for a woman to satisfy your lust."

Nathan sighed. "It's more complicated than that."

Eyes widening in surprise, Justin remarked, "I can't imagine how. Mimi Sinclair may be a widow without a man, but she's hardly one who would expect advances from you and then act on them happily."

"Actually, I think she would."

For a moment Nathan wasn't certain if Justin heard that whispered reply in the boisterous atmosphere around them, and he was equally uncertain of whether he could repeat it should he need to. The notion alone made his head ache at the temples.

Justin cleared his throat and sat up a little straighter. "What makes you think that?" he asked skeptically, and a little confused.

Disregarding the flush he felt creeping up his neck, Nathan looked to his hands again and tapped the tips of his fingers together in front of him. It was now or never he supposed.

"She did something this morning that I'm not sure I understand."

"Well, of course she did," Justin returned at once. "Ladies frequently do things we don't understand." He reached for his ale once more and took another long drink. "They all baffle me, really."

Nathan drew a long face, his lips tightening with building inner frustration, the smoke irritating his eyes, the noise growing raucous to his ears. "That's not what I mean. She's actually quite . . . knowledgeable to talk to—surprisingly sophisticated for her age. Even . . . I don't know. Intelligent."

"Indeed," Justin replied. "A rarity, to be sure."

Nathan didn't know if the man mocked him, teased him, or spoke in total truth as he believed it, but he ignored the comment. Uncomfortable, he looked out to the blond barmaid again, who had certainly never heard of the word "transmutation," much less offered a definition of it. In a tight whisper, he disclosed, "I think Mimi's trying to seduce me."

Justin laughed outright and heartily. Nathan could feel his skin growing hot beneath his clothes as his body broke out in sweat. He turned his head and gave Marley a hard stare.

Justin raised his mug in toast. "Here's to you, my friend. May we all be one day fortunate enough to have beautiful, needy widows at our heels." Then he swallowed the remaining brown liquid in three full gulps.

Frustrated now, Nathan tightened his jaw and leaned over the table. "You don't understand. She didn't say so in words, and she didn't . . . approach me." He fisted one hand and rapped his knuckles on the table. "She's been far more subtle than that, which is the confusing part. If a woman is asking for a romp, I think I would know. I don't with Mimi. I'm only guessing, and frankly I don't know what to do about it."

Justin exhaled loudly, his dark features growing serious as he eyed him with candor. "What exactly has she done?" he asked, placing his now-empty mug back on the table.

Nathan turned a hunk of bread over twice on his plate, stalling. This was the embarrassing part. How to tell a longtime friend about the slight, innocent view of provocative underthings you weren't certain were meant for you to see in the first place. He dropped the bread and ran his hand over his face. God. Better just to blurt it, he imagined, no matter how foolish he might look for being so completely ignorant about women and their motives.

"This morning, without shame," he began, staring at his half-eaten food, "she unbuttoned the neck of her gown in front of me—four buttons—"

"You counted the buttons?"

"Then she stood and leaned over to work with her clay." He glanced up to find Justin suddenly engrossed, a knowing smirk on his mouth. Nathan dismissed it and continued. "Her gown dropped open directly in front of my face—"

"—You lucky man—"

"—Which revealed a very tight corset—"

"—Lucky, lucky man—"

"—And it was made of blood red satin."

"You—" Justin sat up abruptly, his shoe hitting the floor as his leg fell from the bench, his eyes opened wide in astonishment. "Good God."

"Yes, that's exactly what I thought."

Justin blinked. "Red?"

"Red."

"*Satin?*"

"Right again. As smooth and appealing as an apple ripe enough for picking."

"And did you consider picking it?"

Agitated, he remarked, "I'm not sure that's what she wants."

"Is it what you want?"

"That's irrelevant," he snapped.

Justin blew a slow breath out through his teeth. "Where on earth would she—"

"I've no goddamn idea," he mumbled, exasperated, waving his palm in the air.

Justin slowly shook his head, tracing the rim of his mug with his thumb. "And a widow at that."

Nathan had no notion of what such an absurd statement might mean, but he didn't ask for explanation. He shoved his fingers through his hair again, swiftly glancing around them for eavesdroppers. Of course there weren't any, but nonetheless he was feeling agitated and hot in the stale, crowded air. The rain fell harder and louder on the rooftops, and its wetness blanketed the window beside them so that the view of the street was now totally distorted. He wouldn't be going out in that anytime soon, and finding an empty hansom cab in this weather would be impossible.

After a moment, he sighed. "You see my problem?"

"Um..." Justin cocked his head thoughtfully, mouth twisting, forehead creased, staring at what remained of his meal. "You've got yourself into a sticky situation, to be sure, though it certainly can't be an unpleasant one."

Nathan's face flushed fully now, and he sat up again quickly, turning his body forward, feet flat on the floor, forearms resting on the splintered wood of the table.

"Indeed," he answered formally, trying to regain some gentlemanly composure with his calm demeanor. "And yet I'm not sure if her tempting manner is purposeful or accidental."

"Why should you assume it's accidental?" Justin chuckled again and lowered his voice. "It's my experience that women don't do anything accidentally. From the common wench to the perfectly bred lady, every part of their little minds is spent on entrapment of the male sex." With a twitch of his mouth, he added succinctly, "A corset in red satin must be a marvelous thing to behold, I wouldn't know. But that aside, no lady would unbutton her gown in front of a man who was not her husband if she didn't want him sexually. You know that, for God's sake. She's not an innocent miss. She knows *precisely* what she's doing."

That, Nathan finally admitted to himself, was exactly what he wanted to have confirmed for him. And with such a categorical confirmation came an unexpected, and totally unwanted glowing warmth in the pit of his stomach. It actually took all his strength not to reveal a triumphant smile.

Justin raised his mug toward the barmaid, a motion requesting two more. "Seems to me the Widow Sinclair definitely wants you to pick those apples of hers. The question now is, do you have a taste for apples?"

"I've always had a taste for apples," he replied without thought, then amended, "all apples."

"But if you're standing in an orchard with ripe red ones at your fingertips do you cross the road for the green ones when they might be out of reach? Likely not. You eat what's there."

Oh, yes. Eating Mimi's apples. What a thought.

"I think Mimi's apples might be out of reach as well," he murmured, gazing absentmindedly to the dark gray rain-coated window.

Justin understood at last and sat back heavily against the wooden sill. "Not because of her, but because of your ongoing trouble with her father."

His jaw tightened. "I simply can't trust her. I don't know if she was involved in stealing the jawbone—

if she was *ever* involved—but it worries me." More than it should, he decided. The thought actually sickened him.

Justin drummed his fingers on the tabletop, staring at him, his gaze forthright. "You're in a tight spot, to be sure, my friend, but if I were you, I'd be very, very careful. Mimi Sinclair is a determined lady. If she wants you, I don't think it's possible for you to deny her. I've seen you with her. If you intend to continue working with her professionally, my advice then is twofold: do not, in any way, get her with child, and watch your back around her family. I've known her father for years, as you have, and you know as well as I, he's a cunning man who looks out very nicely for the interests of his daughters. Mimi is a widow still in mourning, and Sir Harold has already asked me of your intentions toward her."

Nathan's brows rose with that, but Justin waved off his curiosity with his palm before he could comment.

"I did my best to brush it aside as nothing, but he's clever, Nathan. If I see the attraction between you and Mimi, so will he, and so will the lovely widow's sister, and they won't take kindly to you getting involved."

Nathan said nothing because there was nothing more to say. Justin understood his concerns on the matter, his intentions to attend the New Year's Eve party where he would reveal the Megalosaurus to all in his country, in his profession, who mattered. The fact that he needed Mimi and her skill if he was to accomplish his intended coup was turning out to be more than an unforeseen hindrance, but a very real problem if he didn't play his relationship with her carefully.

But could he afford to get involved? And why did she want him, of all men, anyway? These were questions he just couldn't answer for now. One thing, however, was certain: he'd come this far in returning his honor and name to the forefront of science, and he refused to allow a lovely, perhaps even lonely, widow to undermine that achievement.

Chapter 8

~∽◯◯∽~

Mimi had been restless all morning. Nathan still wasn't expected to arrive for a good twenty minutes, yet she'd been in her studio since breakfast—nearly an hour—gathering the day's necessary tools, laying them out in an order that was *not* necessary, and more or less passing the time by glancing at the clock.

Finally, when she couldn't take any more pacing, she had retreated to her garden from the studio entrance, walking the brick path around the back of her home to the far corner of the yard, where she now sat on a stone bench, staring at the small but secluded fountain as clear water trickled down white marble. She adored these surroundings, isolated within the walls of tall lilac bushes and rose-covered trellises that filled the air with the scent of flowers from early spring until late autumn. It was her own small area of privacy that allowed her moments of peace and solitude, a place that had held no interest for Carter but that she cherished. Nathan probably would not find her here if he looked alone, but one of her servants would no doubt direct him when they discovered her absent from the workshop. Her garden was where she always went when she wanted, or needed, to think. As she did now.

She and Nathan would sculpt again today, although she'd finished the first molding of the lower jawbone yesterday after he'd hastily left her, again, before luncheon. Annoyed with that, she'd decided that getting him to eat a complete meal with her would be her immediate goal for this afternoon. She wanted to spend time with him, talking, away from work.

Admittedly, just the fact that he'd left her so quickly and abruptly had bothered her more than it should have. She didn't understand the need for him to do so, especially when it had been her ultimate desire to entice him to stay. She knew she'd been too forward by unbuttoning her gown in front of the man, but the technique of subtle seduction was not in her repertoire. Still, it had subdued her when he hadn't appeared to be impressed by her rather suggestive conduct. Then again, maybe he had been, and that's why he'd left. Could it be he'd had trouble controlling himself? Mimi had no idea. She really didn't understand men all that well, and she'd never before risked seducing one of them. Getting Carter to notice her had never been a problem.

The thrill of the moment between them yesterday had left her breathless, though, which puzzled her, because nothing much had really happened. But just knowing that Nathan had watched her closely while she leaned over to give him a good, rousing peek at the top of her breasts had thoroughly excited her. Even sexually, which she found perplexing. But more than anything she'd been surprised not only at herself and her actions, but her physical response to Nathan's hot gaze when he'd lifted it to hers.

Oh, indeed. He'd seen what she'd wanted him to see, but instead of mentioning her indecency, or ignoring it, which would have been the gentlemanly thing to do, or even grabbing her for a lingering kiss and—God help her immoral thoughts—reaching out to caress her, he'd stood up and left. Just like that. Mimi didn't think she'd ever felt more thoroughly deflated than at that moment. After his untimely departure, she'd found it difficult to concentrate on her work, but she'd finished the lower jawbone and teeth out of sheer determination in hopes that when he arrived this morning he wouldn't begin to realize what a state of fluster and dejection he'd put her in.

She'd also had trouble sleeping the night through, and that was probably because she'd been restless with her musings about what her approach should be when she saw him today. At last, she'd decided she had two choices: she could be a lady and revert to her former controlled self, pretending yesterday's sensual encounter had never happened, or she could persist with what she wanted. After hours of tossing in bed, she'd decided to do the latter.

Being married had all but spoiled her innocence, she concluded, though in a most delicious way. She knew what she liked and what she missed about intimate encounters, and as the days ticked by, she grew ever-increasingly desirous that those needs be satiated by Nathan. She would probably burn in hell for thinking such a thing, but lascivious thoughts didn't simply vanish because one wanted them to. She just wasn't sure she could encourage his interest in her, although she had, two hours ago, made the very brave decision to try to do so again this morning. If Mimi was anything, she was tenacious.

She'd chosen one of her older, more fashionable gowns, a plain crepe in rich dark silver-gray, with a low scooped neck and cropped sleeves, deciding on it not because it was comfortable, but because it wasn't. She'd lost a considerable amount of weight from the shock of Carter's death, which she'd since slowly regained, and now the gown fit tightly in the waist and bust. Very tightly. She'd also donned a silk chemise in black lace, and a black satin corset. The constriction through the lower bosom lifted her breasts, and the black lace peeking up to the edge of the silver-gray, which only the most observant and close individual could possibly see, drew that much more attention to her pale skin.

She'd changed the style of her hair as well so that it had a softer look to it, braiding it loosely and winding it on top of her head, held in place with a pearl comb. She had a good selection of mourning jewelry given her by her mother-in-law, but Mimi more or less found the pieces too dark and morbid for her individual style. In the end she rarely wore any of it, though she still wore her wedding ring. She supposed she would always wear that.

Closing her eyes, she lifted her face to the morning sun, absorbing the heat of it through the slight autumn chill. Lacing her fingers together in her lap, she breathed deeply of the crisp early air mixed with the scent of lingering rainwater and wet leaves, wondering if it was close to ten yet, if Nathan would arrive on time, smiling when she remembered that she came to the garden to forget all that.

Yes, she brazenly wanted to continue her wanton considerations where Nathan was concerned. He occupied her thoughts, tempted her in too many ways, and nothing sounded lovelier at the moment than kissing Nathan, than feeling his beating heart beneath her palm, than touching his skin with her fingertips and pressing her body—

"What a vision you make, Mimi."

Her lids fluttered open in surprise, as her pulse began to speed just from hearing his wonderfully deep voice penetrate the silence. But it was his candid gaze, the note of fresh evaluation in his eyes when she finally looked at him, that made her breath catch in her chest.

He stood at the edge of the secluded garden, wearing a white linen shirt and dark blue pants, the sun casting a bright glow to the side of his face and shoulder. Again she was thoroughly taken by his marvelous physique, his commanding bearing, but especially by the very masculine hardness of his facial features. She would never tire of looking at Nathan Price. He entranced her in every way and always had.

"Good morning, Nathan," she said at last in innocent reply.

"Indeed it is," he returned softly, his tone somewhat assessing, giving her a half smile as he took a step or two toward her, moving within the walls of her retreat.

He hadn't shaved this morning, which gave his face a scruffy edge where his beard began to grow on tanned skin, and his hair hung loosely over his brow—combed but not groomed. He never wore jewelry or cologne, she'd noticed, and his nails were most certainly not manicured, but were, in fact, cut short over rough, callused fingers. He was the only man she knew who, even when dressed formally, resembled one who'd spent a day of hard work in the sun. Other ladies of gentle breeding would no doubt find his look common, or even disagreeable; Mimi was drawn to it. She'd never known an educated man who carried himself so well and yet looked more like an ordinary worker, as Nathan did. He was a contradiction in personality and image, and she liked it far more than she should. She had, since the moment she'd laid eyes on him for the first time years ago, and all the years in between when she'd grown to adore him during their sporadic but fascinating conversations.

Mimi sighed inwardly as she realized again what she was doing. She appraised his appearance every time they were together, as he usually did hers, she knew, feeling a subtle warmth within. Yet this morning he never moved his gaze from her face. He didn't even glance at her breasts, which, beyond her initial surprise, she found both amusing and at the same time a trifle disappointing after her careful preparation of her person for just such an observation.

In that instant she decided something was different about him. Maybe it was just his relaxed stance, the thoughtful assessment in his countenance, the fresh, intimate surroundings of her flower garden that seemed to intensify the intimate feel of his presence. Maybe it was just the deeply soft, lovely way he'd said her name. However unclear, there was a marked change about him, to be sure, and she felt so strongly attracted to him suddenly, she clasped her fingers tightly at her thighs to keep from standing and going to him. She refused to be embarrassed by feelings not returned.

"Are you ready to work?" she asked pleasantly, deciding to get to the heart of his visit before she disgraced herself by voicing her thoughts.

He chuckled softly and finally looked away from her, to his feet, hands clasped behind his back as he slowly strode to her side. "In a moment," he said. "I thought I'd join you here for a few minutes first."

Mimi blinked, startled by the casualness about him. From the second he'd come back into her life just a little more than a week ago, he'd been driven, intense in his purpose, barely noticing her as an individual of interest. Now, for all practicality, he was relaxed and good-natured and desirous of her company. Perhaps even more so than the Nathan Price she remembered of years ago. This entire unforeseen alteration of their situation made her nervous, but she would never let him know that.

"Of course, Nathan." She scooted to her side a little to make room for him on the bench, pulling her skirts against her leg so that he could sit as comfortably as one could on marble. "I adore it out here on sunny mornings."

"Do you? Even when it's cold?"

She felt the heavy weight of his body as he settled in beside her.

"One can always wear a mantle."

"Indeed, one can."

She laughed softly at that. "What a silly conversation."

He didn't respond to that but sat back casually to gaze at her, amused, one foot crossed over the other. She fought the urge to lean against him, which seemed the natural thing to do under the circumstances.

"Did Carter often sit with you here?" he asked presently.

Again, mention of Carter by Nathan made her skin prickle and her pulse speed up. She didn't understand why he continued to wonder about her relationship with her late husband, but considering that she was daring by nature, she could no longer let such comments pass without answers from him regarding his interest.

Smiling confidently, she maintained, "Carter came here on occasion, I suppose, but I don't recall him ever staying long. His concern with it was nearly always just to find me."

Staring at her, he vaguely smiled. "I've no doubt."

She wasn't certain what he meant by that exactly,

so she waited for more. When it wasn't forthcoming, she pressed, "Why do you ask me so frequently about Carter?"

The mood quickly shifted with her personal question; it wasn't so much an uncomfortable shift, though she felt him tense beside her, his expression going flat.

After a long moment he turned his attention to the fountain. "I didn't realize I was doing that."

His response made her pause. Discussing Carter with Nathan Price seemed almost insensitive to her, as if she were speaking ill of her late husband with a professional rival who knew his comments might or might not be challenged. She didn't want to open old wounds, especially wounds among the three of them. She had cared for Carter and she respected his memory. But, even so, she still desired at least a fair answer from the professor.

"Every time you and I are together, you ask me about him," she acknowledged evenly, smoothing her palms down her skirt to steady them. "I admit I'm curious why."

She noticed the corners of his lips lift minutely again.

"I suppose you are." Seconds later he turned his gaze back in her direction, his dark eyes intense. "I do wonder, however infrequently, how you and Carter were together, Mimi."

Heat suffused her neck and cheeks, their heightened color something she was certain he noticed, and her hands began to tingle in her lap. But she never looked away.

"How we were together?" she repeated. "In—in what way?"

His grin widened as his eyelids narrowed. "In every way," he clarified softly.

His simple statement told her nothing of fact, but his mesmerizing deep voice that trailed off into the quiet, private surroundings implied something profoundly intimate. Her heart pounded in her ears and her body began to perspire beneath layers, even in the morning chill.

Yet perhaps he didn't mean what she thought he meant. Perhaps she was jumping to conclusions. He wouldn't, as a proper gentleman, expect her to think anything else.

Smiling, glancing to the fountain, she said wistfully, "Carter was a very decent man, and I do miss him. He provided for me financially, as a good husband should; was honest in business dealings, to my knowledge; was dedicated to his work—"

"And dedicated to your needs as well?" he interjected.

What needs? she wanted to ask, but thankfully held her tongue. His expression remained impartial, though his tone resonated with deep meaning that made her uneasy in a totally dissolving manner. She tilted her head and gazed back into his candid eyes, their recesses hiding messages she could only begin to measure.

Boldly, gripping her satin skirt tightly with her fingers, she answered, "All my needs, Nathan." After several long seconds without reply on his part, distracted by his warmth and strength beside her, she added, "I'm certain, though, that another man could have done just as well."

He stared at her levelly. "Maybe better."

"Better?" she repeated, daring him.

Shrugging, just above a whisper, he explained, "Perhaps you'll experience that . . . satisfaction again. You're a young woman, Mimi, and quite appealing."

That made her cheeks burn, and her stomach muscles tighten. "Are you speaking of marriage, Nathan, or something else?"

He said nothing for so long she grew physically discomfited, waiting, refusing to break eye contact. At last he was the one to do so by glancing briefly to her breasts. The visual touch, so obvious on his part, made her shiver.

He noticed, and lifted his hand to her. "It's cold. We should probably go inside."

"Ready to work?" she asked, peeking up from the corner of her eye.

He gave her a slight, wry grin. "That's what I'm here for, Mimi."

Bravely, she put her palm in his, and it was just like the week before, when she'd met him in the boarding house and had taken his hand in their agreement. The shock of his skin against hers was overwhelming, exciting, and numbing all at the same time. Just feeling his fingers against hers enthralled her even now, and with that she realized if she did place her lips on his face—anywhere—she would likely faint. Not wise, in her predicament.

Slowly he stood and she raised herself to stand

beside him. But he didn't let go of her hand immediately. Exactly as he'd done it the week before, he ran his thumb along her knuckles, just once, gently, lingering long enough for her to know he meant to do it.

A bird fluttered overhead, landing on a nearby trellis, squawking once before it flew off again. But he ignored the sound—the intrusion—entirely.

He watched her for reaction to his simple caress, and in a moment of burning irritation at herself, she realized she was giving him what he wanted to see. Heat and total captivation. For the smallest second, staring into the dark depths of Nathan Price's eyes, standing inches away from the man in her cool, secluded garden, Mimi was certain he would kiss her.

Kiss me, Nathan . . .

Suddenly he released her hand, stepped back a foot, and casually gestured toward the house.

Mimi blinked quickly and stood erect, then drew her gaze away first. Without word, she lifted her skirts and walked past him, listening to his footsteps on the brick path as he followed.

He couldn't help but stare at her rigid spine as he stepped behind her into her studio, at her perfectly molded backside as it gently swayed in her too-tight gown, feeling smugly amused at this turn of events. And hard of course, which seemed to be his body's natural response whenever he was in Mimi Sinclair's presence. Just touching her fingers with his made him stand at attention, which he rather hoped she might have noticed. Or maybe not. Her knowledge of his state of arousal might make her a bit more cautious in her approach, and he was beginning to enjoy the idea that she wanted him. If he scared her away by becoming open about his need they would get nowhere. He'd seen desire for him in her eyes, even if she wasn't experienced enough to recognize it herself. Still, as Justin had implied, she was a widow. She knew what to expect from intimate relations, and had probably been taking the time since yesterday to consider what she'd been missing from a man for more than two years.

He'd done some thinking after he'd left the pub yesterday, too. On the whole, he rationally knew getting involved with Mimi to any degree was dangerous. Of course he found her difficult to resist when she so obviously desired him, but over and over again, during a restless night's sleep, he kept returning to the fact that he couldn't in any way trust her. It was entirely possible she intended to use him for reasons unclear, to exercise her female charms to lure him into thinking with his cock, thereby controlling him. She wouldn't be the first woman to do that to an unsuspecting man.

Yet Nathan knew himself, and his motives were stronger than mere biological urges. After weighing everything, he'd decided he would take what she gave as she gave it, if it suited his purpose, never for a moment letting his guard down about his real mission and reason for returning to London. She was a widow in need of a man, and he'd be more than happy to satisfy certain needs of hers without emotional involvement; he could manage that. He had his own agenda and plans for his future and they certainly didn't include Sir Harold's daughter.

He suspected the man of so much ill against him that Nathan knew it would only be a matter of time before Mimi would be swayed to side with family.

Nathan remained quiet, watching her as she pulled chairs out for both of them, then moved to a counter in the corner, uncovering the sculpture work she'd apparently done the day before, after he'd left. He shifted from one foot to the other, leaning his right hand on the ugly brown table, inexplicably annoyed that she'd been so unaffected by the sexual awareness between them yesterday that she'd managed to make a very good lower jawbone likeness after his departure.

She moved to his side, carrying the model in both hands, stretched out for his view.

"What do you think?" she asked with an air of pride, smiling.

"It's perfectly . . . adequate," he said. "I'm sure it will all come together when you've completed it."

Her face fell, making him feel like a cad. Wiping a palm across the back of his neck, he amended, "I would not have expected anything less than perfection from Sir Harold's daughter, Mimi."

"Which is the sole reason you're here?"

She'd asked that as an inviting question, making him smirk before he answered exactly as she expected. "Of course."

She tried to hide a widening grin of pleasure. She felt his underlying interest in her, but didn't actually respond to it, which aroused him all the more.

"Thank you, Nathan," she remarked politely, placing the jawbone on the table at his fingertips where they would begin working. "You can help with the teeth today, if you'd like."

"As you wish." He pulled her chair out for her first and she sat daintily, pushing her thick skirts to the side of her legs. When she appeared settled, he lowered his body into his chair and scooted in.

Concentrating on the clay in front of her, as she did yesterday, she began by leaning to her side, toward him, to lift a water bowl. Again, he got a lovely look at her cleavage, that he was now certain she intended for him to see, and he smiled in satisfaction. Of course this gown was far too tight to allow him a view of her breasts worth gawking over, but he could see a hint of black lace. Lovely and enticing. What a marvelous game she played with him.

After sprinkling her clay with water she began to knead it, and he watched the movement of her hands and fingers, mesmerized by the massaging action, clearly imagining those hands on his chest, her hair down and caressing his neck and face while she lay on top of him. He leaned forward and placed his elbow on the table, his chin in his palm, watching her.

"Do you enjoy this kind of work?" he asked, attempting to bring into discussion something that was *not* erotic.

She didn't hesitate in her response. "Very much. It keeps me . . . sane. Gives me purpose." Glancing up to him, she added, "I think I'm very good at what I do."

"I think you are, too," he replied without prevarication. It made her smile again.

"What do you think about when you work, Mimi?"

Seeing the lift of her brows, he knew the question surprised her.

"I've never considered that before. Why do you ask?"

He shook his head a bit as it relaxed in his hand. "Just curious."

She drew a long breath and exhaled loudly, tipping her chin to the side as she examined her mold. "Well, I suppose I think of household matters more than anything, chores that must be done, family situations that must be addressed. Sometimes I think about the parties I'm missing."

That cursory declaration brought another smile to her lips, but Nathan knew she meant it. "What else do you miss?"

Lifting a small knife, she sliced off a portion of the gray material in her hands. "I miss being social, I suppose, but that will come back eventually. I miss the theater, especially the opera. I miss picnics in the park."

He grinned. "If there's one thing I can imagine you doing, Mimi, it's socializing. I'm sure you do so to make the best of London society proud."

Her eyes sparkled in delight. "But I am also a very practical person, not at all frivolous."

"Indeed," he said, his tone revealing surprise. Dryly he added, "I never would have thought so. I suppose you learned such total . . . practicality from your father?"

She laughed at his playful manner—a soft, throaty sound—and it utterly charmed him.

"I know you don't believe me, Nathan, but I'm really much less vivacious and fanciful than he would have others believe." She peeked up at him through her lashes. "He's taught me well."

Nathan paused, regarding her closely as an unexpected wariness pulsed through him. "You love him very much, don't you?"

"Very much," she admitted at once. Looking him straight in the eye, she maintained, "He is a great man, Nathan, and not to be underestimated."

He sat up a little, growing agitated at the implied warning, if indeed that's what it was. "Believe it or not, in many ways I agree with you."

Her lips parted, as if she were about to comment or argue with him. Then she clamped them shut and shifted her attention to her work once more.

Nathan breathed in deeply, smelling dust and clay and her. The combination, to his complete surprise, was altogether inviting. She belonged in this room, and everything about it fit her style—a style, he mused, that he very much admired.

He dropped his gaze to her delicate hands, watching them as she expertly rolled the clay into an oblong shape. Then she pulled half of it away and pushed it toward him.

"You'll want to take off small pieces—like so—and gently sculpt them into teeth," she directed. "I'm going to begin the upper jaw while you're doing this, and you can use that visualization to choose the size as you think they would look to scale. When we get to the life size model, of course, we'll have to be a good deal more careful about accurate measurements."

Instead of reaching for the clay she offered, he sat back, folding his arms across his chest, regarding her with increasing interest as another thought of considerable importance occurred to him.

Lowering his voice, he got to the heart of his concern. "There's one thing you've yet to mention, Mimi."

"And what is that?" She left his portion of clay in front of him and picked up her own.

"Who do *you* think stole my jawbone?"

She fumbled it, and the entire mass fell out of her hands and dropped to the floor.

He stared at her, amused at her sudden discomposure.

"I beg your pardon?" she asked, leaning over to pick it up.

She didn't look at him, but wiped her wrist across her forehead before sitting up straight and digging into her project again.

He chose his words guardedly, repeating the question that filled his mind. "If you're so certain your father didn't take it, you must have some thoughts on who did."

She stayed silent for several lengthy moments, concentrating on her creation, her hands moving with vigor. Then she shook her head negligibly and murmured, "I'm not sure I can answer that, Nathan." She glanced briefly at his face again but added nothing more.

"You're just certain it wasn't Sir Harold," he stated for her, closely observing her reaction.

A trace of a smile touched her lips. "I would not

be helping you now if I thought he was in any way to blame."

True, which was something Nathan had decided already. He readjusted his large form in the small wooden chair and stretched a leg out. "But you do trust that the fossil existed."

He couldn't keep the apprehension that he might hear a negative response from tainting his assertive tone. But although her denial would hurt, it suddenly mattered tremendously that she believed him.

"Yes, I do," she answered forthrightly as she began to roll her clay out with her left palm while reaching over to grasp more water to sprinkle on it with the right. "I've never doubted its existence, and I still wonder why so many of your peers did. Your experience and reputation should have been enough for anyone to believe you'd discovered something scientifically remarkable."

Her reply left him highly gratified for the moment and he had trouble concealing a grin. "Have you ever wondered what happened that evening at the Crystal Palace?"

She eased up on her work, her shoulders slumping forward, brows knitting. "I've often thought about it. I cannot imagine how the jawbone was confiscated without anyone being the wiser." In a gentle voice, she looked into his eyes to add, "I'm just so very sorry that everything you'd worked for, everything you'd envisioned for your future, was so shamelessly stolen from you that night, Nathan. I really am."

Her candor struck a chord in him and for seconds the knowledge of all that he asked of her made him uncomfortable. Sighing inwardly, he reached out and stroked the back of her hand with his index finger.

The contact jolted her a little, but she didn't pull back from his caress, which encouraged him.

"Thank you, Mimi."

"For what?" she murmured, boldly holding his gaze.

His eyelids narrowed with the depth of his sincerity. "For helping me when there are still so many doubts."

She couldn't look away, or didn't want to, hesitating in answer as the gravity of his meaning sank in. Then slowly she straightened, her lips curving up mischievously. "You're stalling."

"I'm what?"

"The dinosaur teeth. Get to work."

She pulled away from him and stood up to lean over the table, concentrating on her clay once more, though Nathan sensed that she remained acutely aware of him at her side. The air positively sizzled around them now, and he knew she had to feel it as he did. The urge to touch her again grew overwhelming.

"You were made a widow too young," he said softly.

She lifted her lashes and her round, brown eyes probed his momentarily before turning back to the table. "I think so, too," she agreed, "but then, that's something I cannot change so I try not to dwell on it. I've often wondered what my life would be like today if Carter hadn't been taken so suddenly. I suppose I'd be a mother by now. I do long for that experience."

She was chattering on, nervous, and he liked the idea that his presence affected her that much. He dropped his arm so that it lay flat on the table surface, his fingertips brushing back and forth on the faded oak. "Do you miss the love?"

Lightly, she shrugged. "Sometimes, I suppose. I would have liked to have had several children."

"I mean the love from Carter."

She refused to glance his way, but he noticed her cheeks flushing with color again. So telling. She had the most beautiful skin of any woman he'd ever known, Nathan concluded in that moment. So creamy and smooth, and not a blemish or scar to be seen save for the tiny birthmark beneath her ear that somehow drew attention and begged to be tickled. Or kissed.

"I miss the intimacy, yes," she mumbled without looking at him.

He wanted to applaud her bravery. This was not a topic for gentle ladies, and yet she answered him truthfully, without pretense or hesitation.

"Were you in love with Carter, Mimi?"

His question was just above a breath, but she heard it.

"I loved Carter, Nathan," she replied in a low, heavy voice, her forehead gently creased in frown. "He was my husband."

That didn't answer at all what he'd asked and Nathan was fairly certain she knew it. She purposely kept this truth from him, but if there was a reason to do so beyond the personal, he didn't understand it. Either she loved Carter for the man he was and didn't want to reveal that to Nathan for reasons of propriety, or she loved him simply because he was her husband and it had been her place to care for him. Nathan suspected the latter and it made him heady with a certain pleasure that he hoped to God he wouldn't accidently convey to her.

Nathan glanced down at last to the piece of material she played with in her hands, paying fast attention as she began to slowly stroke a seven-inch rolled length of clay with water-lubricated palms. He followed the movement for a moment, the warmth within of seconds ago turning to a burning fire.

"Were you . . . satisfied by him?" he managed to ask, his tone husky, daring.

He knew she understood that he'd asked something far more intimate than if she had been satisfied *with* Carter, because she immediately stilled her hand movements on the clay image at her fingertips. For seconds she just stared at it, and then she swiftly raised her lashes and gazed at him again.

She didn't misinterpret anything. Her eyes had grown to large, brown pools of shock mixed with complete embarrassment. She just stared at him, made speechless, and radiantly beautiful, he decided, with pink cheeks and tendrils of blond hair loosely framing her face and throat.

In a brave move, she whispered breathlessly, "Satisfaction is relative, Nathan."

She licked her lips, very slowly and on purpose, he supposed, because he was drawn to the movement.

"Relative to what?" he quietly urged.

In a voice as smooth and rich as fine wine, she replied, "Relative to the moment. To the person one is with. To the circumstances that bring a couple together and to their mutual feelings for each other."

Such a formal response, and yet the air around them crackled with a tension he'd never felt in the presence of a woman. The sensuality she exuded without attempt so impressed him that Nathan felt slightly affronted. And nearly out of control.

Carefully, he raised himself to stand beside her, never breaking eye contact as he nodded toward the clay resting so conspicuously next to her delicate hands.

"Are you satisfied with what you're making here?" he asked intently, probing her recklessly for all the reaction he could get.

She understood the candid questions. If she didn't before, she now realized how much he'd enjoyed watching her stroke, for the last five minutes, what for any imagination looked like a rather large phallus nestled in her palms.

But she didn't back down as he expected her to do. She stilled in breath and motion, and with moist, parted lips, whispered his name on a purely feminine sigh. He couldn't resist it.

From sheer instinct he didn't even know he possessed, Nathan reached out with his free hand and placed his thumb against her bottom lip, just barely, feeling the smooth, tender skin beneath it.

She lowered her lashes in expectation, and he smiled with a marked contentment. Moving his roughened palm around her smooth jaw to clasp her neck, he drew her in slowly, feeling only a fleeting hesitation from her before she accepted his offer without question.

Her mouth felt warm and inviting against the coolness of his, and for a moment he didn't move, just held her motionless, their bodies separated by only the corner of the table. Then she sighed and leaned forward, into him, relaxing against him, and Nathan's last remaining coherent thought was that she didn't have to ask him for a kiss this time.

Gently he stroked her nape with his fingertips, beginning a subtle caress of her mouth with his, opening a little wider, smelling her, tasting her. The tip of her tongue brushed against his upper lip and the sensation brought chills to his arms. He hadn't been kissed so sweetly in ages, and he marveled in it.

In one step he moved around the table's edge so that they were standing with nothing between them. He lifted his free hand and placed it on her lower back, gently urging her forward until he felt her lovely, enticing breasts against his chest.

She reached up and laid her palms flat on his shirtfront, her fingertips, still smothered with wet clay, teasing his muscles beneath the heavy linen. She swayed against him then, her breath quickening to match the speed of his, and suddenly he could hold back no more as the rush of mutual longing became fierce.

He moaned very softly when her kiss became desperate and her tongue searched for his, when she squeezed his chest muscles and leaned intimately against his thick erection, which he fervently hoped she could feel.

He drew his hand from around her back to grasp her upper arm, only to place it, seconds later, to the side of her breast.

She whimpered when she felt that, when she felt him draw his hard thumb across the sloping top. He couldn't feel her nipple but he imagined that it stood straight out, puckered from desire, pearly pink and waiting to be sucked.

"Nathan—" she gasped, breaking free of his mouth.

He drew his lips down her cheek to her throat, pausing to kiss the birthmark beneath her ear.

"Mimi . . ." he whispered at her lobe, flicking it with his tongue, inhaling the scent of her hair. "That was far, far more satisfying than the first time."

Then before he allowed passion to overtake them completely, he withdrew himself, and on weighted, shaky legs, strode from the workshop.

Mimi stood rigidly, eyes closed tightly, encompassed in searing heat, realizing at last that she could no longer hear his retreating footsteps. Then she allowed her knees to give way and she drifted to the floor, her skirts surrounding her in a messy, indelicate heap.

She inhaled as deeply as she could, her palm to her thumping chest, thinking absurdly enough that for the third day in a row, she'd managed to make him leave before luncheon.

Chapter 9

The morning sunlight shone brightly through her long bedroom windows and onto her lacy peach coverlet, proving that the day would be lovely. Mimi hardly noticed.

Her night had been a fitful one, and she'd slept little, or at least she thought so. Her dreams, when she'd had them, had been mixed with luscious kisses and bones of a faceless monster, both in a fog, both drawing her in, both haunting her. Now, as the clock on her bedside table said ten minutes to nine, she couldn't seem to drag herself out of bed. She hadn't slept so long in ages, and yet this morning, for a world of reasons, she didn't want to leave the comfort of her covers.

It had been two long, uncomfortable weeks since

she'd kissed Nathan—a totally numbing and marvelously perfect experience that she relived every
single moment in his presence. She'd wanted it
more than he knew, and had accepted it with an en-
thusiasm completely unbecoming of a widow still
in mourning. But then Nathan was a difficult man
to deny. She doubted that she ever could. It had also
brought back a whirlwind of memory—of that won-
derful-turned-awful night long ago when she'd decided, after being cradled in his embrace in the cool
night, that she would do nearly anything to be with
him. She'd wanted him then, and to her growing
dismay at the excitement she felt, she wanted him
now even more.

The problem, though, was that he hadn't attempted to kiss her again since that glorious afternoon, and it wasn't for lack of trying on her part.
She had, she believed, done her best to tempt him,
wearing subtle perfume, her most becoming gowns
that offered just a slight, enticing peek of suggestive
undergarments, sitting as close to him as possible.
Nothing worked. Their conversations had been superficial as well, and he'd been reluctant to open to
her, to trust her. He'd seemed completely immune
to her charms since that extraordinary kiss in her
studio, and she was beginning to wonder just how
obvious she needed to be. They'd finished the clay
sculpture last week, and even that she'd purposely
created at an almost conspicuously slow pace. Now
they'd begun the real work on the larger, life-size
model that required the most detail and precision,
and when that was completed he would, for all purposes, be finished with her. It had taken her two

weeks to decide she didn't want that. But how could she get him to act again on their shared attraction in the short time they had left together?

She could be more aggressive, she supposed, and go after what she desired, but she was starting to doubt that Nathan would respond as men usually did. The banquet was only a little more than a month away and after that Mimi feared he'd want nothing more to do with her. And always, regardless of what happened between them, in the back of their minds, would be the memory of his professional disgrace, and the ancient jawbone at the center of it, now draped in black velvet and sitting behind boxes one floor above in her very home.

Groaning, Mimi draped a forearm over her closed eyes and sank deeper into her pillows, scooting down farther beneath her coverlet.

She just didn't know how much information about that terrible night to reveal to him. Originally she'd agreed to sculpt the beast because of his overly rude accusations toward her father. Now, after weeks in his imposing, albeit charming, presence she felt doubts seeping in. Every day she remembered what she admired about the Nathan she once knew, and she liked it. Every day she wanted more and more to help him recover what had been stolen from him. Unfortunately, the treasured jawbone in her possession was the only real, solid evidence that would, if exposed, prove to the scientific world that he had been truthful about his find, and more important, that he had been purposefully wronged that night in the Crystal Palace. But by her doing so she would also be revealing secrets long kept, throwing her own family into the depths of social disgrace. The decisions she needed to make regarding her impending actions were all coming much too quickly and weighed heavily upon her shoulders.

Deciding she'd lounged more than would be considered usual for her, Mimi finally braved the cold floor at last with her bare feet. Dressing quickly in black undergarments and her purple gown, she splashed cold water on her face, rinsed her mouth, combed her hair, and braided it in two parts, which she wound into loops around her ears. She then made her way to the kitchen, where she ate only a half piece of toast with strawberry jam and drank a cup of strong tea with milk and sugar, her mind caught up in a storm of contemplation over her predicament, mostly regarding whether or not she would kiss Nathan again today.

At precisely ten minutes past ten, while discussing with her housekeeper, Glenda Simmons, the decision to sell some of the finer china they rarely used to pay for new window dressings that everyone *would* see once the black was replaced again with color, Stella politely informed her that Professor Price had arrived.

Mimi felt the quickening thud in her breast and admonished herself to ignore it. Just the mention of his name made her react physically, and she realized with disgust at herself that she'd never reacted like this toward another man. Not even Carter.

With a polite and polished air, she glided into the parlor where Nathan awaited her, her breath catching as usual at just the sight of him. He stood by the grate, staring down at the small coal fire as he absorbed the warmth of it, arms crossed over his large, fine chest, all muscle and man he couldn't possibly conceal beneath dark, genteel clothing.

Planting a pleasant smile on her mouth, Mimi disregarded the rush of heat to her face and clasped her hands behind her back.

"Good morning, Nathan," she said, stepping toward him.

He turned and quite intentionally, and lingeringly, looked her up and down. She felt totally exposed, keenly thrilled, and utterly satisfied.

"Good morning, Mimi," he replied in a deep, soft murmur, his gaze at last meeting hers and penetrating it.

She paused in stride, not wanting to get too close. After an uncomfortable moment, she glanced at his wide, perfect chest. "Are you ready to work?"

He grinned, then leaned over to lift something from the floor, hidden behind the settee. "I'm at your discretion, madam."

Her skin burned from that insinuation, but she refused to turn away. Crossing her arms over her breasts, she glanced down to his hand, in which he now carried a large white basket covered with a square linen cloth in deep burgundy.

"You brought . . . your own tools, Nathan?" she asked wryly.

His lips twisted into a devilish smile, and he nodded once toward the basket. "A picnic for us."

Her heart sank and her palms grew moist as she considered all the implications. The gesture was sweet and perfect, and impossible. How could he not know that?

She took a deep breath, feeling awful to dampen an eagerness for her company that she would otherwise relish. She had no choice, however, but to decline. "That's very generous and thoughtful of you, Nathan," she said at length. "It's a lovely idea, but I cannot picnic with you. It would be . . . unseemly in my situation."

His smile faded as the lines on his face grew noticeably taut, and gradually he lowered the basket to the seat of the settee. But his sharp gaze never strayed from hers.

"I'm well aware of the social restrictions in your position, Mimi," he replied coolly. "I simply thought maybe you and I could later eat luncheon in your garden. You said once that you miss picnics. It's a nice day so I thought I'd bring one to you."

She couldn't believe he'd done this for her, and she melted within, visibly sinking into her corset. "Oh, Nathan," she said through a softened sigh, "that's—that's a wonderful suggestion."

"Yes, I know," he interjected blandly.

Slowly, she grinned from his sweetness, his kindness, stepping closer so that she stood only a foot away from him, looking up to his face. "Under all that muscle and intelligence, you're still a man, aren't you? Full of arrogance and reserve."

"And tired of feeling such hunger every time I leave you, Mimi," he soothed. "I would very much like to stay today."

His suggestiveness left her breathless, and fairly

gloating inside. "Well, we certainly can't have you walking out so abruptly again. A picnic by the fountain it is."

She watched his eyes darken with a mischief she all but felt herself. Then with a smugness she hadn't experienced in ages, she abruptly turned on her heel, hands clasped behind her back and began walking toward her studio, Nathan following closely behind her.

"It'll be cold outside," she added with challenge.

He snorted—or at least she thought it might be a snort.

"Wear a mantle."

She chuckled and glanced over her shoulder at him. "And you?"

"I'm used to the weather."

"Oh, please, Professor," she chided, stepping into her darkened studio and walking to the drapes on the far wall. "Don't you own a coat of some kind?"

"No."

She stopped short and turned. "You own nothing for winter wear?"

"I didn't need any in the south of France, Mimi."

Yes, he would have, and she knew it. He would have needed the protection at least for winter nights, even there. But he was completely serious, and she didn't know what to say for a moment.

He stood in the doorway, the basket placed on the counter to his side, eyeing her tentatively. "I was hoping," he said slowly, "that I could sit very close to you instead."

Her nerves jumped at the thought, from the deep, seductive timbre of his voice, and she swiftly turned away from his probing eyes, hoping to hide how she suddenly oozed with longing from such simple words. She felt his lingering stare on her back as she lifted the russet colored drapes and pulled them to the side to allow the sunshine to flow through the tall windows.

"I suppose I could always lend you one of Carter's—"

"No."

The sharp, vehement protest made her whirl around to look at him again. He stood stiffly, arms held so tightly at his sides she could see the muscles bunch beneath his shirt, his eyes thunderous as they held her own. That such an innocent gesture on her part could anger him so intensely took her aback and she felt slightly affronted.

"I only meant that while you are here you could borrow—"

"I will not borrow anything that belonged to your late husband, Mimi," he cut in tersely. "I refuse, so we will not discuss it."

She faced him squarely, hands on her hips, annoyed at his unwillingness to be logical where men always seemed to be. And then she questioned her initial response. Did he react so bitterly because of professional or personal jealousy he felt for Carter? Or something more, something deeper that went to the place in each man that held his wealth of pride and dignity. Possibly both, but she wouldn't argue his determination because she doubted she would win.

"I see," she quipped in concession, raising her chin just enough to let him know she thought his rejection of her offer utterly ridiculous. "Then since I doubt my lavender woolen shawl would be suitable to your style, you may sit as close to me as you like for needed warmth. I certainly wouldn't want to be responsible for you catching your death in my garden."

He laughed deeply at that, dissolving the tension between them instantly. Hiding a triumphant smile on her face, Mimi walked to her sculpture, lifted it carefully, then carried it to the table where they began their morning work.

Nathan watched her spread out the linen cloth on a spot of grass near the fountain then sit upon it gracefully, spreading her skirts out and away from her legs, next to which he expected to sit. The day proved to be perfect for late November, the sun shining high in the sky and only a gentle breeze to be felt around them, though the hedges and trees helped to seclude the area. The air was indeed chilly, but not unbearably so, and with the sun on his back, Nathan hardly felt it. His blood ran so hot in his veins now anyway it didn't matter. Looking at Mimi did that to him.

It had been a difficult two weeks for him. She'd been beside him for hours on end, smelling like Mimi did, wearing clothing to entice, whether she knew it or not, and his fingers had itched to undress her, carry her to her settee, and probe her with his hands and mouth until she sighed. Or screamed. Nathan wondered if she screamed when she climaxed, and for the last two weeks he'd been unable to think of little else. After long hours of contemplation he decided that she did. She had to. It would be just like Mimi to scream, and even now his heart thudded hard in his chest with the notion of finding out with certainty.

But he wouldn't. She was out of reach, and had to stay that way, and teasing her about sitting close to her, and his continued hunger for her, was wrong. As much as he wanted to get physically intimate with the lovely widow, he had to remain detached, for his good as well as hers. Their shared kiss of two weeks ago had been unexpected, a moment of abandonment, and an amazing revelation to him—that he still wanted her and that she would respond with an unquenchable eagerness. But in another month's time his name would be restored, to the detriment of her father, who would likely be ruined. That prospect now troubled him more than he could put into words, which, in turn, made him angry. He'd come back to London with a far-reaching purpose and his feelings for Mimi, whatever those were exactly, were getting in the way. He should have never allowed that to happen.

He would not kiss her again, however much he wanted to take her to his bed. His vivid dreams of watching her cry out with her release, under his scorching, aching body, would have to remain just that.

"My goodness, you're so serious, Nathan," Mimi teased with a smile, cutting into his erotic thoughts as she opened the basket.

He lowered himself to the grass beside her, stretching one leg out, the other raised so he could rest his elbow on his knee in a pose of relaxed indifference, hoping to conceal his erection. She'd been married, and would know exactly what it was if she looked closely, which would be thoroughly embarrassing for him under the circumstances.

"I was just thinking you look very . . ." He hesitated for the right word, watching her brows lift in question as she waited.

"Very what?"

Delicious. "Nice . . ." he said, flicking his wrist in her direction. "In purple."

She grinned and went back to lifting items from the basket. "Thank you. I think you look very *nice* without a coat to cover your marvelous physique. It's easy to look at you like this."

Nathan felt the steady rise in his pulse—and stupidly giddy from that, which irritated him because giddy wasn't something men were supposed to feel. But he also realized, very matter-of-factly, that he'd never been so sweetly complimented by a female. Or maybe he had, but this was the first compliment to come from Mimi's lips, and for reasons unknown, that's what mattered to him.

"I'm glad you think so," he replied smoothly, picking a blade of grass and twirling it with his fingers and thumb.

"I've always thought so, Nathan," she admitted without pretense. "You're smart and attractive. I'm surprised you haven't married."

He paused again, uncertain how to respond to an innocent statement he was certain required an answer.

"I haven't the time, really, or didn't have," he

replied blandly, trying to remain aloof about such a subject, as a man should in the presence of a lady.

She shrugged daintily, arranging cold tomato slices on a plain china plate for him. Softly, concentrating on her task, she asked, "Do you think you will eventually?"

Not without the means.

"I'm famished," he said in evasion, suddenly agitated, sitting up a little and reaching inside the picnic basket. He removed a bottle of wine and two glasses, then worked the cork loose with a screw, all the while knowing she'd stopped what she was doing to watch him. His evasion annoyed her, perhaps puzzled her. He could feel it. But he chose to ignore her silent stare and disregard her current mood. One had to be so damn careful of women and their shifting moods.

Seconds later, without further comment, she focused her attention back on the contents of the basket, lifting one of the ample meat and vegetable-filled pastries and placing it on the plate, next to the sliced tomatoes, then setting it beside him. He kept track of her movements from the corner of his eye as she did the same for the second plate. After serving both of them, she closed the basket and moved it off of the blanket away from them.

"Have you ever tried *pasties*?" he asked lightly, deciding to be as charming as possible, pouring her a half-full glass of burgundy wine and handing it to her. "They're a typical lunch where I come from, but quite good. I thought you'd enjoy something different."

She took a sip of the dark liquid at her fingertips, then graced him with a rather prosaic smile. "I'm not sure that I have, though I'm looking forward to trying one. They smell heavenly." She lifted her glass to her lips again, entirely disregarding the food now while she continued to gaze at him speculatively. "So I suppose, in essence, I'm sipping fine wine with a common workers' luncheon, both served to me by a reserved, educated gentleman. How amusing."

She wasn't at all amused, which made him uneasy. He poured himself a generous amount of the dark red drink, then shifted his body away from her a little and leaned back on his free hand.

"Tell me, Nathan, why do you study science?"

That certainly came from nowhere. "I thought we were discussing food."

Her lips thinned to a flat smile. "It's a lady's prerogative to change the subject."

His eyes widened. "Is it?"

She said nothing to that, though a brow rose faintly as if to challenge him to prove it wasn't.

A second or two later he returned the cork to the bottle, squinting up at her bland, patient expression as the sun peeked out from behind a tree branch to warm his skin, and to illuminate hers beautifully.

"It's what I've always wanted, what I enjoy, I suppose," he finally replied, indifferently.

"That's a very good, prepared answer, Nathan," she immediately returned with a gentle nod. "But I could have guessed that. Now, be honest with me and tell me the real reason."

For a long moment, anger burned in the pit of his

stomach, and then her tender manner and the candid way she probed him for explanations subdued him. She was genuinely interested, and he liked that. Probably more than he should.

He blew out a heavy sigh, then took a long swallow of wine. It was excellent, as it should be by the price he'd paid to impress her with it, and he let the warmth of it linger in his throat before he began.

"It's a sorry tale, Mimi," he admitted, lifting his eyes to her inquiring ones, searching for evidence of her recoil.

Her smile became sincere at that, and she relaxed into her corset. "I'm sure I'll not be repulsed, Nathan, no matter what you've done. Tell me."

She didn't understand. She assumed he meant he had a shadowed past, one of a common thief or pickpocket, perhaps even just a society beggar. Her misinterpretation troubled him more than he could say, but something about her manner assured him she wouldn't let the subject lie. He would have to reveal his past, however uncomfortable it would be for him.

"I will tell you everything, but only if you start eating before your food freezes."

Immediately, she reached for her pasty and lifted it to her lovely lips that curled ever upward in triumph. "You may begin, Professor."

He watched her bite into the crust, saw her eyes light up when she started chewing, and he couldn't help but smile in return.

"It's marvelous."

"Undoubtedly," he replied, casually crossing one

ankle over the other. "Mrs. Sheffield's cook rarely disappoints."

"You're stalling," she pressed in a sing-song voice.

He chuckled and rubbed his tired eyes with his fingertips. Then following another deep swallow of wine to warm his cooling body, he began at a most appropriate part.

"Let's see ... I'm originally from Newcastle-Upon-Tyne—"

"I assumed you were from the north country," she cut in, licking her lips before taking another large bite. "Did your father work in industry, then?"

That irritated him. Not that he found her knowledge of it irritating, but that he hadn't been able to competently conceal the fact of his common birth into a working family.

"Yes, my entire family—father and three brothers—works in some capacity in the steel industry," he maintained a little coolly, and without elaboration. "My father's father, and those before him, were miners." Coal miners—dirty, dark, and deadly work. Nathan had sworn that whatever happened with his life, he would never set foot inside a mine.

Mimi nodded without remark, without looking at him, enjoying her pasty with every bite, either ignoring the fact that his family were all common laborers, or dismissing the entire disclosure out of pity. Nathan assumed the former. He despised pity.

"When I was little more than sixteen," he continued, "I left for Oxfordshire with twenty-nine shillings, sixpence in my pocket."

She raised her lashes again and glanced up to

him, eyeing him with a combination of disbelief and amazement. At least he thought it might be that. With another sip of wine, he turned to stare at a vine-covered trellis to his left, its branches brown and empty of life and color.

"I had no immediate goals except that I wanted to work in the field of archaeology, then paleontology, both of which had fascinated me from the first time I'd heard the terms as a schoolboy. If I was going to dig, I thought, it would not be for coal, but for something unique and monumental. Something worthwhile beyond its monetary value. Unfortunately, I quickly learned that important work for a man in my financial and educational position was not to be found anywhere. I was escorted onto a field where I was allowed simply to dig. I couldn't even touch or help to remove the finds, couldn't catalogue the discoveries, was not allowed to contribute anything to intellectual conversations between the scholars. I was a digger, nothing more." He shook his head sharply and took a long swallow of wine, no longer tasting it. "I hated that."

"I'm sure you must have learned a great deal, even in that position," she said at length. "It all sounds very fascinating, actually."

He shifted his gaze to her once more, noting the look of concentration on her features, a few strands of hair laying across her cheek from the gentle breeze that she didn't appear to notice. "It could have been, Mimi, but not for someone of my social class. I was not expected to be a man of intelligence. I came from a family of lowly workers. Frankly, this assumption of my stupidity and ignorance due to the station into which I was born made me furious."

She watched him as directly as he did her, waiting for her condolences, her insincere patting on the hand, whether real or figurative, while she trumpeted the reasons for class distinction. But it didn't come. Nothing about Mimi Sinclair was as expected.

"So what did you do?" she asked instead, eyes probing his with keen interest. "How did you go from being a common laborer's son with no education to Professor Nathan Price, scholar and expert in paleontology?"

When put like this, his jump to her social level sounded utterly ridiculous, and his head ached at the temples from simply thinking about it. So much of his personal past was embarrassing, frustrating, and so very difficult for him to reconcile, much less discuss.

He drew a deep breath and squeezed his glass with his hand, which in turn kept him from reaching for that strand of long, silky hair now very near her lips.

"My mother, as it happens, married beneath her when she met my father. She was born into a middle class family of modest wealth, a banker's daughter, who was always a bit too assertive for her own good." He shoved his fingers through his hair. "When she met my father at the bank, by sheer coincidence, they fell in love immediately and were married within a month."

"How romantic," Mimi interjected, her voice a cross between a breathless sigh and cheerful excitement.

He snorted. "Yes, well, perhaps at the time, and for her especially, but her family did not approve of the match." He tipped his glass to his lips and finished the contents in two easy gulps. "She was more or less rejected by her family after that. I really don't know my aunts and uncles, or grandparents, at all."

Mimi didn't say anything to that, as he knew she wouldn't. She couldn't possibly understand because her life was so simple, so ordered. Nobody married outside of class, therefore one didn't have to worry about prestige, or money, or society and family disdain. Life, for her, had been so easy.

The air grew colder as they sat on the garden grass, in the tiny alcove, fairly sheltered from the world outside and the northern breeze. The food apparently forgotten, Mimi wrapped her mantle around her tightly, though she didn't raise the hood, and for that he was glad. He liked looking at her hair. It reminded him of sunshine.

"So, as a boy, your mother took it upon herself to educate you," she stated, as if already knowing the answer.

At last he picked up his pasty and took a rather large bite. The crust was cold but the contents inside were still warm enough—a marvelously simple combination of beef and vegetables that melted on his tongue as he chewed. He really was hungry, and it gave him something to do while he considered what and how much to tell her.

"Not formally, mind you, but she was persistent," he admitted after a moment. "She corrected my grammar whenever I misspoke, addressed my manners, tutored me in proper social behavior, as she did for my brothers, James and Kendall. My father, though not cultured, adored her and let her do as she pleased when it came to rearing us as gentlemen, probably because he never believed we'd succeed in living above our station."

"And yet you have," she said, smiling. "How did you manage to become formally educated, then?"

He was afraid she'd ask. It humiliated him to take charity as he had, but to get to the top of his field, it had been necessary. It was suddenly very important to him that she understand that.

"My mother knew of my interest in science when I was very young," he revealed, his voice low and tight. "She had . . . connections, shall we say, through her family that didn't acknowledge me, and knew of ways to get me involved with the right tutors."

"She found you a sponsor," Mimi said for him.

He fidgeted, picking off a piece of the crust and flaking it onto the plate between his forefinger and thumb. "Yes, exactly."

She waited, and when his explanation wasn't forthcoming, she opened her arms wide and fairly gaped at him. "Well? Who?"

"Who what?"

"Who is your sponsor, Nathan? Do I know him?"

After all this he supposed it wouldn't matter that she knew. With tight lips, he revealed, "John Marley, Viscount Durham."

"Ahh. Justin's father. Well, that makes sense."

He had no idea why it should, but he wasn't about to ask her to explain her thoughts. He truly felt ill at ease now, talking of this not only with a woman, but with Mimi Sinclair, Sir Harold's daughter.

With a deep sigh, he attempted to put the matter to rest. "My mother did the only thing she could," he replied solemnly. "Without a direct sponsor I wouldn't be here today. I wouldn't have my education, I would not have had the opportunity to work with Owen and his colleagues, I would not have had the chance to meet those of supreme intelligence within upper social circles, who, in turn, have so much influence in this profession. I simply would not be a scientist. I would undoubtedly be digging at the quarry for a minimal wage so others could collect accolades from *my* finds, or worse, working alongside my brothers at the factory in Tyne."

"Oh, for heaven's sake, Nathan, you're being so dramatic."

His eyes snapped up to meet hers in challenge. "It's not drama, Mimi, it's the truth," he readily rebutted. "To see me succeed, my mother had no choice but to petition a family who deserted her and solicit funds and backing from a social acquaintance."

She scoffed. "You make it sound as if your mother did something awful by seeking to help you."

"I never said that, but I don't necessarily want everyone to know. I do have my pride—"

"Don't be absurd," she countered quickly. "The way men discuss their pride as if it's some great . . . *thing* to be won or lost for all eternity continually annoys me. They use that excuse when it's the easy one." Irritation emanating from every movement, she reached for a tomato slice, dropping it in her mouth from above. Her pert little tongue darted out to catch the juice, and he stared at it, feeling the most unusual mixture of arousal and anger pulse through him.

"I don't think you understand," he asserted coolly.

"Don't I?" She wiped her lips and fingertips daintily with a white linen napkin. "I could tell the first night I met you that you were uniquely intelligent, Nathan. You are a smart man who's had a chance to rise above his station because you belong there and were fortunate enough to have someone care. You *are* a scientist, and that is something I would *know*, not something I'm guessing. Your mother did the right thing by finding you this opportunity because she could, because you didn't have it handed to you by birthright. Frankly, I think she sounds very loving and wise."

Mimi's interest, he decided, was positively charming in its innocence, but it annoyed him nonetheless. He bit off another smaller bite of the meat pastry in his hands, regarding her head tipped in thought, her brown eyes large in an attempt to convince, her beautiful face flushed with eagerness and exasperation.

"And yet this wise woman married my father," he said, his tone a bit harsher than intended. "What an illogical, stupid thing to do."

Mimi's eyes sharpened with a frankness he found almost intimidating. "How can you say such a thing?"

He shook his head. "Do not misunderstand me, Mimi. I admire my father, his hard work, his physical efforts to provide for a family. Likewise I adore my mother, primarily because she has always cherished me, and wanted the best for me and my brothers. My parents are honest and admirable people." He leaned toward her, and to his complete satisfaction, she didn't pull away, but faced him squarely. "However, this love of family simply cannot negate the fact that she should not have had to 'find' me a sponsor for anything. If she had not married beneath her—"

"Was she happy?"

The soft question startled him, and he jerked back a little. "I can't imagine why that matters. Happiness is a relative thing. One is happiest when life is easiest. Life would have been easier for everybody had she married someone of her class. I, as her child, would have been accepted in that class, I would have been able to study on my own, with my own funds. I would never have had to rely on someone else's generosity—"

"And you would also not be *you*."

At that moment, sitting face to face, Nathan couldn't decide if he wanted to argue with her logically as he would a man, or kiss her silly for being the clever, beautiful thing she was right now—all sunshine and heat and shimmering radiance that made even the cold air surrounding them a forgotten presence.

Mimi snickered at him, but never pulled away

from the magnetic stare they shared. "I find you too levelheaded for your own good, Nathan."

He tried not to look surprised. "How can one be too levelheaded?"

The left corner of her mouth turned up coyly and her eyes narrowed minutely.

"It's very disheartening, isn't it?" she noted softly. "To be so desirous of something you adore and be told time and again that it's not for you? I know that anger you felt inside, Nathan, though I must admit I'm extremely jealous that you've been able to rise above the shadow of adversity with such success and style. So much grace. I admire you more than you possibly know."

Nathan was totally baffled. He had no idea how they'd arrived at this subject, or even what the subject was, exactly. And how could she possibly understand his feelings of rejection and inferiority? His features must have expressed his confusion of thought, for at that moment, she smiled and leaned toward him, her face so close he could see a tiny bridge of freckles on the tip of her nose.

"It's amusing, I think," she added in a sultry voice, "that you don't see it."

See what?

Then without dropping her intense gaze, she reached up with her forefinger, and dragged it across the side of his mouth.

Her sizzling touch shocked him, partly because it was so unexpected, partly because just the idea of having Mimi touch him purposely was the first part of his perfect erotic fantasy. Even if only on the mouth.

Her grin deepened and she pulled her finger back enough for him to see a smidgen of gravy on the tip. He'd been talking to her, so serious and rationally, he'd thought, about manners and rising above his class, and all the while he'd had food on his face.

Before she could move, he grabbed her wrist, holding it before him for a second or two. Then, prior decisiveness to avoid her forgotten, he slowly, deliberately, drew her finger into his mouth, past the crook of the first knuckle, to the second, and beyond, until nearly her entire finger rested on his tongue. Then he began to suck, purposely, smoothly, his eyes melding with hers, his grip tightening even as she tried to pull away.

It was amazing, really, how quickly her expression of triumph turned to one first of astonishment, then smoldering heat. He drew the tip of his tongue along the tender skin between her fingers, to the nail, then back down again. He heard her steal a sharp breath, and could have sworn she squirmed beneath her skirts. Her cheeks flushed pink and she bit her bottom lip, her eyes growing glassy, and Nathan could take no more.

Gradually, he pulled her finger from his mouth, kissed the tip, and lowered her hand to the blanket.

Why are you doing this, Mimi? Why are you testing me with forbidden fruit when you know I can't resist?

He couldn't ask her; he wouldn't let her make a fool of him, no matter how hard she tried. She now played not with his feelings of inferiority, but with his desires as a man. He didn't understand her motives and couldn't begin to speculate on them right now. He needed to think things through.

Chapter 10

The cold dampness clung to her cheeks as Mimi descended her front brick steps for her short walk to May Street Gardens, the park closest to her home. The hour was early, the air very still after nighttime showers, a slight drizzle remaining. Yet she wanted to get this meeting over with as soon and as quickly as possible, before she lost her nerve and retreated to the safety of her studio. She also wanted to be away from prying ears, and of course the dreariness of the day would keep most casual strollers indoors where they belonged. She was glad for that. She didn't need the gossip right now, and although in half mourning one could reasonably ascend, albeit slowly, from the reclusiveness one had been forced to realize, an impression of gaiety could be most destructive to one's reputation. Mimi wanted to avoid that.

Closing her mantle tightly around her, the hood pulled high over her head to cover her hair completely, she held her chin high and walked briskly west, toward the park's south entrance.

Her upcoming meeting with Justin had been pure inspiration on her part, though absolutely necessary in light of yesterday's revelations. Nathan's candor, coupled with his continued restraint, had unleashed something in her, something wild and even a bit foreign, something exotic and forbidden. But she couldn't resist it. To see his need for her, placed so purposely before her eyes, and then to have him walk away from her with such control made her nearly shriek in frustration. Had he no idea what he did to her? Did he not see the heat in her eyes? Yet through all of it, most maddening of all, was that as a respectable lady, she could not act on her feelings and desires. Nathan certainly understood that, and she was positive he took advantage of it.

She only hoped that Justin could somehow help her, in a manner of speaking, which was why she'd sent him a personal note yesterday afternoon, following Nathan's sudden departure. That's why she was here now instead of meeting with Nathan for another day of suppressed desire while sculpting. She needed some . . . assessment, and help, from a friend, a male friend, and Justin was the only man who was not family that she knew well enough to trust with such a delicate issue. She'd known him for years, and she believed that he would, above everything else, respect her privacy in this matter.

Mimi spotted him at once as she rounded the black iron bars that outlined the entrance. The park was empty save for the two of them and a strolling couple with a child on the other side of an oblong pond. Justin sat in front of it, on a wood-framed bench, wearing a black wool coat and hat, looking ever distinguished, as Justin always did. His mouth curled down slightly in a frown, but he hadn't noticed her yet as he stared at the shallow water now topped with dead, russet colored leaves.

Her determination faltered for only the briefest second, but she refused to turn away now.

At last he heard the crunching of her shoes on the pebble pathway and his eyes darted in her direction. He smiled tentatively at her and she returned it.

Strolling to his side, she raised a gloved hand toward him. "Justin, thank you so much for meeting me this morning, especially on such short notice."

He stood, his brown eyes capturing hers rather frankly as he lifted her knuckles to his lips. "The pleasure is mine, Mimi, though I cannot imagine what could be so urgent as to get you outside on such a dreary day."

She laughed softly, appropriately, probably because it was the best way for her to hide, and relieve, some of her building nervousness. "May we be seated?"

"Of course," he replied at once, smiling in true gentlemanly fashion, eyes softening at the corners, which always made him appear younger than his twenty-nine years.

Mimi lowered herself to sit comfortably on the bench built for two, daintily pushing her light brown skirts to the side so that he could fit beside her without touching. She brushed her leather-covered palms down her black woolen pelisse and cleared her throat.

"I've got something . . . personal to discuss with you, Justin," she began, staring not at him but straight ahead. With obvious warning, she added, "It is my expectation that this conversation will not be repeated."

For a second he did nothing, though Mimi could feel his gaze boring into the side of her face.

"If it is indeed personal, then I won't repeat it to a soul, Mimi," he said thoughtfully. "You have my word on that."

Relaxing, she replied, "Thank you."

"Does this have anything to do with Nathan Price?"

She supposed she should have expected that. Shivering, she dropped her gaze to her hands, clutching them together in her lap, thankful that her hood concealed her reddening cheeks that had nothing to do with the cold. "You're quite right, Justin. It does."

He drew a long, slow breath. "I assumed as much."

She didn't want to comment on that; it disconcerted her. After waiting a moment, she chanced a peek at his face. He no longer smiled, and his eyes sliced hers with a slyness she had not expected from him, at least, not before she'd stated her intentions. It intimidated her a little, and she almost stood to make a fast, tactless departure.

"You're wondering what he sees in you romantically, aren't you?" Justin asked very softly.

She pressed her lips tightly together to keep from gasping as embarrassment coursed through her at his inference, her eyes opening wide. He never looked away.

She swallowed. "Well, that's . . . part of it, of course, though it's more than just that."

His right brow rose faintly, but he offered nothing in reply.

"I—I'm more . . . concerned, shall we say, that he's not interested in me at all as a woman. Is this because I am a widow, do you think?"

She could sense that he wanted to laugh. He blinked instead, sucking in his cheeks a bit. Then he angled his large body toward her more, gloved fingers interlocked in his lap, his dark brows drawn in a display of mild confusion.

"I'm sure the fact that you were once married has nothing to do with anything where Nathan's thoughts about you are concerned," he maintained guardedly.

Her heart sank as her mind suddenly acknowledged the obvious. "It's because I married Carter, then. I knew they disliked each other intensely, but I never thought—"

His loud groan cut her off. Closing his eyes briefly, he mumbled, "Why the devil do women always think everything is about them?"

It was a rhetorical question, but she felt slightly affronted nonetheless. "Where men and their stupidity come into play, isn't it usually?"

He shook his head and chuckled, wiping his large palm down his face then glancing out over the still, shallow pond. "Mimi, trust me when I say this is strictly about Nathan."

What is strictly about Nathan? she wanted to scream. Good breeding restrained her, however, though she did tighten her grip on her fingers in her lap, smiling pleasantly.

"Why doesn't he . . ." She paused to rethink and rephrase her question so as not to sound too indelicate. "Why does he not act on his attraction to me, then?"

If Justin were disturbed by her frankness he didn't show it. He continued to stare at the still water in front of them, though she could tell he was deciding what to say to her. The drizzle of the morning now began to strengthen from mist to light rain, but he didn't appear to be bothered by the tapping of water on the shoulders of his coat. And she certainly had more important considerations than a little sprinkling.

"What is it you'd have him do, Mimi?" he finally asked without expression.

She shifted her bottom a bit on the wooden bench. "I want him to notice me."

His lips turned up wryly, though he still didn't look at her. "I know that. But what I asked was what you think he should *do*."

Her face flushed with deep heat. If he looked at her he'd see it. Yet she knew what she wanted and would have to make it clear to him. "I want him to respond when I seduce him."

Justin wasn't nearly as shocked as she thought he'd be. In fact she was certain she noticed a twitch of genuine amusement at the corner of his lips. But she couldn't stop now.

Breathing deeply for inward strength, she admitted, "I've been doing my best to entice him, Justin, and the man is clearly not interested. Those times I've tried to get him to respond he usually just leaves me."

He turned to look at her again, his forehead creased in puzzlement. "Leaves you?"

She endured her deep felt abashment and continued. "Every time the conversation turns personal, or when I make my interest in him more than apparent, he walks away from me. He leaves." She tightened her jaw and looked down to her hands. "It's really getting to be quite funny, if it weren't so annoying. I don't understand the man's actions when I know he's attracted to me. At least I think he is—"

"He's attracted. And interested."

Her gaze shot back to Justin's. That quiet statement sent such an intense jolt of satisfaction through her she almost squealed. Then the warmth of its meaning spread down her spine. "Did he tell you that?" she prodded impishly, grinning.

He grunted, eyeing her candidly. "More or less, yes."

She restrained herself from giggling, which would be entirely too unladylike under the circumstances. Instead, she cleared her throat and murmured, "I see."

His watchful expression grew intense. "But I don't know if he feels it's in your best interest to romance you, Mimi."

Her heart fell and so did her jaw, which he noticed. "*My* best interest?"

Lips thinned grimly, he raised his elbow and rested his forearm on the back of the bench. "Mimi, Nathan realizes where he comes from—"

"Yes, Newcastle-Upon-Tyne," she interjected matter-of-factly. "I've been there twice. An industrial town—"

"You know that's not what I mean," Justin said irritably, cutting her off.

She stared at him straight-faced. "It doesn't matter."

"Yes, it does."

She wanted to hit him. Damnable men and their silly resignation to class and birth. Justin must have seen the anger in her eyes, for his features softened a little and he relaxed into the bench.

"I know you think a love affair with Nathan would be what's best for you now, but you've only been widowed a short time—"

"Don't you dare treat me like an imbecile, Justin, or a child," she voiced heatedly, her eyes locked with his in pure determination. "Yes, I'm a young widow, but I know exactly what's best for me. I've been half in love with Nathan for years, but the man was destroyed the night I gave him fair warning that I would welcome his intentions and that my father would accept an offer from him. It's what I'd wanted for months and my father knew it. But due to unfortunate circumstances, Carter Sinclair became my husband instead—a decent man, but not the one I'd yearned for with all my heart." She huffed disgustedly, and sat up rigidly, clutching the edges of her hood at her throat. "I was told what was best for me before and it will not happen again—"

"Mimi—"

"I want Nathan, Justin," she enunciated for his benefit, leaning toward him. "I want to marry Nathan, not embrace him in a casual love affair because I am lonely for the comforts of a man. I know he desires me but is reluctant to move forward. I need your help to convince him to act."

For a moment, Justin just sat there, stunned. She could see it in his vibrant eyes, the way his features went slack. But to his credit he didn't come back with a hand-patting, condescending rebuttal, probably because he knew how infuriated it would make her if he did.

At last he turned his gaze from hers and glanced out over the artfully carved shrubs and barren trees.

"Mimi, I don't even know if Nathan wants to marry at all. You're supposing he'd be interested in something more than a short romance, but I can't say certainly that he would. The two of us have never discussed it."

"I'll worry about that," she said, though the thought had occurred to her on more than one occasion. She just refused to contemplate it.

"I suppose I now understand why you couldn't go to Mary," he remarked after a long, silent moment.

She sighed as she realized with rugged pleasure that he wasn't going to counter her brash statement, or send her home to discuss this with her father of all people. It was a very gratifying moment. "Mary, as you know, is extremely class conscious. I could never discuss this with her, or any other relation. It's a delicate topic, Justin. It's also true that you know Nathan better than anybody."

He inhaled a long, slow breath, focusing his attention on a dormant tree to his side, pulling off a brown leaf to rub to a pulp between his gloved fingers. "I'm not sure what you would have me do."

She blushed but managed a triumphant grin. "I would like you to arrange a . . . meeting place for Nathan and me, without his knowledge."

His astute eyes darted back to lock with hers. "What?"

She raised her chin fractionally and forged onward, heart pounding. "I want to seduce him, Justin, and I'm not sure how else to do it."

He gaped at her, incredulous. "You want me to arrange a romantic rendezvous for the two of you?"

She licked her lips then casually replied, "I can't very well seduce him in my home or his boarding house. Too many people would suspect something, and I would be disgraced."

What followed was the most indelicate moment of her life, and the most intensely frightening. If he said no and repeated her outrageous request to anyone . . .

Slowly, he shook his head. "I can't believe you're asking this of me."

She raised her brows, trying to ignore the heat in her cheeks and the nervous thumping in her chest. "Why? Who else would I ask?"

She couldn't be absolutely certain, but Mimi

thought Justin might actually be embarrassed. His face flushed and he blinked rapidly with the thoughts running through his mind. Through even her own consideration of probable humiliation, she found it all rather charming.

"Are you not even fractionally afraid I will go to your father?" he fairly blurted.

She almost hugged him with that, because suddenly she knew she had him in her clutches.

"Not after I tell you I not only know of an absolute way to save Nathan from further dishonor, but that I have in my power a way to restore his stolen reputation fully. You care for Nathan too much. If you want what's best for him, you'll keep this between us."

Justin shook his head again, then raised a hand to rub his temples with leather-covered fingertips. "God, Mimi, what you're asking—"

She reached out and gently touched his arm. "Nobody will ever know I went to you, or that you helped me with this. Who would believe me?"

Very slightly, he lifted his lips in a smile. Then he chuckled. "You know who took the jawbone, don't you?"

That came out of nowhere, and it should have surprised her, but it didn't.

"I do," she murmured, sitting back a little, knowing that with such an acknowledgment, the final act toward her future with Nathan had been set in motion, whatever the outcome.

He turned to stare at her again, scrutinizing her gravely. "I don't suppose you'll tell me who it was or how it was accomplished."

She grinned smugly. "Absolutely not."

He sighed audibly. "Where is it?"

"Why, Justin," she exasperated with wide, innocent eyes, "it's hiding in my attic."

"You're joking."

"Of course I'm joking. Do you think I would keep it under my nose to incriminate me? Besides, I know the value of such a find."

He was quiet for a long, tense moment, contemplating such sudden, remarkable knowledge, and Mimi got the first indication of indecision and calculation on his part. But, like everybody else, he would never be able to put the pieces together.

Finally, profoundly, he whispered, "I hope to God you were not involved."

She had to expect that, she supposed, but she bristled with irritation nonetheless. "I would never purposely hurt Nathan, Justin, nor will he be hurt by my actions now. I swear it."

A bird squawked nearby; a child laughed in the distance. But he never moved his gaze from her. Seconds later, after scrutinizing every feature of her face, he slumped a little and exhaled fully. "I believe you," he whispered. "What would you like me to do?"

She straightened, feeling enormously relieved, not to mention thrilled at the coming event.

Cautiously she expounded, "I would like you to set up a lovely, secure, private meeting place for Nathan and me, without his knowledge. I need to be alone with him for an intimate . . . discussion. There is simply no place for us to be alone to talk."

His lids narrowed in sly amusement. "Ah. I see."

She squirmed a little, realizing that was a ridiculous thing for her to say and that Justin knew it. Discussion indeed. She felt the blood rush to her face again and she glanced to her lap where she brushed her palms along her gown to avoid his knowing stare. "After you've made the arrangements, please send word regarding when and where, but do so discreetly, if you would. You'll also have to meet the cost for now, but please spare no expense—"

"I'll take care of it, Mimi. When would you like this . . . discussion between you to take place?"

She rubbed the back of her hand along her hot cheek, absorbed in the large silver buttons on her mantle. "As soon as possible."

For an uncomfortable moment, he didn't speak. At last she raised her lashes and boldly looked at him again. His eyes were cautious, but also troubled. What she asked of him didn't shock him so much as it worried him. Realizing that subdued her a little.

"Do not get yourself with child to force him into marriage, Mimi," he warned very softly, but with a marked hidden strength. "If you do, I will come forward and tell him everything we have discussed here today."

His underlying meaning quickly pierced her, first with shock, then with burning anger. She never expected such a measured statement from him, but she understood it. Frankly, she hadn't considered such a thing, mostly, she supposed, because she'd never managed to get pregnant with Carter's baby. Still, she and her late husband hadn't been together intimately for very long. Barrenness wasn't something she could determine about herself yet. She would take Justin's counsel to heart, without telling him that, of course.

Leaning very close to him, she narrowed her eyes with fortitude. "I would never be so shameless, Justin, as to do that on purpose. It would humiliate Nathan, and I would never put him through that again."

"You care about him very much, don't you?" he asked, sounding a bit amazed by such a revelation.

She set her jaw firmly. "More than you could possibly know."

Justin studied her for a few seconds longer, then raised one side of his mouth wryly. "I do believe Professor Price has met his match in you, Mrs. Sinclair. I wish you both the best."

The tension winding through her body disintegrated in a rush, and Mimi laughed quietly in relief. "You're a good friend, Justin."

His smile faded only enough for her to know he remained skeptical. "Be careful. This is a serious manipulation on your part."

"And yours," she said abruptly, challenging him.

He exhaled loudly through his nostrils. "Let me be very clear, Mimi. I would never agree to such a scheme if I didn't think so highly of both of you, or that you could ultimately help him."

Mimi melted within. "Thank you, Justin, for everything." She reached out her hand and he grasped it gently.

"Tell me where the jawbone is, Mimi."

Her mouth turned up coyly. "I can't possibly do that, but you will see it again, I promise."

"Will Nathan?" he asked dryly.

She grinned, eyes gleaming to admit in whisper, "Nathan will be the most surprised."

His lids narrowed; the rain came down harder still and he never noticed. Then understanding lit his face and he sat upright, back from her, shaking his head in disbelief. "God help you, Mimi."

She took that with fortitude, chin high. "I'm counting on it, as I'm counting on the fact that as a gentleman and a friend, you won't tell a soul what we've discussed here today."

Before he could comment, she squeezed his hand once, then stood, turned, and with confident bearing, walked away from him toward the entrance to the park.

Chapter 11

Nathan was restless. Restless and bored, if it was possible to be both at once. He'd spent the better part of the day in his room at the boarding house, reading material he'd already read, looking through written proposals for funding to be used when his name was at last restored, pacing his floor and staring at the ceiling. He hadn't been used to so much inactivity in years, and it was getting the better of him. He needed to return to work, *real* work, because sitting within grabbing distance of Mimi every single blessed day was proving to be a very real strain.

He needed them to be finished with their project so that he could get back to his former life of research and lectures and prestige. So that he would have something to do besides sit next to her every day and restrain himself from leaning in to smell her neck, or brushing his lips against her soft skin, wanting to make love to her.

Yes, it was obvious to both of them that they needed each other physically, and wanted each other mutually. But of course she would never know how much he craved her touch. It was something he didn't understand himself. He'd always been attracted to her, he supposed, especially since the night of the Palace opening, but she'd been, in more ways than one, out of his reach. Now she approached him subtly, and used everything in her power to seduce him each time they were together. As he regarded it thoughtfully, Nathan had to wonder about that. Why did she want him? Why now? She had nothing to gain from a relationship with him, and everything to lose. A love affair would be nothing less than scandalous, regardless of whether his reputation were restored, and blacken her name overnight should those of her station discover it. He could never live with that.

But could he afford a torrid affair? Was that what she wanted? He didn't know. It wasn't beyond the scope of rational thought, though Nathan simply didn't see it in her. Mimi didn't seem the type of lady to offer her body in return for a few weeks of lustful pleasure. He also didn't know if he'd really want that with her. He liked her, and beneath her polished front, and that center spring of attraction between them, he found her witty, smart, engaging, and playful. Those were not, he decided, traits he admired in a good mistress, although sometimes a personal enjoyment of the woman one bedded made the experience that much more satisfying, he admitted rationally. Still, as much as his mind and body ached to be intimate with Mimi Sinclair, he found every reason to avoid it. In the end, Nathan came to the conclusion that a dalliance with her simply wasn't wise.

He was tired. Tired of the wait, tired of feeling useless, tired of being alone. He could return to Tyne, visit indefinitely with family, but he would never stay there. It wasn't his home anymore, and underneath his restlessness, Nathan realized this was the core of his longing. He needed a stable force in his life again. Living outside of quarry fields wasn't it, roadside inns and the King's Boarding House in London proper certainly held no special charm for him. He had to find his home again, and until he did, his restlessness would only get worse. New Year's Eve couldn't come fast enough.

Finally, at nearly seven in the evening, Nathan dressed in his finest suit, adjusted his frock coat over his shoulders, straightened his tie, and walked to the door. This would be one of his last visits with Mimi, and although that would be for the best, the thought saddened and frustrated him because he enjoyed her now more than anyone he knew. But such feelings were irrelevant when they had nothing in common beyond the Megalosaurus sculpture.

Nathan descended the stairs to the parlor below, and, without a word to anyone, walked out into the cold, still night.

Mimi decided the bold approach would be necessary. After her meeting with Justin this morning, she knew she wanted Nathan more than ever. To be honest with herself, she hadn't viewed their relationship as actually leading to marriage until she'd brought it up to their mutual friend. Now everything made sense to her. She wanted him because she couldn't have him easily, yes. That had to be part of it, because it would be just like her nature to do so. But she also wanted to be with him intimately because she realized this morning, when she finally said it aloud, that she was falling in love with Nathan anew. Of course her feelings for him weren't as simplistic and romantic as they had been three years ago, but perhaps that was a good thing. It was probably better that she'd aged a little, matured a lot, and understood herself so much more. Her approach to him would be realistic now. Not laced with that particular tenderness that came with virginity, as her magical kiss with him at the Palace opening had been. Tonight it would be hot, and spiked with awareness. She would see to it.

She'd been preparing all day for this encounter. She'd written Nathan a note yesterday afternoon, after feeling so uncomfortable at his untimely departure, informing him that she had an unexpected appointment this morning and wouldn't be able to work with him today. She also requested that instead, he come to her home later in the evening, after dark, so that he could see the nearly finished product in lamplight, as it would be presented at the banquet. She'd asked for a reply if this arrangement was in any way unsatisfactory, and to her complete delight she didn't get one.

Now, at just a few minutes past seven, she

awaited him in her studio, dressed more formally than usual in a satin gown that tightly delineated her waist and bosom, in the most becoming shade of lavender. She hadn't worn this particular dress for its color, however, but for its large black buttons that went from the top of the neck to the floor for easy access. She didn't want to have to ask him for help when she unfastened them before his eyes. At least, that was her plan.

At the sound of footsteps in the hall, Mimi turned from the counter where she'd been drying tools, and stared at the doorway, grave but determined, brimming with excitement and anticipation, trying not to express such optimism on her face.

Stella walked in first and introduced him with bland countenance, as she should, then turned and made her quick departure. When he entered the studio and stopped short, looking her up and down through narrowed, assessing eyes, Mimi's knees nearly gave way, making her reach out to the counter for support.

He looked so wonderfully handsome by lamplight, so large, solid, and masculine, dressed in his dark olive suit that he'd worn so splendidly the day he'd come back into her life. Nathan Price might not have been born of good family, but he certainly conformed to it, as his formal attire and groomed appearance gave off a trace of distinction that she found not only acceptable on the surface, but deeply sensual beneath it as well. This perfection of form was what he wanted, what he'd strived to attain for so long, and he became it naturally and definitively.

"Good evening, Mimi," he drawled.

"Good evening, Nathan," she whispered huskily in reply.

For a quick moment his dark eyes captured hers and a hint of a smile lit his lips. Then he slowly strolled into the studio proper to stop at the table just facing the dinosaur sculpture.

It sat upon the wooden surface, nearly finished in form, a full Megalosaurus jawbone roughly two feet long, with two hollow eye sockets and sharp straight teeth top and bottom. She'd placed gas lamps on either side—near the front right and back left corners of the sculpture—to create a mood, offering a simple yet haunting look of a frightening past.

His fingers touched it lightly as he examined her creation. Admiration, perhaps even the inner acknowledgment of dreams lost, caused his forehead to crease with his long sigh, his mouth to curve in a frown, as he skimmed the rough edges, drew his thumb down the dinosaur's flat, center brow ridge.

"Your talent surpasses even your father's," he conceded with an awe he couldn't hide.

It was the loveliest compliment she'd ever received, and for a moment she couldn't breathe. Then, with a smile full of pride, she sauntered toward him, hands behind her back.

"You flatter me, Professor," she remarked, "though I do think it's accurate, at least from the drawings you provided."

"It's perfect, Mimi."

He said her name in a low and husky tone that made her fingertips tingle and her mouth go dry. He still hadn't moved his gaze from the sculpture, but she knew he felt her presence beside him.

"Will you tell me of your intentions now?" she asked softly.

"Why do you live alone?"

That abrupt change in topic surprised her and she pulled back a little. "I'm not sure I understand the question."

He squinted at her from the corner of his eye and drew his hands up, rubbing his jaw with his fingertips. "Why don't you move back into your father's house? What holds you here?" He glanced around the room. "Certainly you can have a studio anywhere."

She grasped his manner of thinking now. A widow alone with servants wasn't necessarily a bad thing, but she really should be living with a man to take care of her, regardless of her wealth or self-sufficiency. Gossip, however innocent and well meaning, could be damaging to one's spotless reputation.

"I adore my studio, Nathan. It was made specifically for me," she replied, watching him closely. "I'm comfortable here as well, and although my father would prefer that I live with him again, he has Mary to care for his needs as hostess. My home isn't far from his, either, so I do visit frequently. The situation is reasonable for us all right now." He didn't appear to be impressed with that explanation, so she tried another by way of question. "Why are you suddenly curious about my living situation?"

He dropped his gaze, scrutinizing her figure again, slowly, caressing her breasts lingeringly before he locked it with hers again. "It's not sudden, I assure you."

Those words, or perhaps only the way he said them, inflamed her within. She took a step closer, so close the edges of her gown blanketed his lower legs. "Were you perhaps wondering if it had anything to do with my feelings for Carter?"

His smile faded almost imperceptibly. "No."

That fast answer satisfied her immensely, because under all that solid masculinity she was certain he lied.

She'd had enough evasion and amiable talk. It was time to get to the heart of the confusion he felt. "I didn't love him, Nathan."

A stark silence followed that admission, enveloping them within its depths. For seconds he didn't move, or speak. Then she noticed how he swallowed, how his nostrils flared. But he never looked away.

"What did you want me for this evening, Mimi?" he whispered gruffly, standing rigidly still, pulling her again from her intimate thoughts for the second time in as many minutes. "Why am I here?"

She refused to show her vulnerability, or her indecision.

Grasping him gently by the jaw, she steadied his face so that he couldn't help but look directly at her only inches away. The touch surprised him, as his eyes widened minutely, but he didn't jerk away or grab her hand.

"Tell me what you're planning to do with the

sculpture, with the head when it's completed," she enunciated in whisper.

His jaw tensed beneath her fingertips; his cheek twitched. "I did tell you, Mimi. I intend to show it to everybody."

That's what he'd said to her the first day in her studio, she remembered.

"Trust me, Nathan," she murmured slowly, with a depth of feeling she couldn't hide.

His hesitation to do so, to confess all, troubled her, and that's when she knew his intentions without any remaining question.

He planned to unveil it and simply watch for reaction among his former peers. Logical, and it would be the only way for him to discover the thief, the person, or persons, responsible. Everyone innocent of his downfall would be amazed, or surprised, even doubtful. But the thief would be infuriated, and would question the authenticity, or at least show it in his eyes, his silence. That's what Nathan intended to discover at the exact moment he revealed the sculpture of his stolen treasure. He might not be able to prove anything immediately, but after that night he would know, and the speculation would begin.

But Mimi was the only person alive who knew beyond question that his scheme wouldn't work because she knew what had happened that night almost two and a half years ago. Nathan would be humiliated again, this time solidly and with castigation of the cruelest kind. She felt a chill seep into her bones, so icy and seizing that she shivered violently.

Nathan, still watching her, letting her touch him, felt her reaction. He reached up and pulled her hand from his face, clasping her knuckles in his palm.

"Cold?"

Was this an opening? She didn't know, but instantaneously, inside every feeling of anger and anguish over the unfairness surrounding him, she felt the desperate need to be with him, to comfort him always.

"Not exactly," she whispered, peering directly into his eyes.

His brows rose, and his gaze swept her flushed face, but he never dropped her hand.

His was warm and large and strong. Just as he was. "Actually, I'm feeling so hot right now, Nathan, I think I might burst from the inside."

He didn't move a muscle at her dark, breathless confession. The stillness of the house pervaded the space between them; the light, from only the two gas lamps, created a soft, lingering glow that enhanced the harsh lines of his face and the strength of his hard, tightened jaw.

"What do you want, Mimi?" he asked huskily.

Her stomach fluttered with uncertainty, but she clung to his hand. "I think you know what I want."

His lids narrowed and his lips thinned. "Here? Now?"

His boldness, his unspoken yet lascivious suggestions, cornered her and her nervousness grew. "I've given strict orders not to be disturbed for any reason while we are working. But of course I—I don't want to move fast—"

"You don't want to move *fast*? Move fast where?" He squeezed her fingers and jerked her against him, his face flushed with controlled anger and only an inch from hers.

"Why are you teasing me with something I can't have?" he whispered thickly. "Why are you doing this? Do you want me, Mimi, the fallen son of a commoner? Or do you simply think to undermine my chances of success with the only thing that matters to me, the only thing I've ever achieved?"

She gasped and pushed against him, but he swiftly wrapped his free arm around her, pulling her even closer.

"Your professional disgrace means nothing to me!" she whispered harshly. "I would never hurt you, Nathan—"

"You already have," he said gruffly through clenched teeth, "and I think you know it."

Mimi went numb in his arms as exasperation flooded her. "How can you say that? How could I have ever done anything—"

"You exist," he breathed, face taut, lips tight. And then he slammed his mouth down on hers, knocking the breath from her lungs and stifling a cry from her throat, pulling her tightly into his rigid body.

Mimi resisted his carnal assault until his hand came forward and cupped her breast. Then she melted and went limp against him, welcoming his boldness as he squeezed her in his palm, flicked her nipple beneath satin, and searched for her tongue with his.

Nathan, Nathan, Nathan . . .

He grasped her with a hand to her bottom, massaging it, softly moaning once as she responded to the igniting heat within her. Then he lifted her briefly and shoved her against the large wooden door that led to the garden. She slumped against him, pinned on all sides, pushing her breasts into his waiting hands as he cupped them both, squirming with need, melding her lips with his.

He continued to demand the attention from her, in his touch, his light groan of pleasure. She felt his erection low on her stomach, thrilled her as she marveled in it, frightened a little by its bold insistence. But in the back of her mind she knew he wouldn't last long. He wanted her as much as she wanted him.

"Nathan," she gasped against his mouth. "Please—"

He didn't hear her. Or didn't want to.

His hunger grew and he tore a short cry from her lips as he lightly pinched her nipples over her gown. Then just as quickly as she reached for him, he grabbed her hands in one of his, and held them above her head while rubbing her breasts with the other.

She couldn't help herself. She squirmed, whimpered from pure need, a primitive desire he unleashed in her.

He responded to it by dropping his hand from her breast to her skirt. Quickly, he lifted it in bunches, teasing her tongue, exploring her mouth, their short breaths mingling. Her heart banged against her chest, but she was powerless to stop him.

She didn't want him to stop. She pushed for more as he released her wrists at last and reached low for her gown with both hands, lifting it easily. She grabbed his frock coat at his shoulders, fisting the material in her palms, clinging as she continued to kiss him hungrily.

Suddenly she felt his fingers on her thighs, over one layer of silk petticoats, and then he pinned her tightly to the door again, an arm lying across her chest, above her breasts, a hand holding her shoulder.

Abruptly, he released her mouth, and after a second she raised heavy lashes to look into his eyes.

They were heady with desire, and a marvelous intensity, probing hers.

He touched her intimately between her legs, covering her mouth with his free hand to keep her from crying out with pleasure, or shock. He watched her blatantly as he rubbed her over thin silk, the tip of one finger quickly probing the tiny slit where she grew slick and hot with need.

She whimpered softly as the tiny thrusting action of his fingers, the fast flicking of the tips, brought her quickly to the edge.

It scared her, captivated her, and made her move her hips against him in total abandonment. It had never been so fast, so sharply pleasurable, so consuming before.

She felt herself coming. So did he.

"Give it to me, Mimi," he whispered in a hot, thick breath against her cheek. "Make me feel it."

In a blind wave of ecstasy, she climaxed from his touch. Her head jerked back against the door, her throat tightened, and she bucked against his hand, holding the scream inside, clutching him against her, as the throbbing continued to pulse, and then gradually subsided between her legs.

He moved his hand from her mouth and kissed her again, hungrily, as he slowed the rhythm of his fingers. Then he grazed her cheek and jaw and temple with tender kisses as he breathed heavily from his own unfulfilled lust, pushing his fingers through the soft hair between her thighs, cupping her a final time before pulling back and allowing her skirts to drop to the floor once more. He grabbed her shoulders with both hands and forcefully held her to the garden door, sucking her earlobe, making her shiver.

"Is this what you wanted, Mimi?" he whispered in a thick breath of his own desire. "A moment of pleasure? A man to satisfy you physically? You think I can give you what you need?"

Her breathing came fast and heavy and she couldn't speak. Or he didn't let her have the chance.

He shoved her shoulders hard against the wood then pressed his hot forehead against hers. "Do you have any idea how much I dream of being inside you? How difficult it is for me to resist you every day? How I crave to take you to bed, to explore your body with my own, to get physical pleasure from you?"

"Nathan," she breathed on a sigh, but she couldn't open her eyes.

"Now I carry your scent on my fingers, teasing me, torturing me, making me crazy. All night it will be there, with the memory of how warm and wet you were where I stroked you, how hot I made you. All goddamn *night*." He squeezed her arms to the point of pain. "Are you going to take care of my needs, too, Mimi?"

"I want to," she heard herself say in a far off voice. "I want to feel you so much."

"And then what?" he pressed. "*Then* what?"

She couldn't answer him, and he knew it.

Suddenly he released her and took a step back, wiping a shaking hand across his brow.

"This can't go on."

He stepped to her side, unbolted the garden door, and walked out into the cold night.

Mimi stood where she was for minutes, eyes squeezed shut, legs trembling. She shouldn't have allowed that to happen, not without giving him something in return. He couldn't possibly know what he did to her, how crazy he made her, how she, too, wanted to feel him inside her. It couldn't go on like this for her, either.

Lifting her lashes at last, she slowly straightened with grace, and moved with a marvelous dignity out of her studio and toward the front of her home, to her small parlor where her desk sat, cluttered with household lists and various papers that she completely ignored.

Her note to Justin remained simple but to the point.

Hurry.

Chapter 12

She hated the fact that he kept *leaving* her. What on earth made him do that? She couldn't understand his actions, except to assume it had something to do with his masculinity, his inability to confront his feelings and then respond to them. Mimi knew gentlemen sometimes had trouble with that. Of course there was always the possibility that his rapid departures—when the conversation turned personal or the intimacy intensified—had something to do with her, but on the whole she disregarded that notion. She was certain he wanted her physically, yet if he felt such longing and walked out on her one more time, she was also quite certain she'd go mad.

Mimi stood in front of the fountain at the edge of

the brick path that meandered through her garden, in the morning air that was more damp than cold, trying to keep her mind focused on the various bushes and dead flowers and leaves in front of her that she needed desperately to cut back, rake, and clear for the coming winter frost and spring planting. Yet today she felt too jittery to care about the approaching season, or the condition of her backyard.

It had been a week since the night of Nathan's quick departure, since the night she'd been held by him, felt his lips on hers, reveled in his hands caressing her body, seen him last. It seemed like years. Every day she missed him more, spent indefinite periods of time thinking about him, and the uncertainty ahead of him. Their situation together was precarious, and it worried her tremendously, especially as the weeks progressed toward the banquet on New Year's Eve.

She had yet to hear from Justin regarding any arrangement he might have made, and as the days passed without word, she grew increasingly agitated. She expected a note of confirmation soon, but until that time, she would simply have to make due with all the unknowns nagging at her conscience and floating through her mind. And the loneliness created by Nathan's intentional absence.

"Well, I didn't expect to find you outside on such a bleak day," came Mary's lighthearted voice from behind her.

Mimi twirled around in surprise as her sister approached with a breezy smile on her lips, her hair parted in the middle and set with ringed curls at her ears, her peach satin morning gown cut conservatively but enhancing a trim figure. What she wouldn't give to be able to wear such tasteful, elegant clothing in such an utterly appealing color.

"Good morning, Mary," she replied affably, running her palms up and down her upper arms to stay a shiver. She nodded briefly toward a brown spot beyond the fountain. "I was just having a look at my overgrown and shameful garden."

Mary chuckled and strolled to her side. "I really expected to find you laboring ambitiously on one project or another. Only you would actually want to openly experience an ugly, gray December morning." She looked up and squinted at the sky. "It's freezing out here."

It was Mimi's turn to smile. "Where's your cloak, or did you give it to Stella?"

"I gave it to Stella. I never expected to be out here. There's no reason on earth a lady in her right mind would be wandering about in the open air under such nasty conditions."

Typical of Mary to scold her in such a loving, sisterly way, and she didn't take a word of it critically.

Mimi looked back to the dry fountain. "I find it rather refreshing."

"And yet you're shivering," her sister pointed out, amusement coloring her tone.

"I'll move indoors in a minute."

"I'm sure you're not looking at me," Mary returned without pause, "but I'm rolling my eyes at your ridiculous argument, dear sister."

That made her smile brighten. "I know that, of course."

Mary stood silently next to her for a second or

two, arms crossed over her breasts, then sighed. "I noticed the jawbone sculpture sitting on the table as I came through your studio. Naturally I would never see such beauty in a thing. It's rather rigid and grotesque, I think. But the attempt at duplication in this case is exquisite."

Mimi wanted to laugh at such a qualifying comment about her work, but she restrained herself. "Thank you," she said humbly, glancing sideways at her sister. "I'm very happy with it myself."

Mary stared at the brickwork at her feet, shuffling the sole of her shoe along loose pebbles. "Is it complete?"

Mimi glanced down at the dry marble in front of her, her forehead crinkling in thought. "Essentially. It took me all of last week to decide where to place the neck. Nobody is certain what the beast looked like, so I had to guess at its location and dimensions from Nathan's drawings. But I think he'll approve."

Mimi realized immediately that she shouldn't have used Nathan's given name. That was a mistake. But she wouldn't comment on her blunder for now.

Mary walked away from her a yard or two, stopping directly in front of the stone bench, running her fingertips across its smooth back. "So Professor Price hasn't yet seen the results?"

After a few seconds of continued silence, Mimi turned her body to face her sister directly, feeling warmth creep into her cheeks that would likely tell a world of indelicate tales, or perhaps just fantasies, to Mary as it would no one else. But she refused to hide under false accusations or mere insinuations.

"No, not the completed beast," she answered

evenly. "He hasn't been here in more than a week, though he seemed pleased with the results he saw at his last visit."

"I see." Mary crossed her arms over her chest again, nervously massaging her elbows with her fingertips. "How pleased?"

Mimi knew that was coming, but indignation flooded her nonetheless. She stood erect, lips thinning to a hard line. "What exactly are you asking, Mary?"

"Nothing. I just don't want to see you hurt by him."

"I'm not hurting in the least," she shot back.

Mary didn't believe that for a second, she realized. Her sister's expression conveyed concern as she gently bit her bottom lip, her eyes narrowed with troubled thoughts and conjectures that had no grounding in fact. It made her fiercely mad but she held her tongue.

"I'm sure you and Professor Price have been quite proper in your business association," Mary muttered cautiously, voice lowered. "But he is a man you are attracted to physically. Men will be men, and not all of them are gentlemen when alone with a lovely woman who expresses that attraction, even in her innocence."

"I haven't expressed an attraction."

"Haven't you?"

Mimi said nothing to that.

"He *has* been a gentleman, hasn't he?"

"Of course he has."

Mary sighed, softening her voice to add, "Still, it's altogether possible that he's using you—"

"Oh, for heaven's sake, Mary, he's not using me," she interjected with exasperation, tossing her palms in the air and rolling her eyes. "Don't be so *dramatic*."

Mimi watched her sister press her lips together to suppress a laugh. Mary had never been accused of being too dramatic, whereas she lived and breathed drama in everything about her, and everybody knew it. Her outburst embarrassed her now, but thankfully Mary brushed over it.

"He *is* using you if he still thinks Papa had anything to do with his professional disgrace."

Mimi stood her ground. "You and I both know he didn't do anything of the kind, so I don't see how helping the man regain some of his stolen dignity could be detrimental to Papa's reputation. We just have to be very careful in how we go about it."

She'd said that softly, but with conviction, and it had its effect. Mary's eyes ignited with an anger she rarely expressed as she began to pace.

"I just don't understand how he can possibly be so bold as to ask *you* to help him, the daughter of the man he accuses." She shook her head sharply. "It's rather insulting."

Mimi knew her sister meant well, but the words ground into her like gravel on skin. She'd spent the last week, since the night Nathan brought those wonderful feelings front and center, thinking the same thing, having the very same worries Mary did.

"He needs me," she replied softly, hoping she sounded more confident than she felt.

A gust of cold wind made the leaves rustle and

swirl on the ground, around their skirts. Mary stopped pacing and hugged herself against the chill again, then sauntered to her side. "Tell me what's bothering you, really," she insisted, gently.

"Nothing is particularly bothering me," Mimi replied after a moment. "Though I am worried about Nathan Price and the outcome of his showing at Professor Owen's banquet in three weeks' time."

Mary shook her head again and briefly closed her eyes. "Why, for goodness' sake? That man and his professional problems are not your first consideration, I assure you."

Mimi whirled around to face her squarely, hands on hips, her eyes dark and hard with frank stubbornness. "Then what *is* my first consideration, Mary? What would you have me do with my time? Needlepoint? Write letters to those I'm not supposed to visit?" She lifted her skirts and brushed by her sister to begin her own pacing around the fountain. "I'd grow bored from such trivialities, and you know it. It is in my nature to be sociable and to help and care for those in need. Professor Price needs my help, and I want to help him."

Mary sighed audibly, not in the least daunted by that outburst as she attempted to remain matter-of-fact. "I simply think it would be best if you carried on your life with a fair showing of ladylike discipline—"

"Ladylike discipline?" Mimi repeated incredulously, coming to an abrupt halt. "In what manner am I not being ladylike, Mary? You've never been married, or widowed, therefore you are allowed to wear a lovely gown in peach or sunny yellow on any day you choose. You are allowed to go to the opera, or travel, without thought to what others will think. You are allowed to make social calls on any acquaintance or friend of your choice. Social restrictions forbid these things of me."

She clutched her hands in front of her chest and lowered her voice with intensity. "Do you have any idea how I envy you, Mary? That you could choose a husband of your own if you wanted? That you can accept invitations to parties and openly laugh and dance at a ball in a bright pink dress? Can you not understand that I need just a little conversation right now?" She straightened, raising her chin a fraction. "I find a certain companionship with Nathan. I do my best to be properly disciplined where he is concerned, and I haven't done a thing to be ashamed of."

For moments Mary did nothing, just stared at her through crystalline blue eyes that Mimi had always found exceptionally revealing. But she wouldn't give in this time. She refused.

Finally, Mary looked away, toward the trellis to her side, picking a dead leaf off a vine. Inhaling deeply, she said, "Is he pleased with you, or with your work?"

Without pause, she maintained, "I am my work."

Mary huffed and shot her a quick glance, suddenly annoyed. "Don't give me that rubbish, Mimi. You know what I'm asking. He certainly makes quite a pretty prize."

"How dare you say that to me," she hissed in a lowered voice. "You know what I feel for him—"

"No I don't know what you feel for him," her sister cut in, an arm swinging wide. "I don't know that you *feel* anything except attraction to a man who is wrong for you in every regard. He is a challenge because you can't have him, a man who will break your heart if you get too close. I only want to protect you, you know that."

"I'm a twenty-three-year-old widow, Mary, who has lived and managed on her own for two years. You have my permission to stop protecting me now."

That stung deeply, Mimi observed with a shadow of regret. Mary pulled back with eyes wide, her mouth opened on the brink of a biting retort. Then she clamped it down forcefully, bringing her palm to her forehead and rubbing her temple.

"Regardless of your passions, Mimi," she said soberly, "nothing you've said can negate the fact that as a social companion, Professor Price is a poor choice. He doesn't strike me at all as a charming man. He hasn't a title or a fortune, or even simply a good name to which a genteel lady could attach herself." She drew a deep breath and opened her eyes, glancing up. "Yes, I suppose he's handsome, but so are a hundred other gentlemen of your station. I have never witnessed what it is you find so fascinating about him."

If Mary expected a stern rebuttal, or a spot of anger, she didn't get it. Mary had always loved her protectively, especially since their mother died, and every concern she expressed now was honestly felt, not meant to hurt. Mimi did her best to remember that. Crossing her arms resolutely over her stomach, Mimi turned her back and walked to the other side of the fountain.

"Everything about him fascinates me," she finally revealed, her voice quiet, her head down. "He likes me as a person, listens to me, and responds to what I say as if my thoughts and feelings as a woman actually matter. He doesn't make judgments about my desire to sculpt dinosaurs, and in fact finds me talented and says so. He possesses a great intellectual mind, regardless of his arrogance, which, as it happens, I find quite charming for reasons completely unknown to me. He provides . . . stimulating conversation, I suppose, a bit of humor and playful satisfaction I haven't felt in a very long time." She exhaled fully and glanced up at last, looking straight into Mary's probing but compassionate eyes. "He makes me smile, makes me think, makes my heart melt when he's near me. He gives me things I never had with—"

Mimi quit talking abruptly as her attention darted to a flash of color on her right. Suddenly her blood ran cold in her veins, her heart seemed to stop. Then she felt her cheeks flood with warmth.

A throat cleared loudly, behind the hedge. A deeply male voice.

Mimi couldn't bring herself to move. Mary jerked around, following the sound, and took two steps forward to face the intruders.

At that moment both Justin and Nathan walked forward, stiffly, hands behind their backs, features unreadable.

God. How much had they heard? She wanted to crawl into a hole.

Justin's mouth twisted into a vague grin as he eyed them both. Nathan simply ignored Mary as he stared at her intently, try to steal her thoughts, she was sure, causing the heat in her face to saturate her entire body, which she ignored to the best of her ability.

Mimi instantly noticed the change in Mary's demeanor. Her body grew rigid, hands at her sides in tight fists, lips thinned to a flat line, eyes glaring. But although her sister felt justifiably incensed that these men should be eavesdropping on a private conversation, she played the polite hostess during the extremely awkward moment that lingered, taking the initiative to speak first.

"Good day, gentlemen," she said with an overly courteous air, moving her body closer to the hedge so that she partially blocked their view of Mimi. "How nice that you found your way to the garden unannounced."

Justin coughed and had the good grace to look away. Nathan shifted his head so that he could continue to gaze at Mimi, his eyes dark, features expressionless.

"Actually, Miss Marsh," Justin explained congenially a second or two later, and much too formally for someone who knew their family well, "we were escorted to the studio by a parlor maid who then directed us to the garden. I hope we're not intruding."

That never should have happened, and Mimi at once regretted it. Any respectable gentleman would know that he should be properly introduced and received, not allowed to wander into private grounds without first being announced. Ordinarily she wouldn't care, but Mary would only read this as a violation of propriety, and although Nathan might be one to defy proper behavior, Justin should know better. It didn't help her argument at all.

"Of course you're not intruding," Mimi declared after another silent disconcerting moment, standing gracefully erect, smiling subtly, as was expected of a proper lady. "It's a lovely day for a visit by two very distinguished gentlemen."

She felt Mary's glare on the side of her face, but she ignored the warning.

"Yes, well," her sister chimed in, returning to the point of her visit, "I merely came by to invite you to dinner this evening, Mimi. Papa is anxious for the three of us to have a good talk."

"Yes, lovely," she returned at once. "I'll be there early."

"Good." Mary drew her shoulders back and stated brusquely, "It's cold in the garden, and I can't stay. Perhaps you gentlemen could wait in the parlor—"

"We can't stay either," Nathan interjected, still looking at Mimi through narrowed lids, arms held stiffly at his sides.

"Actually, we just came by to view the finished jawbone sculpture," Justin explained congenially, rubbing his chin with his palm. Smiling, he then shoved both hands in his coat pockets and added, "It's a marvelous replication, from what I briefly saw. I would, however, like to examine the detail."

"The detail is perfect, I assure you," Mary said, a little too defensively.

His brows rose. "I'm certain it is, Mary. I would expect nothing less than excellence from a Marsh."

The silence droned after that, the moment growing increasingly awkward. The wind picked up, rustling the trees and stirring the chill in the air. Mimi wiped a palm over her cheek in an attempt to secure loose ends of hair. "Perhaps it would be best if we go inside."

"Very good idea," Justin agreed as Nathan remained unusually silent.

Justin turned toward the house first, then quickly stopped in mid-stride, forcing the rest of them to pause behind him.

"Before I forget," he articulated slowly, head down, "I wanted to ask you to meet me tomorrow evening, Nathan, at Parker's Terrace, a lovely hotel and dining establishment in Holland Park. I'll be doing some late work with Owen in the afternoon, getting ready for the New Year's dinner, so I thought you and I could discuss it later, over a late brandy. Say . . . nine o'clock?"

Nathan grunted something neither she nor Mary could understand, and Justin laughed before he proceeded to walk again.

In that slice of a second Mimi realized that Justin had just informed them both, at the same time, of the scheduled rendezvous he'd arranged at her asking. The man was a devil, and of course she would be forced to pay him back for his unusual humor at her expense someday. She only hoped to God her face wasn't so red right now that her sister would deduce fever.

Chapter 13

Nathan climbed the white marble steps to the entrance of Parker's Terrace, a large three-story brown brick hotel on the outskirts of Holland Park. At nearly nine it was fully dark outside and he was tired. The day had been long, full of increased boredom, which probably explained his eagerness to meet with Justin, if only for a brandy and a round of good conversation, even at this hour.

A winter array of potted greenery and vines that hung off white trellises surrounded the large front door, defined only by two glowing gas lamps. He pushed the hard metal handle down and stepped inside to stand in a bright foyer with blood red walls and hard wooden floors that gleamed from a recent polishing. The light cigar smoke in the air teased his nostrils, the warmth from the parlor fire warmed him, and the scents of roasting game drifted from the kitchen.

On his left, a wide spiral staircase curved up to the second story, and just in front of him, inside the great room decorated in yards of red and green velvet that covered both windows and furniture, he took note of several people mingling, men and women, dressed elegantly, as was he, for dinner and brandy and conversation.

He walked in a few steps and surveyed his surroundings, glancing at the patrons, expecting to see Justin among them. When he didn't, after a moment's curiosity, Nathan stood erect and strode casually to a tall man in tastefully fashioned black evening dress whom he assumed was the hotel's concierge, working behind the long oak desk beneath the staircase.

"Good evening, sir," the hotel employee said with a staid smile. "Are you by chance with the Hubert party?"

Nathan assumed the man meant those laughing and chatting in the parlor. "No, actually I'm here to meet a Mr. Justin Marley—"

"Ahh . . . yes, you must be Professor Price," the concierge maintained with an arrogant air, his smile deepening. He reached over and grabbed a key to his left. "Everything is arranged. You'll be in room three. Up the stairs and to your left. I believe your party is awaiting you."

Admittedly, Nathan was a little puzzled. An hour or two of brandy and cigars didn't typically necessitate a separate room, yet perhaps Justin simply wanted private discourse. That made sense, he supposed.

With a curt "thank you" to the concierge, Nathan took the key, turned, and walked to the staircase, climbing it without notice by anyone. At the end of the carpeted hallway, he stood in front of room three. Inserting the key into the lock, he opened the door and stepped inside.

The smell of flowers struck him soundly, slapping him with the knowledge that all was not as it seemed, or what he expected. The room appeared empty at first, small and square, with a moderately sized four-poster bed to the right of the door, framed with a sheer lace canopy and covered with a quilted red coverlet. The modest grate took up much of the opposite wall, now with only a low fire burning, next to which stood one tall brass lamp, softly lit, illuminating the room.

But it was movement behind a sheer red screen, only a foot or so in front of the lamp, that caught his eye. Secreted behind it, he spied the shape of a woman as she slowly lifted her body from a water-filled tub and reached for a towel.

The sudden realization of what was to transpire made him dizzy, and a little angry, if he was honest with his feelings. Justin had evidently hired him a woman for the evening, and although he supposed he should be thankful for the company and female attention, he really felt a little affronted. After the episode with Mimi only a week ago, where he brought her to orgasm with nothing more than fingertips and whispers, leaving her hot and unsettled and needy, and his lust at the bursting point, he was really not at all ready for a tryst with a stranger. And that was laughable. What the bloody hell was wrong with him? He should be jumping at this opportunity, but instead he felt only tired. And deeply confused.

But there was no turning around and making a hasty exit, as the woman had apparently heard him enter, and had to be expecting him. If he'd walked into the wrong room she would have screamed. He didn't particularly want to leave either, after noticing the outline of her curvaceous figure as she stepped out of the tub, then wrapped herself in the towel.

He sighed, feeling only the slightest reaction in his nether regions, though it was more than he expected. At least his body worked properly when charged with erotic thoughts and veiled images of the female form. Still, a paid whore didn't appeal to him. At least not now, when hard, crucial professional and personal decisions of his own were about to be made.

Nathan cleared his throat. Then, getting directly to the point, he said, "I believe there's been a misunderstanding."

The sheer screen could not conceal the long hair that the woman brushed aside with her fingers as she covered her body with a wrap of some kind. But she said nothing.

He softly closed the door behind him, so that others in the hall wouldn't hear or see them, but he stood beside it, ready to take his leave before his body took control of his senses. "I'm very flattered that my good friend thought to find me . . . entertainment for tonight, but—"

"You're doing very well so far, Nathan," came a throaty murmur as the lovely silhouette moved to the edge of the screen then appeared in the figure of a flesh-and-bone woman. "That's exactly what I would like you to do under similar circumstances. Say 'no' to opportunity, that is."

Nathan blinked several times at the stunning vision. His mouth dropped open in astonishment, his forehead beading in perspiration as the room began to spin before him.

"But if you leave me again now," she continued huskily, slowly sauntering toward him, hands behind her back, "as you always seem to do when the situation gets intimate between us, I swear by all that's holy I will hunt you down and cut off every body part of yours you treasure."

Nathan could do nothing but stare. Mimi stood a mere foot away from him, enclosed in this luscious, red room made for total intimacy, bathed in the scent of flowers, long blond hair flowing over her shoulders, wrapped only in white satin that, although tied loosely at the waist, dipped open between her breasts and spread wide again at the thighs, exposing every smooth inch of her legs.

Holy Christ.

Her eyes, locked with his, narrowed in the realization of his profound shock, and her lips curled up coyly.

Huskily, she whispered, "Surprised, Professor?"

Surprised? *Surprised?*

"That's . . . um . . ." He swallowed. "That's quite a threat you promised," he remarked in what sounded like a croak in his throat. "I'm . . ."

"At a loss for words?"

He had no answer for that.

She tossed her hair back purposely, seductively, enticing him. Amazing, he thought, that she even knew how to do that.

"I thought you might be," she answered for him, stepping closer. "Would you like a bath yourself? The water's still warm."

He went hard without further taunting. Rigidly hard. She stood close enough to touch, to smell, to stroke, which he controlled by fisting his hands at his sides. God . . . what bedding her would mean to them when the passion faded, when they were finished with each other, when they shared a permanent ending. It simply couldn't happen.

"Mimi—"

"I could wash your body for you," she whispered, gazing up to his face.

Jesus. How could he say no to that?

Her warm breath brushed his chin, her lashes closed halfway over her shining, brilliant brown eyes, beckoning him to go within, to touch and discover. Her skin glowed from dim light reflecting off the dewy moisture that lingered. Her blond hair, combed thick and shiny, hung over her breasts and down her back, stopping at her curved waist. Her moist, full lips parted and begged . . .

Mimi's lips.

The taste of them, the smell of her sex on his fingers, pervaded his mind, drawing him in, summoning detailed thoughts and marvelous memories. Suddenly permanent endings and fading passion ceased to matter.

The room turned dark for him; quietness prevailed save for the snapping fire in the grate. The laughter and noise below stairs disappeared as the outside world faded to nothing.

She waited, watching him, knowing he swayed at the brink of a grave decision. A defining moment. And then her inhaled breath caught on her lips, barely heard, when he reached up with one finger and glided it gently, slowly down her neck, her chest, between her sloping breasts, to the edge of the silken material that covered her nakedness.

"Make love to me, Nathan," she pleaded in whisper, in heightened boldness, laying her palm directly on his shirtfront and rubbing the coarse material with her thumb.

"Do you know what you're doing?" he managed to murmur, his voice intense and dangerously low. "What you're asking?"

She didn't smile slyly or display a sense of confidence in her ability to seduce him, as he expected. Instead, she pushed her body against his, molding herself to him, flattening his hand at her belly and his back against the door so that he had no choice but to feel the softness of her every gentle curve, every remarkable hint of the woman she was.

Her features showed longing and a deep sense of an inner acceptance, and then she closed her eyes, lifted her lips, and softly spoke against his mouth.

"Yes, I know. Don't turn away from me now. I've been waiting so long for you."

He groaned as she rubbed her hips against his, as her tongue stroked his upper lip, and that was all it took. No more uncertainty.

"Damn."

Fisting the belt of her silk wrap in one hand, the hair down her back with the other, Nathan stared at her beautiful face for one final second before claiming her mouth with his in a subtle show of possession, holding her tightly against his solid form.

Swiftly, he coaxed her mouth into a rhythm of its own, playing her tongue against his, noting her supple softness as she leaned against him. They stood like that for ages, his hand in her hair, hers resting on his shoulders. He fingered the tie at her waist until he felt it give way and loosen, opening the wrap enough to expose her to the navel.

He broke free of her lips then, and began a trail of soft kisses from her mouth to her ear, his lips brushing her cheek and jaw and temple.

"I need to see you," he whispered, skimming her lobe with his lips, tracing it with his tongue.

She whimpered very softly, almost inaudibly, but he knew she reacted to those words of honest need because she shivered in his arms.

Reaching up she ran her fingers through his hair, caressed his neck with her fingertips, rubbed her nose and lips along his jaw. And then she backed up a step and lowered her arms so that she could grasp the sash at her waist.

Her hand covered his, and as she opened her eyes to gaze into the lonely, wanting depths of his, she pulled at the tie with one hand and opened her wrap with the other so that it draped to her sides, exposing her naked flesh to his view for the very first time.

He stilled, gazing down to her in firelight. Then, with suddenly shaking fingers, he grasped the wrap's edges at her shoulders and pushed at them until they fell down her back and gathered in a pool of white silk at her feet.

He sucked in a breath as he beheld her lovely, perfect female form. Her breasts were firm, their pink tips aroused to luscious protruding points that he desperately longed to stroke, to suck and kiss and caress. Her stomach showed the flatness of one who had never borne a child, her waist tapered delicately, her hips spread gently, her lean, graceful legs extended to daintily arched feet. But it was the blond curls at the center of her that drew his undivided attention. He'd never before seen a blond in the nude, and the paleness of her skin, coupled with the glow of fire and dim lamplight, made the hair at her thighs shine like pearls.

Instinctively, he reached out and touched her there, faintly, brushing her intimately with the back of a finger. Mimi closed her eyes and leaned her head back, her breath coming fast as she swayed against his touch.

Nathan's heart pounded in his chest, his body growing hot as it yearned for completion, yet he didn't want this single instant, this simple stroking, to end.

He grasped her by the shoulder, rubbing her warm, clean skin with his thumb while he increased the intimacy, placing all of his fingers there and stroking now. She grew wet at his demand, her breasts heaving with each labored breath she took, face flushed beautifully, licking her lips.

It was as much as he could stand.

"You're more beautiful than I ever imagined."

She sighed, raising her palms to cup his face, though she never opened her eyes. "Did you imagine me like this?" she asked in a feather-soft voice.

He almost smiled. "Every day."

A tiny whimper escaped her and she raised her lashes to peer into his eyes. "Take me to bed, Nathan."

He needed no persuasion.

Drawing his free hand down her shoulder, he cupped it over her breast, brushing the delicate skin back and forth with his fingers, running his palm across her swollen nipple, never dropping his gaze from hers.

The intensity of the moment increased. She was fully wet between her legs now, her breathing as rapid and shallow as his, and his body ached to claim her. As if sensing the rising tension between them, Mimi lowered her palms and began unbuttoning his shirt.

Her fingers trembled; she faltered at the task and so he released his hold of her and pulled back to help her undress him. She stared into his eyes and he never looked away as he worked through each button, untied his neckcloth, and dropped it and his shirt to the floor at his feet.

She reached for his chest then, her palms closing over his muscles that bunched from the initial contact, massaging them, her fingers grazing his nipples. That did it for him. Immediately he needed to be inside her. Exploration could wait.

He leaned forward and captured her eager mouth again, urgently now, blending his tongue with hers. Then grabbing her hands in his, he began pushing her backward, toward the bed. She followed willingly, never breaking her lips from his, coaxing him onward.

She pulled him onto the soft coverlet when she reached it, and he followed, spreading out beside her, still clothed to his hips. He quickly kicked off his shoes and reached for the buttons of his pants, his breath coming fast now in anticipation, mingling with hers as she teased his lips with her own.

He knew she hesitated to help him undress, but he needed no aid or encouragement to free himself of the barriers between them. Her hands on his face and neck, leaving feathery soft strokes with her nails, convinced him to discard it all quickly, before she changed her mind, before he lost control. At last he lay beside her as naked as she, and he reached for her, his palm splayed across her back, pressing her perfect breasts against his chest, wrapping one leg over hers to draw her in, never wanting to break the contact.

She moaned softly when he lowered his hand to cup her bottom, caressing it gently in slow circles, pressing his erection into her belly, wanting her to feel what she did to him, how he needed her.

She took the initiative then, brushing her hands up and down his chest, raking her fingers through his hair, kissing him back forcefully in total abandonment, her tongue mating with his, her leg rubbing his as her movements increased with her pleasure.

This was Nathan's last opportunity to stop. He knew that. Apparently, so did she because at that moment she pulled back from the kiss, panting, looking into his eyes with a fresh desire and a need he'd never witnessed in a woman before. She held her feelings before him, her expression so serious but open for his view.

Gently, he traced her flushed cheek and brow with his lips. "I can't hold back any longer, Mimi."

"I know," she whispered.

He felt her warm breath on his jaw, heard the certainty in her reply, noticed how she shivered beside him with her conviction. Of course she knew. She'd been with her husband, knew what it felt like to have a man inside her. In that one second, Nathan experienced an overwhelming ache in his chest from something he could never claim as his, a part of her she had given to someone else. Of treasures lost.

Mimi noticed the reservation in his eyes, understood his restraint, however minimal. But she also saw the look of a man charged with lust and caring and eagerness, and she refused to allow sensibilities to interrupt them now. Not while this most incredible time was finally upon them. Not with Nathan.

"Love me," she pleaded, holding his face in her palms, pushing her hips into his, feeling his hardness against her belly and relishing in it.

He responded to her insistence not by putting his hand back between her legs, as she so fervently yearned for him to do, but by lowering his head and taking her breast inside his mouth.

Mimi nearly jumped from the bed when his roughened tongue expertly swirled over her nipple. He grazed it with his teeth, then began to suck, making her gasp and bite down hard to keep from crying out. She clutched his hair with her fists, pulling him in, lifting her hips to meet his probing erection that he moved ever so rhythmically against her. She wanted to touch him there, to take hold and caress him, but indecision held her back. As did his amazing hands and mouth.

Suddenly his fingers found the cleft between her legs and again he began to entice, to lightly probe, to stroke her slick entrance. She arched her back and pushed into him, whimpering. Nathan breathed hard against her, his lips to her chest, mouth on her breast, teasing, torturing, licking, his face between them, rubbing back and forth, then kissing them reverently as his fingers began to move in rhythm between her thighs.

Mimi matched the tempo, hands on his head, fingers in his hair, her heart racing with each step closer to that wonderful, satisfying edge. She could feel it envelop her, feel it coming, without him even inside her, where she wanted him.

"Nathan—"

He didn't stop. He tormented and teased with his mouth and tongue and fingers. Then unexpectedly he grabbed one of her hands in his and placed her palm on him, shocking her, silencing her, thrilling her.

He was so hard, so hot there. She rubbed her thumb across the tip, feeling a bead of liquid escaping it, and he moaned his pleasure, possessing her heart.

His breathing grew shallower still, as did hers, and he reached again for her mouth, capturing it and kissing her ardently as his fingers stroked the heat between her legs, faster and harder as he brought her closer and closer still to climax. And then it happened.

She opened her eyes as a scream tore from her lips, taken by him with his penetrating kiss as she rocked against him and shoved her hips hard against his fingers that moved and stroked and caressed her intimately. She gripped his erection until she felt him jerk back and grasp her wrist, pulling her from him. Quickly, he positioned his hips between her legs, running his tongue along her lips, playing with her mouth, kissing her cheeks and jaw and temple, opening her with his fingers to accept him.

She lifted herself slightly, and closed her eyes to the feel of him hard against her cleft. Gently he probed the entrance and began to insert himself, inch by inch.

Mimi gasped as he filled her; Nathan groaned heavily and tucked his face in her neck. He reached down and lifted her legs, bending them at the knees to give him deeper access, and she complied.

He whispered her name, over and over, as he began to move, to rock his hips into her. She kissed him softly, curved the tip of her tongue along his ear. He reached for her breast, licking the hard nipple, sucking it. Mimi arched back and found his rhythm, grinding her hips into his.

He exhaled through his teeth, pushing harder, thrusting deeper, taking her up once more with him.

Mimi felt it all again. Nathan touching her intimately. Nathan filling her. Nathan grabbing her breasts, thumbing her nipples, claiming her mouth with his, moaning. Nathan ready to climax in her arms.

It put her over the edge.

Suddenly she gripped him tightly, her nails to his back. Then, with his name on her lips, she reached her crest once more, this time feeling each muscle contraction around him, legs jerking against his, a sob tearing from her throat.

"Mimi . . ." he whispered, holding her, thrusting into her.

He groaned once more as he lost himself to the exquisite pleasure, yanking his head back, lifting his chest as he claimed her again, deeply, holding himself there, eyes squeezed shut. Then, in one fast motion, he pulled himself out from her completely as he convulsed against her thigh.

Mimi felt the warm fluid spill from him and into the crease between her hip and leg, clutching him tightly until he slowed his action and his body calmed, smiling.

Nathan Price belonged to her at last.

Chapter 14

Nathan stared at her sleeping form, illuminated only by lamplight as the fire grew to a dim glow. They lay side by side beneath the sheet and blankets, facing each other, though he held his head in his hand as he rested his elbow on the pillow. She slumbered on her stomach, facing him, her dark blond lashes spreading downward toward her lovely angled cheekbones, her hair splayed out behind her like a river of wavy gold.

He'd been watching her for some time, caressing the skin on her shoulder with his fingers even though she couldn't feel him, amused how she had drifted off to sleep so quickly and soundly after such a showing of passion. He'd been the tired one upon his arrival, and now he felt more restless than exhausted, more troubled than eased by what had just taken place between them.

He'd admitted to himself in the course of the last hour that Mimi's desire for him was real, not imagined, and not a deception of the worst kind, which he had, on more than one occasion in her presence, considered. She wanted him, physically and emotionally, and what stumped him most of all was not knowing why. He'd accused her father of a grievous crime, planning in the end to expose the man, which, strangely enough, didn't seem to worry her at all. And he couldn't offer her even one single thing that mattered, at least not now. He had no money, no title, no name to give her, should he choose to. They shared only a mutual attraction that could come to nothing. Yet she settled for it, and somewhere very deep inside him, Nathan found that not only admirable, but wondrous. Watching her now, bathed in the glow of lamplight, his heart swelled with tenderness he could no longer deny for this remarkable woman, so unique and textured, so beautiful, who enjoyed him with an honest depth of openness and trust.

Nathan moved his elbow and dropped his head to the pillow, snuggling down beneath the blankets, never taking his gaze from her face. She stirred at the movement, and after a second or two, lifted her lashes and peered at him through squinting hazy eyes. He touched her lips with his thumb and she smiled.

"Did I sleep?" she asked in a husky purr.

He felt his body respond to that darkly erotic voice of hers, but there would be time for that later. At least he hoped.

"For a while," he replied softly, stroking her jaw. "How do you feel?"

He had to ask that. He wanted regrets, whatever they might be, to be said to him now, while they were alone together.

Her smile widened and she stretched lazily, her hands and arms above her, her breast peeking out from beneath the sheet. "I feel marvelous."

Nathan hadn't expected that. Undoubtedly she was sore, and probably concerned for her reputation, but he'd expected something a little more factual.

"Marvelous?"

"Mmm . . ." She reached up and touched his cheek with her index finger. "I feel perfect, actually. Better than I have in years."

The honesty she conveyed in those words moved him deeply. Did she mean after lovemaking? That she never felt this good with Carter? He didn't ask because he didn't want to hear her say that she'd meant something else. He only wanted to imagine the best for now.

Leaning over, he kissed the tip of her nose and she in turn wound her arm around his neck, drawing him closer so that they lay nearly touching. He took her hand in his and drew his lips across her palm, gazing into her eyes, totally content for the first time in as long as he could remember.

"Are you proud of yourself?" he asked, his mouth curved up in amusement.

"For what?"

He nibbled on her thumb. "Managing to seduce me?"

She chuckled softly. "I never doubted I could for a second. And I'm so glad it worked."

"So am I," he admitted huskily.

She sighed, pushing her fingers back toward his neck, angling them through the hair on his nape. He did the same with her, brushing silky golden strands away from her temple.

"How did you arrange this?" he asked, hesitating only the slightest bit because he wasn't sure he wanted to know.

"I asked Justin to help," she replied confidently, without pause.

He'd assumed as much, and yet hearing her say it aloud made it all so much more real. It worried him too, because she'd risked everything to be with him for only one night. One extraordinary, unforgettable act—and night.

Exhaling heavily through his nostrils, he closed his eyes briefly, shaking his head. "That was so stupid, Mimi."

"I know," she agreed, caressing his neck.

He looked at her again, and she grinned like one satisfied beyond all measure. It warmed him immensely to see her so content.

"He won't tell a soul," she added in a rather odd attempt to assure him.

Nathan's lips thinned grimly. "I know that, but others might talk, and that, in the end, could be far more damaging."

"Oh, Nathan, have a little faith," she chided, grinning.

He blinked. "A little faith? Faith in what? In society, for shunning a widow who seduces a man? In servants, that they won't spread gossip between neighborhood households?"

She put her finger to his mouth to silence him. "Nobody knows where I am. Everyone in my household thinks I'm visiting a sick friend in Hampstead, and I shall return before my family even learns that I've been away."

He remained quiet for a moment, amazed at such daring on her part, just to be with him. If he considered it, the whole affair made him lightheaded. Mimi was the only woman alive who had a way of turning his insides to pulp.

She waited, uncertainty shining in the clear brown depths of her eyes, unsure if he would scold her, leave her, or perhaps spread the news of his conquest of the Widow Sinclair himself. Nathan truly hoped she thought better of him than that.

With a deep inhalation, he grasped her around the waist and pulled her against him. "How much time do we have?"

She laughed softly at that, wrapping her arms around his back and hugging him close. "All night. All morning. All day," she said wistfully. "How long would you like to lie here together?"

Forever.

He swept that thought aside with annoyance. Such a romantic notion should only be considered by virgin brides on their wedding nights. Mimi cluttered his mind.

"I suppose we could accomplish quite a lot in several hours," he whispered, running his palm up and down her warm back.

"Mmm . . . if that's what the professor wants."

She snuggled into him so that he felt her breasts on his chest, her thighs against his, the hair between her legs caressing his shaft just enough to bring it to life again. She felt his reaction to her touch and pressed her hips briefly against it, stroking it with every intention of inciting his desire.

"You are so perfectly formed, Nathan," she said mischievously, draping a leg over his to hold him close. "I think I'll sculpt you next."

"In the nude?" he asked with raised brows, trying not to laugh.

"Naturally."

"Hard?" he whispered huskily.

She grinned and touched her lips to his. "Only if I can get you in such a state myself."

"You needn't do anything but enter the room, madam, I assure you," he revealed, his voice barely audible.

"The perfect thing to say to a lady, Nathan."

She kissed him fully then, playing her lips against his, and he responded. He teased her bottom with his palm, pushed his erection into her, and she followed in kind, drawing her thumbnail up his spine and then tunneling her fingers through his hair.

She backed away first, dropping light pecks on his lashes and nose, his cheeks and jaw.

"Do you like this?" she asked without pause.

He groaned. "What do you think?"

"I think it's exactly what you've wanted for a long time. Weeks maybe."

"Longer than that."

She looked up, into his eyes, an odd mixture of curiosity and indecision lighting hers.

"So it's been . . . a while since you've done this?" she asked slyly.

He smirked. "A while." Deciding she wouldn't be at all satisfied with that answer, he added, "But I meant I've wanted to do this with *you* for longer than a few weeks. Much longer."

He could have sworn she purred from that and snuggled into him even tighter. "Me, too."

"Really?"

Her lashes fell over her dark eyes as her expression grew cautious, serious. "I've wanted to be with you for years, Nathan. You can't be surprised at that. I even told you that once."

The night of the Crystal Palace opening, he mused. He remembered what she'd said to him outside that night. Every word.

"Did you and Carter ever discuss that night?" he asked, knowing it probably wasn't the time to bring her late husband into the conversation, but doing so anyway.

"Rarely," she murmured after only a moment's thought. Inhaling deeply, she revealed, "Carter was very jealous of you, Nathan, and didn't often want to discuss you. He envied your status with Professor Owen, your analytical ability, the fact that you were treated so respectfully when you'd come from . . . humble means, shall we say. He disliked the fact that you were so—so liked by everyone, if that makes sense. And I think you are probably inherently smarter than he was, and many knew it, including him." She paused for a second or two, fingering his shoulder blade with wispy movements. "I think, in a sense, he pitied you that night, Nathan, and in another, he realized your downfall would be his gain, and in a manner of speaking I think he felt guilty about such feelings. Carter was, in general, a good, honest man. I want to say again that I know he had nothing to do with what happened to you professionally that night. He simply stepped in and took advantage of the situation."

Nathan needed a moment to absorb that, and then the chilling realization of what she was actually telling him began to sink in. He stilled, felling a growing anxiety in the pit of his stomach—and an ache of others also wronged that night nearly three years ago.

"What did Carter feel for you, Mimi?"

She tilted her body back a bit. "He was a good husband—"

"That's not what I asked."

He'd whispered those words low and forthrightly, and immediately noticed the slightest frown tug at her mouth, and a sadness creep into her eyes as she dropped her gaze to his chest.

"Carter didn't love me, Nathan, if that's what you're asking. Not as a woman. Not passionately. But we made the best of the situation, and we were, for the most part, happy together." She peeked up again to add, "He asked for my hand because it was the practical thing to do, as I'm sure you understand. I am Sir Harold Marsh's daughter and Mary was too old for marriage, even then. Asking for me was well considered and appropriate. And he treated me with as much respect as a lady of my position requires."

Nathan doubted it. Carter probably looked after her needs as a husband should, but he wouldn't have concerned himself with respect, and he certainly wouldn't have cared about her wishes. He would expect her to act the proper wife socially, and he would reward her for her efforts—with children, a home, an occasional nicety, and her studio.

"Did he satisfy you in bed?" he asked softly, knowing he shouldn't, that her positive response would irrationally irritate him. Still, he couldn't stop himself.

Her mouth broke out into a slow, sly grin. "Are you sure you want to know, Nathan?"

That annoyed him. Of course he didn't want to know. But he wanted her to tell him anyway. Squeezing her bottom and pushing her into him, he said, "I wouldn't have asked if I didn't."

She leaned forward and kissed his lips gently. "Physically, yes; emotionally, no," she whispered against his mouth.

He had no idea what she meant by that evasive statement. Then again, it wasn't all that evasive, he decided, feeling a sudden, illogical jealousy inside and chiding himself for it. He was a man, a man who had satisfied women in bed before, and hadn't particularly thought about anything beyond the physical. Yet it bothered him more than he could say that Mimi had positive sexual memories of another lover. That the man was her husband didn't matter to him in the least.

In that instant, Nathan felt a fierce protectiveness toward her, one that he wouldn't be able to describe should he try. But she was here, now, with him, and enjoying him in the most physically delicious way. He wanted her to know what he thought of that.

Grasping her with both arms, Nathan turned abruptly onto his back and pulled her up with him so that she lay on top of him. She giggled, running her fingers through his hair but making no attempt to move away. She ground her toes into his shins, the curls between her legs rubbing his sensitized penis, her breasts flattened against him, her nipples making his chest tingle. He drew a hand forward and brushed her hair from her face and shoulders, gazing into her pleasure-filled eyes.

"Did you climax every time with him?"

"Nathan!"

He watched her cheeks darken as she blushed, her mouth drop open.

He grinned, rubbing his palms along her hips. "Did you?"

She shook her head. "It doesn't matter if I did or didn't."

"Did you?" he pressed in whisper, tipping his mouth to her chin, running his lips along her jaw.

Finally, she faintly admitted, "Yes, most of the time, but I . . . made sure of it."

His grin deepened and Nathan couldn't himself believe he was having this conversation with a woman. He never would have considered it with anyone else.

Pulling back he peered at her face again. She flushed with embarrassment, and he adored it.

"You're beautiful," he said taking in every feature.

"*That's* what you should be saying to a woman. Say it again."

He shook his head. "I want you to tell me what you like."

Her forehead creased minutely. "What I like about what?"

"In bed. With a man."

"You're the devil, Professor Price," she muttered, eyes shining with daring and amusement.

It warmed him to note that she didn't take offense, or change the subject. Such encouragement on her part, or what he took as encouragement whether she meant it or not, made him grow bolder. "Where do you like to be touched?"

Her lids narrowed but she never dropped her gaze. "Everywhere," she whispered boldly.

He felt himself growing erect again, which she undoubtedly did as well. "I want to hear you tell me."

She squirmed on top of him, purposely brushing her hips against his engorged member, stalling.

"Where, Mimi?" he breathed against her jawline, smelling the scent of flowers on her skin, relishing the feel of her breasts on his chest.

"I like . . ."

He ran his tongue along her neck. "Where?"

She moaned a little. "On my breasts, my nipples. Carter never did that."

He stilled his actions and pulled back enough to look at her. "Carter didn't touch you there?" he asked, surprised.

She shook her head and closed her eyes, whether out of embarrassment or sadness, he couldn't guess.

"Carter preferred my . . . um . . ."

"Parts between your legs?" he finished for her.

She nodded slightly, squeezing herself tightly to him. "But when you kissed me there, pinched me there, it felt . . . wonderful." She shuddered.

Nathan felt mightily surprised, and hot all over again. "I liked it, too, Mimi," he whispered in her ear. "You have stunning breasts."

She sighed, pressing her hips into him.

"Stunning?"

"Perfect."

She giggled again. "*Perfect*?"

"They fit perfectly in my hands," he said matter-of-factly.

Smiling, she pushed into him again, rubbing her leg up and down the length of his. It was getting to be too much.

"So put them in your hands," she whispered thickly, taunting him with radiant, impish eyes. It was the only suggestion he needed.

Grasping her tightly, Nathan rolled her over swiftly so that she was once again beneath him. He kissed her mouth gently, then sat up a little, staring at her nude form from head to knees in the glow of lamplight. Placing one leg over hers to hold her still, he began rubbing his palm over her stomach in slow circles, then slowly traced her skin with his fingertips until he reached one of those stunning breasts, cupping it, rotating his palm over her nipple.

She drew a shaky breath, gazing into his eyes. "Perfect."

My perfect fantasy.

She reached for him, plunging her fingers through his hair, pulling his head to hers, lifting her lips to meet his in a growing display of need. He leaned into her, matching her kisses breath for breath, each stroke for stroke, probing her mouth with his tongue in a new desire to know, to discover.

He dropped his hand from her breast to her bottom, caressing her, then lifting it toward him to turn her on her side again, facing him, his hips to hers, his erection lying stiff at her belly.

"I can't . . ." He kissed her deeply, grabbing her thigh and pulling it so that it covered his. "I can't take the risk of getting you with child, Mimi," he finished in a whisper, knowing she would understand.

She didn't comment, but he felt the slightest nod as he brushed his lips against hers, back and forth, his thumb stroking her hip bone. He found her breast again with his fingers, pinching delicately, flicking softly with his nails, and that brought a soft moan from her throat.

"Nathan . . ."

"Touch me," he whispered, leaving soft pecks to her warm cheeks, her jaw and the hollow of her neck.

She hesitated for only the briefest second, and then she reached between them to place her palm on the tip of him.

The feel of her hand scorched his sensitive skin; he shuddered against her, moaning without discretion, allowing her to timidly explore with her thumb, her fingers, her nails, while he toyed with her breasts, kissed her mouth and neck, ran his tongue along her jaw to her ear, feeling her squirm beside him as her desire increased to match the level of his.

At last her heightened need and the feel of her hand carried him too close to the edge. In one swift motion, he kissed her soundly while grabbing her and pulling her up and onto him again, her breasts flat on his chest, her silky hair spilling onto his shoulders, caressing his neck, her hands coming forward to hold his head.

He stroked her upper lip with his tongue, adjusting her hips so that her mound of curls fit directly over his erection, enveloping it to perfection, smothering him with warm moisture, her thighs on either side of his as she relaxed into his body.

Slowly, he began to move against her, and quickly she matched the action, her breathing fast becoming as erratic as his, her cleft rubbing him faster and faster as she quickly ascended to her crest.

He placed his hands on her shoulders and pushed her up a little, to stare into her eyes, those brilliant brown eyes that reflected his passion, and expressed a pure depth of trust in him.

She began to whimper again, over and over, the sound throatier now, her cheeks flushed, breath coming quickly. She clung to his chest and he in turn reached forward and cupped her breasts again, thumbing her nipples, watching her drop her head back and close her eyes to move faster against him.

"You're so beautiful," he said quietly, watching

her close in on her release, knowing she was almost there, urging her on with each thrust of his hips against hers. "Come for me, Mimi . . ."

"Oh, Nathan . . ." she moaned, rotating her head, her glorious hair brushing his knees. "Oh, yes. Oh, yes. Nathan—" And then she cried out, circling her hips hard against him, jerking against his body, stroking him rhythmically as she bathed his hot, engorged penis with wetness that pushed him along with her to the brink.

"Ah, God. Mimi . . ."

He clenched his teeth together, shoved his head into the pillow, clinging to her as he let himself go.

In a groan of deep satisfaction, he climaxed beneath her, feeling her every exquisite stroke, hearing every sharp whimper of her pleasure, knowing at that precious, timeless moment that a fantasy could never be quite so perfect.

Chapter 15

Nathan paced the hard floor of his room at King's Road Boarding House, hands behind his back, staring at the ugly, frilly wallpaper, trying to control his nervousness. He had roughly six hours until his departure for the hall to reunite him for the first time in years with Richard Owen, and the colleagues who had once laughed at his find, then abandoned him. It would be a night to remember, a night for the history books, and although he knew without question that Mimi's brilliant sculpture would impress, even shock, the dignitaries and scientists present, he still risked failing once again. This would likely be the most important night of his life.

Yet much of his anxiousness of mind centered on

Mimi, which both confused and maddened him, because he ordinarily wouldn't be thinking of a woman at all at a time like this. She would, by her decision, be here to deliver the sculptured beast momentarily, probably to keep him from journeying to her home to get it, since it would be out of his way to do so as he left for the banquet this evening, but also because she would be saving him the expense of a hansom cab. That underlying reason injured his pride, but there was nothing he could do at the moment regarding his finances.

It did, however, manage to keep the situation between the Widow Sinclair and himself in proper perspective in some remote, rational area of his mind. Although their night together two weeks ago had been both risky and adventuresome, full of the wonder of discovery, he'd been avoiding her to a certain degree since that incredible event because of what lay ahead. Not only did they come from different worlds, when all was said and done this night, he suspected Mimi's father to be ruined.

What irritated him most of all—no, what *upset* him most of all—was Mimi's utter confidence in her father's innocence. How could she possibly know that with such certainty? Because she blindly loved the man? That was possible, he supposed. But how could she have planned such a seduction and a night of blissful passion if she didn't care about *him* to some degree? None of it made any sense—unless, Nathan realized with a sinking feeling in his gut, she was more involved with his downfall two and a half years ago, as he'd suspected from the beginning. It was the only thing he could think of that ex-

plained her willingness to help her father's accuser
as she worked to complete Professor Nathan Price's
ultimate destruction by getting him to fall prey to
her charms as an enticing woman. Still, even this interpretation did not in any way explain the very real
desire he saw in her beautiful eyes the night they finally made love, the very real passion he'd witnessed in her sexual abandonment that he refused
to believe was an act.

One thing was clear: he could not allow himself
to make any decisions about her until tomorrow,
when his name had finally been exonerated, when
he at last perceived a bright outlook for his future.
Until then, as much as the memory of her scent and
feel and remarkable laughter penetrated his mind
and made his body yearn for more, for everything,
he could not allow himself to feel.

Suddenly he heard commotion below, then Mrs.
Sheffield's heavy footsteps on the foyer floor. Mimi
had arrived.

Quickly he stepped to the door and made his
way downstairs before the owner's wife had to call
on him.

"Mrs. Sinclair is waiting for you in the parlor,
Professor," she said brusquely. Then she turned on
her heel and marched into the kitchen, making a
great spectacle of leaving him and his female guest
alone to talk. Nobody else was around, save two of
the proprietor's young daughters setting the dining
table for luncheon. Nathan rather doubted, though,
that Mrs. Sheffield herself wouldn't be eavesdropping if she could find a way to do so. His conversation with Mimi, once again, necessitated discipline.

Proceeding to the parlor entrance, he let his gaze fall first on the large white box, wrapped in a red satin ribbon, placed in the center of the cherry wood tea table. Amused by that, he at last looked at Mimi as she stood next to the window, staring out into the cold and gray late morning, arms crossed in front of her chest, her hair in a coiled braid at her crown, wearing a plain black pelisse over a gown he couldn't see but which no doubt denoted her status of widowhood. Frankly he tired of seeing her in such dark, drab clothing, but convention came first. It always would.

He took the two steps down into the parlor, and she turned to face the sound, watching him as he appeared before her, her smile firmly planted, but, he noted with uncertainty, never reaching her large, hesitant eyes.

"Mrs. Sinclair," he drawled, his lips curving up as he took in her figure, outlined only vaguely in her apparel. A shame, that. "How nice of you to call this morning."

"Professor Price," she replied primly, holding out her hand to him as he approached. "It's lovely to see you again. I've brought your package to you for the banquet this evening."

"Thank you," he said at once, never looking at it, but to her, her soft curves, her bosom fitting so snugly against her pelisse. He knew she realized where his thoughts lay because she blushed then, delicately, her cheeks growing a most becoming shade of pink. But she never lowered her eyes.

He walked to the side of the sofa and grasped her gloved fingers, raising them to his lips, slowly. Then he lowered her hand and lightly squeezed it once before releasing it, sending a clear message of awareness from that one tiny, unnoticeable act.

"Would you care to be seated?" he asked nonchalantly, motioning to the sofa with a flat palm.

"Yes, thank you."

She sat on the cushion to the right, facing the fireplace, her back to the foyer, and although she never removed her pelisse, she did grab her skirts and pull them toward her in implication that he might sit beside her. He did so, regardless of how unseemly it might look when two chairs in the room remained vacant. He wanted to be close enough for intimate discussion and if anyone did intrude he and Mimi would only appear as two individuals sitting side by side on the small peach sofa. Perfectly discreet. From here he could already smell her clean, spicy skin, peer into her eyes so close to his own.

Getting comfortable, he leaned away from her a little, crossed his ankle over his knee, and interlocked his fingers over his stomach.

"So," he began cordially, for Mrs. Sheffield's benefit, "How was your Christmas?"

"Oh, delightful, thank you," she replied, her lips tilted in a smile, removing her gloves, which she placed on her lap. "My father and sister and I celebrated with an early morning church service followed by dinner together, as we do each year. And you?"

"My Christmas was very nice as well," he said. "Mrs. Sheffield prepared a large goose with walnut stuffing for the boarders. Delicious."

"I've no doubt," she returned. "I'm certain it was excellent."

"Yes, it was, especially when those of us staying here had been forced by circumstances to be away from family during such a festive time."

Such staid conversation between them made her suppress a laugh, he could tell, though her eyes sparkled in humor.

"So, do tell, Professor," she remarked with a heavy exhalation, getting to the point of her visit. "Are you ready for tonight?"

His lids narrowed just minutely over keen eyes; one side of his mouth curled upward. "More than you can possibly imagine. I assume the sculpture is in the box?"

Boldly, apparently aware that nobody gazed on from behind them, that they were essentially alone and hidden by the sofa back, she reached forward and squeezed his knuckles. "It's my Christmas present to you, Nathan," she fairly whispered, her expression turned serious.

"That's why it's wrapped?" he asked.

"That, yes, and because as long as you glance at it tonight, until you open it, I want the red ribbon to remind you of recent gifts given to you surrounded by such a . . . vibrant color."

She had to know that would bring untold hunger and innermost emotions front and center, regardless of whether or not he acknowledged them. He wouldn't for a minute assert that he comprehended the female mind to any degree, but he understood all too well, from simply having a mother, that Mimi felt hurt by his avoidance these last two weeks. Yet did she really think he'd forget their intimate rendezvous, or not take it seriously?

He nodded slowly, unsure where to lead the conversation from here, but having every intention of making her appreciate his need to keep their relationship perfunctory, at least for now.

"I see," he said at length. He shifted his body in the sofa, sitting forward a fraction. "Red satin can be very sensuous. Even scandalous."

For a moment she appeared confused, tilting her head to the side a bit, her forehead gently creasing. Then acceptance filled her eyes and she breathed deeply in acknowledgment, sitting straighter, shoulders erect, chin lifting negligibly in defiance.

"You know, Nathan," she disclosed very softly, quickly scanning the parlor for intruders, "I'll never forget the look on your face the day I wore that red satin corset for you."

"Mimi—"

"And you *liked* it."

His jaw tightened. "Of course I liked it," he stressed in a whisper. "I liked making love to you in a ruby red room, I like the red in your cheeks right now, I'd like to see you wrapped up in that red ribbon wearing nothing else at all, but I'm not sure this is something we should be discussing now, today."

She eyed him candidly for a moment or two, flushing fully. Then she relaxed into her pelisse, into the soft cushion, dropping her lashes to gaze at the reticule she clutched in her lap.

"I want you to know some things before you leave tonight, Nathan."

He blinked, surprised by such a sudden turn of topic, but he said nothing.

She glanced at the grate, staring into the slow burning fire for a few seconds before swallowing harshly and turning back to him.

Watching him carefully, she admitted quietly, "I've kept a secret for so many years that I'm ... ashamed of, really. But it's something that, no matter how hard I try, I can neither excuse nor deny." She tensed fractionally and added huskily, "I never loved Carter and never wanted to marry him."

Something stirred deep inside him. Something he couldn't understand, or explain, even to himself. But it was there, forcing him to feel.

Do not feel.

He shifted his large form uncomfortably on the sofa, sitting fully forward, both feet on the floor, elbows on knees, hands clasped in front of him, staring at the peach carpet unseeing.

"Why are you telling me this now, Mimi?" he asked solemnly.

She paused, then whispered. "Do you think I would have let you make love to me without feeling?"

He closed his eyes and shook his head minutely. "What feeling? Whose feeling?"

She grasped his arm lightly. The touch of her skin scalded him, even through his shirt, but he couldn't bring himself to jerk free.

"I didn't love Carter, Nathan, and I—" She

cleared her throat. "As awful as this sounds, there were times with him in bed, intimately, that I closed my eyes and dreamed I was with you."

Jesus.

He looked at her again, incredulous, the tension in the air descending upon them, enveloping them, oppressive suddenly.

"What?"

Her breathing faltered, but she gazed at him starkly, her expression fierce and without the slightest trace of prevarication. "It was wrong, and Carter never knew, but—" She brought her palm briefly to her mouth, in a manner of shielding her words, before she clutched her gloves with both hands to continue.

"I wanted you to marry me, Nathan," she said in a voice barely audible. "That's why I went outside with you and kissed you that night at the Crystal Palace. I wanted you, not Carter. I wanted you."

He stared into her vibrant brown eyes, remembering that night as if it were yesterday—the bright blue of her gown, the brilliant gas lights reflecting off her hair, her throaty laugh, the warm, humid air, that shocking, amazing kiss that he'd thought about for months. And her marvelous, grave voice when she'd whispered, *Think about me.*

His pulse began to pound in his ears; his palms began to sweat. Static charged the air, thick and heavy, emotionally stirring.

Do not feel.

"Mimi . . ."

With a shaky bearing she stood beside him, gazing down, never looking away from him.

Boldly, intensely, she breathed, "You should have been my first."

Her beauty enraptured him; her conviction entranced him. In that instant it told him everything.

I should have been your only.

Swiftly, turning away, she lifted her skirts and walked to the door. He stood then, bracing himself against an inner assault, legs unsteady, remaining silent even as his heart begged her to stay.

With her hand on the latch, she paused, glancing back to him, her features unreadable but marked with determination.

"I love you, Nathan. I *love* you. Remember that tonight."

And then she was gone.

Chapter 16

*D*ammit.

Damn, damn, *damn* the female sex. All of
them. Every last idiotic one of them and their unexpected voiced concerns of romance and declarations
of love at the most incredibly absurd times. This was
supposed to be his night, the night he'd been anticipating, for which he'd been waiting, for more than
two years. Yet now, as he sat in his hired coach,
dressed formally in recently purchased evening attire of white silk shirt, waistcoat, and neckcloth, and
black trousers, jacket, and hat, on the brink of what
he considered his greatest discovery, he could think
of nothing but Mimi. Mimi and her remarkable
laughter and clever, devilish mind. Mimi and her
tantalizing figure created especially for lovemaking.

Mimi and her beautiful blond hair brushed over her perfectly rounded breasts. Mimi and her soft moans and breathtaking eyes that hinted at hidden desires when he aroused her. Mimi and her husky voice and striking, haunted face as she told him she loved him.

Loved him.

Mimi, Mimi, Mimi . . .

Nathan rubbed his aching temples with his fingertips in the darkness, his other arm resting possessively across the top of the white box, crushing the satin bow with each jolt of the coach's wheels as it meandered slowly south to Sydenham along the neglected city street.

A priceless present wrapped in a red satin bow. *I'll never forget the look on your face the day I wore that red satin corset for you.*

Christ, she'd gotten under his skin, as no woman ever had. She played with his emotions, tormented him with her presence, constantly penetrated his thoughts. What the hell was he supposed to do now? And why would she tell him such a thing tonight, of all nights? She had to know how nervous he'd be, how his mind would be centered on making the best impression of his career among fellow paleontologists, anatomists, and statesmen. Was her staggering confession purposefully meant to undermine him during the most critical moment of his personal quest? He didn't know, and couldn't possibly begin to guess. He'd spent the last five hours pacing the floor of his room at the boarding house, stopping himself several times from reaching for the door to go to her, to clarify, to shake the truth out of her.

To make her say it again.

I love you, Nathan.

Nathan clenched his jaw and shoved his fist into the coach's seat back. He didn't need this from her. Not now. There was so much unresolved between them, so much unsaid. So much doubt.

Regardless of what had been spoken between them this morning, the fact remained that nothing could be done about Mimi and her feelings—truth or lies—until this pivotal occasion was over, until he'd discovered, with certainty, who'd initiated his ruin, especially if it meant the end of her father's reputation, as he suspected it would. Until that time he would do his level best to think of nothing but his plan of attack, the moment he would unwrap the box and lift the lid. The moment all in attendance would finally learn what he'd known all along. Then he could allow himself to think of her, to consider tomorrow. Only then.

Please, God, get her out of my mind.

soon to take place. Arranged by the Crystal Palace Company, with an eye toward publicity, the banquet would be hosted by Owen, and artist and sculptor Benjamin Waterhouse Hawkins, as dinner would be served to twenty-one scientists and dignitaries inside an actual mold of a life-size Iguanodon. Although the new Palace would not be officially opened by Queen Victoria for several months, just the speculation of its eventual grandeur was enough to send a surge of excitement through each man here this night. As it did for Nathan right now.

He and Justin stared straight ahead to a short wooden stage of sorts where the life-size Iguanodon rested, its large head and horned snout to the left, its long, winding tail to the right, its middle cut out and replaced by an oblong table where a seven-course dinner would be served after a round of conversation and toasting. Above it, directly in the center, hung a chandelier to provide lighting, and surrounding the mold and lining the marquee hung plaques that bared the names of the great dinosaur discoverers—Cuvier, Owen, Mantell, and Buckland, the distinguished churchman who discovered and named the Megalosaurus in 1824.

"Marvelous, isn't it?" Justin murmured in awe, taking in the scene before him.

Nathan smirked, still holding his heavy, treasured box that would certainly be the highlight of the evening, at least for him. "The society columns said to expect the unexpected at the Waterhouse Hawkins dinner this night, and the night is young."

Justin leaned very close to him to ask, quietly, "Have you properly thanked the lovely widow?"

Nathan felt heat suffuse his body at that, and he shuffled his feet beneath him, the box growing heavy in his arms, never looking at his friend's face. "She's been thoroughly thanked, yes, as I'm sure you can imagine."

Justin laughed and thumped him once on the shoulder. "I'm trying very hard not to. I'm just glad I was able to accommodate everybody's need to be thanked as they desired." Swiftly, without waiting for another response, he stepped farther into the room to begin formal introductions to the men already present and mingling.

Nathan expected it to be awkward for him for the first couple of hours, maybe for the entire evening, and exceedingly so for the other distinguished gentlemen who were not anticipating the ruined paleontologist to be in attendance. To these men, all of good breeding and advanced education, his ineptitude had been revealed the night of the first Palace opening, during the heightened moment when, with the help of his own elevated arrogance, he'd lost every ounce of respect he'd gained through years of scientific research and study. Still, Owen had given the approval for Justin's extended invitation here tonight, and although many might have initial misgivings toward him as an originally uninvited guest, few would display them, or comment openly. It simply wouldn't be proper to do so. And this was precisely why Nathan could never have confronted each individual man immediately following his great ruin. Gentility forbade gross wrongdoing or gossip, and acknowledgment of misconduct by one's contemporaries would be socially disastrous. Coming forward with information wouldn't happen, although Nathan was certain that someone here tonight, maybe several men, knew exactly what had become of his Megalosaurus jawbone nearly three years ago.

For more than an hour, severely nervous but hiding it to the best of his ability, Nathan followed Justin's lead by making his own introductions to these same gentlemen as they arrived, his prized sculpture, still in its box, now sitting fairly inconspicuously to the left of the small staircase that led to the dining table. Quite to his surprise, however, he was actually well received by his former peers, many of whom remembered him, and appeared to think rather well of him regardless of his fall in status. They asked a little of his whereabouts these last two years, and he obliged their curiosity without hesitation or prevarication. Many seemed quite fascinated by his recent finds and accounts of his physical labor in contrast to his scholarly efforts, so much so that he quickly became the center of attention, if not sympathy, though that would never be admitted by anyone.

At last, on the heels of Waterhouse Hawkins, Professor Richard Owen arrived to much cheering and applause, followed closely by Sir Harold Marsh. As expected, Owen's wide forehead and high cheekbones flushed with excitement, his keen eyes waxed triumph in the wake of such an ensemble of England's finest scientists and their utter incredulity at the site of the magnificent Iguanodon in the budding beauty of the new Crystal Palace.

It was Harold Marsh, however, who promptly drew Nathan's undivided attention. Tall and lean, he stood with stately bearing, his white side whiskers flaring with every good-natured smile. But at close observation his face looked tired, his features strained, the creases in the skin a little more pronounced. He avoided eye contact with Nathan until propriety forced him to accept the inevitable introduction with grace, but even after shaking hands and exchanging polite queries on the state of each man's individual health, Nathan felt the odd man out. In a manner of speaking Harold Marsh belonged here and he did not and everyone knew it, though thankfully not everybody knew of his deep animosity toward the sculptor—nor his uncontrollable fixation with the man's bewitching daughter.

What struck him soundly, though, was not Sir Harold himself, but how very much Mimi took after him, in both manner and appearance, something Nathan had never clearly noticed before tonight. They both possessed a charged, compelling presence and charming wit, drawing attention to themselves with a mere voiced thought, a laugh. Each had the same physical features, the same coloring, same square facial structure, and the same intelligent, deeply probing brown eyes. Overall, Mimi's features were more feminine, of course, her skin smoother and somewhat fairer, but if they were put next to each other, it would be obvious to strangers that the two of them were father and daughter.

God, what Sir Harold would do if the man learned he'd bedded her! Such an uncomfortable

thought unnerved him when he knew it shouldn't.
Mimi had seduced him; her needs had come first to
her, though Nathan realized he hadn't been an innocent or unwilling partner in her scheme. He liked
her, enjoyed her, thought about her when he
shouldn't, made love to her because he'd wanted
her desperately, and, he realized with a sudden,
acute awareness, cared about her as a person—her
thoughts and passions and dreams. She meant
something more to him than just a woman to bed,
and admitting that to himself now not only was
confusing and inappropriate; his irrational feelings
would likely be obvious if Sir Harold simply mentioned her name to him. He would need to be exceptionally careful this night.

At last came the call for dinner, as each man took
his designated spot at the table inside the walls of
the Iguanodon. The fit was indeed tight, with little
elbow room to spare, as they all squeezed into the
small space, attempting to find a comfortable position. Justin sat to Sir Harold's immediate right, and
directly across from Nathan, who'd positioned himself by the stairs, better to receive his box when the
time came; Owen took his seat inside the dinosaur's
molded head with Waterhouse Hawkins at his side.

The toasting began with Owen giving thanks to
his contemporaries, fellow scientists, and Prince Albert, who had made the Palace possible for works of
new and speculative science like his. Then others
took to the spirit of the evening as the various good
wines flowed with each man's embellished words
of appreciation for the opportunity to be involved in

such an endeavor, and with such a group of distinguished statesmen, scholars, and nobles, many of whom had to be left off the guest list due to space constraints. Several times his peers glanced his way, but Nathan stayed quiet throughout the saluting, keeping his drink intake to a minimum, observing the spectacle with an ever-growing anxiousness as the evening slowly progressed.

Finally the dinner itself began to arrive. Hired servants in formal black attire first took requests from the rather extensive bill of fare, then delivered each course in a timely fashion. Nathan chose Jullien soup, filet of whiting, and boiled chicken in celery sauce as his first three courses, though he doubted he'd be able to eat much of it with his nerves wound so tightly. For a good forty-five minutes, as the toasting and rowdy laughter settled down with the start of earnest eating, conversation in his immediate vicinity remained neutral and centered strictly on paleontology and the latest finds recently excavated at various English and European quarries.

At last, however, during a superb course of pheasant with Madeira jelly, the topic turned to the original Palace opening in '51, and Nathan knew it was only a matter of time before someone mentioned him. Alas, he had never expected it to be Justin.

"Do tell, Nathan," his friend broke in casually, cutting a tomato half with his fork, "did you ever recover your Megalosaur jawbone that disappeared opening night?"

Silence descended upon the room as they all

stopped eating at once. Someone coughed; another man dropped his fork to his china plate with a sharpness that sliced through the thick night air.

Nathan swallowed a bite of suddenly dry game he'd only begun to chew, then tapped his napkin against his lips, stalling. In that short space of time a low murmur of two or three voices severed the enveloping unrest, inviting comments of an insensitive nature.

"Those shameful skeleton bones," bellowed Clayton Rollingsworth through a half-drunken slur. "Perhaps the thing walked out on its own and is right this very minute terrifying children and women in Hampshire."

Several snickered openly at that. Nathan turned to the corpulent middle-aged anatomist, whom he knew only by name and brief introduction, his expression grim, his heart pounding as he fisted his hands together beneath the table. "Perhaps it had help from someone in this room tonight," he said in reply, his voice amazingly composed. "Maybe you, Mr. Rollingsworth?"

Someone gasped. Then silence settled over the group again, as those who'd found instant humor in the stupid jest now realized with self embarrassment that Nathan took this matter most seriously.

Seconds of uneasiness passed. Owen made a great display of sipping his port; Sir Harold looked at his half-eaten plate of woodcocks, his hands in his lap. Only Justin continued to eat, undisturbed. Nathan found that rather odd.

Professor Owen cracked the tension by suddenly clearing his throat. "Yes, Price," he remarked, sitting up a little. "A shame it was lost. Ever hear a thing about its recovery?"

That the most celebrated paleontologist in England defended his credibility in front of those here tonight provided Nathan a momentary boost of satisfaction.

With the attention in his arena, he replied succinctly, "I've not heard a word, no, but I have my suspicions as to who took it." He looked straight across from him, directly at Sir Harold. "What I don't know is why, or where it is at the moment."

"Can't prove it existed at all," came a voice somewhere down the table to his right. "Nobody's ever found a Megalosaur jawbone *whole*."

It shocked him that a guest would immediately challenge Owen's obvious conviction that the jawbone was real, but Nathan never looked away from his adversary. "Oh, it was intact and complete, I assure you. It certainly existed then, just as I'm certain it does even now, to someone else's advantage."

"Your arrogance is astonishing, Price," Rollingsworth blubbered.

"As is your rudeness," he shot back without moving his gaze.

That started an uncomfortable shifting of bodies as the negative mood elevated.

"Now, now, gentlemen," Waterhouse Hawkins interjected through a forced laugh, his palms out in front of him. "No need to argue about something in the past. Let's enjoy ourselves. The wine is good, the food superb—"

"Are you accusing someone here at the dinner table tonight, Price?" Sir Harold broke in coolly, and very slowly. "Is that why you've come to this otherwise festive occasion? To accuse one of these distinguished gentlemen of science and culture of disgracing *you*?"

Low murmurs began again. Nathan knew this was the moment when all would turn in his favor—or against it. But no matter what he did or said, he could not afford to insult their gracious host for this event to which he had not been immediately invited to attend in the first place—the man who might also make any future career of his possible.

Drawing a long breath, sitting rigidly solid in his chair, he nodded once to Professor Owen, before looking back at Sir Harold. "I'm delighted to be here, sir, as you can well imagine," he articulated, eyes narrowed, features hard with purpose. "I've been excluded from occasions such as this one in the last two years, not by my choice, as I know you're aware, but because, as you aptly stated, someone chose to humiliate me in front of my peers during the greatest moment of my career."

"Oh, rubbish," interrupted one man.

"Indeed," agreed another. "You are an arrogant pup, aren't you?"

Nathan ignored the ridicule, the churning in his stomach, and the doubts in his mind, to press forward. This was the night of his life. He would survive it or he would fail.

Taking a sip of his port to give him a moment or two of control, he decided to get to the reason for his being at the most momentous occasion of the year. It was time.

In one fluid gesture, he placed his wineglass back

on the table and stood, his chair scooting out behind him on the hard floorboards.

"Gentlemen," he maintained, smoothing his frock coat to hide his growing anxiousness, "I would like to take this opportunity to share with each of you something I hope you'll find interesting, if not fascinating."

"Going to give us a showing again, eh, Price?" Waterhouse Hawkins asked, scratching his chin as he relaxed in his chair.

Several chuckled; one or two groaned. Nathan didn't know whether the man mocked him or felt genuinely curious, but he didn't respond. Out of the corner of his eye, he caught Sir Harold shifting back in his seat, but he ignored it all. With everyone otherwise remaining remarkably silent, he nodded again to his host.

"Something for you, Sir Richard, for the time when this marvelous structure in which we now sit is completed and ready to show to the world all you've catalogued, discovered, and taught." Then he turned toward the steps behind him and motioned to a servant awaiting his signal to carry the large white box to the table.

But upon seeing it again, wrapped precisely and prettily in a bright red bow, as only a woman would do, Nathan's heart started beating hard and fast, not with nervousness, but with remembrance. A remembrance of long, flowing blond hair caressing his chest, a beautifully wicked smile, marvelous pink-tipped breasts, and a red satin corset worn for his viewing alone. He swallowed. This was Mimi's moment, too, he realized, and she couldn't even be here to savor it as he would. Suddenly Nathan felt a surge of intense desire to be with her, arguing with her in her sunshiny garden, sitting beside her on a settee in her workshop while discussing opposing scientific theories, watching her work in a moment of peaceful quiet, making love to her during a long night of passion . . .

The low rumble of whispers shook him from his uncomfortable, if not enlightening musings. He straightened as he took the box from the servant and deposited it in his chair, those sitting beside him moving to their sides a little to grant him room—or stay out of his way.

Standing behind it, Nathan faced the group with fortitude on his face, and excitement raging just below the surface.

This was his moment.

He looked into Sir Harold's shrewd, brown eyes. *And your daughter's.*

Beneath the burning gas chandelier, inside a palace of glass walls and a dinosaur mold of magnificent build, Nathan faced the men who'd rejected him once before. Hands shaking, he reached with careful fingers for the red satin bow and slowly pulled at the ends until the center knot loosened and came free. That done, he grasped the lid with both hands and lifted it, placing it gently at his feet.

He first sighted old newspapers, wadded up and stuffed inside to safeguard the sculpture from movement, thereby keeping it intact. Nathan reached in and lifted them piece by piece, dropping each one to the floor behind him.

At last his eyes came to rest on the black cover

cloth protecting his treasure. The men at his side were now leaning over to view the contents out of curiosity, as the air around the table fairly crackled with building intensity, the entire room still and silent with an anticipation Nathan could not only detect, but actually feel.

Cautiously, he grasped the sculpture with both hands and raised it from the box. Glancing to Sir Harold, who sat stonefaced and unaffected, he tugged on the edges until the velvet came loose and drifted down his upraised arm, disclosing his prize to all of them.

Beneath the hissing bright light, the sculpture lay at last in his palms, long and sturdy and remarkable in its appearance, causing a collective gasp from his contemporaries, a moment of awe followed by low murmurs of amazement and appreciation. Mimi had outdone herself. In its final form, the sculpture was positively breathtaking.

"Brilliant," Sir Richard offered before anyone else spoke. "And such likeness. It's simply . . . astonishing."

Likeness? That confused Nathan, but he didn't comment for fear of appearing ignorant. It wasn't the time for ignorance.

Winthrop Bartlett, a paleontologist from Oxford, shook his head in small, sharp movements, his thick, white eyebrows drawn together as one. "Similar, yes . . ." His gaze narrowed as he cocked his head. "Especially the curved teeth."

"Yes, yes," Owen replied, slowly standing to get a better view. "You're absolutely right. It's the teeth."

Suddenly Justin stood, his brows pinched in dismay, staring at the sculpture with pointed interest, as comments between the men began to flow.

Others followed suit, rising to ogle, moving in to get a closer look. All but Sir Harold, who remained where he sat, his elbow resting on the arm of his chair, his palm lingering on his chin, his wide, arthritic fingers covering what Nathan assumed at first to be the man's own stunned silence. Then his gaze locked with Marsh's brown eyes, so candid and fierce like his daughter's, and that's when he realized all was not as it seemed. Those eyes were solid, confident, amused, laughing at him. No, not laughing. Challenging him.

Nathan looked down at his prize again, turning it slowly in his hands.

"To what likeness are you referring, Sir Richard?" Justin broke in after clearing his throat.

Nathan swiftly glanced up to him. Justin looked pale, perplexed. He quickly followed his friend's gaze to their host.

"Oh, the likeness of the Megalosaur jawbone found in Oxfordshire only a fortnight ago," Owen quickly returned, smiling. "By Colin Smith, the American working with the team from Cambridge." He nodded toward Nathan's sculpture. "That one looks nearly identical."

Nathan had heard of Smith, by reputation, but the bewilderment he felt only moments ago now turned to alarm—not because of the dinosaur found, but because of the look on Justin's face.

What the bloody hell was going on?

"Was it intact?" Justin mumbled, clutching his wineglass with tight fingers.

"Good God, no," Waterhouse Hawkins interjected, flicking his wrist. "So far Smith's only found one side of the right lower jaw, certainly not the complete bone back to front." He gestured to Nathan's sculpture with a brush of his fingers. "But it looks very much like that one, with the long tooth coming up from the center. That's never been seen before that I know of, at least, not whole and in one piece like that."

Justin blinked, then turned and looked across the table at him again; Nathan could only stand there, stumped, trying not to appear the bumbling idiot he felt at that moment.

"Indeed," Owen said to Nathan. "If this is a copy of the one stolen from you at the Palace opening, then it's proof of what you found years ago, I should think. Only two or three of us here have actually seen the Smith jaw, and we're the only ones who'd know." He chuckled with genuine pride, shaking his head and raising his glass. "Good showing, Nathan."

About half of the men joined in the toast, one or two murmuring praise and cheerful admiration; Justin sat down hard in his chair.

"But do tell, Professor Price," Bartlett insisted with a crooked smile, leaning forward so that his rotund belly cut into his empty plate. "Who was your sculptor? That's certainly a fine piece of handiwork." He shot a quick peek to his right, down the line of curious men. "You do that, Benjamin? Harold?"

Waterhouse Hawkins quickly answered in the negative, nonplussed; Marsh had yet to make a sound, hadn't moved a muscle, only continued to watch his silent accuser from across the table through perceptive, narrowed eyes.

He knows something.

And it was Nathan's moment to confess, should he want to. His moment to tell the world of Mimi's talent, as it became immediately obvious that Sir Harold was waiting for him to do so.

But he had promised Mimi . . .

Nathan dropped his gaze to the white sculpture, perfectly formed, that still rested hard and cold in his hands. The plaster and steel mold, solid in its construction, was getting heavy now, but he turned it, looking for truth. Something.

What is it?

Then he studied what the others had found so engaging. The tooth. Two of them, actually. The Megalosaurus dinosaur had one long, curved tooth reaching up from each side of its lower jaw, above all its other chewing teeth, that the ancient beast had presumably used to tear at its prey. But he had known that. They had been present on his jawbone of three years ago. It had been evident—

Nathan felt a violent shift within him, from steady trust, to utter disbelief, to complete and paralyzing rage. Within seconds his head began to swim. The room grew agonizingly hot as the air closed in on him, making him dizzy, forcing the breath from him, causing his body to break out into sweat that beaded on his upper lip, his forehead, and his neck.

The teeth had been fairly intact on his fossil, outlined to completion on his original drawings of three years ago, but not on the recent ones. Not the ones Mimi had sketched, the ones from which she'd sculpted the jawbone that now lay in his hands. He'd purposely left them out as the only way to trap the thief. Nobody should have known about the extra two teeth, or at least, not their size and location and perfect curvature, except for the person who'd stolen the jawbone originally. Hers were too good, too obvious here.

Mimi knew.

His head jerked up. His gaze locked with Sir Harold's and held it.

You both knew.

"Professor Price?"

The voice didn't register, only echoed in his mind. Nothing registered but the sounds of laughter at his long-ago humiliation.

Son of a bitch.

His body turned as rigid as stone, and he clamped his teeth shut to keep from spilling his fury and contempt right here at the dinner table on the night of his life, in front of Richard Owen. But he never looked away from the man who had ruined him.

The man and his daughter.

"This brilliant likeness, gentlemen," he breathed seconds later, through a thick, tense silence, "was sculpted by Mrs. Mimi Marsh Sinclair, Sir Harold's very convincing daughter."

Gasps followed; low mumbles ensued. And then, very slowly, Sir Harold nodded almost imperceptibly and lowered his lashes in acceptance, in defeat.

"I beg your pardon," huffed Waterhouse Hawkins, thoroughly shocked as were the rest of them.

"*Ladies* do not sculpt dinosaurs, Price," Rollingsworth barked, appalled.

Without responding to either man, Nathan carefully laid the treasure made from delicate, caressing hands of talent and clever deception once again inside the box. That done, he straightened and turned to his host, chin held high while attempting to keep his dignity intact and the crumbling he felt inside unnoticed by those present and staring at him.

"Professor Owen," he said steadily, voice low, "with my thanks, I give you this sculpture to place on display in the Crystal Palace. I also someday soon expect to present you with the fossil from which this likeness was created, to show alongside it."

He heard remarks and whispers voiced in disapproval of his continued audacity, but he brushed over all of it. Instead, he turned and faced Marsh for a final time. "Forgive me for leaving this lively occasion early, gentlemen. I have important business to settle that cannot wait."

That got him. Sir Harold jerked up in his chair, only to be grasped at the sleeve.

"Harold," Justin warned softly, holding him back.

Confusion rang anew in the Iguanodon. Nobody understood.

Lips tight, eyes bright with purpose and utter loathing, Nathan simply stuck out his arm and pointed at the man who had betrayed him. It was enough.

Then he pivoted violently and stepped from the

table, his shoes clicking on the wooden floor as he walked toward his final confrontation.

Mimi.

She hadn't broken his heart as his lover; she had crushed it as his friend.

Chapter 18

Mimi sat on the settee in her workshop, in near darkness as the dull beam of one low lamp shone beside her, across her black crepe skirt, leaving her face in shadow. Hands folded in her lap, she'd been waiting for more than an hour, listening to the pattering of light rain, freezing, though she knew the mildly chilly house had no bearing on each shiver, that the cold she felt came from within.

Nathan would be here soon, she knew, to confront her, to query her, to push her into an argument. That thought actually made her smile despite her raw nerves. She knew the man so well in such a short time, knew how he'd respond to this shock she'd given him tonight, knew how he'd bait her for answers, knew he'd probe her for secrets she couldn't reveal, knew that he felt deeply for her as a woman, regardless of the fact that he didn't even recognize this in himself.

Taking a long, full breath, Mimi closed her eyes and leaned her head back against the cushion. It was almost ten, yet in anticipation of Professor Price's visit, she'd kept the lights on in the house, had kept the fire burning, and had had Glenda prepare tea for two. Nathan could use the warmth, coming in from the rain, the winter night's air, and she would play the perfect hostess to counteract his outrage and resentment.

All evening, or rather since she'd left him this morning, Mimi had tried to envision the look to grace his face when he finally opened the box. Oh, how she wished she'd been there! What a marvelous sight that must have been for him, when he'd lifted the lid to lay eyes on his jawbone of years ago. Certainly he would be mad at her, furious for keeping it from him and hiding it all this time. But he would also be standing under glaring bright lights in the Crystal Palace, in front of some of the most important men of their day, including the majority of his fellow paleontologists who'd witnessed his original downfall, commanding their attention with a matchless dignity. Mimi knew her best hope for Nathan's ultimate forgiveness of her would be if they'd at last been in awe of his long-ago find, and had finally accepted his somewhat arrogant pronouncements as fact, thus restoring his credibility. Only that, she knew, would soften the blow to his pride and nurture the wounds that had not healed after all this time.

She knew he'd come to her afterward, and that's why she'd paced the quiet, chilly hallway and rooms of her home during the evening hours, unable to work or concentrate on household matters. Now, as the night progressed and his arrival approached, she'd positioned herself in her studio, wearing a severe gown in black that symbolized her mood and exemplified her status, should he forget. It was the only place where she felt she'd be on equal ground during the confrontation to come.

And just as she'd suspected, at long last, she heard a slight commotion coming from the front of her home, a few muffled words, then silence—except for the sound of his long, slow footsteps as they echoed in the narrow hallway to her workshop, growing closer with each step.

Mimi straightened, her posture ramrod stiff, her face shaded behind lamplight by design, her fingers curled together tightly in her lap as her apprehension mounted with every breath.

Then he appeared at the doorway to her workshop, ahead of Stella, rather than behind her to be introduced properly. "Intimidating" was the first word to come to mind, as Mimi finally beheld the marvelous sight of him that instantly filled her heart with joy and the room with a low-burning energy.

He wore a tailored suit of fine black wool, cut to perfection, outlining his magnificent physique with precision. His hat had been left with Stella in the foyer at his entrance, though Mimi could see the outline of it still in his silky hair that she wished she could run her fingers through. He'd indecently loosened his neckcloth, yet such action seemed appropriate for the moment, at least for Nathan. But it was his stance, his overall bearing, that made her pause. He stood as unyielding as cold marble, looking at her not with confusion or basic anger, but with a hollow emptiness piercing her from round, black, emotionally vacant eyes. Not hot and seething as she'd expected, but frigidly enraged.

Mimi shivered again, visibly this time, realizing at that moment that the encounter to come would likely be ugly.

"Um . . . Professor Price to see you, Mrs. Sinclair," Stella announced from behind him.

Mimi didn't move her gaze from his. "Inform Glenda that we'll take tea—"

"I don't want tea," he murmured in a tone of winter ice.

She blinked in surprise at his disrespect, then glanced to her maid, who looked utterly flustered. "Tea, Stella. Now."

"Ma'am," she mumbled, casting a worried glimpse at Nathan before quickly departing.

Mimi sat where she was, waiting, or hesitating, wondering at his mood, his colorless features that told her nothing. She gripped her fingers together tightly on her thighs, doing everything in her power to keep from standing and going to him. She couldn't bear to be physically tossed aside, and she realized that such a fear grew stronger the longer he stood like a stranger of stone and stared at her as if she were a fly in his sherry.

"Well," she began matter-of-factly, her features pleasantly set, heartbeat quickening, "how was the dinner party?"

He didn't move a muscle, though his lips thinned to a flat, straight line.

"Where is my jawbone, Mrs. Sinclair?"

His tone of absolute contempt hit her as soundly as a forceful slap to the face. But it was his words, rather, that sent her reeling. Still, she refused to let him see how unnerved she felt right now.

"I suppose it's where you left it, Professor," she replied coolly, and, she noted, a bit more sarcastically than she'd intended.

He slowly shook his head in disgust. "Where did a gentle, lovely woman like you learn to be so vicious, Mimi? From your father, or your husband?"

Her eyes widened and her hands began to shake. "What happened tonight, Nathan?" she asked with mounting trepidation, her voice low and cautious.

For seconds he simply stared at her. Then he slammed his fist into the wall at his side. *"Where's my goddamn jawbone!"*

She blinked, and her mouth dropped open in shock, in bewilderment, and in sudden fear for the man she loved. She had never seen Nathan like this. Something had gone horribly wrong.

Very slowly, on unsteady legs, she stood to meet his gaze evenly, arms open at her sides, though she never moved away from the settee. "What happened tonight?" she repeated in a near whisper.

Time dragged endlessly, in bitter silence, through every calculated breath as he looked at her, until at last he whispered in return, "No more lies."

Such simple words. Yet it was the way in which he'd said them, in a timbre of repulsion and sadness, that scared her in a manner she'd never felt before. And in one of life's ridiculous moments, Stella suddenly appeared next to Nathan, who continued to stand just to the right of the doorway, pausing as she glanced up at him after undoubtedly hearing his outburst, carrying a silver tray with china cups, saucers, milk, and sugar, waiting to serve him as a guest at the Widow Sinclair's request. Mimi suppressed the urge to laugh at such an absurd scene. How odd that she'd thought tea would be appropriate for the occasion and make things better. Her mistakes of the past would never go away. She would need to accept them now, even if it meant losing him forever.

Regrets, yes. Too many to count. But no more lies.

Standing tall with newfound mettle, she looked at her maid. "We've changed our minds, Stella. Leave us now without interruption."

Nathan ignored the untimely intrusion, said nothing. Stella gaped for a second or two, before recovering herself to nod properly, turn, and walk in the direction from which she had come. Mimi shivered again and hugged herself for strength, the thought of imported, hot Darjeeling mixed with the intimate smells of wood and clay in her cold workshop now as thoroughly uninviting to her as it obviously was to Nathan.

"Close the door and come in," she ordered, no longer desirous of playing the amiable hostess.

His jaw twitched but he didn't move.

Facing him squarely, she repeated, "Close the door, Nathan. I will tell you what I can, but it must be private."

For only a slice of a second, Mimi thought surprise lit his brow at her commanding direction without the customary female timidity. Then he inhaled sharply and reached for the knob, doing as she bid. But he didn't move away from it.

In a steady voice, she decided to get to the heart of the matter so that she'd know where to begin in explaining everything.

"You must first tell me what happened tonight—"

"Why don't you start by telling me who betrayed me two and a half years ago," he cut in ruthlessly as he began to step toward her, his demeanor menacing. "Was it you directly? Your father? Your loving husband?"

She'd had enough. "Damn it all, Nathan, what *happened* tonight?"

That she cursed in front of him stopped him short. His dark brows lifted and his head jerked back with his first look of true astonishment.

She held up her hand, palm out to imply a truce, briefly closing her eyes. "You *must* tell me this first. I appear to be as confused as you." She lifted her lashes to meet his hard gaze once more. "No lies."

The honesty implied in that one simple phrase got him. He quickly looked her up and down, then murmured in a tone of steel, "I was saluted, naturally, honored by Sir Richard for my marvelous find, though apparently you and your father already knew I would be. I suppose you'd like me to thank you?"

Her forehead creased in frown. "What are you talking about?"

He chuckled bitterly and raked his fingers through his hair. "I'm talking about the sculpture and its perfect teeth that only you, your father, and Professor Owen are aware of, Mimi. And oh, yes, the American, too, Colin Smith."

That bewildered her more than ever, and her legs began to shake. "I don't understand."

"Where's my fossil, Mimi?"

Drawing a long breath for strength, her mind churning with horrible possibilities, she clasped her hands together behind her to reveal, "I put the original jawbone in the box that you took to the banquet—"

"*What!*"

He jerked forward, taking another long step toward her, and she took one away from him in a manner of defense, the back of her knees hitting the edge of the settee. She grasped the cushioned arm to stop herself from falling on it.

"I put it in the box," she said again, eyes wide. "You should have seen it when you opened it."

He shook his head, one corner of his mouth turned up wryly. "If I had seen my jawbone, Mimi," he replied as if speaking to a child, "I certainly wouldn't be here demanding it now."

That stung her, but instead of a nasty retort, as calmly as she could manage, she tried another approach. "Then what *did* you see inside, Nathan? Flowers? Table linens? *Dried fish*? I'm aging quickly from this conversation going nowhere, so don't keep me guessing. Explain it to me."

Her caustic comment didn't faze him in the least as his eyes spilled over with loathing. It was enough to make hers fill with tears that she hoped he'd never notice. But her tactic worked.

"All right, Mrs. Sinclair," he soothed dispassionately. "Let me tell you about the banquet." Turning, he walked to the brown table and leaned his hip against it casually, crossing his arms over his chest, gazing at her flatly from across the room.

"I opened the box tonight, that you'd so carefully wrapped, taking pride in showing your work to all. I was not to be disappointed. Inside was a marvelous likeness, a sculpture of that which was lost to me nearly three years ago, only the teeth were too good, too perfectly imbedded. Even Richard Owen noticed and made comment of it." He snorted sarcastically. "That's when I realized I'd never told you in detail about the two curved teeth shooting up from each side of the lower jawbone—two teeth that I'd mentioned only in passing but which you'd conveniently formed to perfection. These weren't teeth like other dinosaur's, these were imbedded in the sockets of the jaw. I'd thought you'd done a brilliant job, Mimi, until I realized you'd simply copied the original."

Mimi fairly gaped at him. No longer able to balance herself on trembling legs, she lowered her body swiftly and indelicately to the settee.

It didn't make sense. None of this made sense. The fossil hadn't been inside when he'd opened it? That was impossible. Even Justin had known, or had at least guessed, what she'd planned to do the day she'd met him in the park. She'd placed it there herself two days ago, tying the ribbon, making sure nobody touched it until she gave it to Nathan earlier today.

Except her father, who'd perhaps seen it the evening before last when he'd come to dinner. Had he been alone with it? And long enough to switch the fossil for the sculpture sitting in her studio? Could he have possibly known her intentions, been so calculating? It was the only explanation. But why? And with her questions came the stunning realization of what Nathan was actually telling her tonight. His priceless jawbone had disappeared once more, because of her, and this time she had no idea where it was.

Oh, God, Papa, what have you done now?

Nathan continued to watch her, his palms resting on his thighs, eyelids narrowed to tiny slits. Finally, he remarked tightly, "Now you're telling me you actually placed this same original jawbone, a dinosaur fossil of immeasurable worth, into a box one could easily misplace? Or *drop*?"

That pulled her from her troubled musings, irritating her a little. "You weren't going to let it out of your sight, Nathan. And of course you noticed how well it was packaged."

"That's irrelevant," he barked. "You know its value. What you did was stupid."

"Stupid, maybe, but I did it for you—"

"Don't," he interjected softly in warning, stiffening so quickly the muscles in his neck visibly flexed. "Don't say that to me. If you cared, you would have returned it to me long before tonight."

The harsh lines of his face that creased from tension, those words that implied so much hurt, nearly made her break down into uncontrollable sobs, because, through every remark, through every anguished breath, she knew he was right. She wanted so desperately to run to him, to comfort, to love him and prove it. Instead, she gripped her hands even tighter and swallowed thickly to stay her worries, and prevent her tears.

"You don't understand anything," she breathed.

"You're absolutely correct in that assertion," he agreed immediately. "I understand very little. All I know is that you supposedly exchanged a sculpture you made for my priceless fossil, which you've had all along, and then at some point unbeknownst to you, the fossil was switched for the sculpture!" He threw his arms into the air, palms up, in feigned amazement. "So where do you suppose it is now, Mrs. Sinclair?"

His sarcastic manner made her mad and she snapped at him. "Stop calling me that."

"Why? Because you don't like being reminded you were married to a cheat?"

That brought her to her feet again. "Carter wasn't a cheat."

He snickered bitterly. "Stop defending the man, Mimi. He cheated me out of three years' wages and funds for my museum project, out of prestige that was due me. You, your husband, and your whole bloody family ruined my name and then laughed at me. I hope you're all goddamn proud of yourselves."

Mimi just stood there, stung by his rancor, anger filling her in places where only sadness had been. "I never did anything to you. And what I find so appalling, Professor Price, is that you have no idea, even after everything we've shared, what I feel for you."

He gradually stood, though his cold gaze never strayed from hers. "What you feel for me? *Feel* for me? I know my future as a respected scientist was stolen by you, or someone close to you, to your *knowledge*, Mimi, on the night I gave in to your wonderful kiss. Until that night I had never been so taken with a woman. I was possessed by the passion, as you knew I'd be, falling for your flirting tone and beautiful eyes, leaving my fossil unattended just long enough for someone you know to steal it." He closed his eyes with finality. "God, and to think I trusted you," he whispered. "I was stupid and foolish and arrogant. But no more. No more."

He could never know how deeply his words sliced through her heart, how she would give everything she valued to return his dignity to him, his honor that was so rudely and horridly stolen from him on that night long ago. But nothing she could possibly say would make it better now. Nothing.

"What do you want from me, Nathan?" she whispered.

He raised his lids and considered her once more, his eyes radiating anger and frustration and even loneliness that was positively palpable.

"I want you to tell me the truth," he demanded, his voice deadly calm. "All of it."

The house had become acutely quiet; the only sound to be heard was the scratching of a low tree branch on the window behind the settee. The wind had picked up with the coming of a steady night rainfall, and low clouds made the gas lampposts on the street shine brightly through the panes, creating a patchwork of light on the wooden floor.

Instead of ignoring these things, Nathan noticed each one, noticed everything without so much as an effort to do so. His skin crawled with nervous energy, his sharpened senses screamed of being trapped in his body of fire, of rage and bitter remorse. It was all he could do to lean against the table and not move, not break things, not go to her and shake her until she confessed what he more than suspected.

Mimi had betrayed him. Certainly then, perhaps even now, and the thought nauseated him. He had loved her in bed, had divulged intimacies he'd never shared with another, and all along she'd been involved in his ruin. He'd known the possibility had existed, and it was entirely his fault for not heeding his own warning. Tonight, after what had turned out to be a spectacular professional success, he wanted to wrap himself in his pity, his outrage and hurt, and never see her again. But as with all things between him and the Widow Sinclair, it would never be that easy.

At last Mimi stood with determination, wringing her hands in front of her, shoulders back, head held high, as she glided to the window to gaze into the night. Dull lamplight illuminated her shiny blond hair that she'd pulled severely away from her haunted face, which looked years older than twenty-three. Nathan grew fiercely mad at himself for sympathizing with her feelings, although there was no denying that he felt a very odd passion for the unfairness caused her in her past, that he felt something beyond the superficial for the woman herself. But then, she'd made sure of that.

He should have known better.

"I'm fully aware of what you wanted from me initially, Nathan," she finally said very softly.

He grunted. "I've never wanted anything more from you than the return of my treasure. That's what I wanted initially, Mimi, and that's what I want now. I never would have come back to you if it hadn't been for the jawbone."

She smirked, though she never looked his way. "Men can be such idiots."

Women and their ridiculous pronouncements. "Explain that to me."

Closing her eyes briefly, she shook her head. "Do you remember the first time we met?"

Her tactic mystified him, cornered him, but he refused to appear the idiot she proclaimed him to be. "I remember vaguely." He pinched the tabletop with his fingers in spiraling agitation. "What does a moment ten years ago have to do with this discussion?"

She once more gazed out into the soggy night. "I remember it more than vaguely. It may have occurred ten years ago and be only a moment in time to you, but I remember the event as if it happened yesterday."

The event? He couldn't imagine why she should remember any of it, but then, that was irrelevant. "Again, madam, what does our meeting have to do with this discussion?"

She remained silent for several seconds, her delicate brows pinched in thought, her eyes staring vacantly outside.

Nathan feared he might be nearing the point of insanity. He suddenly wanted to throttle her, or walk out of her life for a final time with good riddance—forgetting the jawbone, forgetting what they'd shared in bed, forgetting that she'd told him she loved him and that he had, for a few brief hours, believed it. He simply couldn't take any more.

But it was the vision of her at the window, the faint light on her hair, her beautiful body wrapped tightly neck to toe in a black crepe gown, the shadow of cascading rain upon the glass reflecting on her clear, pale skin that kept him entranced. They looked like teardrops, and the picture of her so alone squeezed his heart in a manner he'd never felt before. The woman had bewitched him, and with enough skill to keep him standing before her like a puppy on her firmly held rope. What Nathan desperately wished he knew was if she'd captured him by design, had planned to do so from the beginning, or if it had simply happened by chance. But he refused to ask her. In light of all that had occurred between them, either answer would hurt too much.

"I had always adored sculpting," she revealed at last in a breathless, faraway voice, her arms crossed over her breasts as she hugged herself. "Even as a little girl I'd wanted to sculpt beasts like my father instead of statues and pottery and bird fountains. But of course nobody took me seriously since I was a girl, and girls aren't supposed to have ambition above themselves. Even my father laughed when I brought my desires to his attention. I thought—of all the people who recognized my talent, he would be the one to support my wishes because he realized just how much dinosaurs fascinated me." She smiled sadly and dropped her gaze to her feet. "How could they not? I'd grown up with them, studying their design and strength in his workshop with complete amazement. But Papa was the first to lecture me on propriety and the fact that ladies did not stray from convention. And of course it was accepted that I would marry and become a doting wife, mother, and household manager, accepting with grace, if not joy, my station in life." She paused, sighing as she closed her eyes, lifting her face to the ceiling.

Nathan wanted to tell her to hurry it up and get to the point. He'd grown tired of such an abstract disclosure of past events in which he felt thoroughly uninvolved. He didn't want to care. But something held him back, held his tongue from offering a terse retort. Something in her distant voice, her posture, her hidden strength that he'd always admired and felt even now, kept him centered on the conversation to learn the meaning behind it.

"Do you know what happened to turn my life around, Nathan?" she continued warily. "To make me realize what I wanted from my work? To make me continue where others said I shouldn't?"

Suddenly discomfited, he shifted from one foot to the other, still leaning on the table but feeling the hardness of it cutting into his thighs. "No," he replied shortly.

She shook her head, her face tilted upward, her eyes still closed.

"I met you."

He knew she would say that, and his initial reaction was to tell her to go to hell, that her girlish dreams and fantasies were not a matter of importance, especially to him. Her words left him agitated again, a part of his brain signaling a deeper warning, and acknowledgment escaped him. To be on the careful side, he said nothing, and she didn't appear to expect him to answer, or join in the discussion. She instead carried on as if he wasn't even in the room.

"I remember it rained that day, very heavily, and the streets were sloppy and muddy. My sister and mother had left to make a round of social calls, as they were supposed to do even on ugly days like that one. I'd decided to hide myself away in the morning room, sitting by the grate and the warmth of the fire to sketch a Stegosaurus that my father had been hired to sculpt from the leg bone, partial jaw, and snout that sat in his workshop at that very moment. I couldn't believe its sheer size and what it must have been like for the beasts at the time of their existence, and I remember wondering if the Bible was correct about the beginning of creation, or my father, who'd told me the dinosaurs walked the earth millions of years ago." She smiled and opened her eyes again. "Such heady thoughts for a thirteen-year-old girl."

What is your point? he wanted to shout in frustration, in anger and tightly winding impatience. And yet he didn't. He simply stood there, in the chilly studio, staring at the lovely image of Mimi lost in memories of another time. Captivated, though wishing desperately he weren't.

Finally she turned and faced him, rubbing her palms along her upper sleeves to ward off the chill, gazing into his eyes from across the studio. His demeanor never wavered, but he felt a tenseness that had not been there between them before.

"That's when you walked into the morning room, Nathan," she maintained almost in a whisper. "Right in the middle of those thoughts. You wore a dark blue suit and had perfectly cut hair. I thought you looked so handsome as a man of twenty, and I'm certain I gaped at you. But you just smiled as you walked toward me and introduced yourself as a student of Professor Owen's—"

"I remember this, Mimi," he interjected flatly, though unwilling to add more. He didn't want to discuss that he remembered her, too, and that she wore . . . yellow, he thought. And that her eyes—so beautiful and sharply intelligent for a girl, he remembered thinking—had jolted him. He'd never taken note of their color until the night of the Crystal Palace opening, when she appeared before him as a fully developed woman, but he remembered vividly their brilliance in the child.

She began to stroll toward him, which in turn caused his nerves to jump in acute awareness. He didn't want her close to him, didn't want to detect her spicy scent, feel her warmth. It would be too much. But the arrogance in him kept him from retreating and he gripped the tabletop even harder, the cold wood slicing into his palms.

"Do you remember what happened next,

Nathan?" she asked, her head slanted to one side as she watched him.

He straightened a little. "No, not precisely, but it certainly couldn't be relevant to this conversation—"

"Oh, it's quite relevant, I assure you," she broke in, eyes focused on his as if searching for memories. "You sat beside me on the sofa for a few minutes, very properly, of course, and studied my artistic endeavor of the Stegosaurus, commenting here and there about my proportions, my attention to detail. I thought you were so knowledgeable and so attractive, smelled so heavenly—"

"Mimi—"

"And not once did you say anything to suggest I shouldn't be sketching something for a man's mind and knowledge. I'd found that so . . . odd, actually, and marvelous at the same time."

She finally reached him as he now stood beside the table, legs spread wide, hands folded over his chest to keep her at a distance, to keep himself from reaching for her, refusing to back away, lest she think him a coward for running. But he could detect her scent, feel her warmth as he'd feared he would, and he fought the raging battle within that urged him to take her in his arms, steal the comfort, and forget the past.

"Why are you telling me this, Mimi?" he asked in a rough voice of caution, eyes narrowed as they remained locked with hers.

She didn't move. "The most remarkable thing happened when you sat beside me on that sofa ten years ago, Nathan. I asked you, with a casual air, of your opinions of the dinosaurs and their existence in this world, if God created them to tempt us into straying from his written word, or if the earth is indeed perhaps millions of years old." She dropped her tone to a mere whisper. "You said to me, 'Miss Marsh, you have asked an ageless question. I don't know.' "

Nathan tried to recall the incident to no avail. In reality, his response was likely an answer said to brush off serious discussion with an adolescent girl. And yet he'd never been one to make light of scientific theory, regardless of who posed the question.

"What is your point?" he pressed, gazing into her dark eyes, noting the seriousness to grace her fine-boned features. Her nearness in such total concentration put him at the verge of taking his leave for a final time, and to hell with his priceless stolen fossil, wherever it might be. To hell with all of it.

Before he could stop her, she reached out and skimmed her fingertips along his cheek. He jerked back in surprise, but it didn't sway her.

Smiling softly, she admitted, "Your answer that day was a turning point for me, Nathan. For the first time, I felt true and complete admiration for a man, and it wasn't for my father, even though I've always loved him dearly. I felt it for you."

Nathan, considerably baffled now, reached up to grab her wrist briskly, pulling her hand away from him, though he held to it firmly, if for no other reason than to keep her at a distance. She didn't even appear to notice.

"Just then my father entered the morning room," she continued, stepping closer so that her black gown wrapped around his shoes and shins. "I sat there staring at you and thinking how handsome and smart and different you were, and you turned to my father and said, 'Well, Sir Harold, your lovely daughter asks questions as thought-provoking as Professor Owen's students. And she's so artistically gifted I'm surprised you haven't let her work with you.' "

She swallowed, and he watched the movement at her tapered throat, watched her visibly gain strength as she revealed what he could never guess.

"Don't you understand, Nathan?" she asked in a fervent whisper, leaning forward so that her hot breath brushed his cheeks. "In less than ten minutes of time, you had done three things that were so astonishing to me they changed my life. You had first admitted that a philosophical conjecture perplexed you and you didn't know the answer. I'd never been told that by a man before. Men in my experience knew everything or changed the topic. But instead of waving it off and discussing the weather or my health or society, or some such nonsense, you simply answered me up front and honestly.

"Then my father steps in the room and you tell him, to his face, that you considered me as intelligent as a man who studies paleontology with one of the most forward thinkers in the world. Regardless of whether such a statement was true, which I'm sure it wasn't, you said this to my *father*. Finally, when you have me completely spellbound, you tell him I have a great talent and should be doing what he does! Can you stop for a moment and imagine what these three things could mean to a thirteen-year-old girl who'd been told all her life that she would never be as smart as a man, that she would never be taken seriously as a dinosaur sculptor like her brilliant father, and that men had all the answers and to leave it at that without questioning them?"

She focused intently on him, slowly shaking her head. "You, Nathan, admitted all of these things that I knew were true, and you did it in front of me *and* my father, sincerely and without hesitation. I couldn't believe it, and long after you'd left that day, I thought of you, wanted to see you again, to learn more about you. I thoroughly enjoyed your company each time you came to my home to see my father for professional reasons. You engaged me with your clever wit and candid charm, and over the years I began to ache for a time when I could know you as a woman."

Nathan could feel his heart start to pound hard against the walls of his chest, could feel her speeding pulse beneath his fingertips as he clung to her warm wrist.

"I can't say I was in love with you, Nathan, because I was so young and saw you infrequently. But I will say you mesmerized me, and I'd never admired a person so much."

She took his hand with her free one, closing her delicate palm over his knuckles. He tried once to pull away but she held tightly to him.

"But the night I saw you again at the Crystal Palace opening, I knew your past didn't matter," she revealed in a passionate breath. "I knew your upbringing had made you the man you were, that your class had sculpted you into an intelligent, intense, driven person that I wanted as a woman wants a man. That's why I came to talk to you while you stood alone by your display. That's why I pretended to be hot so you'd suggest a walk in the outdoors—and if you hadn't, I would have. That's why I told you Carter had asked for my hand. And *that's* why I wanted you to kiss me—to see if you held the same interest in me that I did you. And you *did*, Nathan. You *did*, and I *wanted* you."

He couldn't deny that it had happened like that. He'd felt it at the time, her interest, her persistence, the hoping within him that she'd desire him as a red-blooded man. And then, not an hour later, came the awful moment of his ruin, when he couldn't look at her because he feared he'd witness her pity. But he'd felt her gaze on him that evening, as eager and wonderful as he'd felt when her lips scorched his with a most marvelous kiss. It also explained something else, something that had troubled him from the day he'd come back into her life. If she told him the truth now, and he believed at gut level she did, she would not have been the one to initiate his professional disgrace. She'd wanted him, not Carter, and his ruin was Carter's gain—in every way, including having Mimi for the first time, which suddenly enraged him as nothing ever had before. He should have been her first lover, and that precious part of her she could give to only one man had been stolen from him as well. He knew they'd shared something strong beneath the moonlit sky that night in Hyde Park, something different and life changing and wonderful. If only it hadn't been for the person who had taken everything that mattered.

Rain pelted the glass in waves now as the storm

outside grew violent. As savage as the one inside of him. He gazed into her eyes, swimming with uncertainty, with desolation and sadness in light of his reaction to her confession. And in that brief half of a second, his wounded heart betrayed him.

He jerked her against him, releasing her wrist as his arm came around her waist, her breasts flattening against his shirtfront. She gasped in shock at his boldness, but she didn't fight him. She breathed heavily, quickly, staring up to his hardened face, her gaze determined and begging with a hope that tore at him inside.

But instantaneously, and without warning, his desire for her ignited—stronger than his desire to push her away in defense of his fury. He felt the heat of her searing him, inside and out, her breath coming fast, her heart pounding against his chest, in tune to the desperate thudding of his own. The moment between them now enclosed them from the outside world, enraptured him, seized him, enraged him that he couldn't get inside of her deep enough to make her understand, to make her trust. In a blur of frustration and anger, coupled with an ache so suddenly intense, Nathan groaned and covered her mouth with his own—a hard, frenzied kiss of lust, and longing for everything, and despair, above all else.

She responded immediately, as if expecting this reaction from him, with one little whimper, then gasping, clinging, as she frantically teased his lips and tongue. In a fierce drive of passion, Nathan grabbed her bottom covered with thick skirts, and pulled her harshly to him, leaning back against the table at his thighs, the softness of her in sharp contrast to the wood that cut as deeply as her secrets.

The heat grew intense, blurring the details, the thoughts and all too recent memories that warned him against his carnal intentions. He molded himself as tightly as he could to her clothed body, inhaled the unique scent of femininity coupled with the smell of rain and hardwood, clay and cement dust, and the contrast inflamed him. He wanted her now, in the hard, cold studio, amid the bones and skeletons of an ancient past. And she knew it.

Quickly, holding her securely, he turned them both completely around so that her legs backed up against the table, then lifted her to sit upon it.

Their kiss grew fast and furious, swelling to a fervor of erotic taste and scents, of blended moaning and mingled breaths. Nathan caressed her breasts over her gown as she hurriedly reached for the buttons on his pants.

Hard and brimming with need, he felt her fingers on him, and he groaned, pulled back, gazed into her hot, burning eyes.

"Yes," she gasped, licking her lips, encircling him with her palm.

He inhaled sharply, then reached up beneath her skirt, quickly, hoping. Layers of slips and crinolines but no whalebone, thank God. He shoved the material up to her waist, his palms skimming the soft linen clinging to her calves and thighs.

She whimpered, dropping her head back, and through the faded light he noticed the throbbing of her pulse in her neck. He brought his lips forward and touched it, biting gently as she accepted the torment, as she probed him intimately, drawing him closer with each scorching caress.

As he neared his own inner explosion, he pulled away from her touch and lowered his head to the heat between her legs, his fingers fumbling with silky material until it opened, until she opened for him.

Mimi lay flat on the table, breathing hard and fast, moving her hips up to meet him.

He smelled her, craved her, and without warning, placed his tongue on her. She gasped, jerking once, but he pressed her down with his hands on her hips. He flicked his tongue, tasting the sweetness of woman, giving in to her desire. She ran her fingers through his hair, pushing herself closer to him, to that exquisite edge of surrender.

"Make me—" She sucked in a breath. "Please—"

Nathan couldn't take the wait.

Pulling back, he stood, staring at her beautiful face bathed in passion, its softness in bold contrast to the rough wooden table beneath her and the sharp, brittle fossils surrounding them, his intense anger mixing with a rare and wondrous desire for her alone. And then he pushed himself inside of her, slowly, filling her, feeling her inner walls close around him as he encased himself ever deeper, as she loved him with caressing gentleness.

He pulled her hips tightly against his and closed his eyes, pausing only for seconds. And then he placed his fingers where she needed his touch and began to stroke her as he moved within her in a finely tuned rhythm.

He ground his teeth together, squeezing his lids

shut, moving faster, harder, perfectly. She panted, lifting her body with need, urging him closer. And then, as he sensed her rising to her peak, he placed his free hand on her mouth to cover her moans of pleasure should she scream. She was so close, so quickly . . .

She climaxed suddenly, with him inside her, shoving her body up from the table, her hips to his hand, clutching his thighs with her nails, biting down hard on the meat of his palm, sobbing her release that surged from deep in her throat to slice through his soul.

The ravishing pain, the stroking muscles, the feeling of being inside of her as she came for him—

"Oh, God," he whispered to the cold night air. "Oh, God, Mimi—"

And with one final, penetrating thrust, he lost himself deeply within, the heat of the moment and the fulfilling pleasure of release casting shadows of doubt and radiance over a new memory—another heartache—to last a lifetime.

Groaning, he slumped forward, over her, burying his face in her hot neck, feeling the quick pulse against his cheek, her labored breathing.

She gasped for air, shaking beneath him, clinging to him with her arms wrapped around his shoulders.

He didn't want it to end; he wanted instead to wrap her in his embrace forever.

"You told me you loved me," he whispered feverishly, feeling the ache in his chest as the words poured from his mouth onto her hot skin.

She whimpered. "I do."

He squeezed her tightly against him. "Then tell me who betrayed me, Mimi. If you love me, *tell* me."

A low sob tore from her throat. "I can't. Oh, God, I want to, but I *can't*."

For seconds he did nothing. Disbelief and shock sliced into him as he realized that even joined intimately, even knowing he'd left a part of himself within her this night in the greatest of all risks, she still would not confess the truth to him. Nothing in Nathan's experience had ever cut so deeply and hurt so much.

When she added nothing more, when their breathing had slowed, and the passion had subsided to a dull ache of lost hope, Nathan slid from the warmness of her and stood stiffly at the table in the cold night air.

He stared down to her flushed face and pain-filled eyes, adjusting his clothing in a matter of seconds, refusing to look away from her.

Fury tore him apart at the core, as he finally understood that her love for him, whatever it meant to her, held restrictions. Restrictions he could not accept.

He attempted to step away, but she took fast action of her own, sitting up and grabbing his shirt, wrapping her arms around his neck, holding him firmly, weaving her fingers through his hair as she lifted her forehead to touch his.

He didn't move his rigid stance.

"Please don't leave me, Nathan," she begged through a ragged breath, tears of a dying dream now streaming down her cheeks. "Not like this. Not now."

He swallowed harshly to fight his turbulent emotions, bracing his palms on her hips, his breathing shaky, eyes squeezed shut. "I can't accept love with conditions, Mimi," he said huskily. "It has little value. Always, will feelings for your father, and your husband, mean more to you than me."

"No . . ."

He pushed away from her forcefully then, not daring to look at her pleading face that would forever remain in his memory, his heart clinging to her warmth, her scent, her inner loveliness.

And then he turned from the partial gift she offered, and walked stiffly from her studio for a final time, her muffled sobs echoing in his mind long after he'd gone.

Chapter 19

～⁓◯◯⁓～

The drizzle of the morning had turned to a roaring rain. Still Mimi insisted on visiting the site. It had taken a full two days to get here, and she didn't want to waste the time already spent on the journey. Besides, she rationalized, it was springtime. It always rained in the spring.

The dig was a mass of organized confusion, as usual, she supposed. Of course she'd been to a quarry before with her father, but today was different. This time, traveling alone, as an adult lady of quality, she would stand out like a big black beetle on a white marble floor, and knowing that created a sort of calm apprehension within her—which only added to her severe uneasiness at seeing Nathan again.

It had been nearly twelve weeks since their emotional encounter in her studio, and still, whenever she thought about that cold, dark night, she shivered from the memory of desires he'd awakened in her, and the sense of being alone even as he'd made love to her completely and with total surrender. That was the central reason behind her unannounced visit to his place of work today—that, and the fact that she just missed him so much, much more than she'd ever thought possible.

The coach came to a stop at last, its wheels sinking into the muddy terrain. Mimi gazed out the small window, her stomach wound tightly as she gripped her gloved fingers together on her lap. As of yet, she hadn't been noticed by the men at the site, though one or two had glanced up to the coach with curious frowns. She supposed most laborers arrived on horseback or foot for this kind of work, though that was something she'd never really thought about before now.

At last her driver clicked the latch on the door and opened it. A rush of cool, wet wind struck her bare face, but her hooded black pelisse otherwise kept her from feeling the brunt of the steady downpour as she quickly descended the steps.

"Anything else, ma'am?"

"No; wait here, please. I won't be long."

The driver nodded once. "As you wish."

They'd parked close to the center of the quarry's edge, near the base of the operation. Most of the men employed to dig now stood under two large, square tarpaulins supported by steel bars, which kept the rain off them as they waited for it to subside a little to return to their work. Some mingled, speaking in low tones, some sipped from tin cups, others stood silently as they eyed her curiously with a frankness they didn't try to hide. It all but annoyed her. She was a lady here on business, not some prim and proper miss out for a rainy stroll at a scientific excavation, regardless of how out of place she appeared right now.

She had yet to see Nathan, but as she took a moment to become acquainted with her surroundings, she heard the unmistakable droning of his deep, powerful voice.

Her pulse began to race; her mouth went dry. But it was too late to turn back now.

Gathering strength within, Mimi clutched her reticule against her chest with warm gloved hands, and braving the steady rain, began to walk to the second of the two tentlike structures, toward the sound of commanding instructions coming from the man she knew so well.

He stood in the center, with men in dirty overcoats positioned about him—some sitting on logs, some on the damp ground, most standing, listening to him with varying degrees of concentration.

But it was Nathan himself who engaged her attention immediately. He wore an old cream-colored linen shirt, unbuttoned to expose a smattering of dark hair, and it clung to his broad, firmly muscled chest from exposure to the wet air. Old and faded brown trousers hugged his thighs, and his hair, silky and rain-soaked, hung over his forehead as he focused on a large, oblong sheet of paper—a map of the dig, probably—laid out on the top of a wooden water barrel that he used as a temporary table in front of him.

Unnoticed by the men milling around him, Mimi remained quiet in the distance, her hood pulled over her head to keep the rain off, listening to him give directions and orders to those under his supervision. He looked good enough to devour, and stately enough, even as he now stood informally in front of common men, to be in charge of the grandest group of scholars at the most respected of learning institutions in the country. She knew many gentlemen, born into the best families and raised to be intellectuals, who wouldn't be caught dead taking charge of a group of dirty men hovering cold above a muddy hole in the ground. Not one person she knew, she thought proudly, could hold a candle to Nathan Price.

"I don't care what the devil he told you, Charlie, you can't just pull it from the ground without care. If the claw was found at a right angle"—he twisted the sheet of paper to his left, studying it intently— "then the thigh bone is . . . here. No doubt at all." He pointed to the drawing, then looked up to the man in front of him, his features taut and pulled down in annoyance. "Be careful, and slow, even in this godforsaken weather. I want zero damage to the finds, gentlemen. And if you have any trouble, *ask* me. I'm going to be working on the Hylaeosaur on the north end with John Longfellow, and . . ." he glanced around him, "and Phillip Reed." He ran his fingers through his hair. "As you know, we're on a very tight schedule, so there's no excuse for idleness. Pick up where you left off yesterday—"

"What about the bloody rain, Professor," someone grunted in poor English. "Nobody said nuffin' 'bout diggin' in mud."

Nathan's expression hardened as he stared the man down. "Ignore it, work hard, or I'll replace you, in which case you won't have any work at all," he replied flatly.

Low murmurs of irritation—or acceptance—ensued as Nathan stood tall and peered over the drenched and shivering crowd. "Any *other* reasonable quest—"

That's when he saw her, and Mimi's heart nearly stopped.

His mouth dropped open just slightly in surprise, and then he abruptly shut it.

Mimi drew in a slow, deep breath to stay her rapidly dwindling composure as the other men followed his gaze and turned to look at her. But she stood her ground, shoulders erect, her bearing confident at least in appearance, especially in front of strange men of questionable education who studied her with varying degrees of fascination.

Keeping her eyes on Nathan, she was suddenly unsure whether to smile at him vaguely or to appear matter-of-fact about her being at his excavation site. She decided simply to stand there, waiting for him to make the first move.

After a moment's hesitation, he recovered himself and ordered his men to work. In a flurry of movement and grumbles, the group reluctantly left the tarpaulin, leaving him standing there more or less alone. One man asked a question she couldn't hear, and Nathan answered it still gazing at her. The worker glanced briefly in her direction again, then wandered off.

She began to walk toward the shelter, glad for it, as her outer garments were becoming saturated. He hadn't moved, but he hadn't looked away, either.

She approached him cautiously, but determined, unconcerned about the mud clinging to the bottom of her skirts. "Professor Price," she said affably over the sound of pattering rain.

"Why, Mrs. Sinclair," he drawled. "How lovely to see you here."

He was being sarcastic, of course, and even through the awkwardness between them now, she found his tone comforting. "Thank you," she responded politely.

He offered nothing more by way of pleasantries, though he did manage to cross his arms over his damp chest and lean his hip against the water barrel.

She rubbed her hands together, and took a quick peek at their surroundings to be certain their conversation would remain relatively private.

"Have you come with news, Mrs. Sinclair?"

She jerked her eyes back to lock with his, now narrowed and swimming with irritation. It flustered her.

"Stop calling me that."

He smiled wryly. "Of course. I forgot you don't care for the title."

That did it. She took a step toward him so that her rain-soaked skirt rubbed against his dirty pant legs, her lips thinned grimly, eyes flashing annoyance. "I did come with news."

A brow lifted in question, but he otherwise didn't budge. Or comment. That made her rather angry.

Leaning toward him, as closely as possible, she whispered, "I'm not carrying your child, Nathan. I thought you'd be relieved to know that."

That piece of delicate information clearly startled him, filling her with enormous satisfaction. His eyes opened wide and his expression went slack as the meaning of her words sank in. She drew back a little, smiling politely again, reaching up to pull her hood from her head.

"Are you enjoying your work here, Professor?"

He exhaled loudly through his nostrils, recovering himself to murmur, "How do you know?"

"How do I know?"

"That you're not with child."

She paused, embarrassment flooding her as her face flushed hot.

He didn't move his gaze from hers.

Clearing her throat and lifting her chin negligibly, she replied, "I know in the usual way a woman knows, Nathan."

He blinked quickly as if the whole explanation simply dawned on him. Then he looked away. "I see."

Disappointment seeped into her. She'd so hoped for more, to witness some degree of the same in him as she'd revealed the answer to what he'd surely had to have considered these last few weeks. But his voice and expression weren't telling. She supposed, though, that she should be pleased he hadn't said how glad he was to know he wouldn't be a father anytime soon. That would have been too painful for words.

For a long moment they stood beside one another, the tension mounting to a tangible thing, the rain coming down harder still to echo off the tarpaulin in an almost deafening roar.

At last he sighed and ran his palm harshly down his face. "I would hope, Mimi, that you came all the way out here to tell me something more."

That stung, she admitted, but then, she deserved his rancor. She had hurt him terribly these last few months, and although he didn't understand and she wasn't at liberty to explain, she felt his frustration as deeply as he did. She just didn't know how to express that.

Grasping her elbows with her hands, she gazed back to his face with fortitude. "I agonized for months about how to tell you what I knew, Nathan," she whispered passionately.

His jaw hardened as the only sign that he'd even heard her. It brought tears to her eyes, but she didn't look away.

"I know what this has done to you. I know what you're feeling—"

"I sincerely doubt that," he broke in.

She inhaled a deep, shaky breath, ignoring that bitter pronouncement to move on. "I thought that by giving you back your jawbone at the banquet, everything done to you would be reversed and all would start to heal—maybe not be fixed, but at least be healed."

He studied her for a moment, fairly expressionlessly, which worried her. If he felt anything but irritation, he hid it well.

At last he insisted, "You should have given me the jawbone when I first appeared on your doorstep last fall."

"I know that," she agreed without hesitation.

Such an affirmation surprised him just enough for her to notice.

Then he raised his brows to offer caustically, "And why didn't you, if not to selfishly protect your late husband?"

Mimi felt the mounting anxiety pulse through her. "What was your intention that day, Nathan?" she asked frankly, head tilted to one side.

He briefly glanced at her lips, then back to her eyes. "My intention was to discover who ruined me—"

"—And destroy my father doing it."

Rain pelted the tarpaulin now in heavy sheets, keeping them isolated from the outside world, drowning out everything but their heated exchange.

His features grew tight with anger. "You might not have had anything to do with my initial ruin, Mimi, but keeping it from me when I returned was a choice *you* made."

"And perhaps an incorrect one, I'll grant you that, Professor," she admitted sharply. "But what would you have done in my position?"

He straightened, dropping his hands to his sides in a manner of dismissal. "This conversation is pointless."

"Is it? I think it needs to be had." She moved

closer, refusing to be intimidated. "You came to my home unannounced, and after polite introductions, accused my father of stealing your treasure and ruining you. Yes, I had your nasty little fossil sitting in my attic, but if I'd handed it over to you then, what would you have done? You would have filed charges without any explanation whatever."

"That's not true," he countered, fisting his hand and pounding it once on the water barrel.

"Yes, it is," she whispered.

He said nothing but never looked away.

She stood now only inches from his face, sensing the stark, sizzling heat between them, matching his determination with every bit of strength she possessed.

"I love you, Nathan," she expressed in a fiercely quiet tone. "And you know that. But I love my family, too. I did the best thing I knew to do for you at the time without destroying them. I don't expect you to understand, or even to forgive me. But I would like to think you care enough about me to acknowledge that I've realized all along how deeply we've hurt you, and that I've never been more sorry, and felt such anguish, about any injustice done to a man in my life."

The biting wind picked up; the storm intensified as waves of cold rain swept into the side of the shelter to slap against their clothing, a witness to this equally turbulent moment between them that served as the critical junction to any future they might ever share together. Mimi could only wonder if he thought the same.

At last he asked gruffly, "Why did your father

change the fossil for the sculpture the night of the banquet?"

She swallowed, wishing desperately that she could embrace him now, comfort him, tell him everything and receive his love in return. Instead, she inhaled deeply and straightened, lowering her lashes at last. "I think that's something you need to ask him."

With that final note, she turned and stepped out into the icy downpour, letting the stinging drops strike her face without care.

Chapter 20

Nathan stood inside Sir Harold's brightly lit morning room, his side to the mantel, fingers interlocked behind his back, as he waited for the man.

Spring had arrived early this year, and a servant had placed a large crystal vase of fresh lilacs on the recently polished cherry wood tea table in front of the plum-colored sofa. The same sofa where he'd sat beside Mimi for the first time nearly eleven years ago.

Nothing had changed. The room looked exactly as it had for as long as he remembered, the walls covered with ornate flowered paper and painting after painting depicting landscapes, rose gardens, and portraits, all done by Mimi's mother when she was alive. Nathan stared at one now, a formal of Mimi and her sister Mary, that hung over the fireplace, painted when Mimi had been about ten, he surmised, or at least slightly younger than she'd been when he'd first met her.

He quickly took note of the likeness between the girls, although Mimi had a warmth and charm about her that Mary lacked. Mary, ever the cool beauty, smiled serenely, her expression vague as if afraid to reveal feelings and secrets held within for reasons only she would ever know.

Mimi, however, exuded a fiery radiance, a loveliness in her smile that enchanted even the toughest men, a daring in her exquisite eyes that beckoned, that would bring a man to his knees before he'd realized what had hit him. She was, and always would be, someone truly irresistible to him.

Nathan missed her more than he'd ever thought it possible to miss anyone. He craved her touch, her breathless, intimate voice, her honest laughter, her endless questions that made him smile in spite of the fact that his answers were never quite substantial enough to satisfy her stupendous curiosity. Not a day had gone by during the last month that he hadn't wanted to go to her. But his pride—or perhaps just tempered, lingering anger—kept him from responding to her pleas of understanding that she'd offered the day she'd come to the dig.

God, what a surprise that had been! Only Mimi would be bold enough to travel to a filthy place lacking modern conveniences and cluttered by colorful, questionable men. When he'd first set eyes on her that morning, after assuring himself that she actually stood tall in his presence, displaying a unique and dignified grace, he could hardly keep from smiling at her gall. He'd known, of course, that she wasn't pregnant—not because she hadn't told him sooner, but because he'd cared enough about her to track her whereabouts and concerns these last few weeks, through Justin, who admittedly was becoming rather annoyed at having to keep up with the widow's movements for his friend's sake. Nathan knew that the last time they'd made love, regardless of whether the intimacy had been tinged with regret and anger, there had been an extraordinary bonding between them, and if a child had resulted, he would have done the honorable thing. And he would have been relatively at peace with it.

But he refused to beg for something she didn't intend to reveal to him. If she loved him as she said she did, she'd confide in him. Or at least, that was how he'd felt until she'd come to the excavation site. Now he realized with certainty that she wanted him to confront her father, though for what purpose exactly, he couldn't be sure. The thought of meeting Sir Harold face to face, after all the bitterness between them, had kept him from doing just that for weeks since her surprising visit to suggest it. But now, at last, he would learn the truth. It had taken him some time and careful thinking to put the pieces together, and to calm himself enough inside to challenge Sir Harold without breaking the man's good neck, though it remained entirely true that he would never do anything to harm Mimi's father physically, and both the man and his beautiful, conniving daughter undoubtedly knew that.

Sighing, he ran his fingers through his hair, then turned once more to the sofa. That's when he noticed Mary standing in the doorway, hands clasped in front of her, watching him with piercing blue eyes that told him nothing.

"Miss Marsh," he said in staid greeting.

She smiled pleasantly as was customary for the mistress of a house when receiving a guest. "Good afternoon, Professor Price. Would you care to be seated?"

"I think I'd rather stand, thank you," he replied with a curt nod, afraid if he lowered his body onto the sofa seat the tension coursing through him would be noticeable. He also preferred to be standing when at last he addressed his adversary.

"My mother painted that portrait of Mimi and me," she announced with erect shoulders as she slowly glided into the room, her gown of soft pink muslin swishing around her ankles.

"It's a very good likeness," was the most gracious thing he could think of to offer. She would no doubt detect any false adulation on his part when they both had to be aware of his reason for being in her home.

She continued to study him with keen eyes, her hands now behind her back as she rounded the sofa and sat upon it stiffly. She didn't have Mimi's luscious figure, but Mary Marsh had curves in all the right places and carried herself with precision, ever a lovely woman of elegance and shrewd intellect that she undoubtedly used to her advantage. For the first time Nathan wondered why such a lady of twenty-eight years had never married. Clearly she could have any man of her choice. But of course he would never ask. A question of that indelicate nature would be highly inappropriate and none of his concern.

"My father has not yet returned from his meeting with Mr. Waterhouse Hawkins, though he should be arriving shortly," she maintained, a gentle frown crossing her brow as she glanced critically at his attire.

Nathan stiffened, knowing she found fault in his brown morning suit that was not of this year's fashion. Too damn bad, he decided. He'd come to accept that he'd never fit into her social world, and at this point, after everything he'd been through, he couldn't care any less.

"I'll wait."

Her eyes widened just enough for him to know he'd surprised her with his terseness. *But I'm not of your class, Miss Marsh.*

She breathed deeply, folding her hands in her lap, and for the first time, Nathan suspected she wanted something from him herself—or to have a little discussion of their own.

He never dropped his probing gaze, and after a moment, she shifted her body awkwardly, giving him his first real suspicion that she felt intensely nervous to be sitting in the room alone with him. Of course, that was ridiculous. She was perfectly safe with a household of servants no doubt spying on them and polishing already clean silver within hearing distance. So was it something else?

"Are you in love with my sister?"

He felt gut-punched. *Jesus.*

"I beg your pardon?" he blurted.

She raised her chin but her eyes narrowed as they remained locked with his. "I asked you if you are in love with my sister," she said again, crisply.

He recovered himself enough to murmur, "I don't believe that's any of your business, Miss Marsh."

She nodded. "Fair enough, Professor Price."

Yes, this particular lady was very sly indeed.

"She's in love with you, you know," Mary asserted, after a moment of powerful silence.

Nathan suddenly grew hot all over and wished he was anywhere but here, hoped that his face didn't glow as it reddened. "I'm not sure that's a concern of yours, either."

She cocked her head to one side, studying him, or rather evaluating him, he suspected.

"What do you intend to do about it?"

He raised his brows in feigned innocence. "Do about what?"

Her perfectly pink lips turned up in a half-smile. "Come now, Professor. Certainly you've thought about her feelings for you, and yours for her."

I've tried not to.

He remained silent, his expression like stone.

She sighed, exasperated, but she never lost her composure. "What do you intend to do with Mimi?"

"I intend to do nothing with Mimi," he retorted at once, bitterly.

"She'll be out of mourning soon."

He had never clearly considered that fact, which shocked him in a manner he couldn't describe or possibly understand. Especially right now. He didn't want to dwell on such a poignant truth, and on what might have been. But it did make him suspicious that such an acknowledgment came from Mimi's sister, a class-conscious lady who looked upon him disagreeably.

"I suppose she will be," he returned derisively, staring at her frankly, oddly proud that he'd been able to respond with nothing, though adult enough to realize he was being childish and that she knew it as well.

Still, his mood seemed to quell the questions. He could sense her irritation, too, and for a few long seconds she simply looked at him.

Nathan considered himself on display, yet he awkwardly stood his ground, hands clasped behind his back, acutely uncomfortable in Sir Harold's quiet home, agitated by the pungent smell of lilacs, nervous about the encounter to come, and now besieged by a lady of quality too clever for her own good. He'd laugh if he weren't so annoyed.

Suddenly he detected the slightest slump of her shoulders as she dropped her gaze to her lap and began rubbing her thumbs together.

"Why are you here?" she asked, her voice a tone softer.

That was none of her business either, but she certainly knew very well his reasons for an unannounced visit.

"I'm here to confront Sir Harold," he replied without pretense, feeling marvelous just saying it aloud. "I want some final answers that I believe only he can give."

"I see." She waited, then gazed up to him again, her blue eyes penetrating. "He is an old man, Professor Price."

Nathan shifted from one foot to the other, uncertain of her meaning but unwilling to give in to persuasion. "I realize he's not a young man, Miss Marsh, but neither would I consider him old."

She stood abruptly, smoothing her skirt with both palms, eyeing him directly. "He is an old man," she repeated with caution. "His best years are behind him."

He watched her, noting a twinge of sadness in her voice coupled strangely with an assurance of bearing. The woman was a complex creature—but then, most women in his experience were.

"I'll do my best not to shock him," he said dryly.

Her lips thinned, but she didn't offer a retort. Instead, she inhaled deeply and tried to smile.

"I'll have refreshments brought to you, then. It may be a while until he arrives."

With that she turned on her heels and, carrying herself with marked dignity and a lift of her skirts, waltzed from the room.

Nathan stared at the doorway, thinking how very peculiar it was that convention forced a hostess to serve tea and cakes to a guest who had more or less insulted her.

Chapter 21

‹‹‹—◯◯—›››

He waited three quarters of an hour, with growing impatience, drinking two cups of surprisingly good tea because he had nothing better to do with his hands or his time. The room had grown stuffy, and a servant, who never once even peeked his way, had wandered into the morning room to crack open a window to the garden. It helped a little, though this particular April had been rather wet and a light shower had already begun to fall. Still, Nathan had to wonder if Mary had ordered it done. Probably, though he hadn't seen her again since she'd posed her frightfully intimate questions, then left him alone to his musings.

Agitated, Nathan paced the rose embroidered rug in front of the grate, every now and then glancing at the portrait of Mimi as a child, reliving the night the fully grown woman had intertwined her legs with his and given herself to him with a yielding sweetness that still took his breath when he thought about it. He would most certainly never forget it.

Finally he heard the front door creak open, and he braced himself for the confrontation to come, fighting his anxiety by shoving his hands in his suit coat pockets to keep them calm.

It was time.

Sir Harold's footsteps echoed in the foyer, and then the man himself appeared at the morning room door, stopping short as he gazed upon Nathan for the first time since the night of the banquet almost three months ago.

His astute brown eyes opened wide upon initial sight, his features going slack with a startled realization of who stood before him in his home. Then he blinked and straightened a little, gathering his faculties as he pulled his damp overcoat off his shoulders and handed it to a waiting parlor maid. She immediately turned and walked away with it, leaving the two of them alone.

Nathan had to admire how unaffected Marsh appeared at such a disconcerting moment. And it had to be disconcerting for him, since the last time they'd been together, he'd all but accused the man of ruining him. Still, the surprise he now witnessed on Marsh's face had been well worth the wait.

"Sir Harold," he drawled with a tip of his forehead.

The older man's side whiskers flared at his

cheeks as his mouth tightened. "Well, if it isn't the renowned paleontologist Nathan Price."

Nathan had no idea if the man mocked him, but the flat comment sparked his anger anew. "Surprised to see me?" he asked soberly, squeezing his hands into fists in his pockets.

"Not at all," the older man remarked. "I'm actually surprised it took you this long."

"This long?"

"To confront me. I expected you weeks ago."

That Sir Harold used the same word he had to describe their upcoming meeting sucked the wind from him, but he lifted a brow in feigned nonchalance. "Indeed," he returned. "Then let's get to it. I would like a word with you in private."

"I imagine you would," Sir Harold acknowledged, not in the least daunted by that announcement. He turned abruptly and thundered, "Gracie!"

The parlor maid appeared at once as if she'd been standing in his shadow.

"Sir?"

"We'll take tea immediately, in my study."

She curtsied and left.

More tea. Nathan winced. Right now he'd rather have a whiskey.

"Follow me," Marsh ordered with a wave of his hand, turning to stride purposefully from the morning room.

With a deep breath for confidence, Nathan trailed behind him, moving rigidly across the circular foyer and into the man's private study.

It had been years since he'd been in this room, but it remained the same, ever so much a reflection of the man himself. The wooden fixtures and furniture spoke of exotic adventures, with several pieces of fine ivory, jade, and carved wood gracing his dark walnut mantel and bookshelves. Above the fireplace hung a portrait of fine quality, the figure of a gracefully beautiful blond woman in her mid-twenties, Nathan guessed, dressed in deep purple and wearing a serene smile. Mimi's mother, undoubtedly. Both her daughters bore a striking resemblance to her.

"Care to be seated?" Sir Harold offered, walking straight to a walnut and inlaid bronze sideboard beside a tall window.

He stood erect, hands behind his back, next to the grate. "No, thank you."

The older man chuckled without looking at him, reaching inside an opened cupboard. "Sit down, Nathan."

The mood in the room had shifted to one of weariness. No longer did he feel anger and resentment coming from the man, but a tiredness of bone and a softening of heart.

It put Nathan on edge, but he did as told, sitting awkwardly in a cushioned wing chair opposite an oblong, walnut desk covered with papers and an array of charcoal sketches.

Sir Harold raised himself from the lower sideboard cupboard, holding a bottle. Turning to Nathan, he smirked and lifted it. "Can't have tea without brandy at a time like this."

Thank God.

Nathan nodded, but said nothing, observing Marsh's stiff movements and enlarged knuckles that signaled advanced arthritis. No wonder he kept spirits at his convenient disposal. Drink undoubtedly numbed the pain considerably.

In what couldn't have been better timing, a servant gave a shallow knock at the door, then entered carrying a china tray with matching cups and saucers, silver spoons, milk, and sugar, which she dutifully sat on the desk in front of him. She swiftly returned to the door and shut it quietly behind her without a word.

Nathan ignored the refreshments until Sir Harold moved behind his desk, pulled out his chair, opened the bottle, and poured a generous amount of brandy into each china cup, forgoing the tea completely.

"No need to dirty a snifter," he said presently. "These will work just as well." He then took the full teapot, turned to his right, and dumped the contents into the base of a large green plant of unknown variety sitting sturdily next to the window. "This keeps it healthy. Mary gave that to me two Christmases ago. Sometimes she wonders why it's growing better than all the others."

It was, too. Nathan suppressed the urge to smile, noting how the brandy in his cup looked exactly like tea, and wondering if the man had learned this bit of deception when his wife was alive.

Sir Harold at last shuffled a few papers out of the way and placed the bottle on the desk then sat down in his chair with some difficulty, stretching out and taking a long sip of the soothing liquid.

"Well," he began evenly, after a moment of

strained silence. "I hear you've recently been working for Owen at one of the quarries in Tilgate Forest."

So Marsh wanted to begin their little discussion slowly, on cordial terms. Perfectly fine with him.

"We traveled there together last month, yes." He reached for his cup. "I dug for a time, then helped him catalogue a few recently unearthed bones."

"Hylaeosaur?"

"Exactly." Nathan shrugged. "Nothing remarkable, but the work is good."

"I suppose being away is the reason you haven't shown up here until now."

And the reason I have.

He shifted his body in his chair. "Yes."

Sir Harold frowned and looked into his cup. "It must be nice to be working again in so prestigious a manner, and with someone of Owen's reputation."

Nice?

He cleared his throat and sat forward, his feet planted firmly on the floor, elbows on knees, as he turned his cup in his fingers. "I'm relieved, actually. If it hadn't been for Mimi and her brilliant sculpture, I would still be looking for menial labor. As it is, I'm able to again do what I was trained to do. It's very satisfying and rewarding."

"Ah, yes. Mimi."

Nathan felt the urgency within him rise. His moment drew near, the feeling in the air one of bleakness charged with excitement, an odd sensation, to be sure.

He took a swallow of delicious brandy, letting it slide down his throat, warming him on the inside.

Sir Harold watched him carefully, his head tilted to one side, eyelids thinned in assessment. "You know, Nathan, it wasn't the sculpture that had everybody so enthralled at the banquet; it was you, or more rightly, the existence of your original find that you'd at last been able to prove, and at the most splendid of moments."

Sir Harold had told him this? He didn't know whether to be flattered that the man had admitted it to him, or irritated that he would assume Nathan wouldn't have known. "I'm aware of what happened that evening, sir," he retorted somewhat caustically.

The older man grunted. "You made a fool of me."

Nathan felt a sharp pain in his gut, and he made every attempt to suppress the vague presence of guilt. "From the very beginning, I've only wanted to right this wrong," he answered tersely, voice lowered. "It was never my intention to make a fool of you—"

"Oh, good God, Nathan, I knew what the bloody hell was happening, why you were there," Marsh interjected irritably. He tossed down the remainder of his brandy and grabbed the bottle for a refill.

Nathan watched him, unsure. "What exactly *did* you know, Sir Harold?"

Marsh sighed and leaned back heavily in his chair, eyeing him cautiously, swishing his brandy around in his teacup by the dainty pink handle. After a moment of silence, he murmured softly, "What do you feel for my daughter, exactly?"

Why the hell do these people keep asking me that?

He squirmed in his seat and replied coolly, "I thought we were discussing the banquet."

The corners lifted at the older man's mouth, driving his wrinkles deeper into his face. "Isn't everything about Mimi? The banquet? The sculpture? The jawbone?" He paused, then whispered, "The devastation that befell you at the Crystal Palace two years ago?"

Nathan suddenly felt like crawling out of his skin—or exploding in fury and crushing everything in the room. This whole affair from the beginning perplexed him to the point of insanity; the frustration he experienced right now nearly provoked him into jumping across the desk and wrapping his hands around Sir Harold's thick neck. Squeezing.

Instead, as gentility prevailed, he drew a long, deep breath for continued strength and lifted his cup to his lips with good manners, tactfully gulping down the remainder of his brandy, then leaning over to help himself to more. Marsh only waited, watching with a forthright gaze.

"Why is this all about Mimi?" he finally muttered, his voice sounding cold and distant, even to him.

Sir Harold never looked away. "She's always been a little bit in love with you, you know."

That did it. Nathan bolted from his chair, his brandy sloshing over the sides of his cup, which he licked with his tongue regardless of the social gaffe he committed in doing so. He paced the carpet in front of the mantel, clutching the pink handle of his cup, jumbled thoughts reeling in his mind.

"I want to know why you stole my jawbone two

years ago, Sir Harold," he said in a ragged whisper. He turned to the man, facing him directly, his gaze piercing with a final insistence. "I'm so damn tired of the innuendoes and lies and irrelevant excuses for answers. I want the goddamn truth!"

Marsh never faltered. For minutes—or hours, it seemed—he sat unruffled, staring at Nathan candidly from across his desk. And then at long last he gradually dropped his gaze and lowered his cup to its saucer.

"I never stole your jawbone, Nathan," he said huskily, his tone holding a tinge of sadness.

Nathan brushed over that and went rigid again, head to toe, pinching the cup handle with enough force to turn his fingers white. "Then if it wasn't you, tell me who did. I know you know the answer to that one. Give it to me."

Sir Harold scratched his chin, stalling.

Nathan had had enough.

In two quick steps he stood before the desk, lowering his teacup with a hard *clink* to the saucer, then gripping the edges of the walnut wood as he loomed over his adversary of nearly three years. It was a very gratifying moment.

"What happened," he articulated in deadly quiet, "the night of the Palace opening?"

Sir Harold appeared undaunted, but he adjusted his body a little where he sat. Finally, in a tone cracking with hidden emotion, he whispered, "You were deceived by my family. For me."

At long last . . .

Nathan stood where he was, still and silent, staring into the man's tired, pain-filled eyes. If he'd expected the truth to feel liberating in nature, he'd been wrong. Horribly wrong. In a manner of speaking this truth, the truth that his honor had been deliberately stolen from him by someone he'd admired personally, an intelligent man with whom he'd worked, challenged, and socialized on a professional level, hurt more than he had ever expected it would.

Sir Harold wiped a palm down his face. "You've got to understand that this was never about you. She never meant to do *you* any harm, to ruin *you*," he stressed gruffly. "And after everything happened that night, she truly wished it had never taken place." He shook his head in negation and swallowed. "But love for an aging father is blind."

Nathan felt a dark coldness deep inside of him, felt his heart stop in his chest, his throat tighten, his breath press against his lungs.

Mimi.

Oh, God, and she had told him she loved him . . .

The room began to reel before him and he clutched the table with both hands, his mouth dry, unable to say anything should he try. Then he stumbled back a foot until he fell once again into the chair, his mind overflowing with disbelief—and an ageless sorrow. The knife thrust couldn't have been any more real.

"Why?" he managed to mumble on an aching breath.

Sir Harold stared at him openly, pressing his lips together to prevent tears, before replying, "Look at my hands, Nathan."

It took several seconds for those words to seep in.

And then, very slowly, Nathan lowered his gaze to the table to observe the rugged, aging arthritic hands of a distinguished, gifted sculptor. Hands that could hardly move, much less nimbly create. In that observation lay the answer. Sculpture, not science, had been the motivation behind his disgrace. Sculpture had been the key.

He should have known.

He glanced up at Marsh, speechless for the first time that he could recall, knowing the poignant moment between them now would be ingrained in his memory forever. Suddenly the reality of what had happened that long-ago night at the Crystal Palace began to shine through the fog as the missing pieces fell into place.

He'd been right from the beginning. Carter didn't have the nerve, the cleverness to steal a jawbone of significant worth, nor did he realize at the time that Owen's money would come to him should the arrogant Professor Price fail in his new endeavor. Money had never been the issue, nor Mimi's desire to sculpt, nor even the unpretentious decision to ruin purposely a pompous man who'd pretended to excel within a class in which he did not belong. The answer, simply enough, lay in the love of a child for her adored father, her famous father, who was slowly losing his ability to create, to maintain his prestige and respect while earning a living as a sculptor for the greatest scientists of their time.

Nathan rubbed his palms along his thighs, horribly distressed, fidgety, and at the same time inexplicably moved. Unable to comment, he stood abruptly and turned away from Sir Harold's steady gaze, raking his fingers through his hair as he stepped once again toward the cold fireplace. Arms at his sides, palms fisted, he stared down at the empty grate, lost in his own musings, realizing how little his sense of self-importance had really mattered to anyone else, and how, in an instant of time, his future had been markedly and forever changed by a woman who had befriended him, tamed him, seduced him, and then professed to love him.

The pain he felt inside at that moment was beyond anything he could ever have imagined.

"When did she do it?" he asked quietly, minutes later, studying the ornate brass andirons, trying to distance himself from the part of him that had fallen under her spell, the part of the man who'd made love to her.

"The afternoon of the opening," Marsh disclosed, his chair creaking from his weight as he slumped into it. "She'd gone in when the display rooms weren't yet full and the Palace not yet open, lifted it onto a rolling board, covered it, and walked out. Just as simply as that. I imagine she thought if anyone asked, she could easily say she was taking it to Sir Harold Marsh to sketch before sculpting, and that it would soon be returned. As it was, nobody even noticed her."

Nathan began to feel anger burn anew. "When did you learn Mimi was involved in its theft?"

Marsh sighed heavily. "Just after Carter's death, when she came to me and suggested she start sculpting for me, with no one the wiser. I'd never thought of such an unusual idea before, but it had merit. Mimi is very talented and understands Dinosauria better than any artist alive." He lowered his voice with meaning. "It also gave her something to do with her time. She was disturbed by her husband's swift and untimely death, and very lonely."

That statement made his chest constrict, but Nathan refused to let it in. Instead, he stood quietly for a moment, thinking rapidly, trying to come to terms with all he'd learned in the last ten minutes that he'd wanted to know for years.

Suddenly he looked at the older man, his brows drawn into a deep frown. "Why did you switch the jawbone for the sculpture before the banquet?"

Marsh slowly closed his eyes, features taut, but said nothing.

Nathan turned to face him fully, shoulders back, arms dropped to his sides as he fisted his hands. "You set out to ruin me again? When everybody could have seen the jawbone—the real jawbone— for the first time?"

Sir Harold thumped his palm on the table, startling him.

"What would you have me do, Nathan?" he asked briskly, sitting forward and looking at him again, irritation coloring his voice. "Tell my employer and contemporaries, including Waterhouse Hawkins, my professional rival, that I'd dishonored you in the most insulting and devastating manner? That my *daughter* had dishonored you without thought to your reputation because she worried, as any female would, that I could no longer work?" He waved his palm and pulled down hard on his waistcoat. "You know I could never allow that to happen."

"But you knew she would switch the sculpture for the jawbone the night of the banquet?" he maintained, incredulous. "How is that, sir?"

"She loves you," he spat vehemently.

Nathan felt slapped. So much so that he physically jerked from the words, his jaw tightening even as his insides liquified. For the first time before any of the Marshes, he acknowledged his deepest feelings for the woman who had betrayed him.

"You realized how I felt about her," he whispered, "and that I would tell one of the most distinguished group of gentlemen in all of England that she'd been the one to sculpt my Megalosaur."

It was a moment of sorrowful truth. For both of them.

Then Sir Harold lowered his lashes, looked blankly at his hands, and admitted in one still breath, "Yes."

And that was the answer.

Bitter silence descended upon them, enveloped them in its own intensity. Nathan couldn't bring himself to move. He stared at the man he had once so admired, had grown to hate, and whom he now respected intensely for the one secret he would always keep that revealed his deepest love for his daughter.

"You did it for Mimi," he said softly. "You did it to keep her and your family from being suspects in its theft, and so I would expose her as the magnificent Megalosaur sculptor, thereby making everyone at the banquet aware of her talent." He swallowed. "But it cost you."

Sir Harold shook his head, his lips turning upward faintly. "It's time for me to retire, to let my aching joints speak for themselves. I would have had to do so eventually, but now it can be with a purpose." He waited, then added, "I won't have to hide my affliction anymore."

Nathan inhaled deeply, resentful that he had been so used, but accepting it as well. Slowly he strode back to his chair and lowered his body onto the softly cushioned seat again, reaching for his teacup of brandy. He'd drained it earlier, so he helped himself to more of the smooth, sweet drink, taking two or three swallows before glancing up and across the desk to Marsh, to the tired, aging face that had finally revealed the lies that would lead to an ultimate good.

But it didn't negate the fact that he'd been cheated out of years of reliable work and excellent pay, out of his own museum project, and that his reputation had been severely, if not irreversibly, damaged. The resignation Nathan now experienced only slightly dimmed his resentment.

"Do you know how hard I worked, Sir Harold?" he asked passionately, replacing the cup on the saucer and sitting forward, elbows on knees, fingers interlocked in front of him. "Can you imagine how much effort someone of my station must take, how much ridicule one of my class must endure, to get where I had in my professional career, only to have it stolen from me?" He absolutely despised the necessity of revealing his long-felt indignation at having to try harder, to submit to more prying questions, to be judged more harshly, even unfairly, and then to be accused of his own downfall. All because one of his class was never expected to succeed.

But those dark, penetrating brown eyes that were so like his daughter's never once wavered in embarrassment, pity, or disgust. They expressed only an honest remorse, and perhaps a distant sadness.

"Of course I know," the older man replied gruffly, intensely. "But the scheme—the theft—was executed without my knowledge. When at last I'd learned of what had taken place that night, it was too late to do anything. The damage had been done. You'd left the country, Carter was dead, Mimi had already begun sculpting. The affair had been over for more than a year." He rubbed his brows with his fingertips, then added, "Perhaps I was wrong, but at the time I felt it should all just rest."

"But that doesn't explain why she took *my* fossil," he articulated with fervor. "And why then?"

"So I wouldn't have to sculpt it."

Of course. The sculpture commission would have gone to Sir Harold. All major finds of that size did. Yet he'd worked since then, though it was true that Mimi had taken over his assignments only a few months later. Undoubtedly Marsh could handle creating works of singular ease such as simple thigh bones. But the jawbone was a magnificent find, a one of a kind fossil that would prove to be a spectacular addition to the Palace display, and if sculpted by Sir Harold's aging hands, the world— or at least, those who mattered in the field—would learn of his growing incompetence.

Nathan closed his eyes, hanging his head low, listening to the roaring thunder in his mind, the ticking of a clock on the mantelpiece, the thickening of the afternoon rain as drops of water struck the windowpane.

"Where is my treasure now?" he asked quietly, moments later.

Marsh exhaled through his teeth. "I gave it back to Mimi."

His head popped up. "You did what?"

"I gave it back—"

"I heard you," he cut in, annoyed. "But why? Why the devil did she want it?" *And why hasn't she brought it to me?*

He knew the answer to that.

Because you didn't want her.

"I don't know," Marsh replied with flat features. "But she insisted." He raised a brow. "Maybe you'll need to ask her for it yourself."

Nathan didn't know whether to laugh or to break things. What an absurdity his life had become. Mimi Marsh Sinclair, in all her lovely sneakiness, would someday be the death of him. Of that he had no doubt.

With silence raging between them once more, Nathan placed his palms on his thighs and pushed himself up, standing in front of the desk, tall and unyielding. Sir Harold did the same, with a great deal more difficulty, and for the first time Nathan took note of the grimace that crossed the man's face, the acute discomfort. Sadly, his daughters had no doubt witnessed his deteriorating body for years.

He faced Marsh, nearly eye to eye. "Thank you for your time, Sir Harold."

The older man squared his shoulders, but didn't offer his hand, for which Nathan was grateful. The healing, if there was to be any between them, would be gradual, and with so much still at stake, it wasn't the time to mend wounds. Not completely.

"I've never told this to anyone," Marsh disclosed quietly, "but I knew of Mimi's romantic feelings for you years ago, when she would eavesdrop on our conversations, would speak of you in a dreamlike manner, ask about you constantly." He shook his head in wonder, in remembrance. "Girls."

Nathan ground his fingers into his palms, uncomfortable as he felt a warmth creeping up his neck again. But he didn't move or look away.

Through a sigh, Sir Harold continued, undaunted. "Like Mimi, I would have preferred you to Carter, Nathan, as a son-in-law. I wish things had been different between you and my sweet but crafty daughter."

Nathan blinked, startled.

Suddenly Marsh turned and walked around the desk, toward his study door. "Forgive me for leaving like this, but I must speak to my cook about the damn pheasant he served last night. Too tough. Any good cook worth one-tenth what I pay mine knows if the bird is tough, serve gravy!"

With that bellowed pronouncement, Sir Harold quit the room as Nathan simply stared at the doorway in astonishment.

He left the Marsh home immediately, lost in reflection, seeing no one upon his departure, unconcerned with the pelting rain that hit the brim of his hat and the shoulders of his morning suit. In truth, he hardly noticed it. He was numb inside from the afternoon's revelations; the chilly air did nothing to alter his state of being.

He heard footsteps behind him, but the pedestrian walkway, even in certain downpour, remained heavily congested anyway, and with his head down, he didn't notice the woman approaching him from behind until she called after him rather loudly.

"Professor Price!"

He stopped short and turned, thinking, for the slightest of seconds, that it sounded just like Mimi, then realizing with arresting expectation that it was Mary instead.

"Professor Price," she said again, gulping for air as she paced after him, clutching a scarf around her head with one hand, her skirts with the other. "Forgive me, sir," she gasped, "for not catching you before you left. Standing in the rain is not the best place to converse, I realize, but I must speak with you."

Nathan simply stared at her. This family was nothing, if not confounding.

He stood his ground without comment, on the sidewalk beneath a full budding tree, hands in his pockets, uncaring as sprinkling raindrops tapped his face.

Mary quickly walked up to him, ducking beneath the heavy branches. "Nasty weather, isn't it? I adore springtime, but it's rained for a week now, and—"

"What can I do for you, Miss Marsh?" he cut in curtly.

She blinked. Then, realizing this was not a time

for casual conversation, she drew herself up, still clinging to her scarf, and got directly to the point.

"I suppose my father explained to you what happened the night of the first Crystal Palace opening."

He felt his body tense. "He did. In agonizing detail." He hadn't meant that to sound so sarcastic; frankly, he found it amazing that he could even talk to a Marsh right now. But she didn't appear at all affronted by his tone.

Mary sighed, her shoulders drooping slightly as she glanced toward the busy street, her delicate features troubled. "I'm so very sorry all this has happened to you."

Nathan had no idea what to say. She uttered common words he'd heard numerous times, but her voice held a note of sincerity that made him pause.

A large woman in heavy hoops bustled past them, and they both moved farther under the tree, near a wrought iron fence that paralleled the sidewalk.

"Did you come out here to offer condolences, Miss Marsh?" he asked pointedly.

She drew a long breath and shook her head, lowering her gaze to the wet ground, still clutching her scarf around her neck. "No. I—" She fidgeted. "Actually, I came to tell you I know how my sister feels about you."

Nathan felt irritation bubble to the surface again. What was he supposed to say to that? Thank you? "I think at this point feelings are irrelevant. Let's leave it at that, shall we?"

Her lips thinned to a straight line and her blue eyes sparked with displeasure of their own. "Don't patronize me, Professor Price. I may be unmarried, but I am not naïve. I realize you and she have likely . . . been on friendly terms."

"I see," he replied after a moment's hesitation, watching her fair cheeks pinken even as he felt his own heated response to the thought. But she continued to stare at him with resolve, if not determination to get her point across.

"Are you planning on attending the new Palace opening in Sydenham?" she asked seconds later.

That she changed the subject so suddenly surprised him a little, but he didn't comment on it.

"I'm not certain if I'll even be available, or in the country four weeks from now," he answered vaguely, shuffling from one foot to the other.

She shivered from the chill in the air, hugging herself even tighter. "My sister loves you, Professor Price. I think it would be in your best interest to be there."

That made him fiercely mad again, though he couldn't be certain if it was because he'd grown tired of members of her family telling him what Mimi felt, or that she'd more or less ordered him to attend the opening. But in the end, he realized, none of it mattered.

Standing rigidly, ignoring the buffeting rain on his skin and the biting wind whipping around his legs, he countered, "If your sister loved me, Miss Marsh, she would have told me what she'd done months ago."

Mary's eyes flashed hotly. "Perhaps she wants to know you love her, Professor, in spite of the fact that she didn't."

That said, she abruptly turned and made a quick departure, leaving him to stare after her as he stood in the driving downpour that he no longer noticed at all.

Chapter 22

Nathan wasn't entirely prepared for the on-
slaught of emotions, both painful and tender,
that went through him the moment he stepped from
his hired hansom cab and onto solid ground on
Sydenham Hill in South London.

The newly built and soon to be officially opened
Crystal Palace stood before him, a magnificent
structure of glass and iron glittering in bright sunlight. The marvelous surrounding grounds of sculptured hedges, statues, and numerous water
fountains fairly burst with activity as finely clad patrons awaited its dedication by Queen Victoria later
in the day. This Palace would be much like the first
temporary one, though already touted as having
even greater exhibits to be viewed by those world-

wide. It would display art and architecture from ancient Egypt, the Middle Ages, and the Renaissance, examples of modern industry and the natural world, including, of course, life-size restorations of extinct animals, of which his Megalosaurus jawbone would be a stunning part. A substantial crowd had gathered already, mingling outside in the warm, sunny morning, curious onlookers and writers for society pages and journals alike, and even now he could hear a symphony of music coming from the Palace's huge, arched Center Transept.

The party had begun.

Controlling the nervousness within him, Nathan inhaled deeply, stood erect, and walked with a controlled agility down the foot path toward the great front doors.

He hadn't fully decided he would attend the magnificent celebration until just a few short days ago, when he realized the notion of what Mary had intimated on the rain drenched street intrigued him more than his desire to remain distant from Sir Harold's lovely, infuriating daughter, and what she'd done to his life that had changed it irrevocably.

He'd thought about her constantly these last few weeks, or at least it seemed so to him. It had been difficult to work, to concentrate on the marvelous opportunity offered him by Professor Owen and his contemporaries, because somewhere deep inside his relationship with Mimi did not feel finished. But above it all, beyond every emotion he didn't understand within himself, he didn't want to be distant from her any longer. Or at least, he didn't think so. He would have to see her one last time to know for sure. It would be the moment for a real good-bye, or the shaky beginning of a future together.

He wanted her—body and soul and mind—and forgiving her for what she'd done to him would be the most difficult part to come. He only hoped he would be able to do so, that when he laid eyes on her again after all these weeks, years of resentment would wash away. Yet he didn't know if a cleansing like that was possible, which is what saddened him most of all.

Nathan didn't see anyone he knew as he neared the building's wide open doors, and for that he was thankful. And relieved. He didn't need the distraction of casual conversation about the weather and his health. No doubt Sir Richard Owen, Waterhouse Hawkins, Sir Harold, and Mimi would all be at the grand opening of the official Dinosauria exhibit, and he intended to make his way to it without delay, lest he change his mind and leave England to return to his simple life on the Continent post haste. Somehow sleeping on the ground and digging for scattered bones in France seemed more appealing at the moment, or at least his easiest option for avoidance.

Upon entrance into the massive structure, he first noticed the smothering heat, the echo of laughter, the music and rumbling voices, and the smell of people, plants, and cigar smoke mixed with vinegared glass, which combined to assault his senses and turn his stomach. He ignored the unpleasantness as he strolled with purpose down the great hall, now filling with elegantly dressed gentlemen and ladies, whose wide, brightly colored skirts vied for room on the cluttered, decorated floor.

At last it came into view—or rather, the magnificent Iguanodon, inside which he'd shared one of the most memorable evenings of his adult life, stood tall in the background, towering over the crowd. Nathan hesitated for only the briefest moment as he realized this could very well be the most important day in recent memory. The day he hoped he'd be accepted as a renowned scientist by all in attendance. The day he would look his betrayer in the eye and tell her he loved her. Yes, even in spite of all she'd done.

Pushing his way into the actual dinosaur exhibit in the furthermost corner of the enormous building, he heard the distinct voice of Sir Richard Owen as the man spoke to the crowd on behalf of all England's finest paleontologists and anatomists, dedicating the magnificent work on display in this section of the Palace to Her Majesty's exhibition and all the world.

Then at last, as Nathan tunneled through guests applauding Owen's broad pronouncements, his gaze fell upon the gathering host of scientists, distinguished statesmen and their wives, Waterhouse Hawkins, Owen, Sir Harold, and the lusciously stunning Mimi Sinclair.

Nathan stopped short to stare, his chest tightening, throat constricting, as he looked upon what had to be the most incredible sight he'd ever witnessed.

She looked like radiant sunshine, more intensely beautiful than he'd ever seen her, her glossy dark blond hair curled and pinned loosely atop her head, secured with a pearl comb to match a small chain of them around her neck, wrist, and the teardrops hanging from her ears. She wore a full day gown in luminous yellow, corseted tightly, with royal blue flounces and a scooped neckline revealing only a hint of bosom.

Smiling up to her father and Owen, she looked positively breathtaking, and . . . free. For the first time, free. That was the greatest, most spectacular change of all. No more black and gray. No more severe braiding of her hair. No more confining herself within the walls of her home. Mimi had officially come out of mourning.

It melted him to see her like this, as he'd seen her as a woman for the first time three years ago at the original Crystal Palace gala. Now she shined again, more mature, certainly, and possessing a confidence of character he'd not witnessed in her before. She had yet to observe him among the hordes of people crowding the display, and he held his ground, waiting for the perfect moment to go to her, to whisper in her ear, to make up for the months he'd missed her with an ache he would never forget, never wanted to experience again.

And then she turned and stepped aside so that all in the vicinity could see behind her.

Nathan stilled as a wisp of incredulity swept through him.

The great Megalosaurus, made from little more than steel rods, brown paint, and chiseled cement, stood before them, about six feet tall, hunched over like a bear in a four-legged crawl, its tail hanging low and thick, its long snout sticking straight out and snarling. It was his dinosaur, in flawless form, though likely reconstructed from meager evidence, indeed—some ribs, a toe bone, the hips and thigh bone, and of course, his jawbone—its large body in a line of perfect proportion, the now infamous teeth jutting out from its mouth as it stalked its prey. Then his gaze shifted to the side as Marsh moved back from the sculpture a little for viewers to note the likeness. And suddenly before him, on a pedestal of bright red velvet, inside a clear glass case, sat his magnificent fossilized Megalosaurus jawbone.

He sucked in his breath.

It was here. His jawbone was here. Six feet from him. All of it, in one perfect piece, alongside her brilliant sculpture. Mimi had sculpted the whole bloody thing, and had brought her artwork, and the fossil, to the Crystal Palace for him. She had done all this for him.

Nathan had never felt a moment like this in his turbulent career. Time stalled around him suddenly as he gaped in wonder at his lost treasure next to a perfectly magnificent creation, made from gifted hands, that stood in the Crystal Palace for the nation, if not the world, to see and admire in the years to come. That's why she'd wanted his jawbone returned to her. The swell of emotion inside of him now nearly incapacitated him and brought him to his knees.

"Professor Price, so glad you've joined us at last," Owen announced from across the floor, lifting his champagne glass.

Nathan shook himself as reality struck, his senses returning enough to urge him to straighten with self-possession and move forward, even on awkward legs, spellbound by the vision as Mimi turned to gaze at him for the first time.

Her eyes widened in surprise, just a shade, and then she smiled hesitantly, unsure.

His heart nearly shattered.

Mimi. Do you know how beautiful you are?

It took every ounce of strength he possessed to direct his attention to Owen as he approached the group of mingling scientists and spectators. "Sir Richard, thank you for that warm welcome," he said, with far more calm than he felt.

A low murmur of voices began to rumble through the crowd, some no doubt remembering his showing of three years ago, perhaps embarrassed, mystified at his attendance.

Nathan remained dauntless. "Good day, Benjamin," he added in greeting to Waterhouse Hawkins, then boldly, "Sir Harold."

"Price," the older man replied with a casual nod. "A pleasure to see you here." He turned to Mimi. "You remember my daughter, Mrs. Sinclair."

He wanted to laugh at such absurd formality. Instead, with an instantly pounding heart, he bowed gently, hands behind his back, carefully probing her eyes with his. "Mrs. Sinclair," he drawled, scanning her briefly up and down. "You look . . . well."

She pressed her lips together, in what Nathan assumed to be amusement, or perhaps in a simple manner of holding her tongue from a biting comment. He hoped it was the former.

Reaching out with her hand, she returned politely, "As do you, Professor Price."

He took her warm, supple fingers in his palm, brushing her knuckles against his mouth, then reluctantly, for the sake of propriety, releasing them before he managed to disgrace both of them by sucking on the tips or licking her palm.

"Well," Owen directed to the entire group, "now is as good of a time as any for my partner and me to make our formal announcement." He cleared his throat and shot a quick glance toward Waterhouse Hawkins. "As Mrs. Sinclair and her distinguished father, Sir Harold Marsh, noted, this magnificent sculpture of the Megalosaurus reptile would not be sitting in our presence today if not for Professor Nathan Price and his perfect find at the Oxford Quarry nearly four years ago. A find unmatched to date."

The low whispers began again, giving Nathan an uncanny feeling of going through these motions once before, under similar extraordinary circumstances. But this time he refused to allow inflated arrogance to rule him. He had learned much in the last three years.

"This excellently produced sculpture, ladies and gentlemen," Owen continued, gesturing toward the Megalosaurus with his free hand, "is one that I would like to donate, along with the jawbone of its likeness, in the name of Professor Nathan Price, to my latest endeavor, the English Natural History Museum and its intended exhibit of the giant ancient lizards. The science venture at the museum will run side by side with the displays here at the Palace—those of the museum to be more scientific in nature, naturally." He smiled at Nathan, perspiration beading on his wide forehead, eyes glowing proudly. "Nathan, you said once before that you'd enjoy taking charge of it for me, cataloguing finds and promoting in England and abroad for the necessary funding. I realize the museum won't be as large as we'd originally envisioned, or entirely at your direction, as it might have been three years ago—but that was another time, with different available opportunities. Now, today, I'd be very pleased indeed if you'd consider this position." He nodded to Mimi. "With Mrs. Sinclair's talented fingers at your disposal, of course."

Several men chuckled. "He meant as your sculptor, I'm sure," Waterhouse Hawkins intimated in a whisper for his ears alone. Then he lightly slapped him on the shoulder, grinning. "Jolly good show, Nathan."

"Yes, indeed," added Sir Harold with marked sincerity, lifting his champagne glass in toast.

Nathan was speechless. Absolutely speechless. He'd never expected anything like this to occur here today, although if the truth be told, the offer came at the perfect time. He also realized he'd not be receiving any better propositions anytime soon with his reputation still in the mending stages. Accepting this work would never provide the greatness he'd once envisioned for himself, but it would be close. Damn close.

With a nod toward his host, the man he admired most in the world for his sagacity of mind and generosity of spirit, he replied with a cultured air, "I would be most honored to begin the project at once. You have my deepest thanks, Sir Richard."

"Nonsense," Owen bellowed with a wide grin, stepping forward so that he stood directly next to Nathan and Mimi. "I should be thanking you. Both of you." He glanced at the crowd. "Ah. Justin Marley and his father have arrived. If you will excuse me." With that he stepped away, strolling toward the center of the room as more paleontologists and curious visitors made their way from the great entrance to the end of the hall to witness the astounding exhibit that displayed the beasts of ancient times.

Nathan stared down at Mimi, who blushed a lovely shade of pink. Instead of commenting, she took a sip of champagne and he watched the movement of her throat, entranced, remembering that he'd done the very same thing the night they'd first kissed.

"Perhaps I'll leave you two alone to chat," Sir Harold announced from beside him, straightening and brushing a palm down his morning coat before taking a timely leave.

Nathan had forgotten him and never glanced his way.

"It's hot in here," he said softly.

"Yes," she returned without pause, wistfully.

"Care to take a stroll with me in the out of doors, Mrs. Sinclair?"

Seconds later, she whispered, "I thought you'd never ask, Professor Price."

Chapter 23

The day had been a glorious one thus far, but nothing could compare to the feeling Mimi experienced when she walked out into the bright spring sunshine on the arm of Nathan Price.

She'd been surprised, of course, the moment she'd noticed him in the exhibition hall, but not shocked that he stood among the other scientists. She'd half expected it, since she knew the man intimately and understood that he'd feel the need to relive, as it were, the night of the opening three years ago. But seeing him stride forward from the crowd after Professor Owen's speech had sent a tingle of anticipation up her spine. Especially when he couldn't take his eyes off her. What a most marvelously gratifying moment. And she immensely enjoyed the look to grace his solidly handsome face when he'd first noticed his lost jawbone and the sculpture she'd tirelessly produced to accompany it for this grand occasion.

Now, traversing silently along the curved pathway toward a small pond with a large spouting water fountain in its center, she felt a vibrant energy radiating from his body so close, sensed his strength that she'd missed for so long, and her mouth went dry with uncertainty as her heart began to beat fast in her breast from the possibilities of a profound moment to come. Nathan was here, beside her, and she would do whatever she deemed necessary to make everything right with him, even if it meant their short, sensual, intense love affair had finally and irreversibly come to an end.

Meandering through the growing crowd of gentlemen and ladies in elegant attire, Mimi avoided close contact with others by swaying against him on the stone path, as close as physically possible without appearing indecent, feeling the tightness of his muscles in his arms, the rigidity of his body. He smelled woodsy, wonderfully masculine, and never had she been so close to publicly attacking a man for the sake of sexual satisfaction as she was right now. The thought made her shiver, even in the stifling heat.

"Cold?" he asked formally.

She chuckled. "Of course not. The day is lovely."

He said nothing to that, but directed her toward the edge of the fountain pond to sit upon the surrounding white marble. She did so, spreading her gown out properly, then nervously running her palms across her lap to smooth it.

He stood beside her for a moment, unconcerned that her skirt gently brushed his legs. He crossed his arms in front of him, squinting from the brightness of the day as he gazed out to the white cherub statues and birdbaths that lined the pond floor behind her.

She looked up at him for a moment, admiring the way his shirtfront tightened over his chest muscles, noticeable even beneath his dark green morning suit, waiting for him to speak first, uncertain where his thoughts lay, but allowing him to set the mood. She was certainly anxious and he more than likely knew it, but with the sun on her back and the scent of flowers in the air, she could sit here for hours staring at him, if it took that long.

"The Megalosaurus sculpture is a masterpiece," he said abruptly, pulling her from her lascivious thoughts.

She interlocked her fingers over her thighs, suppressing a wide grin of pleasure. "Thank you. I don't know if I'd call it a masterpiece, exactly, though it did come together nicely, considering I had very little to work from by way of factual evidence and sufficient information about the creature."

He nodded without looking at her. "Much of what you do is creative interpretation, I'm sure."

"Oh, naturally," she agreed. "But then dinosaur sculpting in itself isn't much of a science."

He frowned. "Some days I fear the same about paleontology."

She laughed softly, but added nothing to that.

He shifted from one foot to the other. "Mimi, I have something to tell you."

Her heart thundered in her breast, but outwardly she remained calm, composed, smiling gently. "Yes?"

He wiped a palm down his face, glancing away for a moment. Stalling. Then suddenly he drew a deep breath and looked into her eyes for the first time since walking outside.

"I—love you."

Oh, *God*, she'd been wanting to hear him say that to her for years, and she nearly started crying on the spot. Instead, she forced herself to remain centered, holding her emotions in check, clutching her hands together, to reply innocently, "Yes, I know."

His head jerked back a little, brows drawing together in confusion, obviously unprepared for such a staid answer. But what did he expect? That she would jump into his arms? Confess her undying devotion as well? Here by a public fountain and a mass of people? Men, in general, were so very odd.

He rubbed his palm along the back of his neck. "I suppose I'm not doing this well."

"Oh, you're doing just fine, Professor," she replied at once, choking back tears.

He hesitated, eyeing her shrewdly, his gaze dropping ever so subtly to her breasts and back again to her face.

She beamed inside, waiting.

"Oh, hell." He turned and sat beside her, heavily, slumping forward and resting his elbows on his knees, clasping his hands in front of him.

"Your whole family knows I love you; I suppose it would be asking too much that you didn't."

She did laugh at that, wrapping an arm through his and pulling him close. "They're guessing, Nathan. I'm the only one who knows for sure because I witnessed it in bed. And I've never actually told anyone but you."

He sighed. "I guess I should have seen it there, too."

"In bed? I think you did," she countered. "And it scared you."

She thought he might have smiled as the corner of his mouth lifted minutely.

"I don't scare easily, madam."

She thoroughly adored his defensiveness, but she wouldn't tell him that. Instead, she huffed in feigned disgust. "Men are always scared of love."

"This from a lady who's never been in love?"

She had no idea where he got that notion, but she supposed the fact that she'd admitted to never truly loving Carter had made him assume as much. It occurred to her that men were also very one-sided thinkers. But she'd keep that to herself as well.

"I'm in love with you, practical or not," she said evenly. Growing somber, she lowered her voice to add, "I have been for a long time, Nathan."

He remained silent for a minute or two, and Mimi could read the concern in his dark features, observed the crinkles to the side of his eyes that told of worries he held within.

"I know you're troubled by the class difference between us," she whispered, gazing down to her skirt and running her thumb and fingers over the gauzy material, feeling horribly awkward and embarrassed to be the one to mention it. "It's immaterial, as far as I'm concerned."

He actually chuckled at that, lifting his head to stare across the park, studying a group of children playing with a ball on the other side of the finely cut lawn.

"Mimi, that has never been a consideration of mine."

She blinked, a little startled when her experience with Nathan Price told her otherwise. "I don't understand," she replied cautiously.

He turned to look into her eyes. "One of the most beautiful things about you, Mrs. Sinclair," he declared in a deep, husky voice, "is that you are so passionately forgiving of one's shortcomings. Even sometimes when you shouldn't be." He sat up a little, though he never dropped his gaze. "I know my station of birth matters little to you, but it matters to others who are close to you. In this way, any association with me beyond the casual could ultimately hurt you socially. That matters to me, and being in love with you is irrelevant."

Mimi stared into his dark, mesmerizing eyes that she'd missed so much these last few weeks, hers filling with tears even as he spoke. She squeezed his arm fervently. "Nathan, none of that is important—"

"Of course it's important," he interrupted gently. "It may not be important to you, but it *is* important."

She pulled her body erect, breathing in sharply with fortitude. "You are a professor of paleontology, a very distinguished gentleman in a very distinguished profession, sir."

"Yes," he retorted at once, "and everyone who cares about that will know how I got here and where I came from."

That was true. Gossip spread like wildfire in the upper classes of society. Still she wouldn't let it rest.

"But what ultimately matters?" she articulated slowly. "That we are happy together or that others show us social disfavor?"

He paused in thought, then said brusquely, "Your social life will probably change."

She tightened her jaw with determination. "Good. My social life has been nearly nonexistent in recent years. I think I would welcome a change of any kind."

He sat back even more, pivoting so that he looked directly at her, shaking his head at her tenacity. His eyes grazed every feature of her face, his expression softening, as he raised his arm and placed his thumb on her mouth. Lowering her lashes, she was suddenly filled with warmth and a far-reaching joy, and she kissed the tip of his finger, then rubbed her lips back and forth across the rough skin.

"You're so beautiful," he whispered.

She sighed with closed eyes, marveling in the feel of him again, the sound of his deep, resonant voice. "Not as beautiful as the man I've always known you are, Nathan," she returned with longing. "The man you are inside."

She heard him suck in a breath, felt his thumb still its movement at her lips.

Seconds later she raised her lashes to gaze into his eyes only inches from hers, to witness the depth of every emotion he possessed boldly centered in them and in every remarkable line of his face. If she ever knew anything in her life, Mimi knew he loved her at this moment.

"I have something for you," he whispered thickly after clearing his throat.

She pulled back a little, blinking to keep the tears from streaming down her cheeks and making her look ghastly in front of him. She didn't need him running away in fright from her now.

He reached into his coat pocket, then carefully pulled out a small package, about two inches by two inches squared, wrapped in white paper and decorated with a tiny red ribbon tied into a bow. Her heart melted; her breath caught in her throat. Then her pulse began to race.

"A gift for you," he said, holding it up with his fingers in offering.

She stuck her hand out and he placed it in her palm, though she never uttered a sound because she couldn't think of anything appropriate—and because she feared a scene if she broke down in front of strange pedestrians in the park.

Reaching for the bow, Mimi pulled at the ribbon until it came loose, then quickly discarded it. With nimble fingers, she tore at the paper, then lifted the top of the little box.

Inside lay a tiny hinged jewel case made of ivory, carved on top into a breathtaking scene of flying birds that soared above trees.

"It's lovely," she murmured.

He smiled smugly. "It is, isn't it? It's from Persia, but I bought it in France, to hold my pocketwatch, things of that nature."

She lifted it from the outer box. "It looks too small for a pocketwatch."

"Exactly," he said, adding sheepishly, "I discovered that. And I don't wear jewelry, so I don't very well need a case." He lowered his voice. "I want you to have it."

Mimi glanced up to him, unsure. His hard, flat, masculine features told her nothing, but in his eyes she observed a hidden mischief, a sparkle of excitement that made her desperate.

With delicate fingers, she lifted the lid.

The inside, except for a patch of black velvet, was empty.

Her heart sank, and he no doubt witnessed her disappointment as her face fell. She didn't know whether to tell him it lacked a bloody ring or thank him politely for his generous gift in which she would delightfully place a pair of her earrings.

She'd evidently paused long enough for him to notice he had her stumped.

Suddenly he reached for her, clasping his large, warm palm over hers as she held the box.

"You noticed it's empty," he maintained faintly.

She swallowed. "Yes, but it's—"

"I thought," he cut in, rubbing her knuckles with one long finger, "that you might use this box, as my treasured gift to you, for a place inside which you could keep the ring you wore when you were married to Carter."

Mimi stilled, eyes widening as clarity enveloped her. And then her entire body began to shake.

"Nathan . . ."

With his free hand he reached into another

pocket, his tone calm and thoughtful, as he finally revealed his purpose. "I was rather hoping you'd wear mine on your finger instead."

That said, he held out to her a small, brilliantly cut emerald set upon a thin band of gold.

Her eyes filled with tears again and this time she didn't stop them from flowing. She couldn't speak, and he accepted that. Reaching for her hand, he gently removed the ring that Carter had placed there nearly three years ago. Then he turned the ivory jewel case toward him and placed her late husband's ring inside on the black velvet.

"I love you, Mimi," he whispered passionately. "I love your charm and your joy. I love that you were loyal to a husband who left you lonely. I love your talent and honesty." He inhaled deeply, and swallowed with a force of emotion. "But most of all, I love that you love me in spite of my failings. Please say that you'll marry me."

In spite of my failings . . .

"You will never fail me, Nathan," she murmured huskily. She reached for his cheek with her palm and gradually drew him down so that his forehead touched hers.

For moments they stayed like that, oblivious to passersby around them, the birds chirping on the water, the bubbling of the fountain. Finally Nathan took her hand in his and slid the perfectly formed emerald betrothal ring on her finger. His ring.

"I love you," she whispered.

He said nothing, but his lips grazed her forehead and temple. She clutched the ivory case in her hand, feeling the gold ring on her finger, loose and lighter than Carter's, but there from a deeply felt passion that she trusted would never die.

"I'm sorry I didn't believe you, come back to you sooner," he said after a long moment.

She sniffed. "I knew you needed time."

He grunted. "I didn't need that much time."

She smiled, still leaning against him. "Perhaps, but I needed time to sculpt the Megalosaur."

He placed his fingers under her chin and lifted it to delicately kiss her lips. "I should have forgiven you anyway, for the support, the caring you've shown me, the challenges you've given me. I should have known."

Forgiven her? And then she understood . . . he still didn't know the truth about that night long ago, the total truth about his ruin. Suddenly she felt a pulsing joy within that he'd confessed his love and proposed marriage even as he thought she'd betrayed him that night long ago.

She skimmed her palm across his warm cheek, her thumb across the bone. "Oh, Nathan, my sweet love. I didn't steal your jawbone years ago."

He tried to pull away, though in shock or offense, she couldn't be sure. But she clung to him, squeezing her eyes shut to whisper, "Mary did it."

Nathan sat there, in stunned silence, hardly breathing, not speaking as he absorbed the shock of her words. For moments he didn't understand, and then, with hard-hitting incredulity, he again felt the weight of lies and deception against him. He held to the woman he loved, adored inside and out, smelling her distinctive scent, feeling her, absorbing her heat as he did her devotion, even as he gradually came to realize that the truth he had accepted in the last few weeks was never the truth at all.

That's when the forceful words uttered between him and Mimi's sister during their last verbal encounter shrieked within his mind and total understanding dawned.

If your sister loved me, Miss Marsh, she would have told me what she'd done months ago.

Perhaps she wants to know you love her, Professor, in spite of the fact that she didn't.

Mimi could have told him everything at the dig, easily, but she hadn't, because not only did she love Mary and want to protect her father's reputation; she knew it would be the only true barrier between them and any future they might have together. If he wanted her, he would have to accept her knowing she might have betrayed him. It would be the ultimate forgiveness, and he had done it.

Finally, through the still spring air, listening to each nervous breath she exhaled, he accepted everything with a peace inside that he hadn't felt in a very long time.

"Does your father know?" he asked, his voice raspy, running his fingers along her soft neck.

She shook her head. "No."

She sounded pained, and he lifted her chin, pushing her back a little so he could see her clearly.

"Look at me," he insisted in a whisper.

She inhaled deeply and opened glittering eyes to his—eyes that would forever make him weak.

"It happened exactly like your father told me, only Mary took the jawbone instead of you?"

"Yes . . ."

He paused, then said, "And she did it for him."

Mimi nodded negligibly, never glancing away, her expression twisted into one of deep sorrow. "Nobody knows, Nathan. Mary gave it to Carter soon after she'd taken it, and I found it after his death, in the attic, with his things. I eventually told my father, because I knew he always suspected. To protect everyone involved, I simply took the blame. Only Mary and I know the truth, and I found out when she told me. The guilt over what she did has stricken her for years." She pinched her lips together in budding anger. "But I screamed at her, naturally, when I discovered it."

God, he had to smile. He would expect nothing less from her. "Good for you."

She tried to laugh, but it sounded more like a wail. "I would have given it back to you when I discovered it, but you'd left the country. I didn't know what to do, or who to tell, to go to, so I—I kept it."

He seethed inside with smoldering agitation anew, but he never let it show. "Mary did all this so your father wouldn't have to sculpt it?"

"Yes. She—she loves him so much, Nathan, and in many ways, he's all she has. She's wanted him to stop sculpting for years, and then when his arthritis got so bad, she didn't want him to ruin his reputation in front of Owen, Waterhouse Hawkins, Prince Albert. He could still sculpt thigh bones and ribs, but a jawbone like that one—" She shook her head sharply in denial. "Oh, God, Nathan, I'm so sorry."

She still held the jewel case he'd given her in her hand, still clung to the box. He reached for the lid and closed it over the top in a sharp manner of finality.

"I have an idea," he remarked very slowly, sitting erect once more and glancing around the pond, noticing how the crowd had grown as the hour of the queen's grand arrival approached. The party would be a memorable commemoration, a beginning for his science, his career, and his life with Mimi. In the end, this would be a perfect day, indeed.

She wiped her eyes with the back of her hand, squaring her shoulders in an attempt to regain some lost poise. "And that is?"

He grinned wryly, looked back into her eyes, and with sly humor, rubbed the toe of her shoe under his boot, back and forth, in a private gesture nobody could see.

"Let's have a marvelous night of celebration, a toast to us, and plan this wedding." He leaned very close to whisper, "I'm about ready to ravish you here on the spot."

She softly brushed her lips against his as she replied, "I've been thinking about that very thing, Professor Price."

"Have you?"

She grinned against his mouth. "But next time you may linger intimately inside of me on our own soft bed. That should give *you* something to ponder for the next few weeks."

His body jumped in response to that silky, verbal caress. With gentlemanly smoothness, he stood, grabbed her arm, and quickly drew her to her feet, pulling her close to him with her elbow. "I can't take the pain. Back to the party now, Mimi," he ordered, amused, "before I'm arrested for easing it right here beside the pond."

She laughed outright and linked her arm through his, and they began the short stroll back to the new Crystal Palace, just as they had the night it all began.

Acknowledgments

From an early age dinosaurs fascinated me. But it wasn't until I began researching this book that I realized what a profound effect the discovery of dinosaurs had on Victorian society. In the mid-1800s, science and technology invaded all walks of life in Europe, and, humans being an inquisitive bunch, the discovery of giant "beasts," as they were called, became a huge spectacle in which everybody wanted to take part.

All characters in this book are fictional, with the exception of Sir Richard Owen and Benjamin Waterhouse Hawkins. Owen was indeed an historical anatomist and the central figure in the major dinosaur excavations of the mid-nineteenth century. He was the person who coined the phrase "Dinosauria" and his work was generally accepted as factual and astonishing—until later in that century when new and more accurate information proved many of his earlier observations incorrect. Waterhouse Hawkins was Owen's actual dinosaur sculptor, and the dinosaur sculptures that were displayed in the Crystal Palace were created by him.

The banquet at the new Crystal Palace on New Year's Eve, 1853 was an historical event as well, and, to the best of my ability, I used all information gleaned to recreate it in this book. In my research, I was able to find a copy of the dinner menu, the invitation (which was, in fact, displayed on the wing of a drawn Pterodactyl), and even a picture of the gathering inside Waterhouse Hawkins's Iguanodon mold. I'm sure the real historical dinner was a fascinating event!

I'd like to thank my editor, Lyssa Keusch, and my agent, Denise Marcil, two of the best in the business, for their patience and understanding during a tough writing year.

And finally, I will admit that this book never would have been finished if not for the support and inspiration of my great friend and critique partner, Michele Albert. She's one of a kind and I can't help but love her!

Dear Reader,

Warm up with Avon romance! There's something for everyone . . . and I guarantee these books will heat you up on a cold winter's night. And, if you live in a balmier climate, you'll just have to turn up the A.C. . . .So, if you like the Avon romance you've just finished, check out what we have next month.

Let's begin with January's Avon Romantic Treasure, *Too Wicked to Marry* by Susan Sizemore. Lord Martin Kestrel can have any woman he desires . . . but the only woman he'd ever deign to marry is the woman he knows as Abigail Perry. But as a woman in the service of the queen, Abigail has deceived Martin, and when he discovers her ruse she must handle the consequences . . .

Remember that rhyme you said as a kid? "First comes love . . . then comes marriage . . ." Well, sometimes it's the other way around, as we discover in Christie Ridgway's *First Comes Love*, an Avon Contemporary romance. What would *you* do if you found out you were accidentally married? I know, it sounds crazy, but in a romance by Christie anything is deliciously possible!

If you love romances by Lisa Kleypas, you're going to love Kathryn Smith's sensuous and dramatic Avon Romance, *A Seductive Offer*. Lord Braven has saved Rachel Ashton's life once . . . and when she accepts his offer of a marriage in name only, she knows he has actually saved her yet again. But what happens when her passion for him turns to true love?

A bride sale! How can it be? But in *The Bride Sale*, an Avon Romance by Candice Hern, Lord James Harkness stumbles upon this appalling practice, and stuns himself by bidding on a beautiful gentlewoman being auctioned off. James knows he's not fit to be a true husband, but how can he resist her?

I promised these would be hot! I hope you enjoy them,

Lucia Macro

Lucia Macro
Executive Editor

Avon Romantic Treasures

*Unforgettable, enthralling love stories,
sparkling with passion and adventure
from Romance's bestselling authors*